WHEN THE DAWN BREAKS

Jessie, the young daughter of a local midwife, is determined to become a nurse one day, but family loss and heartache jeopardise her dreams. Isabel, the doctor's daughter, is planning to follow in her father's footsteps – even though medicine is not considered a fitting career for a woman. And then there's Archie, Jessie's older brother, who Isabel just can't stay away from. One encounter in the woods, Archie disappears and all their lives are irrevocably changed... Years later, Isabel is a qualified doctor and Jessie is a nurse and when their paths cross again, neither is certain what the other woman knows about the fateful day.

WHEN THE DAWN BREAKS

WHEN THE DAWN BREAKS

by

Emma Fraser

Magna Large Print Books
Long Preston, North Yorkshire,
BD23 4ND, England.

British Library Cataloguing in Publication Data.

Fraser, Emma
    When the dawn breaks.

    A catalogue record of this book is
    available from the British Library

    ISBN   978-0-7505-3803-9

First published in Great Britain in 2013 by Sphere
An imprint of Little, Brown Book Group

Copyright © Emma Fraser 2013

Cover illustration by arrangement with Arcangel Images

The moral right of the author has been asserted

Published in Large Print 2014 by arrangement with
Little Brown Book Group Ltd.

Magna Large Print is an imprint of Library Magna Books Ltd.

Printed and bound in Great Britain by
T.J. (International) Ltd., Cornwall, PL28 8RW

Dedicated to the memory of my parents,
Anne and George, and my brother, Peter.
Gus am bris an là, agus an teich na sgàilean.

Acknowledgements

First and foremost thanks to my sisters Flora and Mairi for their support, encouragement and insight. Without you the book wouldn't be what it is.

Thanks also to my daughter Rachel who read the book so many times she can practically recite it by heart and my other daughter Katie for being so proud of me.

To Stewart, for his help with the medical detail and for listening to a wife who must have seemed quite mad at times.

Thanks to my agent, Judith Murdoch, and my editor, Manpreet Grewal, for believing in me and my book. Thank you to Hazel Orme for the copy-edit.

Finally thanks to Karen, Hugh, Sandra, Theona and Isabel. A writer's life can be lonely but, as you can see, mine is not.

Serbia, winter 1915

Jessie and Isabel stood over the shallow grave with their heads bowed.

Jessie blinked the snow from her eyes and looked around. Bodies littered the ground as far as she could see yet they had left thousands more behind them – dead not from bullet wounds, shrapnel or even disease – but cold and starvation.

A few feet away, a woman lay curled around the body of her child. Her shawl, still wrapped around her head, fluttered in the breeze, revealing a face that might have been beautiful had her mouth not been frozen in a frightful grimace of death.

Not far from them, propped against a tree, the stiff corpse of a soldier still held his tin mug as if he were about to sip some beef tea.

An infantryman left the column and crunched across the field, his footsteps leaving pockmarks on the snow. He bent over the woman and child and for a moment Jessie thought he was going to bury them, but instead he removed the shawl and wrapped it around his neck. Too exhausted to protest, she watched as he continued towards the dead soldier and dispassionately relieved him of his coat and boots.

On his return he passed close by them and hesitated. He tugged the scarf from his throat and held it out to Jessie. 'For you, Sister.'

She took it from him, her numb fingers seeking

the warmth of his skin that still clung to the material. The soldier touched his hat to them and rejoined the dead-eyed men trudging along the path.

The sound of Bulgarian cannon to the east was louder now, and to the north were the advancing Austrian and German armies – perhaps just hours away.

Their only hope lay to the south and the narrow track through the black Montenegrin mountains; hundreds of miles of mud, snow and almost certain death.

Jessie's feet were frozen. Last night she had tried to thaw her boots over a fire made of straw, but within an hour of pulling them back on they were solid again. Isabel's, she knew, would be the same.

'We must go on,' Isabel urged. 'One day we will return and mark the grave properly, but there is no more we can do here now, and the longer we wait the greater the chance that the Germans will be upon us. We have to make the most of the daylight.'

Jessie sucked in a breath. Isabel was right. If they were to survive, they had to keep moving.

Isabel passed the haversack with what remained of their supplies to Jessie, then picked up her medical bag.

Once three and now two women, Jessie thought, depending on each other for their lives and bound by a secret, that, even if they survived, could yet destroy them both.

She pulled the haversack onto her shoulders and raised her head to the snow-darkened sky. 'Lord have mercy on us all,' she whispered.

PART ONE

SKYE 1903–8

Chapter 1

Skye, summer 1903

Jessie MacCorquodale looked up as Miss Stuart entered the room and banged on her desk with a ruler. The children shuffled their feet and giggled nervously as they took their seats. Quiet fell. Miss Stuart was young but she was strict, and many of them, Jessie included, had suffered the leather tawse on their hands to prove it.

Their teacher wasn't alone. Standing next to her was a tall girl with plaited golden hair and eyes that were much the same colour as the chocolate velvet collar of her smart cream frock. Clutched in her hands was a narrow-brimmed hat with a cherry-red band. Although she couldn't have been more than a couple of years older than Jessie, she wore stockings instead of knee-length socks. Her buttoned, calf-length boots were polished and, as far as Jessie could tell, without holes. Jessie placed one of her feet over the other to hide the toe that was poking out of the front of her left tackety boot. Her own mud-coloured dress was a hand-me-down from an older cousin and had been darned so many times by Mammy that it was more thread than cloth. She ran a hand over her own wayward curls, which refused to lie flat. For the first time she was embarrassed by the way she looked.

'Isabel is coming to join us for the last couple

17

of weeks of term,' Miss Stuart said. 'I hope you will all make her welcome. Her father is Dr MacKenzie.'

So this was the doctor's daughter. Mammy had been talking about a Dr MacKenzie coming to Skye to replace Dr Munro, who had gone to Glasgow to start a new practice. In Mammy's opinion, Dr Munro was dangerous.

'Dr MacKenzie is not long back from the Boer War,' Miss Stuart was saying. 'Who can tell me where the Boer War took place?'

Jessie's hand shot up as her admiration for the new girl grew. Isabel's father had been in a war – just like her own daddy! Except his war had been against the Earl of Glendale's father and Daddy had gone to prison, along with the other martyrs from Glendale. Mammy had said that usually people would be ashamed of having a father in prison – like the McPhees, whose daddy had been taken to Portree and locked up for a couple of nights for being drunk and disorderly – but Jessie had to be proud of hers because he'd been locked up for a Good and Righteous Cause.

Miss Stuart picked on Archie, who didn't even have his hand up, to answer the question and who, of course, answered correctly. It was so unfair. Her brother was three years older than her and bound to know more. Archie should be in a separate class but there was only one teacher, two if you counted the head, Mr MacIntyre, for almost seventy children, so they were all taught together.

Miss Stuart turned back to Isabel. 'Find a seat, my dear. I'm sure you'll get to know everyone's names in time.' She frowned at the class. 'Isabel

18

doesn't have the Gaelic, so when you speak to her, mind your manners and talk in English, please.'

Jessie smiled at Isabel, hoping that the new girl would choose the empty seat next to her. Fiona wasn't at school today. Indeed, half the class was missing. It was a good day and most of them would be out with their mams and dads helping to turn the hay. It was only on a bad day, when the rain and wind lashed the land, that there was full attendance at school. Not that her daddy ever let Jessie miss school: he wasn't having his children scrape a living from a land that bled the life from a man. He said education was the only way out, and Jessie planned to work hard enough to win a scholarship to the secondary school in Portree. Clever-clogs Archie had already won one and was going to Inverness after the summer to study for his senior school-leaving certificate.

Jessie closed her eyes and sent a quick prayer heavenwards: *Please, please, let the new girl sit next to me.*

She heard a rustle and opened her eyes to find that Isabel had taken the seat right at the front. God hadn't listened. Probably because she shouldn't have been asking for things for herself. It served her right. Daddy said she should only pray for other people.

Even from two rows behind the new girl, Jessie caught the scent of oranges. Isabel was like one of the heroines out of the penny novels she borrowed from Fiona's mam, although she was bound to be more interesting. And she already had breasts! Jessie was always studying her own flat chest, wondering when they'd start to grow and be big like her mammy's. Mind you, some of the women Mammy helped birth had breasts that hung almost to their belly buttons. Too many children, Mammy said.

Miss Stuart had laid aside the cue she'd used to point to South Africa on the map and was ready to start the lesson.

There was more rustling as everyone cleaned their slates. Flora McPhee, who was sitting to the left of the new girl and right in front of Miss Stuart, so the teacher could keep an eye on her, spat on her cloth to clean her slate. Jessie hoped Isabel hadn't noticed. She didn't want her to think they were all like the McPhees. The Mac-Corquodales might not have much money, her mammy said, but that was no reason not to be clean and mind your manners.

She was glad when Mr MacIntyre clanged the bell for playtime. Hunger had been gnawing at her for a while – the porridge and boiled egg she'd had after she'd milked Daisy had been hours ago.

As the class spilled outside, Jessie scurried to the outdoor toilet, hoping to make it before the big boys. They spent ages in there and left it smelling worse than ever. By the time she'd come out and washed her hands under the tap in the courtyard, everyone was in the playground. As usual Archie was organising a game of football. It irked her no end that he always ignored her when he was with his friends. He wasn't like that at home.

Searching the crowd of laughing, squealing children for Isabel, she spotted her sitting on a rock, her back straight, knees and feet neatly together as she unwrapped her lunch from a piece of brown paper. Flora McPhee, who wasn't in her usual spot behind the wall, well out of Miss Stuart's and Mr MacIntyre's sight, said something in Gaelic to her friends and they laughed and pointed at Isabel.

'Who does she think she is, with her fancy ways?' Flora said loudly, in English this time. 'That just because she's the doctor's daughter she's better than the rest of us?'

Jessie's heart started to pound. Flora McPhee was a bully, but if you stood up to her she'd back down soon enough. Isabel was ignoring Flora, seemingly intent on the package that lay open on her lap.

Flora and her gang moved closer until they were standing in front of the new girl. Isabel looked up at them with steady brown eyes.

'What fancy food do you have there?' Flora asked, curling her lip in a way that made her look ridiculous.

Isabel smiled politely and held out the package. 'It's a scone with cheese. The maid gave me too much. You're welcome to some, if you like.'

Jessie cringed. Isabel shouldn't have mentioned a maid. Now there'd be no stopping Flora's spite. Flora's older sister, Agnes, had applied for a job at Dunvegan Castle and been turned down. The only people this had surprised had been the McPhees, who had boasted to anyone who would listen that their Agnes would get a job there and be set up for life. The McPhees had a terrible reputation and should have known that no one in the big house would employ anyone without checking with the minister; he was hardly likely to recommend any of the McPhees since they were the only villagers who didn't attend either one of the two Sunday services – a shame even worse than Mr McPhee being in gaol, her daddy said. Mr McPhee had hated Daddy ever since Daddy had warned him not to hit Flora's mam.

Jessie dithered, not knowing what to do for the best. Should she go over or would her presence make it worse for Isabel? If Flora had an audience apart from her friends she might be less likely to back down. Jessie spun around, hoping to see Miss Stuart or Mr MacIntyre. No luck. Her eyes shifted to her brother. Archie, expertly dribbling the ball between his feet, glanced in her direction before his gaze slid past her. He trapped the ball under his foot and narrowed his eyes.

Flora was too intent on her prey to notice Archie watching. She grabbed the scone out of Isabel's hands and tore it in two. She offered some to her friends, who shook their heads. Flora popped a piece into her mouth, made a show of turning up her nose and spat it onto the ground. She flung the rest after it and a seagull swooped, snapped it up and flew off with it in its beak.

It might still have been all right, if Isabel hadn't stood up. Now she towered over Flora, who, although stocky and strong from lifting peats, was forced to look up at the doctor's daughter.

'I don't mind if you want to share my lunch,' Isabel said, 'but I do mind if you waste it.'

The wind had dropped and her voice carried across the playground. The children nearby stopped what they were doing and turned to stare.

22

'You can mind what you like,' Flora said. She moved closer to Isabel, but the new girl was either too stupid or too brave to retreat. Instead she held her ground, looking at Flora as if she were a cowpat on the sole of one of her highly polished boots. Now there was bound to be trouble. Flora was a dirty fighter.

'Leave her alone.' Archie's voice was quiet.

Jessie's attention had been fixed on Isabel and Flora so she hadn't heard him approach. She let her breath out. Archie was there. Everything would be fine now.

Although he was a year older than Flora, Archie wasn't much taller and a lot scrawnier. But Flora knew better than to take on Archie. A year ago he had lifted her bodily and dropped her in the burn after she had hit Jessie. And it wasn't just that. Jessie had seen the way Flora looked at him – in the silly way that the girls who had breasts seemed to look at all the boys, and at Archie in particular. Mam had said it was because he would be a fine catch for any woman when it was time for him to take a wife – he'd inherited his father's good looks and grit and would, no doubt, with a good education behind him, make something of himself one day. Jessie didn't consider her brother good-looking. He had the same wide mouth and wild dark hair as herself, and was far too skinny. His hands and feet looked too big for his body, but Mam said it was only a matter of time before he grew into himself. Admittedly he had a nice smile and his eyes were a deeper, much nicer shade of blue than her own – cobalt, according to the label on a discarded box of almost finished water-colours she'd once found on the moors.

'I said, leave her alone, Flora,' Archie repeated softly, in Gaelic.

Flora looked at him and flushed a deep red. She was pretty under the grime, with her jet-black hair and light blue eyes, and Archie might have walked out with her if she wasn't so dirty – or so nasty.

Flora tossed her head. 'I was only having some fun, Archie.'

'Well, away you go and have fun somewhere else,' he replied.

Flora muttered something under her breath to Isabel before she moved away, her friends following in her wake.

Archie grinned at Isabel and said something to her that Jessie couldn't hear. Whatever it was, it made Isabel smile, and the transformation in her face, from shy and almost plain to quite beautiful, made Jessie ache inside. Why couldn't she look more like Isabel? Why had she inherited her mother's curly brown hair that wouldn't do as it was told, blowing this way and that when it was windy, which was pretty much all the time? Why couldn't she have unusual brown eyes instead of the boring blue shared by most of the village? But, most of all, why couldn't she have a smile that made people look at her in the way that Archie was looking at Isabel?

Chapter 2

Isabel curled up on the window-seat in her bed-room and gazed across the water at Dunvegan Castle. A shaft of sun split the clouds and wrapped the castle in a golden, mystical light. She would ask Papa who lived there. Perhaps a girl of her own age. Someone like Lucy, the heroine of Sir Walter Scott's *The Bride of Lammermoor*. A girl she could be friends with. Whatever Papa said, he couldn't expect her to be friends with the local people. Most didn't even wear shoes. And the girl who had snatched her scone was simply vile. Thank good-ness she'd be going to a proper school in Edin-burgh after the summer.

Skye was a funny place and she wasn't at all cer-tain she liked it. So far, the only good thing about being here was that Papa was living with them again. She was still a little shy of him, although she'd missed him terribly when he'd gone to South Africa to help look after the wounded soldiers. He'd been away for three long years and she'd almost not recognised him when he'd returned six months ago. Oh, it had been Papa, all right, even if his whiskers were now grey at the edges, but in her memory he was a tall man with a vigorous walk and a ready smile. The man who'd come back to them seemed smaller and, although he still laughed and teased her, so much sadder. And now he walked with a limp. A sword wound to his leg, he'd said. He'd got one to his chest too, and it sometimes made his breathing loud and harsh; the smog that hung over Edinburgh worsened it. That was why they'd come to live on Skye. The air here, he said, was much cleaner.

Her mother hadn't been happy to leave Edinburgh. Before they'd departed for Skye, Isabel had overheard her telling Papa that he had no right to uproot them and take them away from all her friends and her work. She wasn't sure what Mama meant by 'work' unless it was the endless committee meetings she attended. But Papa had put his foot down. He had said that he was the head of the household and would make the decisions. Andrew would stay at school in Edinburgh and live with his and Isabel's older brother, George, and his family but Mama and Isabel's place was beside him in Skye.

'You don't intend that Isabel should go to the local school? Really, William! What are you thinking of? Have you forgotten that your daughter is the great-granddaughter of a countess?'

'No, my dear. I doubt I could forget,' Papa responded drily. 'There are only a few weeks left of school before the summer holiday. In the autumn she will return to Edinburgh to complete her education. Until then I want my daughter with me.' There was a rustle as he shook his newspaper. 'You've overindulged her, Clara, while I've been away. If she still wants to be a nurse, it will be to her benefit to see how the common people live. They will be the people she'll look after – not countesses and ladies.'

Although Isabel heard the smile in his voice, his

26

words made her burn with indignation. How could Papa say she was overindulged? And she *was* used to common people. They had servants, didn't they?

'I have the impression our daughter thinks nursing is about mopping fevered brows and little else,' he added.

Isabel's cheeks became hotter. Of course she knew that there was more to nursing than *that*. She'd read the stories about Florence Nightingale. Papa didn't know her at all!

'William, I have no intention of allowing Isabel to become a nurse.'

'I don't imagine you'll have to worry about it for long, but our daughter is headstrong, so perhaps it would be as well not to forbid it.'

Every word made Isabel more determined. She would show him. He would find out she was not a girl who could be put off her course once she'd made a decision.

Not long after that conversation, they had packed up the house in Edinburgh and taken the train to Kyle of Lochalsh, then a small boat across to Skye. It had been almost dark when they'd arrived and Isabel had had only the briefest impression of clean air, scented with sea and a sweet smokiness.

After spending the night at a local inn they'd continued their journey, by carriage, the following morning. The mist had lifted and on either side of the road the sea and lochs glistened in the sun, sending sparks like miniature shooting stars into the air. Mountain ridges, their spines like the backblones of prehistoric animals, loomed over

27

them. They passed several villages with people working outside, mending creels or carrying enormous baskets laden with clumps of dark earth on their backs. Small boats, some with their sails unfurled, bobbed along the shoreline.

As the carriage trundled along in the shadow of the mountains, Papa pointed to his left. 'There are fairy pools over there. One day soon, Isabel, we must come to see them and have a picnic.'

'Don't be silly, Papa. I'm almost fourteen and I know perfectly well that fairies don't exist.' Really! Sometimes he treated her as if she were a baby.

'You can't know anything for certain, Isabel.' Her father's eyes creased at the corners. 'A lot of people here still believe in things they can't see.'

Several hours later, the carriage turned down a tree-lined track. Isabel craned her neck, eager to catch the first glimpse of her new home, but, hidden beyond a wood of ash, oak and beech, it was several more minutes before it came into view.

The lichen-encrusted house sat, hugged by the sea, on its own small peninsula. If she threw a stone from where she was sitting it would land in the water.

The carriage drew to a halt and, while the servants lined up to greet them, Papa jumped down to assist Mama, who was studying their new home with a frown of disapproval.

Inside, the house was big – bigger even than the one in Edinburgh – although much plainer. On the ground floor there were the usual reception rooms, and another room, close to the front hall, with a desk and a long, narrow steel table.

'This will be my consulting room,' her father said. 'The patients will wait in the hall.'

Mama's mouth twisted as if she'd sucked a lemon, but she didn't say anything.

Upstairs there were seven bedrooms, one for each of them, including Andrew when he came home from school; Mama would use another as her sitting room, and the remaining two, she said, would be kept for visitors. 'If anyone ever comes to this god-forsaken place to see us,' she'd added, but quietly so Papa wouldn't hear.

Now, only a week after they'd arrived, Isabel had already had enough of sitting in her room after school was over, doing nothing except read, read, read. As the discordant cry of a seagull came from outside her window, she let her book drop to the floor and uncoiled herself from the seat.

Deciding not to ask Mama's permission, lest she say no, she slipped out of the house, found a narrow, well-trodden path behind the stables and set off up a hill. It would have been easier to take the dirt road but then people would have seen her. Although it was unlikely that Mama would be talking to the villagers – or even notice that she'd left the house – someone might mention to her father that she'd been out on her own and he wouldn't be pleased either. He'd been very insistent about her staying close to the house and not wandering off, telling her that the cliffs could be dangerous, especially when the mist came down. Papa and Mama worried too much. The sun was shining, with barely a cloud in sight, and Isabel could see for miles.

Skye was so different from Edinburgh. Here, it

was as if someone had come along with a big broom and swept away the hustle and bustle until there was nothing left but land, sky and water.

The track became increasingly overgrown with bracken, making it much more difficult to find her way. Sometimes the hill fell away sharply, and when she'd peered over the edge she'd been alarmed to find that the cliff dropped vertically into the sea.

On her other side, huddled in the shoulders of the hills, she could see a scattering of croft. At times a house would disappear from sight with only the chimney smoke to identify its presence; then it would come suddenly and dramatically back into view, as if the fairies the islanders believed in had waved their magic wands. Even when she lost sight of the cottages, the clanging of metal on metal, the dull thud of an axe on wood, the voices of women calling to one another over the occasional squeals of children were reassuring.

Then, from the direction in which she was heading, she saw someone walking along the track towards her.

As the figure drew closer, she recognised him. It was Archie, the boy from her class. He was wearing the same wool jacket with patches on the elbows, but his trousers had large holes in both knees and were held up around his waist with a piece of string. His bare feet were stained with peat and grass. However, if he felt discomfited by his appearance he didn't show it. He might have been wearing a dinner jacket, complete with starched shirt and bow-tie, if his bearing was anything to go by.

He carried a gun in one hand and a brace of rabbits in the other. Although Isabel hadn't spoken to him since that first day, she'd been aware of him watching her in class and in the playground where she spent the breaks reading.

'Hello,' he said, with a smile. 'What are you doing out here?'

She liked the way he spoke, almost as if he were singing, or as if each word was a precious object to be savoured.

'I was just walking,' she said.

'On your own?' He lifted an eyebrow.

As if it were any of his concern! '*You're* on your own.'

'But I know these hills like the back of my hand,' he said. 'There are places where you could sink to your knees in a bog or go over a cliff, if you don't look out. Anyway, I didn't think girls from the big houses were allowed out without a chaperone.' The way he said it, with a sarcastic curl to his mouth, made her bristle.

'I'm allowed to go where I please,' she lied. 'Now, may I pass?'

Instead of moving aside, Archie fell into step beside her. 'I might as well come with you.'

She considered ordering him to leave her, but there was something about his otherness and his casual acceptance that he was no different from her that she found intriguing.

'How do you like it here, then?' he asked, his eyes tracking the flight of a crow with evident displeasure.

'I prefer Edinburgh.'

Archie whistled through his teeth. 'I can't imagine anyone liking a place better than Skye.'

'I take it you've been to Edinburgh to have such an opinion?'

His eyes darkened. 'I haven't, but my dad was there and one day I may go too. After Inverness.'

'Inverness?'

'I've won a bursary and will take my school leaving certificate there. After that, I may do anything I like. Go anywhere.' There was no mistaking the pride in his voice.

'You don't want to live here? In the place you love so much?'

'Pah! Remain here? As a crofter? To work all the hours God sends just to have enough to eat, yet not enough to buy proper clothes? No, it's not for me or for my sister, Jessie. She'll win a bursary too and go away to school. She's determined to be a nurse and she'll make a fine one – if she can keep her head out of the clouds, that is.'

'I'm to be a nurse, too,' Isabel told Archie. It didn't seem quite as interesting now she'd discovered Archie's little sister was to become one. 'I might go to university first, though.' The idea had just come to her. She didn't want Archie to think she was going to be an *ordinary* nurse.

His mouth turned up at the corners. 'Girls can't go to university!'

'Yes, they can. If they want to badly enough.'

'And if they have a father who can pay for them.' Despite his words, the look he gave her was one of admiration. 'My dad says it's good to have ambition – that nothing in life is ever achieved without people wanting to improve

32

themselves. I wish I could go to university,' he added wistfully, 'but there'll never be enough money for me to do that. Not until I've worked for many years.'

They had been walking up a hill as they talked, and as they came to the top, Archie pointed to a clearing.

'This is Galtrigill,' he said, with a sideways look at Isabel. 'Or, at least, what's left of it.'

Instead of cottages with people bustling around, the houses were roofless and empty, their stone walls crumbling into the nettled ground.

'What happened?' Isabel asked. 'Where did the people go?'

Archie's lips twisted. 'The Earl of Glendale's manager forced them out about forty years ago.'

'Forced them? What do you mean?'

'He needed the land. For his sheep.'

'*His sheep*?'

'When the price of wool soared, the landowners could make more money from their sheep than they could from the rent.' Archie sat down on a rock, carefully placing his rabbits and his gun at his side. 'They tried to stop the crofters using the grazing for their cattle back in 'eighty-four, but my dad and a few of the other men made a stand against them. They were taken to prison in Edinburgh. It was before I was born, but it's still talked about.' He smiled.

His father had been to prison! And he didn't have the sense to be ashamed! He really was a strange creature.

'My father was one of the Martyrs of Glendale,' he continued. 'He's known throughout Skye. One

33

day people will know my name the way they know his.'

Isabel sat down on a patch of prickly heather. She had the feeling that this boy, with his ragged clothes and bare feet, could do anything he wanted to. She pointed to the rabbits with distaste. 'Why did you shoot them?'

'To eat, of course.'

'But they are only babies!'

Archie eyed her with amusement. 'The smallest are the tastiest. Killing that which you can eat is never wrong as long as you do it quickly and cleanly. In fact,' he jumped to his feet and held out his hand, 'I'll show you how to get a tasty meal. C'mon, the tide's on the way out so it's the perfect time.'

She ignored the proffered hand and scrambled to her feet. Without looking back to see if she were following, Archie set off towards the cliff with long, easy strides.

Curious, she went after him. He stopped at the edge and waited for her. It dropped steeply into a little bay with a narrow stretch of powder-white sand. Looking down made her feel giddy.

'If we go down to the bottom we can pick mussels from the rocks,' Archie said, tugging off his jacket and tossing it onto a clump of purple heather.

'How do we get down there? Fly?'

'We climb. I've done it thousands of times. Just do exactly as I do and you'll be safe.'

The sun beat down on her back and she was uncomfortably hot in her long-sleeved cotton dress. She longed to feel the cool water on her skin but, more importantly, she didn't want Archie to think her a coward. Her heart was pounding with fear and excitement in equal measure.

'Of course, if you're scared...' His blue eyes glittered like the loch. 'You're a girl, after all – although my sister Jessie's climbed it often.'

'I'm not scared,' Isabel retorted. 'I can do anything a boy can – but it isn't seemly for a girl to be scaling cliffs.'

His grin grew wider. 'Suit yourself.' He draped the brace of rabbits around his neck and slung the shotgun over his shoulder.

He was whistling as he disappeared over the edge. Isabel hesitated. Then she sat down to take off her boots and thick stockings. Realising her skirts were going to get in the way, she tucked them into the knee elastic of her drawers. If Mama could see her now she'd have a fit of the vapours.

She took a deep breath and followed Archie over the side.

How she made it to the bottom without falling she didn't know. But make it she did.

She turned, expecting to find Archie looking at her with admiration, but instead he was using a rope to pull a small, blue-painted rowing-boat towards him. In front of her was a sandy, shallow bay, where the boat was moored, and to her left a ramp that sloped gently upwards from the shore.

'We could have walked down that!' Isabel said, pointing.

Archie grinned. 'We could.'

'Why didn't we, then? We might have fallen.'

35

'*I* wouldn't have fallen and I was watching you. You were in no danger.'

Isabel resisted the urge to stamp her foot. He had risked their lives for nothing.

'Anyway, where would have been the fun in coming down the easy way?' Archie continued, passing her the rope. 'Hold this while I fetch your boots.'

Hiding her annoyance, Isabel did as she was asked. She noticed that Archie took the easy way up and down when he went for her things. Had he been testing her? If so, she hadn't been found wanting.

After he'd handed her the boots and stockings, he took the rope from her. 'Let's leave collecting the mussels for another day. Mam wants some salmon for dinner and the tide is right for fishing.'

'Then I shall come with you.' She hadn't risked her life just to go home.

'Very well. But we have to be quick. There's a storm on its way.'

She glanced up. Some clouds had gathered but most of the sky was still bright blue. 'Why do you think that?' she asked.

'Because I can smell the rain in the wind.'

'That's a funny thing to say!' She lowered her voice to a mocking whisper. 'Did the fairies tell you?'

Archie glowered at her. 'Don't ridicule me.'

She was instantly contrite: if anyone knew how to behave correctly it should be her. 'I'm sorry. Of course, if you think a storm is on the way then it must be.'

If he had heard her apology he gave no sign of

it. He brought the boat right up to the edge of the water and helped her in. It had no sail, just oars. There were two planks to use as seats and she took the one at the rear.

As he pushed away Isabel leaned back and trailed her hand in the water. 'Do you like school?'

'I like learning,' he replied. 'Except poetry – that's for girls.'

'But poetry's wonderful! I read it for pleasure. I particularly like Tennyson's "Now Sleeps the Crimson Petal".'

'"Now Sleeps the Crimson Petal",' he mimicked. 'That doesn't make sense! What's the use of learning something that doesn't mean anything?'

'I don't care what it means. I like the sound of it.'

Archie rowed with sure, steady strokes. 'I've read Tennyson. The only poem I like is "The Charge of the Light Brigade". At least it's about something.'

Isabel sat up and propped her elbows on her knees. 'And what do you think that is?'

'Duty. Honour. Courage. The things that matter to men.'

'They matter to women too!' Isabel protested. 'But I hate that poem. It's about acting without considering the consequences – about throwing one's life away on a lost cause.'

Archie regarded her through narrowed eyes. 'A person shouldn't think too much. Sometimes a man has to act because it's the right thing to do for the good of others. A man has to have honour – even if it means losing his life – or he's not a man at all.'

She folded her arms and glared at him. What

37

could a simple country boy know about honour and duty? But then she remembered the way he'd intervened when Flora McPhee had been so horrible. He'd acted like a gentleman. Could she truly say she was behaving like a lady now?

He cocked an eyebrow. 'You don't like to be disagreed with.'

She flushed. For all his talk of honour, she wouldn't put it past him to throw her out of the boat and make her swim to shore.

After rowing for a few minutes longer he pulled the oars from the water. 'I dropped a net here last night.'

When he stood the boat rocked and Isabel squealed. 'Mind you don't tip us out.'

'You've no need to tell me how to keep a boat afloat.' He tugged at the net. 'It's heavy. I could do with your help.'

Isabel picked her way across the rocking boat until she stood next to him.

'Try not to fall in. I might not be able to save you. I might not *wish* to save you.' The last was muttered under his breath. Isabel chose to ignore it.

Together they heaved on the net until, finally, they had it clear of the water. As Archie had said, it was full of wriggling fish.

'One more pull and we'll have it over the side.'

The wet rope bit into her palms and strands of slimy seaweed were clinging to it. Nevertheless she braced her feet against the side of the boat and pulled as hard as she could. Archie must have been stronger than he looked: the net came onto the boat with a rush and, losing her footing on the slippery wood, she fell backwards, landing clumsily in the bottom of the boat. 'Now I'm soaked,' she said, mortified.

If she'd expected praise for her endeavours or sympathy for her fall, she went unrewarded; Archie grinned at her. 'You'll soon dry out.'

She scrambled back to her seat at the stern and eyed the flapping fish with distaste.

Archie handed her a thick stick. 'Help me bash their heads.'

'I will not! Poor things.'

He eyed her incredulously. 'They're fish. They won't feel it.' She winced as he lifted his stick and brought it down hard on a fish's head. It flapped once more, then lay still.

'I can't do that!' She wished she'd never agreed to come on this expedition.

'I thought you were going to be a nurse.'

'I am.'

'Then you should get accustomed to putting living things out of their misery.'

'I shall be healing people, not killing them.'

His grin widened. 'In that case, I'll kill these and you can gut them.'

She shuddered. Gut a fish? The very idea. That was what cooks did.

'What are you waiting for?' he asked, when she made no move to do as he asked.

'I don't know how to gut a fish.'

Archie looked exasperated. 'Then I'll show you when we get back to land. Every woman should know how to prepare a fish.'

Perhaps the women he knew. Certainly not her.

Archie studied the sky, where thick clouds were

gathering now. 'The storm's coming.' As he spoke, drops of rain fell and the boat rose on the swelling waves. Between the smell of the fish and the choppy sea, Isabel began to feel queasy. 'Can we go home now?' she asked.

He peered at her and his eyes softened. 'You don't look well. I'll land the boat near your house. It'll be quicker for you than walking home.'

'My house?'

'Yes. There it is.' He pointed to the shore.

Sure enough Borreraig House was only a short distance away. It was much closer to Galtrigill by sea. To its left, almost hidden in a copse, was a small brick building Isabel hadn't noticed before, with a small jetty in front of it.

'What's that?' she asked, as Archie headed towards it.

'Don't you know? It's the boathouse belonging to your house. The women used to change there for swimming.' He smirked. 'So no one would see them in their swimming costumes.'

'I know what a boathouse is,' Isabel objected. Did he think she knew nothing at all?

Archie tied the boat to the jetty, and as the rain began to fall in earnest, they left the fish where they were and ran towards the boathouse.

Inside there were two armchairs, with most of the stuffing missing, a small table and three wooden chairs, one of which lacked a leg. Cobwebs clung to every rafter and stick of furniture, and although there was a fireplace at one end, the place reeked of mildew. But it was shelter and it wasn't as if she could invite Archie into the house.

When she shivered, Archie frowned. 'You

should change out of those wet clothes.'

'They are not too bad.' She wasn't ready to go back inside. Whatever this boy's faults, she couldn't say he was dull.

'In that case,' Archie picked up an intact wooden chair and set it on its legs, 'sit here while I make a fire.'

He went outside briefly and returned with sticks and lumps of peat. He took a box of matches from his pocket and soon had a blaze going.

'Can you light a fire?' he asked.

When she shook her head, his eyes crinkled with amusement. 'What *can* you do?'

She lifted her chin. 'I can play the piano, embroider – oh, all sorts of things.' Although right at this moment she couldn't think what. When he grinned, she decided she didn't like the way he made her feel, as if *she* were the inferior. She held out her hand. 'Good day to you. My mama will be looking for me. I must leave you now.'

He took it in his strong, calloused fingers and bowed slightly. 'Certainly, Miss MacKenzie. If you want to come fishing again, you have only to say.'

Chapter 3

The next morning, Isabel's father was at the door when she went downstairs for breakfast.

'Please let Mrs MacKenzie know that I have been called to see a patient and I'm not sure how

41

long I'll be,' he said to Seonag, their maid.

'May I come too, Papa?'

When he hesitated, she played her trump card. 'I missed you so much when you were in Africa. Please let me come – I'll be company for you and you'll be company for me.'

'I don't think Mama will approve, Isabel.'

'But as I intend to become a nurse, wouldn't it be good training for me? I know neither you nor Mama believe I have the aptitude for it, but this way you'll see that I do.'

'Have you been listening at keyholes, Isabel?'

'No, indeed, Papa!' She tried to sound shocked. If people spoke in loud voices and left the door open they couldn't expect not to be overheard. 'I simply happened to be passing when you were talking to Mama.'

Papa placed a hand on her shoulder. 'Sometimes you're too clever for your own good, my dear.' Although he sounded cross, she knew he was amused by the way his eyes were smiling. 'Very well. You may accompany me. Let's see what it does to your wish to become a nurse.'

Outside, the cook's husband, Mr MacDonald, had brought round the horse and trap. Her father levered himself onto the seat next to Isabel and passed her his doctor's bag to hold on her lap.

When they topped the rise the village of Borreraig lay before them.

'The houses are so small, Papa. They look as if they're made for fairies, not real people. Couldn't they have made them bigger?'

He frowned. 'The people here aren't rich, Isabel. At least, not as far as money goes. They each have

42

only a small bit of land to work and live on. They build their houses themselves from whatever stones they can find and thatch the roofs with heather and reeds. They might be small but they're warm and dry. Not everyone is as fortunate as you are.'

Isabel flushed. She hated it when he scolded her.

A couple of children detached themselves from their play and ran alongside the cart, giggling and pointing shyly. Their clothes were full of holes and they had no shoes, but they looked as if they were having fun. Isabel felt a pang of envy as she smiled and waved. Papa would see that she knew perfectly well how to behave towards those less fortunate.

When they came to a cluster of crofts, Dr MacKenzie pulled on the horse's reins to bring the trap to a halt. A rusting plough lay outside one of the doors and a child sat on it, pretending it was a horse and cart. Each home had a neat peat stack to the side and a pile of creels. Several children stared at the visitors with open mouths. Anyone would have thought they hadn't seen people before.

A boy of about ten rushed to hold the horse as her father helped Isabel down then looked at her sternly. 'Now, my dear, if I say you have to go outside you must do so immediately. Is that understood?'

The boy, whom Isabel recognised from school, tied their horse to a post. 'My mam's waiting for you, sir.'

The house had only one window and it was so small it let in barely enough light to see. The

43

darkness was made worse by the pungent peat smoke belching from the open fire at the end of the room. It was impossible to think that this was someone's home.

As her eyes adjusted to the lack of light, shapes slowly distinguished themselves. A woman wearing a full grey skirt and a tight-fitting blouse, a plaid scarf covering her hair, came forward and said something in Gaelic.

The boy who had taken the horse hurried to her side. 'My mother doesn't have English, sir,' he said quickly. 'She thanks you for coming.'

Papa smiled briefly and gave the woman a nod of acknowledgement. 'And your name, boy?'

'Alasdair Beag, sir.'

'So, Alasdair Beag, where is the patient?' he asked, setting his bag on a rough-hewn table.

Alasdair pulled back some thin curtains to reveal a boy of about twelve lying on a bed recessed into one of the walls. 'It's Ian, my brother. We were out with the sheep and one of the rams butted him. His leg was bent at a terrible angle so I ran to get help. We took him home on the back of a cart and he screamed all the way.' Alasdair's face was almost as white with fear and shock as his injured brother's.

Ian scowled at him. 'I did not!'

'Ask your mother to light a lamp,' her father instructed Alasdair, 'and bring it here so I can see better. My eyesight isn't what it used to be.'

Isabel knew he was being kind – there was nothing wrong with his eyesight. Anyone would find it difficult to see in the gloom. She suppressed a cough. The smoke made her throat

44

hurt, but she didn't want to give him any reason to send her outside.

The mother lit a paraffin lamp and passed it to her younger son, who held it over the bed. Isabel crept closer until she was standing at her father's elbow. She could see something white sticking through Ian's leg.

Her father's expression didn't change. 'He's broken his tibia – that's one of the bones in his lower leg – and it's come through the skin.'

Alasdair translated briefly and waited for his mother's reply. 'She asks if you can mend it,' he said.

'I'll do my best.'

The woman spoke hurriedly to Alasdair. Her brow was knitted with anxiety and she was twisting her hands together. Alasdair heard her out and turned to Isabel's father.

'My mother says she has no money,' he said. 'She can give you a chicken and some potatoes from the garden. She says I must tell you this now.'

'Tell her that is most acceptable,' Papa said. 'I'm very partial to roast chicken.'

The woman smiled shyly, looking relieved.

Her father turned to Isabel. 'My bag, please. First, I shall straighten the broken bone before I can set it. It will hurt so I will give Ian something to lessen the pain.'

He washed his hands with strong-smelling carbolic soap in an enamel basin of boiled water that the boy's mother had filled from the kettle on the stove. Then he laid out the equipment he would need on a freshly laundered white cloth. Ian's

45

eyes, wide with dread, followed his every move.

'Now, the important thing is to keep everything as clean as possible,' he said, with a glance at Isabel. 'An open wound such as Ian has can become infected very quickly and we don't want that.' He took a thermometer from his bag and shook it. 'From looking at him, though, I think his temperature is normal at the moment. A doctor has to use his eyes as much as his instruments.' He smiled at Isabel. 'A nurse too.'

She liked the way he was explaining everything, as if she were a proper assistant.

He placed the thermometer under Ian's tongue. Then he mixed something together until it was liquid before drawing it into a syringe. 'Morphine is expensive and difficult to come by,' he told Isabel. 'If Ian were an adult, I'd be tempted to straighten his leg without pain relief. Now, Alasdair, do you think you can help me?'

'I can help, Papa,' Isabel said, stepping forward.

Her father looked surprised. 'You're not frightened?'

'No, Papa.' She *was* a little frightened, and she didn't like being in the gloomy house with its strange smells, but she wanted to be the one to help Papa with the boy's leg.

He pushed the needle into Ian's arm and depressed the plunger. 'In a few minutes you'll feel sleepy and your leg won't hurt so much.'

Papa seemed so relaxed. All the tension that had been in his face since he'd come back from Africa had gone. It was as if what he was doing gave him joy from somewhere inside him. A joy, she realised with a pang, that nothing and no one else could give him.

Whatever he had given Ian appeared to be working: the boy's eyes were unfocused and his mouth slack. Her father removed the thermometer and looked at it. 'Good. As I thought. No sign of fever that would indicate sepsis, although that is not to say that he isn't harbouring bacteria that will lead to an infection. We must keep a close eye on him over the next few days.'

Isabel was thrilled when he said 'we', as if she were really helping him.

'The first thing that needs to be done is to straighten the broken bone. Alasdair, could you hold Ian's shoulders? Make sure he doesn't move.'

'And me, Papa?' Isabel asked.

'I need you to hold tight to Ian's thigh. Grip very hard. Keep holding until I say you can stop.'

He waited until everyone was ready, then pulled Ian's leg so hard that Isabel thought it would come off in his hand. Ian moaned and Alasdair winced. A couple of minutes later the leg was straight. After that he cleaned the open wound with something he poured from a bottle, then placed cotton pads soaked in the same solution on top. 'Normally I would stitch the wound together, but not in this case. I'll splint it and apply a bandage.'

While he talked, he was working with graceful, precise movements. There was no hesitation: it was as if his hands knew instinctively what to do. When he had finished, he gave a satisfied smile. 'All we can do now is let nature take its course. I'll show the boy's mother how to change the bandages and clean the wound, and come back to see him in a day or two. Alasdair, could you tell your mother that? If Ian shows any sign of infection – a red face, or if he is sweating and throwing the blankets off – she must send for me immediately. Is that understood? She must only touch his leg when her hands are clean, and she isn't to use any of her own remedies.'

'I'll tell her,' Alasdair said. 'She says thank you and God bless you. She asks if you'll take a cup of tea while I fetch you a chicken and some potatoes.'

'No, thank you,' he said, to Isabel's relief. Now that they'd finished with Ian's leg, she couldn't stay in that room a moment longer. 'I have another patient waiting for me.' He began to pack his bag. 'Perhaps when I come back to see Ian.'

'That was wonderful, Papa,' Isabel said, as soon as they were on their way again, the chicken and potatoes in a sack at the back of the trap.

'Did you think so? Why?'

'You mended that boy's leg. He was in pain and you made him better. That's why I want to become a nurse. I'd like to be able to do that too.'

Her father smiled. 'Nurses don't set legs, Isabel. One needs medical training to do that. I wonder if you will still think it's wonderful if the boy dies. He's not out of danger, my dear. There is a very real possibility that his leg may yet become infected. When a wound is open like his was, there is nothing to stop the germs getting inside.'

'He's not going to die! Don't say that, Papa. Surely people don't die from a broken leg.'

'Once infection gets into the bloodstream we

48

have no way of stopping it, except...' He paused.

'Except what, Papa?'

Suddenly he looked tired. 'I've taught you enough about medicine for one day. But I'll tell you about our next patient. The Countess of Glendale has been suffering with her stomach all week. I suspect she hasn't been eating enough vegetables. You will see that the job of a doctor isn't always exciting.'

Isabel's ears pricked up. Wasn't the Earl of Glendale the landowner whom Archie's father had argued with? 'Where does she live?'

'They're renting Dunvegan Castle while their home in Glendale undergoes renovation.'

'Does the countess have children?'

'I hear so, but as to their ages and whether there'll be an opportunity for you to meet them, I have no idea. I don't know the family well, although I have met the earl once or twice in Edinburgh – they have a house in Charlotte Square as well as one here and another in London. I understand they don't spend much time in Skye.'

Isabel was disappointed. It didn't sound as if there was a girl of her age, also lonely and wanting a friend.

When her father stopped the cart at the side of the road to let a boy herding cattle pass, a thought was forming in her mind. Why shouldn't she become a doctor instead of a nurse? She wanted to do exciting things, like set legs and perform operations. Papa always said how clever she was. She could go to university and study medicine. It was so obvious she wondered why she hadn't thought of it before.

'Papa, I've made a decision. Instead of becoming a nurse, I shall be a doctor like you.'

Her father laughed. 'My dear, it's difficult for a woman to become a doctor.'

'Why? Aren't girls as clever as boys? Aren't there female doctors already? I read in the newspaper that there is a whole university in Edinburgh just for women medical students.'

Now her father was looking at her with speculative eyes. 'I never thought of you as a doctor, but perhaps you are better suited to medicine than nursing.'

'So I *could* become a doctor.'

'It's possible.' He touched her cheek with the back of his hand. 'I'm not sure what your mother will think of your latest scheme. I suspect she'll care no more for your desire to become a doctor than she did for your wish to be a nurse. I know she would be happiest if you made a good marriage.'

'I have no intention of marrying, Papa.'

He laughed as if he didn't believe her. 'Many women find satisfaction in getting married and having a family. Perhaps, one day, when you're older, you will too.'

Isabel knew that she would never change her mind. She would be a doctor one day. Of that she had no doubt.

The trap pulled up outside the castle and a groom hurried over to take the horse. Isabel looked around, eager to see everything. Some of the windows were boarded up, giving the place the appearance of a Gothic ruin. She shivered with delight.

A footman led them up the staircase and into a large drawing room. He announced them and withdrew. At the far end of the room, next to the fireplace, was a woman with a pale face and a large nose. She reminded Isabel of one of the sea eagles that circled over Borreraig House.

'Dr MacKenzie, how kind of you to come.' The voice was strong, the tones perfectly modulated in the English way. 'Please forgive me if I don't get up. Now, who is this you have with you?'

'May I introduce my daughter, Isabel.'

Isabel bobbed a curtsy.

The countess's hand sparkled with diamonds as she beckoned them closer. 'Please, do sit down.'

Once they were seated, Lady Glendale continued, 'Are you finding the work here suitable, Dr MacKenzie? We're not keeping you too busy, I hope.'

'Not busy enough – yet.' Isabel's father answered with a smile.

'And your wife? How does she find Skye? Where is she from?'

'Mrs MacKenzie is from Edinburgh. You may know her father, Colonel MacLean.'

Lady Glendale frowned. 'Not the MacLeans who own the distillery?'

'Yes. Do you know them?'

'We have little to do with the merchant class,' Lady Glendale said, wrinkling her nose. Now she looks like a crow, Isabel thought.

'My wife's mother was Lady Olivia MacLean and her grandmother the Countess of Arbroath,' Papa replied, after a small pause.

Lady Glendale's brow cleared. 'Oh, yes. I'd forgotten. In that case I must invite Mrs MacKenzie to tea and introduce her to some of the others who are here for the summer.'

Isabel suspected she wasn't referring to the crofters' families.

The countess rang a bell that stood on the small table next to her. Within seconds a male servant appeared. 'Ah, Burton, could you bring us some tea?'

'Is there anywhere Isabel could wait while you and I talk?' Papa asked.

'My eldest son, Lord Maxwell, will keep her company. He is with us for the summer. My other children remain in London. Burton, could you take the child to Lord Maxwell and ask him to entertain her until her father is ready to leave?'

Isabel stood. She would much rather have been let loose on her own to explore the castle, but she could hardly refuse what was clearly a command. She followed the servant from the room.

Burton paused in the corridor and pointed to a chair. 'If you would wait here, Miss, I'll let his lordship know you're waiting.'

Isabel sat down, but as soon as Burton disappeared from view she jumped up and opened a door to her right. A little peep couldn't hurt.

It was a dining room with portraits on every wall. She went in and stopped at one of a man wearing a white wig and dressed in red tartan.

'*The Red Man*,' she read aloud. 'The twenty-second Laird of Dunvegan.'

'He looks rather ridiculous, doesn't he?' a voice said, and she whirled around to find a boy of about sixteen standing behind her. He was good-looking in a way that Isabel wished she could be. His features were refined and his blue eyes challenging. The only thing that marred his otherwise perfect face was his mouth. It was small, almost as if it couldn't stretch far enough to smile.

He sketched a bow. 'I gather I'm to keep you company until your father has finished talking to my mother. I am Lord Charles Maxwell.'

Isabel felt unexpectedly gauche in his presence. 'I'm Isabel MacKenzie,' she replied. She pointed to the painting. 'Why is he dressed like that?'

He came to stand next to her. 'I wondered that too,' he said, 'so I asked. Apparently he was the laird when Sir Walter Scott came to stay. There was to be a meeting of all the clan chiefs in Edinburgh and Sir Walter persuaded him that he should dress all in tartan. I think Sir Walter was teasing, but it appears the laird took him at his word.'

'Sir Walter Scott? The writer? He stayed here?' Isabel could hardly believe what she was hearing. Perhaps this castle was the setting for the Wolf's Crag? How perfectly marvellous if it was.

Charles raised his eyebrows. 'You've read Sir Walter?'

'I'm reading *The Bride of Lammermoor* at the moment. I only have a chapter or two left. It's wonderful – although I do think Lucy might have had a little more backbone.'

'I find books tedious,' Charles replied. 'I would much sooner be out riding and hunting.' He smiled slightly. 'If you like I can show you the dungeon.'

A real dungeon? She had to see it. 'If you wish.' She tried to keep her voice from betraying her excitement.

The glint in Charles's eyes told her he wasn't fooled.

'It's here,' he said, opening a door at the other side of the room. Isabel followed him along what appeared to be a servants' corridor and into a small, stone-flagged room. In the centre a grid covered a hole. It was so heavy that Charles grunted with the effort of lifting it. She peered down as he dragged it aside. The hole was at least twenty feet deep with stone walls that were smooth with age. At the bottom there was a space no more than four feet square.

'How did they get out?' Isabel asked.

Charles was standing close enough for her to feel the heat of his breath on her neck. He laughed. 'The idea was that they didn't get out. At least, not until they were dead.'

Suddenly his hands spanned her waist. 'I could give you a shove,' he taunted. 'You could see what it was like for yourself. Of course, I might not be able to get you out again.'

She didn't like his tone – she could almost believe he would do it.

Twirling out of his arms, she stepped away and glared at him. 'That wasn't funny. I believe I would like to go and wait for my father now.'

Her heart was beating fast as Charles studied her with amusement. She'd seen that expression before. On a cat just before it attacked a sparrow. She lifted her chin and returned his look steadily.

'Very well, little Miss Doctor's Daughter. You can go. I've had enough of playing nursemaid, anyway.'

Isabel was quiet on the way home. She had decided she didn't care for Dunvegan Castle now that she'd been there. She didn't tell her father about Charles. What was there to say? That he'd teased her and threatened to throw her into the dungeon? Papa would just laugh. But he hadn't seen the look in Charles's eyes: she had the distinct feeling that he really would have pushed her into the dungeon and left her there.

Skye was a very strange place indeed.

Chapter 4

The remainder of the summer passed quickly. When Isabel wasn't with her father, either helping him in his surgery or going with him on his visits, she was with Archie. She had enlisted Seonag's help to clean the boathouse and Mr MacDonald had repaired the broken chairs. Then she brought down some cushions from her bedroom and a rug she had found in the attic. The boathouse was now her favourite place – especially for reading. No one, apart from Archie, ever disturbed her there.

He was like no other person she had ever met yet she was at ease with him in a way she was with no other, except for Papa. Archie teased her all the time, particularly about her fancy Edinburgh ways, but she soon grew accustomed to it and no longer took umbrage.

Sometimes, when the weather was poor, they met in the boathouse and she would read to him from *The Bride of Lammermoor* but he would soon become impatient with her 'romantic nonsense', as he called it, and insist that they did something more to his liking.

He taught her how to fish, how to lay a fire and, once, he'd even tried to show her how to catch a rabbit. Naturally she'd refused. There were things she would not do – even if doing them would have raised his opinion of her.

All too soon it was time for her to return to Edinburgh where she would start at Miss Gray's School for Young Ladies. Soon after she had gone Archie would leave for Inverness to continue his education.

Her trunks were packed and her travelling outfit for the morning was laid out on the bed. Mama was to accompany her to Edinburgh and would stay for a week or two to spend time with her sons and see Isabel settled. Now, in preparation for the long journey, she had retired to her room to rest. Papa was out on a call.

Pulling on her coat, Isabel slipped down to the boathouse. The winter weather had set in and cold rain lashed the land, bending the branches on the trees and obscuring the view of the hills.

She'd had just enough time to light the fire, a miserable affair, when Archie appeared at the door. 'Do you call that a fire?' he said, by way of greeting. 'It's not enough to keep a family of mice from freezing.' He crouched next to it, added some peats and stoked them until they flamed brightly. 'You go tomorrow, then,' he said, when it was burning to his satisfaction.

'Yes. I am all packed.'

He took the seat by the fire that had become his and stretched his legs in front of him. 'But you'll come next summer?'

'Papa wants me at home whenever it's possible but I shan't be back at Christmas or Easter. What about you?'

'I'll come back when I can. Certainly for the summer. There's too much to do on the croft for my father to manage without me.'

She would miss Archie almost as much as Mama and Papa. She reached up to the mantelpiece, picked up the book she had brought with her and held it out to him. 'I have something for you.'

'What is it?' he asked, turning it over in his hands.

'It's a volume by Yeats. You said you didn't like poetry but I'm determined to change your mind. I thought you might find one in it that you liked.' She shot him a smile. 'One that might *mean* something.'

'I won't be converted. You know that.' He slipped it into the inside pocket of his threadbare jacket. 'Thank you. I'll read it when I'm in Inverness.'

He hunted in the pockets of his trousers, pulled out his hand and examined the contents: a piece of rope, a crumpled handkerchief and a sweetie paper. His cheeks were red. 'As you can see, I've nothing to give you in return.'

57

'It's all right. You don't have to give me a present just because I gave you one.'

'It's not all right.' His eyes glittered and she knew she had offended him. She twisted her fingers together.

'Shall I see you next summer?' she asked.

'If you're not too full of your Edinburgh ways.'

She tipped her head to one side. 'You say the strangest things. Friends don't forget each other.'

'Aye, well, perhaps. We shall see.'

He was still cross with her. This was not the way she'd imagined their parting, but she didn't know how to put it right. 'I must go. Mama will be looking for me.' She stood on tiptoe and dropped a kiss on his cheek.

He flushed a deeper shade of red and rubbed the place where her lips had touched his skin. 'Go, then,' he said, not looking at her. 'I'll dampen the fire before I leave.'

That night she was unable to sleep, regretting that their last minutes together had been so ill at ease. He was too proud, she decided, and there was little she could do about it.

The next morning, when she went to check the boathouse for anything she might have forgotten, she found, in front of the door, a single wild rose from which all the thorns had been carefully removed.

Chapter 5

Skye, summer 1904

Life in Edinburgh was not to Isabel's taste. She liked the school well enough but the other girls weren't interested in discussing things that mattered. They preferred to talk about teas and parties, dresses and future husbands, and she found herself counting the days until the summer holidays.

Finally she was back on Skye, and at the first opportunity that presented itself, she went down to the boathouse, wondering if Archie would seek her company again. She knew he, too, was back for the summer as she'd seen him in the distance, striding across the moors when she was in the trap with her father on their way to visit a child with a sore throat. Papa had promised that this year she could help him in his surgery and go with him on visits – as long as there was no sign of infection.

She needn't have fretted. Almost as soon as she'd lit the fire, which took her far longer than it was supposed to, Archie appeared at the door.

'Did you see what I've done?' she said, gesturing towards the fire she'd made.

'You did that? Without help?'

She picked up a cushion and flung it at him. 'You know I only need to be shown once – twice at most – how to do something!'

When he laughed and threw the cushion back at her, she knew everything would be fine between them.

They talked about the time they'd spent at school, then Archie delved into his pocket and brought out the volume of poetry she'd given him the summer before. 'I brought your book back.'

'It was a present. I meant you to keep it.' She wondered whether to mention the rose but decided against it. Even if he remembered, he might be embarrassed. 'Did you read it?' she asked.

'I did.'

His hands, she couldn't help noticing, were scrubbed, although soil still clung to his finger-nails. At least, since he'd been in Inverness, he had taken to wearing boots.

He returned her scrutiny with a mocking smile. 'Am I smart enough for you, my lady?'

'You'll do.'

'Anyway I still think poetry is girls' stuff!'

She held out her hand. 'Pass it to me. How can you say you're educated if you can't appreciate it?'

'I prefer science and mathematics. They make sense. They're what I need to know if I'm to get on in this world. You should prefer them too if you're to be a doctor. Poems don't help sick people get better.'

'On the contrary, poetry helps people, all people, understand the world.'

'If they can afford the books in the first place. Most folk I know count themselves lucky to own a Bible.'

'A doctor helps a body to heal but poetry is good for the soul. Take this one, for example. How can anyone not feel better after listening to it?'

He leaned forward in his chair, propping his elbows on his knees and his chin on his hands. 'Read it to me, then. Convince me.'

'Very well. I shall read one that reminds me of us.' She found the poem, slid him a look and began:

'When you are old and gray and full of sleep
And nodding by the fire, take down this book,
And slowly read, and dream of the soft look
Your eyes had once, and of their shadows deep...'

When she stopped, she looked up. He was staring at her with the oddest expression. An unfamiliar sensation gathered in her chest. It was as if her heart were being squeezed.

'Go on,' he said, leaning back in his chair, but keeping his eyes on her.

She took a deep breath.

'How many loved your moments of glad grace,
And loved your beauty with love false or true;
But one man loved the pilgrim soul in you,
And loved the sorrows of your changing face.'

She closed the book and placed it on the arm of her chair. Apart from the flickering flames of the fire, there was little light in the room and Archie's expression was concealed from her by the shadows.

61

'"Loved your beauty with love false or true",' he repeated, almost as if he were speaking to himself. 'I wonder which applies to you.'

She laughed. 'I shall always love truly, of course, when the time comes. As you shall.' She looked at him from under her lashes. 'I am sure many of the village girls already have their hearts set on you.'

To her dismay, he muttered something under his breath that sounded like a curse and sprang to his feet. 'Don't talk nonsense, Isabel. What do you know of love?'

She rose to her feet and stared at him. 'As much as you.'

'I doubt that,' he said grimly. He stepped towards her and placed his hands on her shoulders. 'Be careful, Isabel. You're young yet. You don't understand as much as you think you do.'

'I am but a year younger than you!' What could he mean? To cover her confusion she knelt by the fire and added some lumps of peat. Although she couldn't see him, she knew his eyes were on her.

The room was deathly quiet, with only the sparking of the fire.

It seemed for ever before Archie spoke again. 'I'm sorry, I must leave you now. I have work to do.'

When she turned, he was gone.

But if she'd thought their disagreement would keep him away, she was delighted to find it did not. Like the summer before, she saw him whenever she could. It wasn't every day as Archie was kept busy on the croft and she was out frequently with Papa most days.

The islanders became accustomed to seeing her with the doctor and sometimes, if they telephoned or called at the house looking for him but he was out on a visit, they told Isabel their complaint. She learned to ask the right questions. How long have you been ill? What is your cough like? Is there blood? Does your child have a fever? Sometimes she'd advise them to come to the surgery, at others, if she wasn't sure, she'd tell them her father would call to see them as soon as he was able. He was pleased with her. The information she gathered helped him decide which patients required his help more urgently.

Whenever she wasn't helping her father, she was with Archie. He was full of what he was learning at school and they talked for hours, arguing over Darwin's theories or books they had both read.

She became accustomed to him disagreeing with her – more than that, she enjoyed the way their minds clashed and parried. No one at school challenged her as he did, and she told him so.

'They say it's not feminine to be well read and knowledgeable,' she complained.

'Why does it matter what they think?' he replied. 'You must learn to be your own person and not care so much about the opinions of others.'

Of course she didn't care about what other people thought – except Mama and Papa.

Archie told her about the ceilidhs at which everyone met to exchange gossip and news before the singing and dancing started. Now and then the sound of voices, accompanied by fiddles and accordions, soared across the hills to Borreraig

House. She often longed to join in, but Archie had never asked her, and even if he did, she couldn't have gone. Mama would never have tolerated it.

He was her friend. Her only true friend. If she didn't completely understand his moods, it was only to be expected.

Chapter 6

Skye, summer 1906

Life in Edinburgh with her older brother, George, and his family was stultifying. If possible, George was even stricter than Mama, allowing Isabel to go out only with him and his wife, Gertrude, to the theatre or to one of their tedious friends' homes for dinner at the weekends. Happily, Gertrude considered Isabel too young to require her company in the drawing room after dinner so she used the long, empty evenings to study every textbook about medicine she could find. She intended to learn as much as possible before she started her medical studies.

Grateful to be back on Skye, she wondered if Archie would be there. Last summer, to her disappointment, he had stayed in Inverness. Perhaps it would be the same this year.

On the first fine day she went looking for him. When she crested the hill near Galtrigill she was pleased to find him, sitting against a rock and chewing a stalk of clover.

He was dressed in wool trousers – without a single hole, she noticed – and a white shirt with the sleeves rolled up to the elbow. He was also sporting a small moustache. She felt curiously shy of him. Since she'd last seen him, the boy she'd known had grown into a man.

'Isabel! I heard you were back.'

'Of course you did,' she teased. 'Probably the moment I stepped off the boat.'

They shared a smile. Over the years, Isabel had come to realise that there was very little the islanders didn't know about what happened on Skye.

'I knew you were coming before you even left Edinburgh. Dr MacKenzie told my mother you were expected. He also said you're going to finishing school in Switzerland after the summer.'

Isabel grimaced. 'I know. It makes me sound like a piece of incomplete embroidery, doesn't it? But it will allow me to brush up on my German and French. Mama says all women, even if they plan to become doctors, should speak at least one other language fluently.'

There was an uncomfortable silence between them as if they had forgotten how to talk to each other.

'How are your parents? And Jessie?' she asked.

'Mam is well, and Jessie won the bursary right enough but...' his blue eyes darkened, '...she can't take it up. Dad's not so well and Jessie has to stay at home to help Mam look after him.'

They had talked often about Jessie's desire to become a nurse and Isabel knew that she required at least a year's further schooling and her inter-

65

mediate certificate before a reputable hospital would take her on for training. 'I'm sorry about Jessie. Is there nothing to be done?'

'Not for the time being. Maybe in a year or two.'

'And you? You didn't come last year.'

'I was helping to teach at a school for the summer while I studied for my school leaving certificate.' He glanced at her. 'I have it now.'

Isabel frowned. 'I thought you were going to find work as a schoolmaster once you had it?'

Archie shook his head. 'As I said, Dad's not keeping well and I'm needed on the croft.'

'Has my father seen him?'

'Aye. But he can't find anything wrong. He thinks that the time he spent in prison might have weakened his chest.'

Once more silence stretched between them.

An eagle mewed like a cat above their heads. The sun warmed Isabel's face, and from the east, the smell of peat smoke drifted on the wind. One lungful was enough to make her feel at home.

'Mrs MacDonald tells me the people here still look up to your papa for standing up to the Earl of Glendale. You didn't tell me the whole story the first time we met. I'd like to know what really happened.'

Archie jumped to his feet. 'Let's walk while we talk. I've sat long enough.'

He hadn't changed altogether, Isabel thought, smiling to herself He was the same restless, lively Archie she'd always known.

'There's nothing much more to tell than I told you before,' Archie said, as she fell into step beside him. 'Back in the eighties, many of the landlords were clearing the land of people so they could put sheep on it. They reckoned sheep would make them more money than the rents they were getting from the crofters.' His lips twisted. 'They were probably right. It's hard enough to make a living as a crofter without having to pay rent too.' He gestured to the fields. 'They even stopped us gathering heather to thatch our roofs and fill our mattresses. As you can see, there's plenty of it just lying around.'

'That's dreadful!'

'They wanted us out of our homes and off their land. After that it got even harder to make a living and most of the crofters on Skye couldn't keep up with the rent, especially when the factors kept increasing it. You've seen how we live. There's little to spare. And if crofters tried to improve their houses, making them bigger, for example, the landlords wanted more rent.'

'Didn't they care that the crofters couldn't afford it?'

'Most of them don't even stay in the big houses they own. And those who do leave it to the factors and managers to look after their business. I doubt many of them give us much thought.'

No wonder he sounded bitter.

'One day, the earl's factor tried to stop the crofters using the common grazing for their cattle – even though they didn't use it themselves. But the men of Glendale wouldn't accept it. They held a meeting, which was against the law, and decided to ignore the order. My father's croft wasn't in Glendale but he knew that whatever the factors did to them they would do here too, so he joined in the protests. Dad wanted it known that no one could ever put him and his family off his land. Mam was expecting my older brother then.'

Isabel frowned. 'You never told me you had a brother.'

'He died.'

She touched his hand lightly. 'I'm so sorry.'

'It was a long time ago. Before I was born.'

'Tell me more about your father,' Isabel said, 'but let's stop walking so I can concentrate on what you're saying instead of watching where I put my feet lest I step in a cowpat.'

Archie removed his jacket, with the flourish of a man wearing the best that money could buy, and laid it on a patch of grass. The air was heavily scented with clover and freshly cut hay, and splashes of bright purple heather punctuated the hills.

'Where was I?' Archie said, staring out towards the sea. 'Anyway the boat arrived with policemen from the mainland. They wanted to arrest every-one who had been at the meeting. Instead, my father and four others put themselves forward to take the blame. They sent the gunboat packing and insisted on making their own way to Edin-burgh on the RMS *Claymore*.'

Archie was a natural storyteller, Isabel thought. She could imagine the meeting, the men dressed in their kilts (whether they had worn them or not she had no idea, but the image appealed to her), their women clutching at their husbands. Or had the women stood stiff-shouldered and proud? An image flashed into her head. The one from near the beginning of *The Bride of Lammermoor* where, with a flash of steel, the men pulled out their swords after the Keeper threatened to stop Edgar's father's funeral. Isabel had read the book several times and still didn't much care for the pliant Lucy. Edgar, on the other hand, would always be her ideal of a romantic hero. Come to think of it, Archie reminded her of Edgar, except that he wasn't nearly so dour. Not that she would ever see Archie in *that* way.

'The men were sentenced to two months in Canton gaol in Edinburgh for sedition,' Archie continued. 'At first they were treated like any other prisoners, but eventually they gave them proper soft beds to lie on instead of the hard beds the others had.' He smiled. 'Most of them were used to sleeping on straw mattresses at home, or on the mud floor of bothies, so the hard beds wouldn't have bothered them, but they were also allowed a fire and newspapers and the hotel across the road sent them hot meals. To the annoyance of the government, they were treated like heroes. When they were released, almost every islander who could walk was there to greet the Martyrs of Glendale when their boat berthed at Portree.'

'Then what happened?'

'The government set up a commission to look into the problem. That resulted in a change to the law that gave crofters security of tenure. They can't throw us out of our homes any more. It was a victory for the ordinary man, and my father was part of it.'

His voice rose. 'It doesn't change the fact that most of us can't vote and still have to scrape a living from this land, but at least now we have rights that can't be taken from us. Never again will families be forcibly removed from the only place they know, their cottages burned to the ground, and the people put into the cargo holds of ships, like cattle, to be sent to lands they know nothing about, only to die in their hundreds on the way there.'

He smiled ruefully. 'Listen to me! Jessie says I should be a politician. Fine chance when I'm still not allowed to vote.'

'It infuriates me,' Isabel said, 'that only certain men have suffrage. Everyone, including women, should have the right to vote on the affairs of this country. Every person over the age of twenty-one at least.'

Archie tossed aside his stem of clover. 'Well, men should.'

'You don't believe in votes for women?'

'I didn't say that. I just think that if all men, men like my father, had the vote, things would be different. Women wouldn't need the vote then. Their men would look after them.'

Isabel decided to let that pass for the moment. 'How would it be different?'

'We'd be equal. We wouldn't have to work for rich, ignorant men who don't know anything about the land they own. We could make something of ourselves – fight for decent wages and decent living conditions. We could start businesses, make proper money, become politicians, even. Why shouldn't we do anything they can?' He paused. 'Things have to change.'

His words made Isabel feel ashamed, as if she were responsible too. But women had even less power than men. All she could do was try to forge her own future.

'When I was in Edinburgh I saw the suffragettes march in Princes Street. There were hundreds of them – and thousands more women lining the street and waving. One of the leaders rode a horse astride, like a man, and she was dressed in a uniform, like a soldier. I thought she was wonderful. They say they won't stop marching and fighting until women get the vote. Perhaps we're not that different, Archie. Neither of us can do what we want. Not yet, anyway.'

She smiled at him, wanting to banish the darkness in his eyes. 'Whatever happens, we'll always be friends, won't we?'

He frowned. 'I doubt that. You'll be a fine doctor with your own practice, and I'll...' He tugged a clump of grass from the ground and threw it in the air. 'Who knows? Perhaps I'll be a rich man. One thing I do know, I'm not going to be a crofter all my life.'

They sat in silence for a bit, listening to the murmur of the waves on the rocks.

'I'm thinking,' Archie said finally, 'that one day I might go to America. There's talk in the newspapers that a man can make his fortune there if he's prepared to work hard.' He stared into the distance as if imagining this new life for himself.

America! The thought of him going so far away dismayed her. In her mind he was part of Skye and she hated the thought of returning and not finding him here.

'What about the croft?' she asked.

His gaze locked on hers as he leaned back on his

71

elbow and propped his head on his hand. 'Dad will get better and he and Mam will manage. As soon as I make money I'll send it to them. It'll be enough so that they won't have to work so hard, and perhaps enough to pay Jessie's way at school.'

'You have it all worked out, don't you?' Her heart ached at the thought of him leaving. But he was right to think of the future. Archie had always wanted more than the island could offer. And it was too sad that his brother had died. She couldn't bear it if anything happened to Andrew.

He pulled another blade of grass and tickled her under the chin, making her laugh. 'That's better,' he said. 'I don't like to see you sad.'

'I was thinking of what I would do if my brother died. What happened to yours?'

'Mam said a fever killed him. She never knew what it was exactly. She still tends his grave. He's buried at the back of our house.' He shook his head. 'Almost every family here has a brother or sister, or both, buried on their land.'

Isabel felt a pang of guilt – almost as if it were her fault that people like Archie and his family suffered. But her father would never behave towards anyone as the landowners had behaved towards their tenants. He treated everyone with kindness and courtesy, no matter how poor they were.

'Mam says my brother is in a better place,' Archie said. 'She believes we'll all meet again in the next life.' He murmured something in Gaelic she couldn't understand.

'What did you say?' she asked.

'It is a line from the Bible. From the Song of

Solomon. "Until the dawn breaks and the shadows flee." It's written on most of the graves here. Do you not know it?'

'I don't think so, although I like it.'

'Why?' He stared at her intently as if her answer really mattered to him.

She thought for a while. She wanted to tell him exactly how the words made her feel. 'Because it promises so much more than a life with God in Heaven after death. It promises that when pain seems without end, almost beyond bearing and without the possibility of happiness, that it *will* end, and just as the dawn will surely follow even the darkest night, happiness will follow sorrow.'

She took a deep breath when she'd finished. She hadn't known that she'd been going to say all that. Would Archie even understand?

But judging by the way his eyes creased at the corners, he was pleased with her reply. 'You know poetry yet you don't know your Bible. Not so learned, after all,' he teased.

'Just because you know one line from the Bible doesn't mean you know it all.'

He leaned towards her. 'That's where you'd be mistaken. I know the Song of Solomon by heart. I had to learn a book from the Bible and that was one of the shortest.'

'Say it to me, then.'

He raised an eyebrow. 'I will not. It's rude. When I discovered that, I learned another instead.'

'The Bible rude?' She laughed. 'Now I know you're only pretending to have learned it.'

He smiled slowly. 'Don't say you didn't ask for it. Are you ready?'

When she nodded, he continued: '"How beautiful are thy feet with shoes. O prince's daughter! The joints of thy thighs are like jewels, the work of the hands of a cunning workman."'

Heat flooded her cheeks. He was right. It *was* rude.

For a moment the air seemed to shiver between them. As his eyes held hers, Isabel stared back, noticing for the first time that they weren't simply blue but had flecks of navy in them, reminding her of the different colours of the sea. The way he was studying her, as if he could see into her soul, made her heart race.

His voice deepened as he continued. '"Thy neck is as a tower of ivory: thine eyes like the fishpools in Heshbon."'

He reached up a hand and gently touched her cheek. Her skin burned under his fingertips. His arm, she saw, was covered with fine dark hairs.

'"I charge you, O daughters of Jerusalem, that ye stir not up nor awake my love, until he please,"' he continued.

She knew she should pull away, but she couldn't make her limbs move.

'I like your mouth,' he said softly. As his thumb traced the curve of her lips, a strange sensation gathered in the pit of her stomach. 'Have you ever wondered what it would be like to be kissed?' he asked.

She shook her head, unable to speak. It was difficult even to catch her breath.

He cupped her face in his hands. 'Would you like to know?'

She had thought about it, of course she had.

But kissing was for married couples.

However, when he drew her towards him she couldn't bring herself to resist. At first his lips were gentle. Just the merest breath on hers. She opened her mouth in a little gasp – 'Oh' – and his tongue flicked against her teeth.

She liked it. And she liked the way he smelt of sea and the wind.

She leaned forward, pressing her mouth to his. He sat up and wrapped his arms around her and she buried her face in his shirt. Closer now, she could smell the salty, musky maleness of him and feel his chest hard against her face. His hands were entwined in her hair. '*Mo ghaoil,*' he whispered. 'You are so beautiful.'

Frightened by the strange sensations running through her body, she drew away and jumped to her feet. She glanced around, worried that someone might have seen them, but to her relief all she could see were flocks of sheep, grazing contentedly. 'I should go. Mama will be looking for me.'

He studied her through half-closed eyes. 'One day, when you're older, perhaps you'll find the courage to be your own woman.'

She tossed her head and glared at him. 'I'm my own person now, Archie MacCorquodale. A woman already. And you should have known better than to kiss me.'

His eyes were pools of fire and ice. 'A kiss you returned with more passion than a man could hope for.'

Her face burned. 'If you're going to try to kiss me, perhaps it's better if we don't meet again,' she said stiffly. 'It isn't seemly.' And, with the feel of his lips still imprinted on hers, she hurried away.

The kiss changed everything. Afterwards, she could no longer see Archie just as a friend, and they could never be anything else. For all that she cared about him, he was still a crofter's son and it wasn't as if they could ever be together. Not in that way.

Even if that alone hadn't made it impossible, she was going to be a doctor and there was no room in her life for anything else.

For the rest of the summer she kept away from the hills and the boathouse, instead remaining with her mother in the drawing room when her father didn't require her assistance. Although she missed Archie horribly, and longed to return to the easy camaraderie they'd once shared, she knew it could never be the same between them again. And for some reason the realisation made her heart feel like a handful of dust.

Chapter 7

Skye, August 1908

Jessie's life was over. Dad was dead and, although she was only just sixteen, she might as well be dead too. Of course she still had Mam and Archie, but could she really spend the rest of her life here when her heart cried out to be in the city so that she could work as a nurse? But what choice did she have?

Using the pitchfork her father had made, Jessie gathered up the remains of the cut hay and threw it onto the cart. She placed her hands on either side of her aching back, knowing she was a long way from finishing for the day.

Although it was more than six months since he had died, she still missed him terribly. He wasn't the only one to have been taken in the typhoid epidemic that had swept across Skye last winter. In their village alone, Peggy Ban had lost two of her children, and Jessie's best friend, Fiona, had lost her mother. With Dad's death, all the light had gone out of Mam's eyes. At least Archie was home to stay.

He'd changed. His hopes of leaving Skye were over too, and they no longer spoke of him going to America. Without the money Dad had brought in from fishing, there simply wasn't enough to be made from the croft for Jessie and Mam to pay the rent and keep food on the table. Archie had had to take over the responsibility of providing for them. Sometimes he'd be away fishing for days at a time and Jessie would be left with all the croft work as well as her own chores.

But that wasn't what she minded. Her dream of going away to school was in shreds too. Although she'd won the scholarship there was no money spare for her to go to Inverness.

It was wrong to think like that. Daddy was dead and she shouldn't be caring that his death had destroyed her dreams, but she couldn't help it. How could she become a nurse without the proper schooling?

Even Flora McPhee had managed to get what she wanted. To everyone's astonishment, she had succeeded in securing a job as a maid at Dunvegan Castle. The earl and countess were still there, although the renovations to their house in Glendale were finished. People said that Lady Glendale had become accustomed to living in a castle.

Life at the castle seemed to suit Flora too. Her figure had become voluptuous and her breasts the envy of the other girls in the village. She had taken to washing herself and, on the rare occasions she had come back to the village to see her mother, had looked almost beautiful in a dress that was obviously a castoff from Lady Glendale or her daughter, Lady Dorothea.

But Flora's triumph had been short-lived. Her pregnancy had caused a scandal when it had become known. She'd tried to claim that Lord Maxwell had made her fall, but no one believed her. What would a man like him want with a below-stairs maid? Flora was always trying to make herself out to be better than she was. When her pregnancy had become evident, she'd been turned away from the castle and sent home in disgrace. A few days later she was seen in the village with a black eye.

Archie had gone to see Lachie, Flora's father, when he'd heard he'd returned to his old ways, and had told him that if he ever lifted a hand to one of his womenfolk again, he would personally throw him over the side of the cliff. Jessie wouldn't have put it past him. Archie could be hot-headed.

She gathered up the reins and set off for the barn. After she'd finished unloading the hay, she unhooked the horse from the cart, rubbed him down and gave him water. By the time she was able to make her way home the sun was low in the sky.

Despite the light from the fire and the oil lamps, it took her eyes a few moments to adjust to the darkness. Mam was alone, sitting in her chair by the fire, staring into space, with her usually occupied hands empty. It made Jessie feel uneasy.

'What's wrong, Mam? Are you ill?'

In the last few months her mother's hair had turned white in places. She had lost weight, too, and stooped now when she walked. Jessie could see how much her mother had aged and it frightened her. What would she do if God decided to take her too?

'I'm all right, *mo luàidh*. Just a little tired, that's all.'

Jessie knelt by her mother's side. 'Can I make you some eggnog? Or warm some porridge on the stove?'

She shook her head. 'I'm not hungry. Where is your brother?'

'I don't know, Mammy.'

Her mother plucked at the folds of her dress. 'I wish I could have let him stay in Inverness,' she said. 'It's not right that he had to come back here.'

What about me? Jessie wanted to cry. How can it be right that I had to give up my chance too? Of course she didn't say anything. It wouldn't change the way things were.

There was the scraping of boots outside and Archie appeared at the door. Over the years he had shot up to almost six foot and had to duck to avoid hitting his head on the lintel. He shrugged out of his wet jacket and set it next to the fire to dry. He ignored the empty chair next to their mother, which had been Dad's, and took a seat on the wooden settle by the window. 'She's back,' he said, tugging off his boots.

'Who?' Jessie asked.

'The doctor's daughter. Isabel. Their motor-car passed me on the road to Dunvegan.'

'Did she talk to you?'

Archie's mouth twisted in a smile that didn't reach his eyes. 'She waved.'

'Archie,' their mother said gently, 'the days when Isabel MacKenzie and you could be friends are past. She's a young woman now and you're a grown man. You mustn't expect that things can continue as they were when you were younger. It wouldn't be right.'

Archie lifted his chin. 'Not right, Mam, because she's a woman or because she's the doctor's daughter and I'm a crofter?'

'Oh, Archie, don't tell me you have hopes of her. It's impossible. You must know that.'

'You and the doctor's daughter? She'll never give any of us the time of day now she's been to that fancy finishing school,' Jessie scoffed.

Archie scowled. 'Be quiet, Jessie. You know nothing about her. She might consider herself above most, but she doesn't see me like that. She knows I have ambition, that I won't always be a crofter.'

80

So that was the way of it. Archie had feelings for Isabel. When Isabel had first come to Skye, he had spent a lot of time with her. As soon as work on the croft was finished he'd be off, sometimes without either his gun or a fishing line. Jessie had followed him once, curious to know what he was doing, and had seen him meet the doctor's daughter, then stride along with her as Isabel, with steps almost matching his, chatted non-stop. Every so often, Archie would nod and laugh as if whatever she had said was the funniest thing he'd ever heard. But the last time Isabel had been back for the summer Archie had gone out and returned with thunder in his eyes. Jessie suspected that the doctor's daughter had grown tired of him. Poor Archie. He was a fool if he thought she would ever let him woo her.

'Anyway, I'm still going to go to America when I get the chance,' Archie continued.

'You can't go to America and leave Mam and me!'

'I'd send for you, once I'd made my way.'

'I'm not going anywhere,' their mother said quietly. 'This is where Dad and your brother are buried. I'll not leave them.'

A look of resignation crossed Archie's face, and when he smiled, Jessie could tell he was making an effort for Mam's sake. He pulled their mother out of her chair, placed his hands on either side of her waist and swung her into the air, making her giggle. 'In that case, I'll have to stay where I am, won't I?'

'How did Isabel look?' Jessie asked.

'She looked ... grand. But different. You'll see

her yourself soon enough, I reckon.'

Whenever Isabel had been back on Skye she had helped her father, either at his surgery or on his visits, and more than once Jessie and her mother had met her on the road when she'd accompanied Dr MacKenzie to see a patient. Everyone had heard that she was leaving shortly to start her medical studies at Edinburgh University and Jessie envied her with all her heart.

'I imagine I will,' she said.

Unless Isabel had become too grand to come to the villagers' homes with her father, sooner or later their paths would cross.

Chapter 8

'The Earl and Countess of Glendale have agreed to host your coming-out ball,' Isabel's mother said, looking pleased.

'Oh, Mama, is it necessary?' Isabel flung herself onto the sofa beside her mother. What was the point in a coming-out do? It wasn't as if she had any intention of marrying. At least, not until her studies were over and she was a fully qualified doctor.

'Please don't loll around as if you were a sack of potatoes, Isabel. Didn't the school in Switzerland teach you anything? The moment you're back on this island you seem to lose all sense of decorum.'

'I'm sorry, Mama.' Isabel sat up straight and smoothed her dress. She smiled at her mother. 'Is that better?'

'A little. Do you know your hair has come loose?'

'Oh, never mind that, Mama. Aren't you just a little pleased to have me back?'

Her mother patted her hand. 'Of course I am, darling. You know how much I miss having my children with me. If only Andrew could be here too.'

Andrew, the younger of Isabel's two brothers, was supposed to have joined them, but had been invited to tour the continent with the family of one of his friends before returning to Cambridge after the summer break. Isabel still hoped he would come to Skye, or Edinburgh at the very least, before the new term started. She'd seen too little of him over the last few years.

'He couldn't turn down the chance to see Europe, Mama. I'd love to be in his shoes – I wish I could go to Florence and Rome!'

The truth was, Isabel had been invited to stay with a friend in Italy but had turned it down. This was to be her final summer on Skye. She had missed the island – and her parents – and hadn't told them about the invitation. Mama would have insisted she go.

'And even if I do have to have a coming-out ball, why can't we have it here at Borreraig House? It's big enough. How many people do you propose to invite?'

A look of distress crossed her mother's face to be replaced quickly with a tight smile. 'This house is too small for even the small number of guests who will be coming from Edinburgh and London. Besides, the countess says she'd like nothing more than for you to use the ball she is giving for your coming-out.'

When Isabel opened her mouth to protest again, her mother held up her hand. 'I know it's not quite the same as having a proper coming-out ball in London, or even Edinburgh, but given Lady Glendale's connections, it will suffice.'

'You know I don't give a fig about a party, Mama, but if it makes you happy, then do thank the countess for me.'

Mama fixed her pale blue eyes on Isabel. 'Just one thing. Please don't mention the fascination you have with medicine. It is neither polite nor interesting. Find something more suitable to discuss with the other guests.'

'Of course, Mama. I shall talk of nothing but the latest fashions, even if I get my silk mixed up with my chiffon. Will that please you?'

'Don't be sarcastic, Isabel. It's not becoming. And speaking of fashion, we must have new gowns for the occasion, although goodness knows how I'm to go about it when I'm miles from a decent dressmaker.'

Leaving her mother to fret over what they would wear, Isabel went to her room to bathe and change. She wondered whether she would see Archie. She'd often thought of the way he'd kissed her when she was sixteen and it still made her feel hot and strange. But the kiss had spoiled their friendship. Even at sixteen she'd known that Archie could never be anything but her friend, and that had been two years ago. Surely he would understand now that he had mistaken her friendship for something that could never be.

As her maid helped her out of her dress, Isabel sighed. Perhaps it was better to avoid Archie while she was here. What could they possibly have in common now they were adults?

On the evening of the ball, Isabel and her parents set off for Dunvegan Castle. Her father had been away on the mainland so she had been confined to the house, with only her mother for company, over the last two weeks. It had made her long for the ball. That, and the way she'd looked when she'd seen herself in the mirror. The ivory silk her mother had had made up for her suited her complexion perfectly, and although she wished she had more curves, the tight bodice and the fashionably narrow skirt flattered her rather boyish figure. With her hair upswept into a chignon, but for a few loose curls framing her face, and crowned with the ruby tiara her parents had given her for her birthday, Isabel knew she wouldn't be out of place at the castle.

Her father had bought one of the new motor-cars and had insisted on driving them there himself. Isabel, in the seat next to him, held on tightly to the door handle to keep her balance as it lurched over the potholes. Her mother was in the back seat with her eyes screwed tightly shut. Her father told Isabel that Mr MacDonald had refused point-blank to have anything to do with the vehicle so he had taught himself to drive, but unlike the gentle touch Papa had with his patients, he tugged the steering-wheel this way and that, as if it were a badly behaved horse.

'You should teach me to drive,' she suggested, as

the car tipped onto two wheels when her father mistimed another pothole.

'I don't think so,' he replied. 'It takes strength to keep these beasts under control.'

It wouldn't if he would only keep out of the holes. She'd teach herself to drive when he was otherwise occupied. It couldn't be that difficult. In the meantime, she'd watch exactly what he did so she could try on her own later.

At least the car roof prevented the rain from soaking them. It had eased off in the last hour, but now a thick mist mingled with the smoke coming from the crofters' chimneys and obscured the views of the sea and cliffs, which she missed whenever she was away from Skye.

At last the car pulled into the long driveway at Dunvegan Castle. Although, like the rest of Skye, the castle had no electricity, it was lit up as if a thousand fires burned within. A frisson of excitement danced up her spine.

After the butler had taken their wraps and her father's coat, he showed them into the already crowded ballroom.

The countess came across to them and kissed her mother's cheek. 'My dear Clara, how well you look tonight. And, Isabel, you've grown since I last saw you. You're quite the young lady now.'

Why did people always say that? Did they honestly think people got smaller as they grew older? Come to think of it, perhaps they did. She certainly never remembered her father being so small. Anxiety gnawed at her. Despite the unpolluted air of Skye, his cough had worsened over the years and he was pale, his cheekbones increasingly prominent. He should take some time off. Even doctors needed rest.

Mama, on the other hand, was glowing. She was wearing a dress ordered especially from London that emphasised her still tiny waist and long neck. Her eyes glittered with suppressed excitement, although no one besides Isabel and perhaps her father would have noticed. Mama was too adept at portraying the slightly bored, languorous air that women in her position seemed to think was the only acceptable expression in polite company.

'My dear Henrietta, how kind of you to have us. Is Glendale well?' Mama asked.

'Busy as always. It keeps him in London, I'm afraid. Our eldest son, Charles, is here and my daughter Dorothea too. Her twin, Simon, and our other son, Richard, are occupied in England.' She looked around as if expecting one of her children to appear at her elbow. 'There are other young people too, Isabel, so you shouldn't be bored.'

'I am rarely bored, Lady Glendale,' Isabel replied.

'Bored? Did someone say they were bored?' A man appeared at Lady Glendale's side. Isabel recognised him immediately. It was Charles.

As he greeted her parents, Isabel studied him surreptitiously from under her lashes. He was even more handsome than he had been when they had first met and a lot taller, topping her father by at least six inches. He wore his blond hair a shade longer than was fashionable, and Isabel suspected he knew it gave him a reckless, devil-may-care look. Unlike his contemporaries he was clean-shaven and a smile played across his narrow mouth.

He bent over her hand and she was aware of the faintest pressure of his lips through her silk evening glove.

'How do you do, Miss MacKenzie?' He raised his pale blue eyes to hers. She read admiration in his gaze and her heart cartwheeled. 'We have met before, I believe.'

'You threatened me with the dungeon, Lord Maxwell,' she said, with a smile, pleased that her voice didn't sound as breathless as she felt.

'I know. I was unkind to you, and you must promise to forgive me.' With a quick glance at his mother, who was introducing Isabel's parents to a man with a well-oiled moustache, he leaned towards her and whispered, 'If I'd known you were going to turn into such a beautiful woman, I would never have risked your anger.'

She knew she was blushing and, for the first time she could remember, she was speechless. Was she beautiful? But men said that all the time, didn't they? She had no idea. The only men she knew were her father, her brothers – and Archie. And they weren't suitors.

She turned away to hide her consternation. 'This is a charming room, and this...' she stepped over to a painting of a woman with a mischievous smile holding a small child's hand, '...is truly a beautiful woman. Is she related?' As soon as the words were out of her mouth she wished them back. She might as well have called him beautiful to his face.

The implication clearly didn't escape him. He grinned. 'She was the wife of one of the lairds and was considered a beauty, although she had, shall we say...' he dropped his voice again, '...a reputation.'

He widened his eyes theatrically and she had to laugh. 'I like the sound of her,' she said. 'I confess I feel an affinity with women who do not conform.'

'You are your own person, then,' he said. 'I, too, prefer those who can think for themselves. It's so dull always to be doing what is right, don't you agree?'

'I do.' She found she wanted to impress him with her sophistication. 'Society is too rigid, some might say stifling. Too many believe that women exist only to be admired and looked after.'

'But you don't?'

'I would like to be free of convention. Indeed, I have decided to follow my own way.'

'And what way would that be?'

Before she had a chance to answer she heard the rustle of silk as someone came to stand next to them.

'Speaking of women who spurn convention, have you been introduced to my sister, Dorothea?'

If Charles was good-looking, his sister was exquisite in a way that took one's breath away. Her hair was a deep red that seemed to glow in the light from the candlelit chandeliers. She was wearing an emerald dress that complemented her colouring, and the neckline of her pearl-studded bodice – lower than was normal in polite society – exposed the swell of her creamy breasts. Her mouth was wide, her nose straight, and she had an impish look in her blue-green eyes.

'Don't believe a word my brother says.' She laughed, holding out her hand. 'How do you do? You must be Miss MacKenzie in whose honour we're holding this ball. My only regret is that we haven't met sooner. I don't come to Skye very often, I'm afraid.' She lowered her voice. 'I find it a little tedious, don't you?'

For a second, Isabel was tempted to agree. It would make for a more amicable exchange. But fiddlesticks! When had she ever cared about making herself agreeable?

'Actually,' she said, 'although Edinburgh has its charm, I feel most at home here on Skye.'

Dorothea lifted a perfectly shaped eyebrow and smiled. 'You don't miss the balls and the operas? I find Edinburgh less to my liking than London, but at least it has some entertainment. Apart from dining with the other families from the Houses, and riding one's horse, there's simply nothing here to keep one occupied. Don't you like to be occupied, Miss MacKenzie? But I have heard you plan to be a doctor. I could scarcely believe it. You must be very clever.'

Isabel was feeling increasingly gauche and wrong-footed. But she would not let this woman treat her as if she were an eccentric blue-stocking.

'I enjoy my studies,' she said stiffly. 'As much, I suspect, as you enjoy balls.'

'Please, Miss MacKenzie,' Dorothea responded, 'don't take offence. I admire you. I sometimes wish I had something to feel passionate about, although I do find passion rather draining.'

'My sister is easily bored,' Charles put in. 'She

changes her mind from one day to the next as to what amuses her.'

Isabel didn't care for the derision in his voice, but it didn't appear to annoy Dorothea.

'Would you excuse me, Miss MacKenzie? I have other guests to welcome. Perhaps you will come for luncheon one day. I should very much like to get to know you better.' The glint in Dorothea's eyes suggested she would be more interesting company than most.

'Unfortunately,' Isabel replied, 'I shall be returning to Edinburgh shortly to take up my studies.'

'Then we must meet there. My parents have a house in Charlotte Square and we stay there frequently in winter.'

She smiled again and left Isabel with Charles.

'I thought the castle belonged to the MacLeods, but your sister resembles the woman in the painting so much that I feel certain you must be related to them.'

Charles pretended to glance around to see if anyone were listening, then bent to whisper in her ear, 'It's all kept quiet. The woman in the painting divorced the laird. She then went on to have a child – my maternal grandmother. Some say that the child was the result of a relationship with royalty. My mother can't make up her mind if she wants it to be true or not.'

Isabel laughed, but before she could respond a hand cupped her elbow and she looked around to find her father standing beside her.

'My child, we monopolise Lord Maxwell. I believe he has other guests to attend to.' Although his voice was light, there was an undercurrent in his tone that alerted her: he wasn't best pleased to find her talking to Charles. She wondered why. It wasn't as if they were alone. 'Will you excuse us, sir?' her father said and, taking Isabel by the arm, steered her towards the other side of the room. 'Would you care for some lemonade, my dear?'

'Yes, please, Papa.' She was perplexed. 'I'm sorry,' she said, 'if I did something wrong.'

He beckoned to one of the servants holding a tray. 'You did nothing wrong, but you're still very young,' he said. 'There are things I cannot tell you, but I would prefer you not to spend time with Charles Maxwell.'

'I shall soon be nineteen, Papa. Many women are married when they're younger than I.'

They took drinks from the tray and waited until the servant had moved away.

'My dear, as you're always telling me, you have no ambition to be married. Or have you changed your mind about your medical studies?'

'I'll never change my mind about that, Papa. Perhaps one day I will choose to marry, but that day is such a long way off, I can barely conceive of it.'

'I'm glad to hear it. I'm not yet ready to lose my daughter to another man – if I ever shall be.'

She squeezed his arm. 'Dearest Papa. You shall never lose me, no matter how hard you try. Don't you know that?'

The rest of the evening passed in a blur. When the dancing started, a mix of waltzes and Scottish country, Isabel was never short of partners. Usually she preferred the rhythm of the swirling reels and schottisches to the more sedate pace of the waltz, but when Charles claimed her for a dance and she placed her hand in his, it was as if she had entered a different world. Until now, most of her dancing practice had been with other girls at her school in Switzerland, but instead of the soft palms and curved waists of her friends, Charles's hand was firm, his body hard and masculine. He smelt different too, his cologne musky and faint but no less appealing than the perfume women used.

As they moved together Isabel's heart was pounding. 'There's a shooting party tomorrow. Will you join us?' Charles murmured.

'I don't care to watch the slaughter of innocent animals,' she said.

'Not even birds? They hardly count, surely.'

'I don't wish to see anything killed just for sport.'

He twirled her around and the other guests faded into the background.

'If you cannot be persuaded to join the shooting party may I call on you and your mother?'

She hesitated. Papa had made it clear that he wouldn't like her to associate with Charles, even if he was the earl's son. Nevertheless it was time he realised she was grown-up and able to make her own decisions. Yet she couldn't ask Charles to the house in direct opposition to her father's wishes.

'I go out walking most days. I suppose if we should chance upon each other...' She shrugged her shoulders, terrified but excited by her own daring.

His eyes held her gaze. 'I don't walk for the pleasure of it, although sometimes I ride out to look at my father's estates. Happily they are near where you live and it might be that I shall ride that way on Monday.'

'Then if we chance to meet, I shall not ignore you.'

The string quartet brought the dance to an end. It was almost midnight and time for the guests to depart. Charles released her and bowed.

'I look forward, Miss MacKenzie, to seeing you again,' he said. 'Soon.'

Chapter 9

'Jessie, hurry up and get ready. It's her first, so it'll take a while to arrive, but her mam says she's been labouring since this morning.' Flora's baby was coming a little early and Jessie had been out on the far croft when her mother had whistled for her.

'You go on, Mam. I'll follow when I've finished here.'

After she had left, Jessie laid aside some cold mutton and potatoes for Archie when he came down from the fields and covered it with a cloth to keep off the flies. On another plate, she put a slice of clootie dumpling she'd made the day before and covered that too. Then she wrapped a shawl around her head and went out into the wind.

The McPhees still lived in a blackhouse, one of the few remaining on the island. Unlike their home and most of the other houses, it had no windows and the open fire was in the centre of the room, with only a hole in the ceiling to let the smoke disperse. The arrangement didn't work as well as a proper chimney and the house was so filled with smoke it was almost impossible to see, even with the light from the oil lamps.

Although the wind was driving the rain in horizontal sheets, Jessie's mother had cleared the house of the remaining six children and Jessie guessed they would be taking shelter in the byre. They would be cold and damp but there was no room for them inside as well as Jessie, her mother, Flora and Flora's mam. Happily, Flora's ill-tempered father was nowhere to be seen. Men didn't stay about the house when a baby was being born – not if they could help it.

Flora was cursing under her breath. 'I don't want this baby. Get it out of me!'

'Now, Flora, all women say that when they're giving birth,' Mam said mildly. 'You'll feel different when you're holding it.'

'I won't,' Flora grunted, through gritted teeth.

'Hush now. Save your strength for what's ahead.' She leaned over the bed and, using her hands as Jessie had seen her do so many times before, felt for the baby. 'The baby's on its way, Flora. It won't be long now. Could you open your legs so I can have a wee look down below?'

When her mother raised her head, Jessie saw alarm in her eyes.

'Now then, Flora, you just lie there for a minute.' She stepped away from the bed and beckoned Flora's mother to her. 'Jean, we need to get the doctor.'

'What is it, Mam?' Jessie asked. For all the babies she had watched her mother deliver, she had never seen such a look of fear in her eyes.

'The afterbirth is lying in front of the baby.'

Jessie's heart lurched. When that happened, it often caused massive bleeding that couldn't be stopped. Her mother had told her that this very thing killed women and their babies.

'I don't know what that means!' Jean cried.

'It means she needs more help to deliver this baby than I can give her,' Mam replied, her voice calm. 'We need to send for the doctor.'

'The doctor! We don't have money for the doctor!'

'Never mind about that now, Jean. He'll come whether you have money to pay him or not. Now, who can you send?'

'Hector will go.'

'Tell him to run as fast as he can. He must tell the doctor to come straight away. Will he do that?'

Jean shouted for her son, and a scrawny boy with sad eyes hurried into the house. After a few curt words to him, his mother gave him a none-too-gentle shove out of the door.

Flora was writhing in pain, but her lips were clamped together as if she were damned if she'd let Jessie see how much it was hurting. Jean returned to the bed to sit by her daughter's side and, taking a damp cloth, pressed it to her forehead.

'What can we do, Mam?' Jessie whispered.

'I didn't want to tell Jean but Flora's bleeding badly. All we can do is keep her comfortable until the doctor gets here. She asked to get up and walk around, but I said no. This is one time I don't want to hurry the baby along.'

'How far apart are her pains?'

'Three minutes and getting stronger. If the doctor doesn't come soon...' She shook her head. 'I don't know if I can do this for much longer, Jessie. I have little heart for it any more.'

Jessie took a deep breath to quell her rising panic. Although she and Flora had never got along, she wished her no ill. She had never seen anyone die before and she didn't know how she would cope if it came to that.

Jean had set a pan of water over the fire to heat. Jessie found a bowl and tipped some in. She washed her hands thoroughly, using the carbolic soap her mother always carried with her, then dried them with the clean towel she had brought too. Jessie knew that this time her mother needed her help more than ever, and if the doctor didn't arrive soon, they would have to do the best they could.

But as she laid aside the towel, the door opened and the doctor entered, bringing with him a lash of rain. Isabel was with him. Jessie hadn't seen her since she had last been home on Skye and was taken aback by how much she'd changed. There was no sign of the schoolgirl who had once tramped the moors. Instead, with her hair up and her long dress of deep blue silk, she looked every inch the young lady. Jessie felt more in awe of her than ever.

She bobbed her head at Isabel, who smiled back. The doctor peeled off his greatcoat and placed it over the chair. 'Can we have more light in here?'

'Thank God you've come, Doctor,' Jean said. 'I'll light another lamp for you.'

'You should go and see to the other children, Jean,' Mam said softly. 'You could take them to our house. Perhaps you could give them a bite to eat. Archie will bring you back later.'

Jessie suspected she wanted Flora's mother away from what might happen.

Jean hesitated, but then, with a final whisper to her daughter, left the house.

'What do we have, Mrs MacCorquodale?' the doctor asked.

Jessie liked the respectful way he addressed her mother.

'The afterbirth is lying in front of the baby,' she said. 'As soon as I realised, I didn't touch her.'

'Placenta previa,' Jessie said, using the correct term. She couldn't help showing off, especially in front of Isabel.

'Well done, Jessie.' The doctor rewarded her with a smile, then turned back to her mother. 'You did the right thing. Many a woman has suffered from interference born of ignorance. Isabel, what do you know about the condition?' As he spoke, he rolled up his sleeves and washed his hands in the basin of clean hot water Jessie had placed by his side.

'When the mother bleeds heavily it can be difficult, if not impossible, to stop it. I have read that delivering the baby through a cut in the uterus is the only way to prevent this,' Jessie said eagerly, before Isabel could answer.

'That's right, Jessie.' Dr MacKenzie gave her another nod of approval before bending to examine his patient.

Flora was so immersed in her pain, Jessie doubted if she'd been aware of a word they'd said. She hoped not, for her sake.

'Open your legs, Flora, and let the doctor have a look,' Mam said, helping her to spread her knees apart. Jessie took the lamp and held it high so that the doctor could see. She was conscious of Isabel's perfume as she leaned over her shoulder.

Dr MacKenzie straightened and placed a hand on Flora's abdomen.

'The pains are coming two minutes apart,' Mam told him.

Dr MacKenzie nodded. 'I'm going to have to deliver this baby by Caesarean section and un-fortunately I shall have to do it here. I'll need help. Mrs MacCorquodale, if you could get everything ready for the baby – warm towels and so forth. Jessie, you can help with the anaesthetic. Don't worry, I'll guide you as we go along – it's really quite straightforward. Isabel, you will be my assist-ant.'

'Very well, Papa.'

'I can't operate on her on this bed. Let's have her on the kitchen table with as much light as possible. We'll also require as much boiled water as you can manage, Mrs MacCorquodale.'

No one said anything as they set about getting ready. Jessie cleared the kitchen table and scrubbed it quickly with boiling water and carbolic soap. Dr MacKenzie took something from his bag that looked like an oversized perfume bottle and sprayed the table, filling the room with the not unpleasant smell of antiseptic. Isabel found a crate and placed it on some bricks to act as a table for Dr MacKenzie's instruments, checking to make sure that it was at the right height and wouldn't fall over easily. Jessie's mother boiled more water and filled clean basins, while talking to Flora in a low voice.

When they had made the preparations, Dr MacKenzie explained to Flora what he was going to do.

'Where's my mam?' Flora asked, looking frightened for the first time. 'I want my mam!'

'She'll be back as soon as she can,' Jessie's mother soothed. 'Don't worry, we'll look after you. In a very short while you'll have your baby to hold.'

'I don't want the baby. I've told you that. I want my mam!' Flora began to wail. 'I should never have let Charles Maxwell near me. Just because he was the son of an earl. He said he cared for me, but when I told him about the baby he saw that I was turned out.' Her words were coming in short bursts between groans of pain. 'He said I must have been with someone else. He knows that's not true. How could he do this to me? I hate him!'

So the gossip had been right. Poor silly Flora. How had she been taken in by a man whose position was so far above hers that there would never be any chance of marriage?

Jessie heard a gasp from behind. She turned. Isabel's eyes had widened and she was holding a hand to her mouth. Didn't she know that women fell to men they weren't married to? It happened

100

often enough. Well, she'd find that out when she became a doctor for real.

Dr MacKenzie passed Jessie a device that looked like a mouse's cage. 'Place it over Flora's mouth along with this lint. Flora, I'm going to give you something to put you to sleep. Try not to fight it. Take deep breaths.'

Jessie did as he asked. Once the contraption was in place and Dr MacKenzie had snapped rubber gloves over his hands, he measured some liquid into a dropper and carefully released three drops onto the mask. 'Now, Jessie, I want you to keep a close eye on Flora. Watch her chest rise, and if anything changes, tell me at once.'

Jessie nodded.

'I'm going to cut Flora's abdomen from the umbilicus to the pubic bone. Then I will cut through the uterus. Once I do that I will use retractors to keep the muscles apart. Isabel, I need you to hold the retractors in place so I can deliver the baby. Mrs MacCorquodale, if you could make yourself ready to take the baby from me? Wrap it tightly to keep it warm and check that it's breathing.'

He raised his eyes and paused at each face in turn. 'Any questions, or is everyone ready?'

Jessie's mouth was too dry to allow her to do more than nod. She glanced at Isabel, but saw only excitement in her eyes.

When Flora's breathing deepened, Dr MacKenzie picked up the scalpel. 'Now, Isabel, when a doctor decides to cut he must not hesitate.' He made one sure slice down Flora's belly. Jessie watched, fascinated, as the skin parted to reveal a butter-coloured layer of fat. He sliced again, more carefully this time. 'The important thing,' he said, 'is to apply just the right amount of pressure. Too little and you have to cut again, which isn't good, too much and you risk harming the baby.'

As soon as he was into the abdomen he placed retractors on either side of the opening. He gestured to Isabel, who took the instruments without hesitation, holding them exactly as she'd been shown. Dr MacKenzie reached in and there was a slurping sound as the baby came loose from its sac. He passed it to Mam who took it from him. Jessie glanced down. Flora's chest was still moving up and down. So far, so good.

Once Dr MacKenzie had removed the afterbirth, he took the retractors from Isabel and threw them into one of the basins.

Isabel cut the umbilical cord, took a length of catgut from her father and used it to tie off the cord.

A cry of outrage came from the bundle in Mam's arms and Jessie caught Isabel's eye. Once more they shared a smile. It was always incredible to Jessie that a baby who had, moments before, been in its mother's stomach could cry seconds later as if it were starving.

Dr MacKenzie sewed up the wound and, as he did so, Flora began to moan.

'I think she's waking up,' Jessie said.

'I just need another minute. Jessie, give her one more drop of ether. Only one, mind.'

Jessie did as she was asked, and Flora settled again.

When Dr MacKenzie had finished repairing the wound, he saturated some lint in the same stuff he'd sprayed the table with earlier and placed it over the stitches. Then he took a bandage and dressed the wound. As he straightened and stretched, Flora mumbled and moved her arm, swiping at her face.

'You can take the mask away now, Jessie,' Dr MacKenzie said. 'The less time a patient is under, the better. I'll give her morphia before I leave.'

He ripped off his gloves and flung them into the bowl beside the retractors. 'Could you wash them in boiling water for me, Jessie? I'll do them again when I get back to the surgery, but I never put anything soiled into my bag. If there's one lesson I can teach you it would be that. More patients die from infection than anything else.'

Isabel and Jessie helped Dr MacKenzie lift Flora back onto her bed. She was awake, although her eyes remained unfocused. Mam placed the baby beside her and turned away as a paroxysm of coughing overtook her.

'How long have you had that cough, Mrs MacCorquodale?' Dr MacKenzie asked.

'She's had it for a long time, Doctor,' Jessie said. 'I've asked her to see you but she won't.'

'Sit down and let me listen to your chest,' he said. 'It'll save you a trip to my surgery.'

Jessie turned her back to give them what little privacy could be had and busied herself washing Dr MacKenzie's gloves while Isabel cleaned the table. Jessie couldn't help admiring the doctor's daughter. She might be a lady, but that didn't stop her mucking in.

'Are you really going to be a doctor?' she asked. 'I didn't think it was possible for a woman.'

'It's not easy,' Isabel replied, 'but I'm determined.' She lifted her chin. 'I don't believe in letting anything stop me once I make up my mind. There are several women doctors in this country already.'

'I wanted to be a nurse,' Jessie said. After helping Dr MacKenzie save Flora and her baby's lives – and as sure as the tide came in twice a day, that was what he had done – she wanted it even more. She had played her part too. Jessie glanced behind her. Flora was awake now, looking drowsily at her baby with a warring mixture of disgust and pride.

'Archie told me. Have you changed your mind?' Isabel said.

Jessie sighed. 'No. I was supposed to go to secondary school after the summer – I won the bursary, you know, but it isn't enough by itself. I need extra for board and lodging. Archie said he'd try to help me – he hoped when he'd finished his own schooling that he could get a decent job on the mainland, something that paid more, but when Dad died, he had to stay to help with the croft. We only make enough to keep ourselves.' Suddenly she realised she'd said too much. In the aftermath of what they'd been through, she'd forgotten herself. Archie would be furious with her for discussing their money problems in public – and with someone like Isabel, who couldn't have the slightest interest in the affairs of the crofters.

'How much do you need?' Isabel asked.

Jessie stiffened. She didn't want charity if that was what Isabel was thinking. 'Enough to cover my board and lodging, I suppose. I'd try to earn it if I could find someone who'd let me work for them after school. I wouldn't care what I did. I'd scrub floors, clean stables, anything.'

'I might have an idea,' Isabel said. 'Why don't you let me see what I can do?' She raised her voice. 'Jessie would make a good nurse, wouldn't she, Papa?'

The doctor turned. Mam was doing up the buttons of her blouse and, for a split second, Jessie saw a look of sorrow on his face that chilled her to the bone. But before she could be sure, he had replaced it with a smile. 'Wouldn't who what?' he asked.

'Wouldn't Jessie make an excellent nurse? I know they're crying out for decent nurses in Edinburgh.'

'Yes, they are, but if you're talking about the Royal Infirmary, they're looking for their probationers to have a School Leaving Certificate, which takes them beyond primary school. Do you have that, Jessie?'

'No, sir. But I want to.'

'We'll help you. Won't we, Papa?'

Dr MacKenzie smiled. 'We shall do our best. Let me have a think how to go about it.'

Chapter 10

Two days after they'd delivered Flora's baby, Charles called on Isabel. Happily Mama was having luncheon with Lady Glendale at the castle. 'Please tell Lord Maxwell I am indisposed,'

Isabel told the maid, 'and unable to receive him.'

She knew now why Papa had not wanted her to become friendly with Charles: he was the father of Flora McPhee's baby. Isabel might have been able to accept that but for the knowledge that he had refused to acknowledge the child as his – and to have stood back allowing Flora to be dismissed when the fault lay with him as much as her, was contemptible. She wanted nothing to do with him.

He'd called twice more over the following weeks and had been told that Isabel was not free to see him. On each occasion neither of her parents had been at home and Isabel was beginning to suspect that he had waited until she was alone to call on her. That made her despise him all the more.

However, soon she'd be free of his attentions. In a few days she was going to Edinburgh to prepare to start her medical studies, but first there was something she needed to do. She had news for Jessie and was looking forward to seeing her face when she told her what she'd arranged.

'Has my father taken any lunch?' Isabel asked the maid, as Seonag helped her into her coat.

'Mrs MacDonald says he managed a little of her chicken broth. Your mama is with him at the moment.'

Her father had been in bed for the last few days and Isabel was a little worried. But when she'd asked whether she should call the doctor from Portree who was covering for him while he was in bed, he had told her not to be silly. 'It's only a cold, child. A few days' rest and I'll be back on my feet.'

Isabel hadn't liked the look of his flushed face, or the way he'd seemed to be struggling for breath, but Papa was the doctor. He'd know if there was something the doctor in Portree could do for him. Nevertheless, if he wasn't better by this evening, she'd take matters into her own hands and call the doctor herself.

She was still feeling uneasy when she arrived at the MacCorquodales' house.

Jessie opened the door and smiled hesitantly. Isabel wondered if she knew how pretty she was, with her dark curly hair and bright enquiring eyes, so like her brother's.

'Miss MacKenzie! Please, come in.'

Isabel had never been inside Archie's home before and looked around with interest. There were two rooms: a bedroom and the kitchen with its open fire and chairs on either side. On one, Mrs MacCorquodale sat, winding some wool onto a skein. There was a curtain, behind which Isabel guessed there would be a recessed bed. The only other items of furniture were an ornate oversized sideboard against one wall and a table in the centre of the room. Mingling with the smell of peat smoke was the delicious aroma of home baking. Indeed, the table was piled high with scones and bread.

Jessie must have been the baker as she had a smear of flour on her forehead. Her pinafore covered a worn but clean dress. Disappointingly, there was no sign of Archie but it was rare to find a man indoors during the day.

Mrs MacCorquodale placed her wool on the floor and rose to her feet. 'Miss MacKenzie, what brings you here? Does your father need help with a patient?'

'No. He's in bed, poorly,' Isabel replied. 'The doctor from Portree has taken over his cases for the next few days.'

Jessie and her mother shared a quick glance.

'Nothing serious, I hope?' Jessie said.

'I trust not.' Isabel held out the package she had in her hand. 'My father asked me to give you this, Jessie. It's one of his medical textbooks. He says you can keep it for as long as you need.'

Jessie took it from her and started to unwrap it. 'Please thank him for me. Will you take a cup of tea?' She indicated the empty chair across from where her mother had been seated.

'Thank you,' Isabel said, perching tentatively on the edge. There were a few moments of strained silence. 'I'm leaving on the steamer on Monday,' she said. 'However, before I go, I have some news for you. I've spoken with my father about Jessie's education, Mrs MacCorquodale, and he knows a family in Inverness. The father is a teacher and he and his wife have five children who are all at school. He is willing to have Jessie to stay if she is prepared to be nursemaid to the children when they're not at school.'

The hope in Jessie's eyes was almost painful to see.

'Jessie will share a room with one of the other maids and have her board, lodging and a small amount for her everyday needs. She will be able to attend school.'

'I can go to school? Sit my exams?'

'And when you've done that, you'll be able to

start your training.'

'As a nurse?' Jessie's eyes shone.

'Yes! Now, what do you say?' Isabel could barely conceal her satisfaction. She had it all worked out. Everything had been thought of.

Jessie jumped to her feet, went to her mother and crouched by her side. 'What do you think, Mam? Can I go? I hate to leave you, especially with Dad gone.'

Mrs MacCorquodale frowned. 'Why should you worry about leaving me, child? I'll have Archie to keep me company. I'm perfectly able to keep house still. It's only your fussing that stops me doing more.' Some of the light went out of her eyes. 'Your dad would be proud to know his child was getting a proper education.'

'Do you really mean it? Oh, Mam, I'd only be away for a year, two at the most, and I'll save every penny I can so that I can come and see you.' Jessie turned to Isabel. 'This means I can be a nurse! A proper nurse!'

'There's more,' Isabel said. 'Papa says if you do well in your exams, and he has no doubt that you will, he'll put in a word for you with the matron at the Edinburgh Royal Infirmary to have you taken on there as a probationer. The pay would be poor, and the hours long and hard, but you'd be able to stay in the nurses' home and have a first-class training.'

Jessie's smile broadened. 'I'm used to hard work. And for the chance to be a nurse at one of the most famous hospitals in the world, let alone Scotland, I'd do anything! Work day and night, if they asked me!'

Isabel laughed. 'I don't think it'll come to that, and first you have to get another year or two of schooling, but as far as I can see, everything is in place.'

She stood up and Jessie's mother did the same. She grasped Isabel's hands in hers with a surprisingly strong grip. 'Thank you, and please thank Dr MacKenzie. We'll never forget this kindness. Anything my family can ever do for yours, you have only to ask.'

Jessie held out Isabel's coat for her.

'Is Archie about?' Isabel asked, as casually as she could, slipping her arms into the sleeves. She wanted to tell him herself about the arrangements she'd made for Jessie. She wouldn't put it past him and his pride to refuse help.

'He's on the croft moving our sheep to different grazing,' Jessie replied. 'You might pass him on your way to Galtrigill.'

'I'll try to find him there, then.' She paused in the doorway. 'If I don't happen to come across him, will you tell him goodbye from me and that I wish him well?'

'Of course,' Jessie said, with a mischievous smile. 'But I think he'd prefer it if you told him yourself.'

After Isabel had left, Jessie could hardly sit still for excitement. At last it looked as if one day she would be a nurse. And not just any nurse! One of the nurses from the Edinburgh Royal Infirmary!

She grabbed some dirty clothes from the basket, thinking she might as well do some washing. While she scrubbed, she would make plans.

As she sorted the clothes, a handkerchief stained

with blood dropped to the floor.

Jessie picked it up and frowned. It was one of Mam's. It had the initials Jessie had painstakingly sewn on the corner last year, before giving it to her for her birthday.

Mam had picked up a basket and was preparing to go out to gather plants to make dye for the wool she had been spinning. She coughed and slid an anxious glance at Jessie.

The truth hit her like a blow to the stomach.

Mam had been coughing for such a long time and she'd lost so much weight that her arms looked like a chicken's wings. Her cheeks were hollow and her complexion sallow.

Now the look in Dr MacKenzie's eyes on the day Flora McPhee's child had been born made sense.

Jessie had seen enough consumption in the village to know that her mother had it. How could she have been so blind? She'd been so wrapped up in herself she'd failed to see that Mam was sick. What kind of nurse would she make if she couldn't even watch out for her own?

'Why don't I make us a cup of tea, Mam?' she said.

Her mother shook her head, surprised. 'There's no time, Jessie. There's too much to do.' She smiled. 'Just wait until Archie hears that you're going to be a nurse.'

Jessie's chest tightened. There would be no going away for her now. 'Mam, please. Sit down.'

As if she knew what was coming, Mam didn't protest, but sat down in her chair and closed her eyes. Jessie warmed the teapot on the stove as she

111

waited for the kettle to boil. She set out two cups on the table and buttered a scone for her mother. When the kettle boiled she filled the teapot and placed it back on the stove to mash. She knew she was putting off what had to be asked.

Finally, the tea was poured and the scone set on a plate. There was no more Jessie could do to delay confirming the truth she already knew.

'Mam, your tea.' Jessie touched her mother on the shoulder and her eyes opened. For a moment she looked at her as if she didn't know who she was. Then her eyes cleared. 'You're a good girl, Jessie. Did I ever tell you that?'

'You didn't have to, Mam.' Jessie's throat felt thick.

Her mother grasped her arm with her free hand. 'Promise me, you'll never give up trying to become a nurse. I'm sorry, *mo bheag*, that we couldn't send you away to school. Dad and I wanted you to make something of yourself. And Archie.' She smiled sadly. 'Although you make me proud already. Both of you. I want you to know that.' She placed her cup and the plate on the table beside her chair as if she hadn't the energy or appetite for it.

If Jessie had had the tiniest hope that she might be mistaken that her mother was ill, it had vanished with Mam's words. Mam wasn't demonstrative and she would never have spoken to her in that way unless – the realisation made her chest hurt – unless she knew she wouldn't be with them for much longer.

'Mam, I know,' she said finally.

'Know what, dear?'

'I know you have consumption.' Unable to hold back her terror any longer, Jessie gave an anguished cry and dropped to her knees, burying her head in her mother's lap. 'Don't die, Mam. Please don't die.'

Her mother stroked her hair in the way she used to when Jessie was a small child. As she waited for her to stop crying, she spoke softly. 'Jessie, I'm not afraid to die. I've known great happiness. I've known what it is to have the love of a good man. I have two children who make me proud, and I've been able to do some of God's work by bringing children into this world. I'm luckier than most. Of course I don't want to leave you or your brother, and I hope I won't die for a long time yet, but when I do I'll be with Dad and God. How can I be sad about that?'

Jessie raised her face to look at her. 'You could go to a sanatorium, Mam. They don't ask for money for people with tuberculosis. Archie and I will look after everything here until you get better.'

Her mother took a handkerchief from her pocket and dabbed the tears from Jessie's eyes. She smiled softly. '*A ghràidh*, I'm not going to get better. It's too late for sanatoriums or anything else. Trust me when I tell you that. And I don't want to leave my home or the graves of your baby brother and your dad. All I have known and all I care about is here.'

'Archie will make you go, Mam, when I tell him.'

Her mother stiffened. 'He's not to know.'

'Why not? He's the head of the family now. He has the right to know that you're ill.'

'Why tell him, Jessie? It will only worry him

113

when there is nothing he can do to change the outcome. It is a woman's job to bear the sorrows and to keep the men free from worry.' She reached out a hand to tip Jessie's chin, forcing her to look her in the eye. 'Promise me, on your dad's soul, that you won't tell Archie. It's the only thing I truly want. That – and you learning to be a nurse.'

Jessie knew she couldn't deny her mother this request. Her mam was still her mam and she'd never disobeyed her before and she couldn't start now. 'I promise.' She wiped her eyes and got to her feet. 'But I can't go away now, Mam. Of course I can't.' She lifted the teacup and the plate with the uneaten scone from the little table. 'The only nursing I'm going to do is here – looking after you.'

Jessie's heart ached as she watched a tear roll down her mother's lined cheek. Mam took the dishes from her with a tremulous smile. 'Of course you must still be a nurse. I've had my life and I won't allow you to throw away yours. Not now, when you're so close to achieving your dreams.'

Jessie forced a smile. 'There'll be time for me to be a nurse, Mam, when you're well again.'

'No, Jessie!' She was getting agitated. 'You must go. Archie will be here to help with the croft, and our neighbours will keep an eye on me. I could have many years left, you know that.' She placed her hands on either side of Jessie's face. 'My child, if you stay here, you will only make me sad. Do you want that?' Her eyes burned into Jessie's. 'At least go to Inverness and finish your schooling.'

'I promise you I'll find a way to be a nurse, Mam. Don't you worry,' Jessie said firmly. And she would. One way or another.

The anxiety cleared from her mother's eyes. She dropped her hands from Jessie's face and picked up her basket. 'Good. Now, enough talking, my girl. There's work to be done.'

Chapter 11

The wind had dropped a little by the time Isabel left the MacCorquodales' house. It had been gratifying to see Jessie's pleasure at her news.

She swallowed. The tickle in her throat that had started that morning was getting worse and the beginning of a headache tugged at her scalp. She felt hot, too, as if she were starting a fever. Perhaps she had caught Papa's cold. She hoped not. Nothing must prevent her leaving for Edinburgh tomorrow.

She crossed the road and followed the path up towards the cliff. At the top, the wind was stronger, forcing the waves against the rocks so that the spray blew into her face.

When, finally, she came over a rise to find Archie, her heart leaped. She had missed him so much.

He had the hoof of a ewe in his hand and was studying it, so engrossed that he hadn't heard her approach.

'Hello, Archie,' she said.

He looked up and, for a moment, she saw the familiar gleam of pleasure her company had always seemed to give him. 'Miss MacKenzie, how are you?' He bent his head back to his task.

His casual dismissal chilled her. '"Miss MacKenzie"? Are we not still friends?'

He placed the ewe's hoof on the ground and the animal ran away, with an alarmed bleat. 'Yet you chose not to seek me out these past weeks.' His eyes were bleak.

'I couldn't, Archie. When I wasn't assisting Papa, Mama wouldn't let me out of her sight.'

His eyes swept over her. 'Of course. You're a woman now, a woman who has a place in society with rules and conventions to live by.'

'Then you understand...'

'You always did as you liked.' He dropped his voice. 'I hadn't thought you would change.'

She didn't like the disapproval in his voice. Before she went, she wanted him to look at her the way he used to. With warmth.

'I've just come from your home,' she said. 'I brought good news for Jessie and thought I should deliver it myself.'

'What news was that?'

'My father has found her a place to stay in Inverness so that she can take up her bursary. She'll have to work for her room and board but Jessie assures me she's happy to do so. Then, if she does well, my father has promised an introduction to the matron at the hospital in Edinburgh.'

As she'd suspected, instead of looking grateful, Archie glowered at her. 'We don't need your charity, Isabel. It's my duty to look after my family. I'm saving so that Jessie can go to school without relying on anyone else or having to work as a servant.'

'But it will take for ever for you to save enough to send Jessie away.' As soon as the words were out of her mouth, she knew she had said the wrong thing. Damn Archie's pride.

His face darkened further. 'That's what I mean. Friends don't give out charity as if they were handing sweets to a child.'

'You're wrong, Archie. Friends help each other. That's not charity. Besides, Jessie's too clever to stay here and work the rest of her life on a croft. She should be a nurse. In a hospital.'

Archie's expression grew even more thunderous. 'So, only the stupid and ignorant stay to work the land? Is that what you're saying? In that case you must despise the man you claim to call your friend.'

'I didn't mean that, Archie! I know, if circumstances were different, you could be anything you wanted. Remember how we used to say that you could be a politician?'

'That was the talk of children.'

'But it wasn't completely wrong, was it? The villagers come to you for advice. You're on the parish council. It doesn't matter where you are, Archie, or what you do, you'll always lead. One day you'll find your true vocation.'

The storm clouds disappeared from his face and he smiled sadly. 'You were always an idealist, Isabel. Comes of reading romantic poems and novels.'

She couldn't take umbrage at his words. At

least he was talking to her as if he knew her. 'I'm leaving on Monday,' she said.

'I heard.'

They looked at each other for a long moment. Isabel doubted she would ever see Archie again and her heart ached. To her horror her eyes filled.

Archie took a handkerchief from his pocket and gently dabbed away her tears. 'Aw, don't cry, *mo ghaoil*.'

She reached up, took his hand and pressed it to her cheek.

The world stood still. He grasped her waist and pulled her to him. Her breath came in short gasps as she lifted her face to his and then his mouth was on hers. A hot flame shot through her and she pressed herself into him.

Gently Archie disentangled her arms from his neck and pushed her away. He grinned down at her. 'I knew my Isabel couldn't have disappeared for ever. But I won't be satisfied with kisses. I want to court you properly. Like a gentleman courts a lady.'

Court her? It was unthinkable. It was one thing to be friends with a crofter's son, but for him to believe... Aghast, she stepped away from him. 'Oh, Archie, that's impossible,' she said.

'Why? You care for me and I care for you. You might be a doctor's daughter and I might be just a crofter's son, but as you've said, I won't always be.'

'I'm sorry,' she said stiffly. 'I don't know where your future lies but I know where mine does. I can't think of you – or anyone – in that way.'

His features settled into a grimness she had

never seen. 'Don't make a fool of me, Isabel.'

Her heart was racing. 'I don't mean to.'

'You won't allow me to court you, yet you kissed me. Is that the behaviour of a lady? If it is, then even the lowest-born woman on this island knows how to conduct herself better than you.'

The censure in his eyes sent colour flooding to her cheeks. It was true, she had behaved badly, but he had no right to talk to her as if she were a naughty child. It was too humiliating. She raised her chin. 'Forgive me. I was wrong. I simply wanted to say goodbye.'

Clouds scudded across the sun and his eyes gleamed in the fading light.

'Lie to yourself, if you wish, but don't lie to me. The way you kissed me was not that of a friend.' He smiled slightly. 'One day, Isabel, you will come to me. As my equal.'

The certainty in his voice shook her. He was wrong. To be with him would mean the end of her dreams and she could never allow that. 'We will always be friends,' she said flatly. 'But only friends.'

His eyes held hers. Then he sketched a mocking bow. 'I shall always be at your service, Miss Mac-Kenzie. If you need me, you know where to find me.' He gave her a last long look. 'You'd best be leaving now.'

Still hot with embarrassment, Isabel left Archie and continued to walk towards the ruined village, wanting time alone to think before she returned home. It was hardly her fault that Archie had read too much into a simple kiss. But she couldn't

119

make herself ignore the voice in her head that pointed out it hadn't been a simple kiss at all. She had pressed her body to his. And she had let him kiss her before. Her face grew hotter. Could she blame him for thinking he could court her when her behaviour had been shameful? But – a man who earned his living from the land! A man who, whatever his prospects might be in the future, was barely able to support himself and his family. Did he think she would give up her chance to go to university and become a doctor to stay with him here? In his tiny house with his mother and sister? Or did he think she'd wait until he had made enough to support her? She closed her eyes, imagining the horror on her mother's face when she introduced Archie as her beau. She knew she had hurt him, though, and regretted it deeply.

She was almost at the ruins of Galtrigill when she heard the thudding of hoofs behind her. She turned and raised a hand to her forehead to try to see better. The rider, whoever it was, was heading straight for her. To her dismay, she saw it was Charles Maxwell. She had no wish to talk to him, especially not when she was so flustered. There was nowhere to duck out of view and, besides, judging by the direction of his mount, he must already have seen her.

She continued towards the cliff, entering a small wood with only the narrowest of overgrown paths. Too narrow and difficult for a horse to follow, she hoped. Perhaps Charles would give up and continue on his way.

However, it seemed he was determined to speak to her. She heard his muffled footsteps behind her and turned to find him a few steps away, leading his horse.

'My dear Miss MacKenzie, how fortunate to find you here,' he said with a smile. His appearance alarmed her. He was dishevelled and had a bruise under his left eye.

Now she had no option but to return home. Anyone seeing them might think it was a tryst and she did not intend her name to be linked with his. She shuddered.

She turned on her heel. 'I was on my way home,' she said.

He blocked her path, which irritated her. Within the bounds of good manners, she couldn't have made it clearer that she wasn't interested in his attentions.

'Stop and talk with me a while,' he said. She stepped back. Was that drink she could smell on his breath? It was only early afternoon.

'You have been avoiding me, I think.' His voice was slurred and his eyes glazed. 'Yet you seem to have no issue with kissing the crofter's son.'

Her heart thumped. So he had seen her and Archie kiss. Well, what of it? It was no concern of his.

'Please let me pass, Lord Maxwell.'

'Lord Maxwell? Why so formal now? You weren't so formal on the night of the ball, if I remember.'

'If I gave you any indication that I welcomed your advances, you must forgive me. Put it down to a young woman's naïvety. I wish you good day.'

Once again she stepped forward, trying to force him to move out of her way. To her annoyance he remained in her path. She made to brush past him, but he grabbed her arm and tugged her towards him.

'One kiss,' he said. 'I bet a guinea that you'll enjoy kissing me more than the peasant. One kiss and I'll let you go.'

Furious, she shook off his hand. 'I have no intention of kissing you. Please stand aside, or I shall be forced to tell my father about your lack of manners and he, no doubt, shall tell Lord Glendale.'

His lip curled. 'Do you think my father would care about a single stolen kiss from the doctor's daughter – especially when I tell him that she was also kissing one of his crofters? You flatter yourself.'

'Then I shall also make him aware that you are the father of Flora's son. I don't imagine Lord or Lady Glendale will be happy to hear that their son put someone in the family way and completely abdicated his responsibilities.' Her heart was racing but she kept her voice even. Bullies like him fed on other people's fear.

He narrowed his eyes, then threw back his head and laughed. 'My father is a man of the world. As long as I never made any promises to the girl, which I didn't, and as long as I continue to carry out my duties as his eldest son and heir, he'll be happy.' But behind the smile, she saw a flicker of doubt.

Suddenly he gripped her arms and pulled her against him. She could feel his heart beating and something else, something that made her feel truly scared for the first time. Her resistance had only excited him.

His hand groped between her legs. His action shocked her so much that, for a moment, she was rooted to the spot.

'What are you doing? Let me go at once!' She flailed at him with her fists but he was far stronger than her. Why had she chosen this path where no one could see them? He brought his mouth down on hers and forced his tongue between her lips. Sour-tasting bile rose to her throat.

She bit his lip and he pulled away with a sharp cry of pain. He drew his hand back and slapped her. Hard. Her head reeled. No one had ever hit her before. But she would fight back. She would not allow him to do what she feared he intended. She would rather die.

He grabbed her arm with one hand and with the other lifted her skirt until it was above her waist. Then he dipped his hand into her drawers and pushed his fingers between her legs. The pain made her gasp. She pounded her fist against his face, but her efforts only excited him more. He used his leg to knock her feet from under her and the impact of her body hitting the ground robbed her of any remaining breath and made her head spin. His hands fumbled at the string of her drawers. Dear Lord, he was going to violate her.

She stretched her hand along the ground groping for something to use against him. Her fingers found what she was looking for. A rock.

She made herself go limp, as if the fight had gone out of her. Her actions had the desired effect. Charles grinned and relaxed his grip. She knew this was the only chance she would get. She swung the stone and hit him as hard as she could on the temple. He clutched his head. 'Bitch!' Mustering all her strength, she rolled him off her.

And then, without a backward glance, she lifted her skirt and ran.

Chapter 12

Jessie was woken by a cry. At first she thought she'd been dreaming. A storm had come up while she'd been sleeping and the wind sounded like ghostly dervishes hurling themselves against the windows and doors.

But the sound that had woken her wasn't the wind.

'No, Archie. No!' It was Mam.

Jessie stayed in bed, straining her ears, but all she could hear was Archie's voice: he was talking in a low, urgent tone.

She pushed away the covers, shivering as her feet hit the cold floor. She pulled her shawl around her shoulders and went through to the other room. Her mother was looking up at Archie with imploring eyes, her cheeks streaked with tears.

'What is it?' Jessie asked. 'What's the matter?'

Mam wiped her face with the edge of her apron. She's so thin, Jessie thought. Why did it take me so long to see it?

'Your brother's leaving.'

'Leaving?' Jessie echoed. 'To go where? Why?'

She stepped closer and peered at Archie's face.

There was a livid mark along one side. 'What's happened? Are you hurt?'

He raised a hand to his cheek, and when he did, Jessie saw that his knuckles were grazed. Her heart started to race. Something bad had happened – she just knew it. 'Archie, Mam. Tell me what's going on!'

Archie looked at their mother and shook his head slightly. He took Jessie's hands in his and squeezed them. 'I'm fine,' he said. 'I tripped and hit my face on a rock.'

The mark on his face wasn't one that would have been made by a rock. It looked more like the lash of a thin branch. 'You're going away?'

'I have to, Jessie.' He glanced at their mother, who was stony-eyed. 'There's nothing here for me. Not any more. There's a ship leaving Glasgow for America on Thursday. If I get the boat from Dunvegan tomorrow morning, I'll be able to get onto it. But I have to set out now.'

How long had Archie been planning this? Why hadn't he said anything before? If he went, Jessie couldn't even go to Portree to school: Mam couldn't be left on her own.

'But you promised,' Jessie cried. 'You promised you'd stay so I could go to school.'

'I know I did, Jessie, and I'll make it up to you one day, but I have to leave here.' He led her over to a chair. 'You know how much I've always wanted to go to America. John the blacksmith has a ticket that his brother, who died from typhus, was going to use for the sailing on Thursday and he's sold it to me. If I wait, it might be months before I can get another berth.'

'But–'

'I'll send money when I can. And as soon as I'm settled I'll send for you and Mam. Don't you see, Jessie, it could be a chance for all of us.'

'I don't want to go to America and neither does Mam. I want to go away to school and then to Edinburgh so I can be a nurse.'

'You can be a nurse in America. They must need nurses there too.'

Mam stood up and started taking Archie's clothes from the drawer of the sideboard. She held his good sweater to her face for a moment before placing it in a paper bag.

'Mam! Tell him not to go!' Jessie cried. If Archie knew Mam was sick he would never leave them. 'Tell him that you're–'

'Jessie!' The word was like a whiplash above the sound of the storm. 'Eisd! Enough!' Her mother's voice softened but Jessie could see the pain in her eyes, even in the dim light from the oil lamp. 'He has to leave,' she continued. 'He's right. There's nothing for him here. Only years of working all the hours God sends just so we have enough to eat.'

Jessie could hardly believe her ears. She knew Archie wanted to go to America, but he'd agreed to wait until she had finished her training. Why was he going back on his promise to her? Was it something to do with Isabel? Had he decided that now she was going away he could no longer bear to be here? Or did he have hopes that, if he earned enough, he would have a chance with her? If he did, he was mistaken. No matter how much money he made, he'd never be able to marry her.

That was just the way it was, and no amount of wishing could change it. She had to make him see that.

'Is this anything to do with the doctor's daughter?'

Archie started and narrowed his eyes. 'Why do you say that?'

'Because I'm not stupid. I've seen the way you look at her. Are you going because you think you'll make your fortune and then she'll court you? Is that it?'

Relief crossed Archie's face. 'Oh, Jessie, do you think I don't know that Isabel isn't for me? At least, not now. But you're right in one respect. In America a man isn't judged by where he comes from but by who he is and what he makes of himself. That's one of the reasons I need to go.'

'One of the reasons?' A sob caught in her throat. Couldn't Archie see that she needed him here?

Archie clamped his lips together as if he'd said too much.

Mam stepped forward and placed her hand on Jessie's shoulder. 'Let him go, Jessie. It's for the best.'

Jessie looked from her to Archie. They had made up their minds. How could he do this to her? With him gone, Jessie would have to stay to work the croft. There was no way Mam could manage it on her own.

'I hate you, Archie MacCorquodale,' she cried. 'I don't care if I never see you again.' She pulled her shawl over her head and ran out of the house.

By the time she returned he was gone.

Two days later the policeman from Portree arrived at their door looking for Archie. Mam was up to her elbows in flour and Jessie was sweeping the floor.

'I'd like to speak to your son,' he said.

His serious expression frightened Jessie. She glanced at Mam who had paled, but then calmly wiped her hands with a cloth.

'He's not here.'

The policeman, a man in his forties with a greasy moustache, frowned. 'Then I shall wait for him.'

'I don't expect him to return for some time.' Mam moved the kettle from the side of the stove onto the heat. 'Will you take a cup of tea? You've come quite a way.'

The policeman shook his head. 'When will he be back?'

'I can't say.'

'Why are you looking for my brother?' Jessie put the broom aside and stepped forward. 'Is he accused of something?'

'You'll have heard that Lord Glendale's son is missing.'

'Aye,' Mam answered, turning away to place the kettle on the fire. 'What of it?'

They'd been aware that he hadn't returned home after going riding. How could they not be? Every man in the village had been dragged from his work to search for him. Gossip was that he'd stopped over at someone's house and was drinking. He'd been known to disappear for days at a time but he always turned up sooner or later.

'Your son was seen fighting with Lord Maxwell

on the day he went missing.'

Jessie's blood ran cold as she remembered the mark on Archie's face and his grazed knuckles. Dear Lord, had Archie harmed the man? Was that the real reason he'd left? She slid a glance at her mother, who was still fussing with the kettle. When she turned back to the policeman her face was white. 'Who is this person who claims to have seen my son fight with Lord Maxwell?' she demanded.

The policeman puffed himself up, like a male swan spreading its feathers. He folded his arms and glared at Jessie. '*I*'m asking the questions here.'

'Was it Lachie McPhee?' Mam persisted.

The policeman consulted his notebook and his eyes flickered. 'What if it was?'

'Lachie McPhee has no reason to like my son.'

'If anyone was fighting with Lord Maxwell,' Jessie said, 'it would be him. He fights with everyone, and his daughter, Flora–'

'Hush, Jessie.'

The policeman ignored Jessie and kept his beady eyes on Mam. 'It says here that it was Flora Mc-Phee who saw your son fighting with his lordship. At least, that was what her father told us. But when we questioned her, she denied saying anything to anyone. She says her father drinks and makes up stories. Others say the same.'

'See, now,' Mam said. 'If Flora says she didn't see it, you should believe her.'

'We might have believed her if we had been able to find his lordship. If we could question your son, we could clear up this matter. If he has nothing to hide, he has nothing to be afraid of. Now, I must ask you again, where is he?'

Jessie's mother glanced at Jessie and clasped her hands together. 'I don't know for certain.'

'Is he up on the croft or fishing? Just tell me where he is and I'll go and find him.'

Mam took a deep breath. 'He's gone to Glasgow,' she said finally. 'There was a difference of opinion between us. You know how sons can be with their mothers. It was over something silly – I forget what. I imagine he'll be back in a week or two, once he cools down.'

Jessie didn't think anything could shock her more than the police looking for her brother, clearly of the mind that he had had something to do with Lord Maxwell's disappearance, but she could never have imagined hearing a lie slip so easily from her mother's lips – in God's hearing. Why didn't she just tell him Archie had gone to America to look for work? Many had gone before him and, no doubt, many would follow.

'What was this "difference of opinion" about?' the policeman asked.

'I–' Mam was clearly struggling to come up with another lie.

'He said he wanted to find work away from this island,' Jessie said quickly. 'He said that he was tired of working his fingers to the bone for nothing.' She forced a smile. 'You're a Skye man, sir, and must know how hard life can be. We didn't want him to go. If it's hard for a man to make a living here, it's even harder for two women on their own. There was a row, as Mam said, but Archie went anyway. He'll be back soon enough.'

130

Jessie sent a silent, prayer upwards, hoping God would forgive her.

The policeman looked unconvinced. 'Mrs Mac-Corquodale, if you know where Archie is, it will be better for you all if you tell me. At the moment we only want to ask him some questions, but if I have to send word to the mainland for the constables there to search for him, it will not look good for your son.'

'As soon as we have an address for him we'll let you know,' Jessie said. 'He won't leave us long without one.'

Jessie's mother placed her hands on her hips and lifted her chin. 'My Archie is a good man. As God is my witness, I swear he would never hurt anyone.'

'Then he has nothing to fear from our questions.' The policeman looked uncertain – as if now he couldn't drag Archie off to Portree gaol, he didn't know what else to do. 'I'll go for the time being, but if you hear from your son, you must inform the police station in Portree. If he's gone to ground somewhere, word will reach us, and we'll know he has something to hide.' He picked up his hat. 'I'll send a telegram to Glasgow and ask them to look for him there. In the meantime I'll bid you good day.'

After he left, her mother collapsed into a chair. Jessie poured her a glass of water from the jug on the table and waited until she had taken a couple of sips and some colour had returned to her face. 'Why didn't you tell the policeman that Archie had gone to America, Mam? Why did you lie and say he was in Glasgow?'

'Because if I told them he was on his way to America, they would have found out easily which ship he was on and would be waiting for him. Perhaps they wouldn't even allow him to travel.'

'You can't think he has anything to do with this, Mam. Not Archie!'

She gave a slight shake of her head. 'All I know is that he didn't harm anyone.'

'Then he has to come back to clear his name. Otherwise they'll believe him guilty and he can never return to us.'

'If Lord Maxwell turns up dead, then someone will have to be held accountable. I cannot take the chance that my son is blamed for something he didn't do.'

Jessie knew she was right.

'I knew nothing good would ever come of his friendship with the doctor's daughter,' Mam muttered.

A shiver ran up Jessie's spine. Lord Maxwell had been on Galtrigill, as had Isabel and Archie. She knew Archie cared more than he should for the doctor's daughter. And there had been the gossip from one of the maids at Borreraig House about his lordship calling on Isabel and being turned away. Not once, but several times. Had he and Archie fought over Isabel?

'What do you mean, Mam? What do you know that you're not telling?'

She looked startled, almost as if she'd forgotten Jessie was in the room. 'I mean nothing. Nothing.'

Jessie crouched by her side. 'Please, Mam, if you do know something, you have to tell me. Did Archie have anything to do with whatever has happened to Lord Maxwell? Is that the real reason he left?'

'I'm telling you the same thing I told the policeman. Archie is a good man – as you well know. Now, leave it alone, Jessie.'

From the determined set of her mother's lips, Jessie knew she'd get no more from her. She made up her mind. 'I'm going out, Mam. I won't be long.' She took her shawl from behind the door and wrapped it around her shoulders. She had to speak to Isabel, before she too left Skye.

Jessie marched down the dirt road leading to Borreraig House with no idea of what she would say when she got there. All she did know was that she had to speak to Isabel – to ask her whether she'd found Archie that day or seen Lord Maxwell. Had she witnessed the fight between them? Perhaps she could vouch for Archie – tell the policeman he had been with her that afternoon.

The truth was, she didn't know what she hoped to achieve by speaking to Isabel, but she couldn't sit at home and spend the rest of her life wondering what had really happened.

But as Borreraig House came into view from behind the small copse that shielded it from the road, the eerie stillness hanging over the house sent a shiver up Jessie's spine. A raven cawed, the sound ringing through the still air, its wings flapping over her head in a black blur. All the curtains were drawn, although it was still light. It was a sign that someone in the house had died. Everyone knew ravens foretold death, and Dr MacKenzie had been ill.

She went around the side of the house to the kitchen door. She knocked briefly and, without waiting for an answer, walked straight into the kitchen.

Chrissie MacDonald, the MacKenzies' cook, was pummeling dough, her face streaked with tears, while Seonag sat at the table polishing the silver. She, too, had been crying. They looked blankly at Jessie.

'Is it the doctor?' she asked bluntly.

'*Ochone! Ochone!* He passed away this morning,' Chrissie replied.

'Oh, no!' Dr MacKenzie had been a fine man and a fine doctor.

Chrissie sucked in a breath. 'We're all at sixes and sevens. There's a lot to do. There'll be folk from the big houses wanting to pay their respects and the house is to be closed up.' She glanced at Jessie and frowned. 'What is it you're wanting?'

'I need to speak to Miss MacKenzie. It's important.'

The cook wiped her hands on a towel and gave Jessie an incredulous look. 'You'll not be able to speak to Miss Isabel,' she said. 'She has the scarlet fever too. Poor mite doesn't know her father has died and we don't know if she'll come through either.' A soft sob came from Seonag. 'But she's strong. Her papa wasn't.' She placed a hand on Seonag's shoulder. 'Enough of your crying, lass. Away upstairs and see what the mistress needs.'

Seonag scuttled off, wiping her eyes with the hem of her apron.

Jessie was uncertain of what to do next. Archie gone, Lord Maxwell missing, the doctor dead

134

and Isabel sick: how could the world have turned upside down in three days?

'Whatever it is you need to ask Miss Isabel will have to wait,' Chrissie continued. 'As soon as she's fit to travel, they're leaving for Edinburgh. The doctor is to be buried there.' She sniffed. 'Seems the island soil is not good enough for Madam. If you ask me, the doctor would have liked to be laid to rest here, with the people who loved him.'

It was no use. Isabel, even if she wasn't sick herself, would be in no state to answer questions.

'Please give the family my respects,' she said. 'Tell them they'll be in my prayers.'

Chrissie nodded. 'I will, lass. Now you'd best be going.'

Jessie pulled her shawl over her head. She couldn't speak to Isabel now, but as soon as the doctor's daughter was better, she'd come back. One way or another she'd find out the truth.

Chapter 13

It was as if someone had placed a weight over Isabel's eyelids. Her heart was pounding, her muscles frozen with fear. Someone was chasing her. She didn't know who or why, but she knew that if she didn't open her eyes he would catch her. Using every ounce of her strength she forced her lids apart.

She was in bed, in her room, and it was dark. What time was it?

The memory of Charles and his hands on her body rushed back. He was the one who had been chasing her. He had tried to violate her. She'd been running, trying to get to Papa. Papa! She had to speak to him. Tell him what had happened.

'Papa?' Her throat was dry and the word came out as a croak. 'Papa,' she tried again, her voice stronger this time.

A figure detached itself from the chair next to her bed and bent over her. Isabel smelt violets. 'Mama?'

Her mother's face swam into view. She was drawn and pale, and her eyes were awash with tears. Did Mama know what had happened?

'Ssh, darling. Don't try to speak. You've been very ill and need to rest.'

She'd been ill? She raised a hand to her throat. It was painful to swallow. She remembered feeling hot back there on the moors. Hot and dizzy.

Her mother pressed a cup to Isabel's lips. 'Drink this, darling.'

Isabel managed a swallow, but lifting her head took so much effort that she fell back on the pillows, exhausted. Where was her father? Why wasn't he here? 'Where's Papa?' she asked. 'I want him.' Terror squeezed her chest. And Charles? Had he told everyone that she had kissed him, even though it was against her will? Did everyone know that his hands had been all over her body?

'Papa isn't here,' Mama said, her voice shaking. 'You need to sleep now, Isabel. We'll talk more when you're stronger.'

Isabel wanted to get out of bed and find her

father, but her body wouldn't obey her commands. What if he wasn't coming because he was angry with her? What if he'd heard what had happened and blamed her? She should never have been walking on her own. Not at eighteen. He was right to be angry. She slumped back on her pillows. She would sleep a little and then she would speak to him.

When she next woke it was still dark and her father still wasn't there. Instead Seonag was in the room, stoking the fire.

'What time is it?' Isabel asked.

'It's four o'clock, Miss.' Seonag left the fire and came to stand by her bed. 'I'll just fetch your mama. She said I was to call her when you were awake.'

Seonag wouldn't look at her. Like Mama, she looked as if she'd been crying. Did everyone know of her shame? 'Don't wake her. It's the middle of the night. Let her sleep.'

'Oh, Miss. It's four in the afternoon. Your mama is in the drawing room. She...' Seonag's voice broke.

Nothing was making sense. Why was it so dark?

'Open the curtains, Seonag, and then fetch Mama,' Isabel ordered weakly. Papa must be out on a call. That was the only reason he wasn't here. Unless... Her heart stuttered as, once again, the memory of Charles touching her, pushing her, forcing his hand down her drawers came rushing back. Unless he couldn't bear the sight of her. She needed to tell Papa what had happened. She'd made a terrible mistake, but Charles had had no right to treat her as he had, as if she were nothing.

Less than nothing.

'I can't open the curtains, Miss.' Seonag was backing away from her as if she, too, couldn't bear to be near her. 'I'll go and fetch Madam.' She hurried out before Isabel could say anything more to her.

Confused, Isabel pushed the heavy bedcovers aside. It was too hot in the room. She needed air. When she tried to stand, her legs buckled and her head spun and she had to sit back down on the bed.

The door opened and Mama swept into the room, followed by Seonag. Her mother was wearing black. Isabel's heart crashed against her ribs. Black clothes, closed windows and curtains... Dear God, no! It was coming back to her. Papa had been ill.

'Mama...' She couldn't continue. She didn't want to hear what her mother had to say. She covered her face with her hands. 'Please, Mama, don't say it.'

Her mother sat on the bed next to her and gently pulled her hands away. She took Isabel by the shoulder, forcing her to look at her. Seonag was standing behind her, twisting her hands. 'My dear girl, you must be brave.'

Isabel shook her head. 'No, Mama,' she whispered. 'Say it isn't true...'

'Your papa was very sick with scarlet fever, my child. As were you.' Her mother's back was ramrod straight. Only a slight trembling of her lips betrayed her distress. Isabel concentrated on her face, trying to block out the words she knew were coming. 'I'm sorry, Isabel, but your papa passed away yesterday. There was nothing anyone could do.'

'Papa's dead?' How was it possible?

'As soon as you're fit to travel we must to go to Edinburgh. The funeral has been arranged for next week.'

'How long have I been sick, Mama?'

'Three days.'

Three days. It didn't seem possible. The last she remembered was running from Charles, reaching home and collapsing.

'We didn't know if you would come through. But you're strong and Papa was weakened from his time in the army. Thank God you survived.'

She didn't know if surviving was a blessing or a curse.

Her mother rose to her feet and smoothed her dress. 'I shall let Mrs MacDonald know you're awake and need some of her soup.'

Isabel's head was throbbing.

Seonag came over to her and put her arms around her. 'Come, Miss. You've had a terrible shock. You're still sick. You must get back into bed.'

Unable to find the strength to resist, Isabel let Seonag tuck her legs under the blankets.

'Oh, Miss, I am so sorry about your papa. We all are. There's five dead in the village, all from the fever. Mrs MacDonald's niece was sick too, but she's on the mend. And then there was all that other fuss. Oh, Miss, you have no idea what it's been like these last days! My grandpa says someone must have upset the fairies for such bad luck to come here.'

But Isabel wasn't really listening. All she could think about was her beloved papa and that she would never be able to talk to him again. The one person she might have confided in was dead.

'Seonag!' Mama's voice rang in from the doorway. 'I thought I made it clear that Miss Isabel wasn't to be troubled with gossip. Away you go and bring up the soup. Then please start packing her belongings.'

'May I be alone for a while?' Isabel asked her mother, when Seonag had scurried away.

'You should have someone with you,' she protested.

'Please, Mama. Just for a little while. Then I'll sleep.'

Her mother hesitated. Then she patted Isabel's hand awkwardly. 'Ring for the servants when you need me. I won't be far away.'

'Thank you, Mama.'

Isabel lay quietly. Papa had died thinking she was good and brave, and for that she was grateful. He would never learn of her shame. She owed it to him to be strong. She was a grown woman, no longer a child. From now on she had to make her own decisions. She had to forget what Charles had tried to do to her.

All she could do now was make her beloved papa proud.

Chapter 14

Skye, winter 1908

Jessie sat alone in the front pew and let the singing of the hymns wash over her. Donald Bàn would intone the first line, then the rest of the congregation would add their voices to his and the music would rise and swell almost to the heavens.

She'd sat here for many funerals before, including Dad's, but today, when she most needed one of her own to share her grief, she was alone.

Mam's coffin was so small and so light she had needed only four pall-bearers to carry her instead of the usual six. With Archie gone, the bit of Mam that had still been there after Dad's death had slowly leaked away. Her breathing had become worse until she couldn't walk the length of herself. When she had taken to her bed, Jessie had nursed her, fitting in her work while Mam slept. When the weather was fine, she had helped her outside to sit in the sun, and although it had improved her breathing for a while, she had grown weaker and weaker until she couldn't – or wouldn't – leave her bed.

When she wasn't working the croft or looking after Mam, Jessie attended to the women in labour and soon she was called out for other reasons apart from birth. They had started asking her about their children's coughs and fevers while they were waiting to deliver, and she had discovered that she had an instinct for telling when a child was truly sick and needed a doctor, or whether a mustard poultice or some comfrey tea was all that was required. The villagers were grateful – they could save the money to pay the doctor for when it really mattered.

She couldn't even tell Archie when Mam was nearing the end.

Over the months since he'd left, they'd received a few letters from him. At least, they'd assumed they were from him because all the envelopes had contained was a few dollars. No message or even a forwarding address. They'd needed most of the money to pay the rent and keep food on the table, and most of what remained had gone on Mam's funeral.

Jessie and Mam never had spoken about what might have happened to the earl's son, almost as if they were scared to share their fear that Archie had had something to do with his disappearance. With Archie safe in America and no way to question Isabel, Jessie decided it was best to leave things as they were.

As soon as Isabel was well, the MacKenzies had closed Borreraig House and returned to Edinburgh. The policeman had come back twice to ask Mam and herself whether they'd heard from Archie or had an address for him, but soon enough he had stopped coming too. Lord Maxwell still hadn't appeared, and Jessie couldn't stop wondering if Archie had had anything to do with it. She hated the anger against him that knotted her insides. He should be here, beside her. He should have been there when Mam was dying.

The singing and prayers were coming to an end. In a little while they'd be putting Mam in the cold ground, next to her husband and the baby who had died. At least she wouldn't be alone.

As the men came forward to lift the coffin, Jessie murmured a prayer under her breath. "'When the dawn breaks and the shadows flee", Mam, I'll see you again.'

With her head held high she walked to the door of the church, feeling sympathetic eyes on her. She wouldn't break down. Not until she was on her own. Mam and Dad were dead. Archie was gone.

All she had left now were her dreams.

PART TWO

EDINBURGH 1909–14

Chapter 15

Edinburgh, February 1909

Edinburgh both terrified and excited Jessie.

She had never been on a train before and even the simple procedure of purchasing a ticket at Glasgow's Queen Street station confused her. In the end she'd followed the example of a mother with two small children and asked for a third-class ticket to Edinburgh. It had taken more of her precious shillings than she'd expected and she was alarmed by how quickly her money was disappearing. As the small family made their way to the platform, Jessie hurried after them, worried that she might get on the wrong train. A man kindly lifted her bag onto a rack above her head and she took a seat opposite them.

She was tired, hungry and beginning to feel sorry for herself. She leaned her head against the window and watched the rain run like tears down the glass.

It was still difficult to think of Archie's leaving without anger. Worse was the constant feeling of dread that he had had something to do with the mysterious disappearance of Lord Maxwell. The earl's son had never turned up, alive or dead.

After Mam's funeral, there had been no reason for her to stay on Skye. Even if she could have paid the rent, it was unbearable without Dad, Mam and Archie. Now, though, there was nothing to stop her becoming a nurse.

She'd sold what she could, which wasn't much, but with what she'd got, and the small amount that remained of the money Archie had sent, she had paid for her passage on the boat from Skye to Glasgow, the train fare from Glasgow to Edinburgh and had a few shillings left over for her lodgings while she looked for work.

'Mummy, I'm hungry.' The voice of one of the children opposite broke into her thoughts. The mother unwrapped some sandwiches from crinkled brown paper. Jessie's stomach rumbled. How long had it been since she'd eaten? Before she'd left, the village women had come to say goodbye and pressed packages of cold ham, salted herring, bannocks and cockles fried in oatmeal, even a penny or two, into her hands. Their generosity had touched her, and more than once she'd struggled to hold back tears. But the boat journey had lasted three days and she'd finished the last of the food last night. She didn't want to spend the little money she had on more until she knew how much she would need for her lodgings.

She had the address of a boarding-house on the High Street that one of the women from the village had given her. Sophie couldn't tell Jessie how much the landlady would charge or how to get there once she had got off the train at Princes Street station in Edinburgh, but had assured her that it wasn't far to walk.

The train eventually arrived with a bellow and puff of steam. The woman with the children was soon swallowed up in the crowd, leaving Jessie uncertain what to do next. She gritted her teeth and hefted her bag onto her shoulder. She was strong. If necessary, she could walk for miles. She stopped to ask a man in a train guard's uniform for directions and he pointed up a steep cobbled road, told her to follow it and to ask her way again when she got to the top.

After the open spaces of Skye, the crowd-filled streets panicked her. She had never seen so many people in one place before. Everyone looked as if they had somewhere to go, as if they belonged.

Trying not to gawp, she wound her way between hawkers and ladies in elegant hats with feathers, clinging to the arms of gentlemen dressed in fine suits and bowler hats as they dodged the mud and dirt on the street. The dress she'd made so she would look presentable in the city was already stained and crumpled from her travels, and her hat kept getting tipped to the side by careless elbows as people pushed by without seeming to see her.

Her new boots pinched her feet and every step she took made her wince. She was tempted to take them off and walk in her bare feet, but she didn't want to look as if she belonged with the ragged crowds of women and children huddled together on the pavement with outstretched palms, begging.

She watched a motor-bus with people sitting in the open-air roof thunder past – the only motor vehicles she'd seen before were the cars on Skye that belonged to the big houses. Not all of the buses had engines: some were pulled by four horses, and the wheels of the heavily laden two-storey carts made a terrible racket on the cobbled streets. Jessie was sorry for the poor beasts, puffing such a weight up the hill, their eyes blinkered and dried sweat scumming their flanks.

It wasn't just the noise that took her by surprise: it was the smell. Coal and soot, dung and other unrecognisable odours coalesced to form a rancid stink that made her want to gag.

But it wasn't all bad. Businesses of every description lined the streets, shops with haunches of beef and pork hanging up outside, covered with flies, and others selling silver, clothes, linen and china. She had never imagined it was possible to buy so many different things. In Skye there were few shops and they sold a mix of everything. Not that Jessie or any other village woman had much call to go into them. Most of their food came from the land and their clothes were hand-me-downs or home-made.

As everyone had said, Edinburgh was truly a city where you could get anything you desired – as long as you had money.

She hugged her bag closer and felt in her pocket for her coins. Still there, wrapped up in a clean handkerchief. She didn't know what she would do if she fell victim to a thief. Sophie had warned her to keep a tight grip on her possessions and she had no intention of letting anyone separate her from her few remaining pennies.

Eventually she found the name of the close she was looking for at a corner of the High Street. The soot-blackened tenements were piled higgledy-piggledy as if a child had been balancing blocks on top of one other, and Jessie had to crane her neck to see the top of the buildings. A little girl of three or four stood just outside the mouth of the close. Snot was streaming from her nostrils and she made no attempt to wipe it away. When Jessie asked if she knew which was Maggie Simpson's house, the child stared at her with blank eyes. Jessie gave up and asked an older boy, who was playing with an old wooden wheel, instead. He glanced at her without interest and pointed to a doorway. She gathered her skirt and adjusted her eyes to the darkness of the unlit staircase. The noise of people going about their business filtered through the walls along with the stale odour of cooking.

Maggie's flat was right at the top. Ignoring the shouts she could hear from below, she knocked on the door.

It was opened by a frazzled-looking woman with one child in her arms and another clinging to her skirt. A man in shirt sleeves brushed past Jessie without so much as a hello.

'Yes?' the woman asked crossly, and turned away. 'Tom, stop yer snivelling or I'll take my hand to you.'

'Mrs Simpson? I'm Jessie MacCorquodale. Sophie from Skye said you were expecting me.' She was beginning to think she had come to the wrong place. It was crowded, with several children sitting on the floor, and a young girl stirring something in a pot on the stove.

Maggie Simpson stepped aside. 'Aye, well, don't just stand there. Come in.'

Inside, Jessie stood uncertainly in the middle of the room. It wasn't so different from her house in Skye, with its one room for cooking and living. It even had the same recessed bed tucked into a wall, but if this was the boarding-house, where was she to sleep? Not with the family, surely.

But it seemed that that was exactly where she was to lodge. Not in the recessed bed, thank the Lord, but in a separate room in a double bed with Maggie Simpson's two daughters.

'That'll be two shillings a week,' the woman said, as soon as Jessie put her bag down on the floor. 'I need a week up front.'

Two shillings! It was more than she'd planned for and more than this place deserved, but she was too exhausted and overwhelmed to search for new lodgings. This place would have to do until she found a hospital to take her on. At least then, hopefully, she would be able to afford her own room.

Anxiety fluttered in her stomach. She had not much more than a pound left. Even if she found a position in the next day or two, it would be some time before she was paid. In the meantime she had to survive on what she had.

Maggie left her in the room 'to sort yourself out'. Jessie unpinned her hat and placed it at the end of the bed. There was no chest of drawers for her clothes, or even a hanger for her dress. The room was filthy. The floor looked as if it hadn't been swept for the last month and the bed smelt of damp and sweat.

She swallowed the lump in her throat and told herself not to be silly. A little dirt wouldn't kill her. Tomorrow she'd start looking for a nursing position, and with a bit of luck, she'd find one. She opened her bag and took out her apron. In the meantime there was cleaning to be done.

Finding a nursing position wasn't as easy as she'd hoped. She tried the Royal Infirmary first. It was only a short walk from Maggie's but the porter laughed at her when she asked to see the matron. Had she a reference? She had to shake her head. He looked her up and down and his lip curled. 'You don't just turn up and expect to be given a job at the Edinburgh Royal Infirmary!' The way he said the name of the hospital, anyone would have thought he was talking about Buckingham Palace. 'You have to apply to the Lady Super-intendent in writing and then, if she thinks you're suitable, she might invite you for an interview. But I wouldn't count on it. Not when there are ladies looking for nursing posts who are willing to pay to be taught here. They don't take the likes of you,' he said, 'unless you're willing to work as a ward maid. They're always looking for them.'

The likes of her! Pay to train as a nurse! It was, of course, impossible. But neither was she going to work as a ward maid. She could just as well have stayed in Skye as come all the way to this un-friendly city to do that.

She wanted to punch him. He was no better than her, yet he was treating her as if she were a pauper. She thought about arguing but one look at the smirk on his face told her she wasn't going to get her foot on the step, never mind all the way to the Lady Superintendent's office. She walked away, holding her head high. She wasn't going to let that stuffed-up jackass see that he had upset her.

She tried other hospitals, too, but they weren't prepared to take her on either, either because she didn't have the right qualifications or because she wasn't the right sort, she didn't know. Eventually someone suggested she try the workhouse in Craigleith. They were looking for nurses in their infirmary wing and it wasn't a sought-after job. Better-educated girls preferred to work in a proper hospital.

And that was how, three days after she'd arrived in Edinburgh, she found herself at her first interview.

Matron Yellowlees was a stern-looking woman in a black dress with a stiff white collar. 'Tell me why you wish to work here,' she said.

Jessie hid her sweating hands in her lap. 'I want to train as a nurse and I know of nowhere else that will take me,' she admitted. 'All I've ever wanted is to be a nurse.'

The matron raised an eyebrow, but her severe expression relaxed a little. 'The work's hard. I've just taken over and the current state of affairs here can't be allowed to continue. The wards are a disgrace, and there is only one trained nurse to cover them all and teach you. We have another nurse but she works in the children's ward. You'll be expected to cover it as well on her day off. The rest of the nursing is supplied by the female inmates and, I must warn you, they have no liking for work.'

'I'm used to hard work, Ma'am.'

'You must call me "Matron". You're in a hospital now.'

Matron steepled her fingers, and studied Jessie

154

with a mixture of hope and resignation. 'How much schooling have you had?'

'Until I was fourteen, Ma'am – I mean, Matron. I was supposed to go away to get more but my mam got sick and I couldn't. But I can read and write, and I even know some Latin.'

'Where is your mother now?'

'She died, Matron, of consumption.' Jessie wasn't sure if that was the whole truth. Perhaps if Dad hadn't died and Archie hadn't left, Mam would have fought harder to stay alive. 'My mother delivered the babies on Skye and I helped her. I never lost one.'

Matron's mouth twitched. 'And why do you think that was?'

'My mother said the most important thing was to keep everything clean, Matron. She said that you could leave it to God after that.'

'Did she indeed?' Matron scribbled something with her pen on a piece of paper. 'Very well, then,' she said, putting her pen down and peering at Jessie over wire-framed glasses. 'I'll give you a trial. The wage is twenty-five pounds a year. You'll buy your own uniform. You'll be woken at five thirty and be on the wards by six thirty. You'll work until eight in the evening with half an hour for luncheon and half an hour for supper. Lights out at ten thirty. You'll have a room in the attic and one day off every two weeks. Any studying must be done in your own time. In addition to your nursing duties you'll have other tasks. We have five wards here, as well as the children's ward, and you'll work on all of them. Sister Hardcastle will keep an eye on you but you'll be responsible for overseeing the female inmates who work in the infirmary, as well as ensuring that the kitchen delivers adequate food to the patients. You'll also be responsible for ensuring that there's a regular supply of clean linen from the laundry. Despite your enthusiasm, you may find the work too strenuous. The last nurse left after a month.'

Jessie's heart was pounding so hard she thought it might jump from her chest. At last she had the chance to become a proper nurse. She didn't care how hard it would be as long as she was being trained. And the fact that she would have her board and lodging was a bonus. She didn't know how much longer she could have put up with the cramped and disorganised – if no longer filthy – conditions in Maggie Simpson's house.

'I won't leave, Matron. I promise.'

'In that case, Probationer MacCorquodale, when can you start?'

Jessie came back the next day with her bags and her nurse's uniform. She didn't even care that it had taken almost all of her remaining money to buy it: it was beautiful and she couldn't wait to wear it.

An inmate took her up to a room in the attic. There was just enough space for an iron bed, a wardrobe and a side table with a basin, but it was all hers. She had to stand on tiptoe to look out of the tiny window but she could see the hospital fields. The anxiety and fear that had been swirling in her stomach since she had left Skye began to ease.

'Mrs Luck says you can have your meals in the

kitchen. Sister Hardcastle and Matron have theirs in the parlour. Breakfast is at six, dinner at one and supper at five.'

'Thank you...?' Jessie prompted.

'Me name's Sally.'

'How long have you been here, Sally?'

'Two years, pet. My man got put to the gaol a while back and I couldn't get no one to take me on, not with the kids and me having no place to stay, so we came here.'

'And do you like it?'

A flash of disbelief crossed Sally's face. 'Naebody comes here if they can help it, Miss, but at least I ken ma bairns are getting fed. They's with a family noo that can feed them and send them tae school.' She dabbed her eyes with a grubby sleeve.

'They're not with you?' Jessie was shocked.

'No, Miss. The littlest children get fostered out. I hasnae seen mine these last twelve months. I keep telling masel they're better aff whaur they are.'

That wasn't right. Surely it was best to keep a child with its mother. 'Don't you have family who can help?' Jessie asked. In Skye, when a mother and father died, someone always took in the remaining children. Usually it was a grandparent or an older sister, but if there was no one a neighbour would do it. Edinburgh was a strange place indeed.

'No, Miss. I did once, but they washed their hands of me when I married my man. They said he was nae guid and it turns out they was right. I'm no gaun tae crawl back to them now.'

'How many people live here, Sally? Do you know?'

'I'm nae guid wi numbers. Hundreds anyway. Maybe as mony as a thousand.'

Jessie was stunned. So many people without a home of their own. How was it possible?

Sally shuffled her feet and looked towards the door. 'If that's all, lass, it's almost time for me supper. If I'm late there might not be any left. Sister Hardcastle said to tell you she'll see you on the fever ward tomorrow morning.'

'Thank you, Sally. I'll find my way to the kitchen when I've unpacked.'

Jessie hung her uniform carefully, standing back to admire the stiff white apron and the starched collar and sleeves. Then she put away the rest of her clothes and laid her hairbrush on the table. Finally she set her notebook and the textbook Dr MacKenzie had given her next to the brush. Her new life was about to begin and she felt dizzy with excitement.

Chapter 16

The next morning, Jessie washed using the bowl of water that had been left outside her door and dressed in her uniform. Her fingers fumbled as she wound her hair into a tight knot. She jabbed pins into the stray locks that wouldn't do as they were told, then spent another twenty minutes trying to coax her nurse's cap into the right shape.

Even though it had taken her far longer to get dressed than she'd expected, she was still twenty minutes too early for breakfast. She held the hand mirror that had belonged to Mam at arm's length and studied herself. Unfortunately she could see only bits of herself at a time. Her cap wasn't perfect, but she thought she looked smart in her light blue uniform – even with the thick stockings and stout shoes. If only Mam, Dad and Archie could see her now! They'd be so proud of her. Thinking about them brought a lump to her throat and she blinked rapidly. She wouldn't cry. Tears never did anyone any good. In her mind's eye, she saw Mam looking down at her and smiling. She could almost hear her saying, 'Well done – but what have you done with your hair, child?' She wanted to giggle as she remembered Mam's shock when Jessie had tried to straighten her hair with the iron from the stove. She'd been silly then, but now she was seventeen and knew better.

After a breakfast of thick, lumpy porridge and toast in the kitchen, Jessie found her way to the fever ward. She paused at the entrance to the cavernous, dimly lit room. Apart from an inmate, who was leaning on a mop, and the patients, who were eating at a long table in the middle of the ward, there were no nursing staff.

She took a deep breath and entered the room. The smell of urine and sweat hit her instantly. The windows were tightly closed and the fire at the end of the room gave out more smoke than heat. Jessie walked to the first window and flung it open. The air outside was cleaner than it was in the centre of Edinburgh and she drew in deep lungfuls.

'What do you think you're doing?' a voice snapped behind her.

She spun around to find a severe woman in a sister's uniform glaring at her.

'Close that window at once! Don't you realise there are sick people in here who can't afford to catch their deaths?'

Jessie was sure that their congested chests were more likely to get worse from the smoke in the room, but she held her tongue. The woman in front of her must be Sister Hardcastle and could dismiss her with a flick of a bony hand if she wished. Reluctantly Jessie closed the window, smoothed her apron and dropped a curtsy.

Sister Hardcastle walked a circle around her while the patients looked on with mild interest. 'Your cap is squint. Straighten it immediately.'

Jessie didn't know how she was supposed to do so without a mirror but she did her best. Sister Hardcastle clicked her tongue, tugged the cap off Jessie's head, did something to it with a few deft movements and put it back. 'Learn how to fold that cap, Probationer, before you come on duty tomorrow.'

It seemed strange that she was more concerned with Jessie's cap than with the stench and the filth on the ward, but she was thrilled to be called 'Probationer'. In a few years, God willing, people would call *her* 'Sister' and probationers would curtsy to *her*. She would put up with anything to have that happen.

'I'm sorry, Sister,' she said.

'I don't know how much Matron explained about how things work here, but I'd like you to start by sorting out this ward and the female fever ward next door. I'll be back to check on you later.'

Jessie bobbed again. She couldn't wait to begin.

As soon as Sister Hardcastle had left, Jessie looked around the ward, wondering where to start. The smell was unbearable. In the middle of the room there was a large pewter tub and when Jessie inspected the contents, she was horrified to find it almost full of urine.

Her shoes sticking to the dirty floor, she walked over to the nearest patient. He was lying in a rumpled bed that stank of urine, sweat and faeces. It must have been days since he was last washed and there were another twenty or so like him in this room alone. For a moment she felt over-whelmed. Then she remembered what Matron had said about the inmates helping. She needed them if she was going to put everything to rights – there would be no assistance from Sister Hard-castle.

'I'll be back in a minute,' she said, to no one in particular, and went in search of the female fever ward. It was only a little cleaner than the male ward but at least six women were doing nothing but chatting to one another. They all looked healthy enough to be out of their beds.

To her relief, she spied a familiar face pushing a grubby mop listlessly over the floor.

'Good morning, Sally.'

Sally stopped her mopping and leaned on the pole. 'Hello, hen.'

'I need some women to help me,' Jessie said.

'Who should I ask?'

'There's no many that can be bothered, lass, although there's a few who could do with getting off their arses.'

'I need as many as you can persuade.'

The other women shook their heads when Sally asked them to help so in the end there was only Jessie and her. First they got rid of the communal piss-pot that the men used in the night. Then, together, they washed and changed all of the beds, demanding that those men who could do so get up and dress. Jessie met with resistance at first, but with a mixture of wheedling, shaming and downright bullying from Sally, only around half remained in bed, tucked under clean sheets and laundered blankets.

'By God, Miss, for such a wee lassie ye ken hoo tae work,' Sally said. 'Ma ain body is aching mair than it has in years.'

'This isn't hard, compared to what I'm used to.'

Just then Sister Hardcastle appeared, but if Jessie had expected praise for her efforts, she was disappointed.

'Have you taken the temperatures and pulses of the patients yet, Probationer MacCorquodale?'

It was on the tip of Jessie's tongue to say of course she hadn't – when would she have had the time? But of course she couldn't say that. 'I'll do that now, Sister,' she said instead.

'You do know how?'

'Yes, Sister.'

'Good. When you're finished here, move on to Women's Fever. After lunch there's the north and south wings. As it's your first day, I'll see to the whooping-cough ward.'

Over the next months, Jessie learned to dress wounds and bathe patients without lifting them from the bed. She had nursed children and adults through every kind of fever and infection, and had even assisted in theatre. She studied every text-book she could lay her hands on and memorised symptoms and treatments until she believed she could recite them in her sleep.

Slowly she had managed to cajole increasing numbers of the female inmates to help her. At first they'd been reluctant, but when they saw that she worked alongside them, only stopping for meals, they gradually came round. Eventually they began to take an interest in the work and developed a liking for teasing Jessie. Increasingly the wards rang with the sound of their ribald humour.

The consultant physician, a man with a florid face and an unnerving squint, came three times a week to do rounds with the lady doctor and Sister Hardcastle. As soon as he'd left, Jessie would write down everything he'd said in her notebook. It was the third she'd filled since she'd arrived and she was proud of it.

She missed the fresh air and big empty skies of home but she'd gradually become accustomed to the noise and smells of Edinburgh. For the first few months she'd been lonely. On her day off she would walk the streets or go to the Botanic Gardens, where she would sip tea in her new sprigged-muslin dress as if she were a lady. Sometimes, when the weather was fine, she'd sit in the work-house gardens and watch the inmates as they tended the vegetable patches. Mr Dickson, the head gardener, had taken a liking to her and she would always leave with a piece of fruit or a tomato in the pocket of her dress.

Her favourite place was down at Newhaven Harbour. Whenever it wasn't pouring with rain, she'd walk down there to smell the sea. Even the squawking of the gulls delighted her. If she closed her eyes she could almost imagine she was back on Skye. She would take off her shoes and wade into the water, revelling in the feel of the wet sand squishing between her bare toes.

A little further up, at the pier, women sold fish from the heavily laden baskets they carried on their shoulders. Although Jessie had no money to buy from them, or the wherewithal to cook a fish, she would talk to them and, for that short time, her loneliness would ease.

She was neither one thing nor the other at the workhouse: too elevated to be friends with the workhouse inmates, but too lowly to be considered company for Sister or Matron, although recently Matron had taken to inviting her to the parlour for tea.

Sometimes Jessie bought farthing sweeties for the children, but apart from the muslin dress, she had spent very little. She saved her wages in a jar on her table, not sure what she was saving for but knowing that one day the money would be useful. She'd discovered the library where she could take out books for free, and in the evenings, when work was finished for the day, she would read by candlelight until she found it impossible to keep her eyes open.

She had been at Craigleith for six months when she met Tommy.

The nurse who usually covered the children's ward was on a day off and Jessie had just finished making the beds when a dark-haired man with a cheeky grin appeared at the door.

'Tommy!' the children squealed, jumping out of bed and running to throw their skinny arms around his legs. Even little Jock, who hadn't said a word since his mother had died three months earlier, was hanging onto the man's hand as he sucked his thumb.

'What are you doing here?' Jessie asked, flustered for some reason she couldn't put her finger on. 'No visitors on the ward without Sister's permission.'

'Oh, I'm not a visitor, am I, Jock?' He swung the little boy into his arms. At the same time Maisy dipped a hand into Tommy's pocket and brought out a paper bag in a way that suggested his appearance with sweets was a common occurrence.

It was on the tip of Jessie's tongue to confiscate the sweets and dole them out at appropriate intervals, but one look at the anticipation on their faces was enough to make her change her mind. The little mites got few enough treats as it was.

Jessie studied him. He had taken off his cap when he'd come into the room, and his thick hair was awry. He had a long nose, which looked almost too big for his face, and a wide mouth that turned up at the corners. His brown worsted trousers were too big for him and were held up with a worn leather belt. His shirt had a hole in the shoulder and another near a button, but his boots were reasonably new, although they were badly scuffed.

Jessie glanced around, but Sister was nowhere to be seen. 'I'm still not sure you should be here. Are you related to one of the children?'

'No, lass.' His accent was interesting. It had a little of Edinburgh in it, but there was something else too, something that reminded her of the islands. 'I work down at Leith docks and it isn't far to walk. I've nothing better to do most Sundays 'cept come here for a visit.'

Tommy sat on one of the beds and lifted Jock onto his lap. 'I was here from the age of eight until I was fourteen,' he continued. 'I come back whenever I can to say hello to my friends and the wee ones.' He ruffled Jock's hair and grinned at Maisy. 'I heard Maisy was in the ward and I couldn't leave without saying hello.'

Maisy climbed onto his lap alongside Jock and wrapped her arms around Tommy's neck.

Jessie saw that Tommy was studying her and blushed. She didn't know very much about men, but the way he was looking at her made her feel funny inside.

'What's your name?' he asked with a grin.

'She's Jessie,' Maisy said, before Jessie could reply. 'We're supposed to call her Nurse Mac-Corquodale but she lets us call her Jessie when Matron isn't here.'

Tommy's grin grew wider. 'A rebel, eh? There's not many who don't do what Matron says.'

Jessie wasn't sure she liked Tommy being here, but he wasn't doing any harm, as far as she could tell, and she needed to get to the other wards.

166

Maisy's mother was in the laundry and wouldn't be coming up to see to the children until later.

'I have to go,' she said. She pointed to the bell on the table in the centre of the room where the children had their meals. 'Maisy's mammy should be along at some point, but if you need me before then, ring that. I'll be in the ward next door.'

He'd come every Sunday since then and he was always the same, polite to her and gentle with the children. At first Jessie wasn't sure what to make of him. Surely he had better things to do than visit the poorhouse.

Then one day, when she had a day off, he was waiting for her by the gate. For once he looked ill at ease, twisting his cap between his fingers, despite the new trousers and shirt he was wearing.

'Hello,' she said. 'Not going in today?'

'I've come to see you.' He dragged a hand through his hair. 'I wondered if you'd care to take a walk with me.'

Jessie hesitated, but only for a moment. She was lonely. On Skye there was always someone to talk to and, most evenings, ceilidhs took place where everyone met to gossip and sing songs. Here in Edinburgh, when her day had finished, she had only her own company and her books to look forward to.

'I'm going to the Botanic Gardens, and if you happen to be going that way, I suppose there's nothing I can do to stop you coming with me.'

Edinburgh was covered with a grey blanket of smog that made it difficult to see even on a good day, far less one like today when rain fell in short bursts from a sky thick with dark clouds. Jessie

167

never let the weather put her off her walk. Apart from the harbour at Newhaven, the Botanic Gardens was the only place she felt she could breathe.

Tommy trudged next to her, apparently lost for words, and Jessie took pity on him. 'What's it like down at the docks?' she asked.

'It's grand,' he said. 'Well, perhaps not grand, but the work's steady. I help build the ships.' There was a note of pride in his voice.

'Do you live in Leith?'

Tommy frowned. 'Aye. I share a room with some others. One day I'll get my own place. When I'm made foreman.'

Jessie lifted an eyebrow. 'And is that likely to happen?'

He grinned. 'As sure as I'm walking beside you.'

Because of the rain, the gardens weren't as busy as they sometimes were. They passed a woman pushing a pram and another one riding a bicycle. Jessie followed a familiar route, the one that took her past the tea-room. She didn't always stop there for a cup of tea. Sometimes she just looked through the misted windows to watch the well-dressed ladies holding delicate china cups and taking genteel sips.

Tommy stopped and felt in his pocket, bringing out a sixpence, which he brandished as if it were a pound note. 'Would you have tea with me, Miss MacCorquodale?' he asked, with his cheeky grin.

Jessie hesitated again. She didn't feel comfortable going inside with Tommy. Even with his new shirt and trousers he would be out of place. But she would hurt his feelings if she said no. Their money was as good as anyone's. She smiled back and took his arm, for all the world as if they, too, were gentry. 'I'd be delighted,' she replied in her primmest voice.

After that, whenever she had a day off she would find Tommy waiting for her. They walked for miles, sometimes up Arthur's Seat, sometimes to the Botanic Gardens or to Newhaven, and once down to Leith docks. She liked Leith. There were women hawking fish, the ring of metal on metal, the shouts of men as they built the ships in the dock and an endless stream of barefooted children playing on the streets or in the narrow closes.

Tommy didn't take her to the place where he lived, and for that she was grateful. It would be unseemly for her to go to his lodgings with him.

Slowly she fell in love with him. She couldn't help herself. Although his life had been hard – he had been brought up in the poorhouse after his parents had died from typhus soon after they had come from Ireland – he never complained or indicated that he was anything but content with his lot. On her day off he'd wait for her at the gatehouse. Once, he wasn't there, and she wanted to cry with disappointment, but a fortnight later he was back. He'd apologised profusely, saying he'd had an opportunity to work overtime and couldn't turn it down, not if he wanted to hold onto his job.

That was the day he'd proposed. 'I want us to wed, Jessie,' he said. 'I don't have much, but I've enough to support us both and, God willing, a baby in time.'

She blushed when he'd said that. But the truth was, she'd been imagining how it would feel to be

169

held by him. He'd kissed her then, his lips soft at first, but when she'd responded, opening her mouth, his kiss had deepened, leaving her shaky and gasping for breath.

'What about my job?' she said, reluctantly tearing herself away from his embrace. 'They won't let me stay if I marry.'

'You'll have plenty to do looking after me – and the wee ones when they come along.' He circled her waist with his hands and lifted her against him. 'Come on, Jessie, say yes.'

She looked up at this man whom she'd come to love almost more than life itself and touched his dear face with the tip of her finger. She hadn't thought there was anything she could love more than nursing until she'd met him – but she had to finish her training. She couldn't stop now. Did she have to choose?

'Do you really love me, Tommy?'

'More than I thought possible,' he replied, gazing at her with an intensity that stole her breath.

'Then will you wait for me? I have two years to go before I can call myself a qualified nurse.'

'Two years! You want me to wait two years?' He pulled her hips towards his, and whispered in her ear, 'Can you feel that, lass? I want you in my bed.' He laughed shakily. 'I don't think I can wait two years. I don't think I can wait two months, I want you that much.'

'And I want to be with you, too.' Jessie blushed. 'But we're both young and we have the rest of our lives to be together. Please, Tommy. Say you'll wait for me.'

He cupped her face in his large hands, looked

into her eyes and gave her a rueful smile. 'If I have to, then I will. But I can't wait for ever.' He dropped a kiss on her forehead. 'Two years, darlin'. Not a second longer.'

Chapter 17

Edinburgh, October 1912

Isabel paused at the door of the lecture theatre and looked around in disgust. The male students were drumming their feet on the wooden floor, like stampeding cattle. Some had managed to get hold of policemen's whistles and added to the din with shrill, prolonged blasts. Through a haze of pipe smoke, she watched a student being passed over the heads of his fellows from the back of the theatre to the front. Those not participating in the mayhem were either filling their pipes or lolling back on the benches with their eyes closed. Only one, a bespectacled, serious-looking fellow, sat upright, his book in front of him, waiting for the lecture to begin.

She tucked a stray lock of hair under her narrow-brimmed hat, took a deep breath and forced a smile. It wouldn't do to show her unease at the first of what was bound to be another series of hurdles. Women doctors had been fighting for years to be allowed to attend lectures alongside the men. To turn tail now would only make the men believe they had been right. Today she was the only woman who had dared to come.

The four years she had been attending the Edinburgh School of Medicine for Women had passed quickly. The work had been harder than she'd expected: despite the holidays she had spent helping her father on Skye, she had found she didn't know as much as she'd thought and had had to study harder than she could ever have imagined, often deep into the night. She had sat exams in botany, zoology, materia medica and physics, and passed them all with merit, except physics, in which she had little interest and had barely scraped a pass. She'd walked the wards, dissected a cadaver, learned how to test urine for sugar by heating a sample with a Bunsen burner and so many other things she wondered sometimes if there was room in her head for it all. At least her studies and her work stopped her dwelling on those last dark days on Skye when her world had changed for ever.

She still missed Papa terribly. All that mattered now was medicine and making him proud.

As she made her way down the steps a man noticed her. He leaned back in his seat and hooked his arms behind his head. 'Gentlemen, we have a lady in our presence.' He had to repeat himself several times to be heard. After a minute or so, the drumming and whistling stopped and the figure being passed around was set back on his feet. Fifty pairs of eyes turned in Isabel's direction and then, as one, the students rose to their feet. For a heart-stopping moment, Isabel thought they were going to walk out in protest, but to her relief, those who were wearing hats removed them and one even sketched a bow in her direction.

Isabel nodded slightly and took a seat. At the front of the semi-circular anatomy theatre a body, covered with a sheet, was lying on the dissection table. Next to it was a trolley with a variety of saws and scalpels. Despite the high-vaulted ceiling, the overpowering throat-stinging smell of formaldehyde filled the room.

She removed her notebook, pen and ink from her bag and placed them neatly in front of her, ignoring the whispers and titters, and the occasional angry cry of 'It shouldn't be allowed!'

The doors to her right swung open and a rotund bewhiskered man, wearing a short wool jacket and grey, slightly rumpled trousers, walked into the room. At last Isabel was finally going to hear the well-known chief anatomist, Mr Forsythe, lecture.

Without saying a word, apparently oblivious to the students in front of him, Forsythe exchanged his jacket for a white gown and his assistant tied it for him. With a flick of his wrist, the surgeon removed the sheet from the operating table exposing the cadaver of a female of around forty, with the emaciated look of someone who had been ill for some time before her death.

Isabel felt embarrassed for the woman the corpse had once been. Stripped naked, apart from a cloth covering her pelvic area, and laid out for the students' curious eyes, the dead woman had a vulnerability that Isabel preferred not to see. She tried not to think of the body on the table as someone who had once been a living, breathing person with hopes and dreams just like the people in the room, or that once she had been someone's beloved daughter, sister or mother. It was easier to think of her as a mass of tissue, organs and bones. Good doctors, she was always being told, albeit by the male professors, focused on the disease, not the person.

Besides, this was the part of her medical training that she had been most looking forward to: a postmortem and the chance to discover whether her clinical diagnosis had been correct. When Mrs MacGillvary had been admitted to Women's Medical two days earlier, Isabel had immediately thought of tuberculosis, which was the main reason the poor of the city were admitted. Her conclusion hadn't been the result of a razor-sharp medical brain but, sadly, born of seeing too many with the disease.

Although medicine had come a long way in the last fifty years or so, there was still so little they could do to fight the toll that poverty took on the city's inhabitants. If the men and women of Edinburgh would only seek treatment sooner, the doctors might be able to save more of them, but those most in need – the unemployed, the poor, those who came from the country in search of work – were the very ones who could not spare the few shillings required or afford the time off work to go to the hospital.

She'd tested Mrs MacGillvary for the tubercle bacillus, but by the time the results came back, the woman had died.

'Obtaining cadavers for dissection is no longer as easy as it was when we had Messrs Burke and Hare to help,' Mr Forsythe said, referring to the infamous murderers who'd made a living by killing their victims in order to sell their bodies to medical schools. He looked pleased with his joke and the students laughed obligingly. They knew it didn't do to be on the wrong side of the man whose patronage they might seek one day. Should they in the future wish to set up practices to attend to the needs of Edinburgh folk, they would be dependent on him and his colleagues to refer patients their way.

'Now, gentlemen,' Forsythe continued, puffing on rubber gloves, 'what can we tell about this woman from looking at her?'

Isabel raised her hand, as did several others. But it was Philip Montgomery who answered without waiting to be invited.

'Apart from being dead, sir?' Only Montgomery would dare risk Forsythe's wrath with a quip. It was well known that his father was one of the major subscribers to the Royal Infirmary of Edinburgh. 'She's malnourished and has the complexion of a person who drinks.'

'Her appearance could have other causes,' Isabel interjected. 'She tested positive for tuberculosis and that would account for the skeletal appearance. Shouldn't we discuss her medical history before we make any guesses?'

Forsythe looked at her and pretended to do a double-take, as if he had only just noticed a woman among the students. 'Why,' he said, 'I was wrong when I addressed you all as "gentlemen". I should have said "gentlemen and lady".' He gave the last word heavy emphasis to underline that he doubted whether any lady would be interested in medicine, particularly when it involved

175

the study of a naked body.

He studied the roll-call sheet in his hand. 'Miss MacKenzie, I presume. I must admit I had my doubts as to whether you would join us.'

His words echoed round the oak-panelled room and Isabel twisted her fingers together. She straightened her shoulders and stared straight ahead. She had a right to be there.

'Not marching with your fellow suffragettes, then, Miss MacKenzie? I would have thought that was more your cup of tea.' Forsythe wasn't done with her yet, it seemed.

She bit her lip, keeping her expression composed. 'I'm happier here, sir.'

Forsythe stopped smiling. 'If you think you might swoon, please feel free to leave,' he said.

As if she would. In the first year of her training, she'd been handed a single leg of a cadaver to dissect. Later on, they'd been taken to the anatomy museum at the Royal College of Surgeons and the exhibits had been gruesome. If the sight of the decapitated head of a one-eyed baby hadn't made her faint, nothing would.

Forsythe took them through Mrs MacGillvary's medical history, from which it was clear that she had had the tubercle bacillus – even without the sputum result. Then he passed around her X-ray.

When it came to Isabel, she could see the cavitations that were a clear indicator of the dreaded disease.

'X-rays weren't available to us when I was a young doctor – we had only our eyes and our stethoscopes to make a diagnosis,' Forsythe said, as if this were something to be proud of.

And the fact we now have X-rays is in no small part thanks to Madame Curie, who just happens to be a woman. Isabel resisted the urge to remind him.

Forsythe was holding a scalpel aloft. 'I'm going to show you how we dissect bodies for post-mortems. It's possible that some of you will be called upon to do this one day. First, I will cut from the suprasternal notch to the pubis – like so.' He made a decisive sweeping incision as he spoke and the skin parted easily. 'Then I cut trans-versely.' Now the torso was open, like a divided cake.

He flung the scalpel into an enamel basin and pulled back the skin, revealing the organs. He nodded to his assistant to cut the ribs.

The snapping noise was far worse than any smell and Isabel concentrated hard so that she did not jump each time the bone-cutters bit through bone. At last the assistant was done and the chest contents exposed. Forsythe made a few quick movements with his scalpel, reached in and pulled out the lungs, holding them towards the students in his bloody hands, as if he were making an offering to the gods.

Isabel placed her spectacles on the bridge of her nose and leaned forward. She didn't need them but she thought they lent her a scholarly air. It was the same reason that, soon after she'd started at the university, she'd exchanged her pastel dresses for dark grey skirts and jackets.

As she had expected, the damage to the organ was immediately apparent. Large cavities had re-placed much of both upper lobes, the normal glistening surface scarred and fibrotic.

Forsythe sliced the lungs longitudinally. 'I will put them on a dish and you may all have a look at your leisure. As it reaches each of you, I would like you to point out a part of the lung and name it. I would also like you to give me a fact about the organ and name another disease that may affect the lungs. Anyone unable to do so must leave the class.'

Afterwards Isabel hurried along the corridor, her shoes echoing on the dark brown tiles. She was in danger of being late for ward rounds. That Forsythe had droned on long after the time allocated to the lecture had passed would not be deemed a good enough excuse.

She ignored the lift at the end of the hall, not trusting the ponderous contraption to reach the third floor without breaking down. Lifting her skirts, she bounded up the stairs two at a time, smiling at the startled looks of nurses as they passed her. She made it just in time to see her fellow students follow Dr Galbraith, the specialist in infectious diseases and chests, through the double doors of Women's Medical. She licked her palms and quickly smoothed her hair. No doubt her cheeks would be bright red from her exertions but there was nothing she could do about that.

Rows of cast-iron beds lined the ward on either side and the patients in them were tucked up with almost military precision, no crease daring to ruffle the starched smoothness of the sheets. Sister always made sure that no patient was eating or, God forbid, requiring a bedpan when the consultant was on the ward. Everything stopped for the Grand Rounds.

After a quick sweep of her pristine ward with a critical eye, Sister hurried over to them. Her nurses were standing to attention, arms behind their backs as if they, too, were on military parade.

'Shall we make a start?' Galbraith barked. 'What do you have for me, Sister Logan?'

'We have a double pneumonia in Bed One, Doctor,' she replied, as she led them across the ward.

The woman's breathing was laboured and she had the cyanotic tinge of death on her lips. A bottle of dextrose and saline fed fluid into her veins, and her head and shoulders had been raised to help her breathing. There was little else that could be done. She would either recover or, as seemed more likely in this case, simply slip away.

'Who can tell me about this patient?' Dr Galbraith asked.

Isabel pushed her way to the front. 'Mrs Campbell is thirty-three. She has four surviving children, all under the age of five. They live in a one-roomed tenement in the Grassmarket.'

Dr Galbraith raised his head and stared at her over the top of his half-moon glasses. He pursed his lips. 'That is all very well, Miss MacKenzie, but I want to know about her medical condition. To be a doctor is to be concerned with science. Physicians must remain detached from the patient and not be concerned with his or her circumstances. If a doctor chooses to become involved, he will seek unique solutions and that goes against what it is to be a scientist. If you wish to see the patient as a person, you should have become a nurse. It is a profession, after all, more suited to the feminine sex.'

Her fellow students tittered. Isabel felt herself flushing with anger and had to bite her lip to stop herself replying that patients could not be seen as separate from their circumstances. Coal miners got black lung because they worked in coal mines; children died because they didn't get enough nutritious food to eat and poor women continued to die in childbirth at a rate ten times that of their richer sisters. That she knew this wasn't because she was a woman: it was because *statistics* proved it. Of course Mrs Campbell's living conditions were relevant. Enlightened physicians, like Dr Littlejohn, knew this. That was why he'd insisted medical students go into the poorest houses in Edinburgh and seek out patients with tuberculosis so that they could be offered treatment before the infection took hold. This practice had fallen away under Dr Galbraith and the numbers dying from the disease had risen once again. Only the female students studying at the Bruntsfield Hospital, for women and children, continued with the visits.

'Mrs Campbell presented at the outpatients department with a three-week history of shortness of breath,' Isabel continued, keeping her voice even. 'She was admitted to the Lister Ward and had treatment with ultraviolet light for fourteen days. At first she showed signs of improvement but five days ago her condition deteriorated. On examination, the right lower lobe was dull to percussion and there were bronchial breath sounds – signs of lobar pneumonia. Over the last twenty-four hours she has had haemoptysis, producing prune-coloured blood when she coughs.'

'Better, Miss MacKenzie. Anyone else?' Dr Galbraith glanced at the other students.

'Not much to add, sir,' one said. 'The prognosis is death within forty-eight hours.'

Although Isabel knew he was right, she winced. She was glad the woman was unconscious and unable to hear her death sentence. Impulsively she took Mrs Campbell's hand and squeezed it. 'Could I ask Sister what the nurses are doing to make Mrs Campbell more comfortable?'

Dr Galbraith's bushy brows snapped together. 'I think we can take it for granted that Sister and her nurses are doing everything they can. As I said, if you'd prefer to be a nurse, Miss Mac-Kenzie, I'm sure that can still be arranged.'

'Nevertheless,' Isabel persisted, 'the patient's extremities are cold. I know we must keep the windows open but it's chilly in here, even with the heat from the stove. Have the nurses tried to keep the blood moving by massaging the patient's limbs?' Perhaps she should have let it go, but Mrs Campbell needed someone to speak for her.

Sister Logan stepped forward and smoothed her apron. 'I would like to answer that, Dr Galbraith. Never let it be said that patients on my ward don't get the best treatment.' The look she gave Isabel left her in no doubt that she hadn't made an ally. 'We are just about to give out the hot-water bottles. And I never heard of massage making a difference. Unless there is something I should know?' Her voice rose in disbelief. 'Besides,' she gestured towards the ward, 'I have fifty-nine other patients to look after. I suggest that my nurses' time is better spent looking after those who have a chance of recovery.'

She was right. Whatever they did wouldn't change Mrs Campbell's outcome.

Dr Galbraith looked at Isabel with derision. 'You may, if you wish, Miss MacKenzie, stay with the patient and try whatever you please. Or you can carry on with rounds. The choice is yours.'

It wasn't a choice. The message was clear. If she wanted to continue studying at the Royal Infirmary, she had to act like the men.

Giving Mrs Campbell's hand one last squeeze, Isabel followed Dr Galbraith to the next patient.

Chapter 18

Edinburgh, October 1913

Jessie wiped sweat from her eyes as another plume of steam filled the room. The washhouse was unbearably hot at this time of year. She plunged her arms into the water and, taking hold of the washboard, started scrubbing vigorously.

She and Tommy had been married for more than a year and a half and their baby, a little boy, was eleven months old. Although she loved being a wife and mother, she found the days difficult to fill and, without her wage, money was tight.

Tommy wouldn't be pleased if he knew she was taking in washing from the houses in Trinity, but what he didn't know couldn't hurt him. She hated keeping secrets from him, but the extra money would come in useful when it was time for Seamus to go to school.

'Hey, Jessie, how's that man of yours doing? Not given you another baby yet?' the woman next to her asked, with a leer. Lizzie Blackstock was all right. Most of the women were. They hid kind hearts under their caustic remarks and Jessie enjoyed their wit.

'One baby's enough right now, Mrs Blackstock. Not all of us are up to looking after six children under five, like you.' And as most of the other women did, if truth be told. Jessie sneaked a glance at Lizzie. She was thirty but looked fifty. Her hair was already going grey, her face lined, and the few teeth she had left were brown from the tobacco she chewed. And judging by the way her worn skirt clung to the mound of her belly, there was another on the way – and in the very near future too, judging by the size of her. Lizzie lived a few streets from Jessie in a similar tenement. One room, a shared toilet on the landing and a small, dirty back close was no place for eight of a family. It was no place for three of a family either, but Jessie was determined that one day she and Tommy would have a house with a separate bedroom. Perhaps even a front room.

She glanced at the other women bent over the sinks. They all had the same exhausted faces, the same peeling red hands and clothes that had seen better days. On the other hand, they were quick to smile, found humour in almost every situation and would give their last penny to help someone if she needed it. Almost all had families the size

183

of Lizzie's. Jessie knew that the more children she had, the less chance there was that she and Tommy would make it out of Pennyworth Row. Thank God she knew how to douche after sex. It was something else she kept from Tommy. She would have another child, but only when Seamus was a little bigger or when they had saved enough money to leave the tenement they were in.

'Maybe he finds your bones too hard for him, Jessie,' a woman quipped. 'Don't you know men like a bit of something to get hold of?'

'He likes my bones well enough,' Jessie replied. If the women thought they could make her blush, they were mistaken. After three years of banter from the inmates at the workhouse Jessie had heard it all.

'"He likes my bones well enough,"' Lizzie mimicked. 'How come you speak so fancy, Jessie? Is there something you're no' telling us?'

Jessie laughed. 'What? Like I'm really the daughter of Lady and Lord Muck who've fallen on hard times? That'd be right.'

'Well, why's your accent funny? Come on, Jessie. Tell us.'

'It's funny because I'm from Skye. And I speak fancy, as you call it, because English was taught to me when I was at school so I learned to speak it properly. We spoke Gaelic at home.'

A wave of sadness surged through her. For a moment she wished she was back on Skye. There she could breathe. On good days, washing was done in the open air at the loch, with her mam and the other women from the village for company. But Mam wasn't there any more. She was

184

with God, and Jessie should be glad of it, although she couldn't bring herself to be. At least she had Tommy. If Mam hadn't died Jessie couldn't have come to Edinburgh to be a nurse, and if she hadn't come to Edinburgh she wouldn't have met Tommy. Mam had always said that no one knew what God had in store for you, so you should look at everything as a chance. It would have been better if she was still alive, living with her and Tommy in Edinburgh, but what was the point in hankering for what you couldn't have?

'Where's Skye?' a younger woman, with pock-marks from a bad case of smallpox, asked. 'Is it near here?'

'It's a three-day journey by boat,' Jessie said.

She rinsed the clothes in the sink and carried them across to the mangle. She'd have time to use the baths next door while the clothes dried in the stove-heated room. It would cost a few of her precious pennies, but it was worth it. Her neighbour Peggy was watching Seamus for her and wasn't expecting her back for another hour or two. Tommy wouldn't get home from the ship-yard until nearly eight. By that time she'd have the washing returned to its owners.

After wringing the clothes, she hung them in the drying room. She frowned as she remembered Seamus's cough. It had kept her up most of the night. She had boiled kettles and the steam had seemed to help for a while, but she wouldn't be happy until it was completely gone.

Maybe she should skip her bath and make do with the tub in front of the fire after she'd put

Seamus down for the night. She shook her head. No, that wouldn't do. If she waited until Tommy was home, he'd want to wash her back, then one thing would lead to another and they'd end up in the bed making love. She couldn't depend on her douche too often.

Suddenly she was anxious to get home and back to Seamus. What if his cough had worsened while she'd been away? What if he was fretting for her? No, it was better to have a wash at the sink before Tommy came home and use the extra time to make him something nice for his tea. Maybe some potted sheep's brain. She cooked it just as her mother had taught her and Tommy liked it. A sheep's head had the added benefit of being cheap and she could also make soup that would last the week.

As soon as she could, she waved goodbye and set off up the cobbled street towards her home. At three o'clock the streets were thronged with people selling from carts and housewives doing their shopping. A fishwife was hawking the day's catch from a basket she wore around her shoulders as she walked the streets, looking for customers.

In the close of Jessie's tenement, barefoot children were playing a make-believe game with sticks and pieces of rubbish they had retrieved from the outside midden. Jessie had tried to tell the mothers not to allow the children to do that but her pleas had fallen on deaf ears. The women were only too glad to have the children out from under their feet and occupied. It was so different from her childhood, spent running across the

186

heather-covered moors, breathing in the fresh, clean air and paddling in the sea. How Seamus would love it on Skye. Eager to see him, Jessie ran up the rickety back stairs leading to her tenement and called in for her son.

'I'm sorry. I know I should have been back sooner.' She looked past Peggy for her child and her neighbour stood aside to let her in. Like Jessie's, Peggy's home was a single room with a recessed bed on one side and the rest of the space used as a kitchen-cum-sitting room. When Jessie saw Seamus sleeping on the bed, anxiety knotted her stomach. He was a lively baby who would normally be playing on the kitchen floor or trying to pull himself up by holding onto the table leg.

'He's no' been himself all day,' Peggy said. 'He wouldn't take the porridge you left for him and he's been sleeping most of the time.' Jessie rushed over to him. Seamus's breathing was laboured and he was flushed. Apart from his cough, he'd seemed normal earlier. Alarm shot through her. Her child wasn't well. There had been a number of deaths recently from diphtheria and it was possible that somehow Seamus had caught the infection. Please God, she hadn't brought it into her home from the washhouse. She'd been so careful to keep her child away from any source of infection.

She gathered Seamus into her arms and, with a quick word of thanks, ran up the flight of stairs to her home. As soon as she was inside she set the kettle to boil. Perhaps she was being overanxious. Maybe another dose of steam would help.

But it didn't. If anything his breathing became worse. He opened his eyes once, smiled weakly, then fell straight back to sleep. Jessie made up her mind. She went to the jar on the mantelpiece and grabbed a handful of the precious shillings inside. She would take him to Leith Hospital, but she had to be quick. They closed the gates at five and it was already after four. She'd have to take a cab.

'Please, God,' she whispered, 'let my baby be all right.'

It was almost five by the time Jessie arrived at Leith Hospital. Hansom cabs were hard to find down by the docks as there wasn't much call for them among people who could rarely afford even to take the tram. In the end she had run all the way, holding Seamus close to her chest.

There were around twenty people in the out-patients department still waiting to be seen. In the time it had taken for Jessie to reach the hospital, Seamus was worse. A lot worse. His small chest rose and trembled with the effort of taking each breath.

Jessie hurried to a nurse who was standing behind a lectern taking names of patients waiting to be seen. She pushed her way to the front of the queue, ignoring the muttered curses from those waiting patiently in line.

The nurse's mouth tightened. 'You have to wait your turn,' she said.

'Please, Nurse,' Jessie said. 'It's my wee boy. He can hardly breathe. He needs to see a doctor right now.'

'Everyone needs to see the doctor right now,' the nurse replied, unmoved. 'It will go faster if you wait in the queue, like everyone else.'

Jessie looked at the patients. None seemed in urgent need of help. 'Please,' she begged again. 'My son can't wait.'

An older woman near the front of the queue spoke out: 'Let the lassie go first. Anyone can see her bairn needs attention.'

There were a few murmurs of 'Aye' from the rest of the line and the nurse gave in. 'Name?'

'Jessie Stuart. My boy is Seamus Stuart. He's eleven months old. Please fetch the doctor.'

'Have you money?' the nurse asked.

Jessie pulled the coins from her pocket and thrust them at her. 'Take this. It's everything I have.'

'Sit over there.' The nurse nodded to an overcrowded bench. 'I'll let the doctor know you're here.'

When she turned to the next patient without calling for the doctor, Jessie's frustration boiled over. 'Nurse,' she said, forcing herself to sound calm, 'my child needs to see a doctor *now.*'

'And I said I'd let her know. She's with a patient at the moment.'

Jessie looked around the cavernous building, and spotted another nurse who was occupied with a trolley. She hurried over to her. 'Please, Nurse,' she said, 'my baby can't breathe properly. He needs to see a doctor *now.*'

The nurse stopped what she was doing. Whatever she saw in Jessie's face seemed to convince her. 'Let me have a look.'

Jessie unwrapped Seamus from his blanket. He was limp and barely conscious.

Alarm crossed the nurse's face. 'Follow me.' She led Jessie into a room with an examining couch and a dressings trolley.

'Undress your child,' she said, 'while I fetch the doctor.'

Relieved that at least this nurse seemed to appreciate the urgency, Jessie unwrapped Seamus from his blanket and gently undressed him. She laid him on the couch and covered him with her shawl.

After what seemed like hours but was only a few minutes, the nurse returned, followed by a woman in a dark suit. 'Where's the doctor?' Jessie asked frantically.

'I am Dr Harcourt,' the woman said stiffly. 'Now, if you will remain calm, I will examine your child.'

'I think it's diphtheria,' Jessie said. 'I don't know where he could have picked it up. I've always been so careful.' Once again, her mind flashed back to the washhouse. Silently she promised God she would never go there again, if only He'd let Seamus be all right.

'Are you a doctor?' Dr Harcourt asked.

'No, but–'

'If you're not a doctor,' Dr Harcourt cut her off, 'then may I suggest you leave the diagnosis to us?' She turned to the nurse, who was looking sympathetically at Jessie. 'Could you pass me a tongue compressor, Nurse?'

The nurse already had it in her hand. She gave it to the doctor and smiled reassuringly at Jessie behind the other woman's back.

Dr Harcourt used a pair of jaw clamps to hold Seamus's mouth open. When her child didn't respond to the invasion, Jessie's chest squeezed so hard she thought her heart would stop beating.

'Swab, Nurse,' the doctor demanded. She swabbed the back of Seamus's throat and placed the sample in a glass tube. 'I shall have this tested for the diphtheria bacillus. In the meantime we'll have to wait.'

Jessie wanted to shake the doctor. She knew it was diphtheria, and even if it wasn't, her child was struggling for breath. When she'd been a nurse she'd seen a doctor cut a hole in a child's throat to help it breathe. It had worked and the child, who had been on the point of collapse, had made a full recovery.

'He's only taking one breath every thirty seconds,' Jessie shouted at the doctor. She knew it wasn't helping but she couldn't stop herself. Couldn't the woman see what was as plain as day? 'He needs a hole in his throat to help him breathe. And he needs it now. If you won't do it, get me a doctor who will – or, God help me, pass me a scalpel and I'll do it myself.'

'If you don't calm down, I'll have to call Matron,' Dr Harcourt said.

Just then Seamus shuddered and stopped breathing.

The nurse stepped forward and felt for a pulse. She looked at the doctor and shook her head.

'Do it now,' Jessie said, 'for God's sake, while there's a chance!'

The doctor paled. Silently the nurse handed her a scalpel.

Jessie could see that the doctor's hands were

shaking. She looked at the instrument in her hand as if she'd never seen one before. 'I need to call the senior doctor. I've never performed a tracheotomy.'

'There's no time to call another bloody doctor!' Jessie yelled. She took a deep breath and forced the anger and fear from her voice. 'Cut just below the carotid cartilage but above the thyroid gland.' Still the doctor hesitated. She looked at the nurse, who nodded.

'Now, quickly,' Jessie said, 'cut that way.' She indicated with her finger, wincing as the scalpel sliced through her baby's skin and blood spurted. 'Now find a tube. Push the thyroid out of the way and place the tube in the hole. Go on!'

The doctor did as Jessie suggested. Jessie heaved a sigh of relief as air rushed into Seamus's lungs. God willing, he would be all right.

Three hours later Jessie was holding her dead baby in her arms.

Shortly after the doctor and nurse had left them, Seamus had opened his eyes briefly, then simply stopped breathing.

Jessie had run into the waiting room shouting for help, but it was too late. There was nothing anyone could do for her child.

She wrapped his still warm body in his blanket and held him close to her heart. Then, not knowing what else to do, headed home. She could barely see her way through the tears.

The doctor hadn't acted quickly enough and now Seamus was dead. Jessie would never see her little boy grow into a man, never see him smile again, breathe in his distinctive smell or feel his podgy hands touching her face.

Why had she gone against Tommy and taken in washing? *Had* she carried disease home with her from the washhouse?

If Mam had been alive she would have said Jessie should be glad that God wanted Seamus with Him. But Jessie wasn't glad at all. It was as if someone had plunged a knife into her breast and removed her heart. She wanted no part of a God who had seen fit to rob her of her only child.

She wanted her mam. But most of all she wanted Tommy.

Jessie sat with Seamus on her lap. He was already cold, his tiny nails tinged with blue.

His cradle was by her side and she lifted his blanket to breathe in his scent. His breakfast bowl was still on the table. His tiny clothes, which she'd washed that morning before going to the washhouse, still hung on the line above the range.

How was it possible that her child had been alive only hours before and was now lying dead in her arms? Where was his soul? Had it gone to Heaven? Were Mam and Dad comforting him? She couldn't bear to think of her baby on his own.

She'd passed her neighbours on the stairs but she'd not told them about Seamus. Not when she couldn't believe he was really dead. If she'd told them, someone would have run for Tommy and he'd be here with her. Tommy. Tommy. Her heart ached with such pain she thought it might shatter. How would he take Seamus's death? He worshipped their baby.

She heard his footsteps on the stairs and sucked in a breath. She would need all her courage in the next few minutes.

The door burst open and Tommy came in. He was whistling and at first didn't notice that she hadn't got up to greet him as she usually did by flinging her arms around him.

He dropped his lunch tin on the kitchen table and went to the basin to wash his hands. 'How is my dear wife today?' he asked. 'And the little man?'

Her silence made him turn. His eyes darkened. 'Jessie?'

She simply could not find the words to tell him.

'Jessie!' He was beside her. He took her hands in his and rubbed them. 'What is it, dear? Tell me!'

'Seamus got sick,' she said. 'I wasn't here. I was at the washhouse. Upstairs was watching him.'

'The washhouse?' Tommy frowned. 'Why were you there?'

'It doesn't matter. All that matters is that I wasn't here when he got sick.' She was still pressing Seamus to her.

Gently Tommy took him from her. He pushed aside the blanket until he could see Seamus's face. The world slowed as she looked at her husband. She watched every second of his dawning realisation.

'Seamus?' His voice was soft. 'Seamus!' Tommy was shouting now. 'For God's sake, Seamus, wake up.' He looked at Jessie in desperation.

'He can't wake up, Tommy. He's gone.' She

knew she didn't have to tell him.

Tears were streaming down his face. 'Not our little boy, Jessie. Not our little boy.'

She held out her arms and her husband, still holding their dead child, came into them.

Chapter 19

Edinburgh, spring 1914

Every bone and muscle in Isabel's body ached. It had been another long, hard day and the thought of waiting for a tram was more than she could bear. She scanned the road for a hansom cab among the horse-drawn carriages and motor vehicles adding to the thrum and noise of the city – not to mention the casualty toll at the hospital. Only today a woman had been admitted after being hit by a motor-car. She had had a compound fracture of her tibia and Isabel had set the bone. The great Dr Inglis herself had watched Isabel work and had seemed impressed. She wasn't to know that Isabel remembered everything that her father had shown her in minute detail.

Under her fatigue she felt the glow of satisfaction. Every day she was acquiring new skills, although she wished she could learn them faster. Soon she'd be on her own with no one apart from herself to rely on. She had graduated MB ChB from Edinburgh University and could now call herself Dr MacKenzie. It still thrilled her every time someone addressed her by that title.

After graduation she had taken a dresser's post at Dr Inglis's Edinburgh Hospital and Dispensary for Women and Children. When she'd completed her time there she would spend a year as house officer at Leith Hospital. After that? She wasn't sure.

Spotting a free cab, she raised her hand.

Ten minutes later, Isabel paid the driver and ran up the steps into the house her brother had secured for her and her mother. In the hall she removed her gloves. The *Scotsman* was on the table and she lifted it, smiling as she read the headline: *Suffragette arrested after breaking windows of Kibble Palace in the Botanic Gardens. Held in Duke Street Prison.*

After years of putting up with the rude and unchivalrous behaviour of her fellow male students, Isabel's sympathy was all for the suffragettes. Men could only conceive of two types of women: the ones they put on a pedestal as the epitome of femininity – and the rest. The only men who had ever treated Isabel as an equal were her father and Andrew. And Archie.

'There you are, darling.' Her mother came into the hall and wrinkled her nose. 'You smell rather pungent. I suggest you have a bath before dinner. Andrew has come up from Cambridge with two of his friends and I've invited them to dinner.'

'How long is he staying?' Isabel asked, immediately feeling happier. She loved the younger of her two brothers dearly and wished she saw more of him. He'd completed an arts degree but had decided to stay on at Cambridge and take another – in law this time. 'I hope it's for more than just one night.'

'Two or three days, I think. You know he doesn't like to be held to his plans.' Although the words were said disapprovingly, her mother's eyes were soft.

She still looked good for her age, with unlined skin and glossy dark brown hair. She had become used to being a widow and, after the appropriate period of mourning, had immersed herself happily in Edinburgh society again.

Upstairs her maid had lit the fire in Isabel's room and was laying out her dress for dinner. 'Shall I get your bath ready, Miss?' Ellie asked. 'You haven't long if you want to be ready by seven.'

'Thank you.' By the time Isabel had undressed, Ellie had the bath ready.

'Could you take away my dress and brush it down, then come back to help me with my corset?' Isabel asked.

'Certainly, Miss. I've laid your russet silk on the bed. It shows off your colouring.'

In the bath, Isabel pulled her knees up to her chest and rested her chin on them. If Andrew hadn't been visiting, she would have had dinner in her room. There were lecture notes that she wanted to go over, but they would have to wait until later.

Her mind wandered back to the newspaper article. She wished she could join in the fight for the vote alongside the Pankhursts and others. She wasn't sure what breaking a few windows and dropping acid into letterboxes was supposed to achieve, but peaceful protests weren't working either. However, as a doctor, she couldn't afford to draw that sort of attention to herself.

Out of the bath, she started to dress and Ellie reappeared to tie the ribbons of her corset, then helped her into her dress and began to brush Isabel's hair. 'I don't know why you cut it, Miss. It's such a lovely colour. Like honey. It suited you much better when it was long.'

'I can't have my hair in my face when I'm working, Ellie. You know that.'

'If I was you, Miss, I wouldn't work. Not if I didn't have to.'

Isabel smiled at her maid's reflection in the mirror. 'And I, dear Ellie, couldn't bear not to.'

Isabel flung open the drawing-room doors. The three men in the room turned towards her, but the only one she was interested in was Andrew. Losing all sense of propriety and decorum, she hurried towards her brother.

'Darling sis! How well you look tonight.' Andrew wrapped his arms around her, then whispered in her ear, 'At least you're not wearing one of those drab suits you've taken to lately. Well done.'

'Idiot,' Isabel murmured. 'You know they make me look professional.'

Even in her second-best evening gown she wasn't nearly as glamorous as her brother. Andrew always dressed in the latest fashion and tonight was no exception. He was wearing the conventional starched white shirt and silk cravat but his jacket was a flamboyant red instead of the more traditional black. His hair was fashionably cut and his fine, almost effeminate features were more beautiful than those of any woman's Isabel had ever seen.

'It's lovely to see you too,' Isabel said aloud, 'but what brings you and your friends to Edinburgh? I thought you preferred London when you were free.'

'We do, but we thought we'd come for the weekend, me to see you and Mama, and Simon to see his family.'

Aware that she had been remiss in greeting their guests, Isabel turned towards the other men in the room.

'May I introduce the Honourable Simon Maxwell?' Andrew said. 'I believe Mama knows his mama, Countess Glendale from Skye. Can you imagine it? It took us until last year to discover we shared a connection.'

The room closed in on her. She reached for a chair knowing that if she didn't sit her legs would give way. Simon Maxwell? Son of the Maxwells in Skye? Charles's brother?

Simon stepped forward, took Isabel's hand and bowed. He didn't look anything like his brother. Where Charles had been good-looking, Simon had tomato-red hair and freckles. She remembered meeting his exquisitely beautiful twin sister, Dorothea. Her red hair had been like burnished gold.

'It's good to make your acquaintance.' She held out her gloved hand, praying that it wasn't trembling. Thank Heaven no one had noticed her agitation.

'And I yours, Miss MacKenzie. May I introduce Baron Maximilian Hoffman?' Simon said, gesturing to the man standing by the fire. 'He's a chum of ours from London.'

Isabel tore her gaze away from Simon. A tall man with a beaked nose and white-gold hair was watching her with narrowed, speculative eyes. 'Dr MacKenzie,' he said, with a bow. 'I have heard a great deal about you.' His irises were an unusual shade of blue – like that of a winter sky. He stepped towards her. 'Are you feeling quite well? You look a little pale.'

'Oh, Isabel is always pale, Maximilian. She works too hard,' Andrew said cheerfully.

Simon had sat down again and was talking to Mama, Isabel saw; he was leaning forward with the appearance of a man who was riveted by what his companion was saying. Dear God, why did Andrew have to be friends with him?

'Your brother tells me you're a doctor,' the baron said, his eyes not leaving her face.

Isabel ran her tongue over dry lips as she struggled to compose herself. Somehow she had to get through the next couple of hours without calling attention to her distress. She forced into her voice a gaiety she was far from feeling. 'Andrew, don't tell me you've been boring your friend with details about your family. I can't imagine that the baron would find us very interesting.'

'On the contrary,' he protested. 'I am very much interested. I, too, am a doctor. I'm here to work with Dr Cairn at the Edinburgh Royal Infirmary.'

Despite her agitation, Isabel was impressed. Many doctors fought to work with Dr Cairn, but few were chosen. 'What is wrong with the hospitals in Germany?' She cocked her head to one side and managed a smile.

The baron lifted an eyebrow. 'Nothing at all. You must know that many of your famous professors studied at our universities and many more continue to do so. It is, after all, where Wilhelm Röntgen made the discovery that led to X-rays.'

'And we have Joseph Lister, James Simpson and William Macewen – among others,' Isabel responded lightly.

The baron grinned. 'You are correct. But is it not better that we share expertise? I am here to teach the latest techniques in abdominal surgery. I trained under Billroth's successor in Vienna. That is why Edinburgh has invited me to work at your famous hospital.'

'You're already a surgeon?' Now she was truly impressed. Billroth and his methods were considered to be at the forefront of advances in surgery. Isabel wished she could be allowed to watch Dr Hoffman operate, but for all the small concessions the hospital had made to the women doctors, access to theatre wasn't among them.

'I am.'

'Then how did you meet my brother?'

'At a London club. Even doctors have to relax.' His blue eyes were teasing. 'And my mother is English. She takes a house in London every summer.'

That explained his accentless English.

'Shall we go in to dinner?' Isabel's mother asked, rising to her feet and taking the baron's elbow. 'You young men must be ravenous after your journey.'

Isabel tried not to flinch when Simon held out his arm for her. She felt awash with shame and guilt, as if the very presence of Charles's brother was mocking her. But why should *she* feel ashamed? She had done nothing wrong. Besides, if Andrew and Simon were friends, Simon was a decent man. That much she had to believe.

As usual only gas lamps and silver candelabra lit the large dining room, the one room in the house that her mother had refused to convert to electrical lighting, deeming it far too harsh for dining. Secretly, Isabel thought the sooty light of the gas lamps on the dark, heavy furniture and the crimson velvet drapes made the room oppressive rather than warm. The only relief was the reflection of the light on the silverware and the polished crystal glasses laid out perfectly on the brilliantly white damask tablecloth.

Her father's chair at the head of the table was, as always, left empty. Instead Andrew sat next to her mother with Simon opposite him, which left the baron to take the chair across from Isabel.

Talk at the table was the usual mix of who was engaged to whom, how the London season was going and whose party had been the most successful. Mama hung on every word. Isabel, on the other hand, could hardly swallow a mouthful of the smoked partridge or the roast pork that followed.

'Andrew and I have news,' Simon said, smiling disarmingly at his hostess. He paused to ensure he had everyone's full attention. 'We intend to train as pilots with the Royal Flying Corps.'

Isabel's mother froze. 'Whatever for? I thought you were helping your father and Richard with the estates. And, Andrew, I thought you were going to do articles?'

He sighed. 'I can do that at any time, Mama. Simon and I have decided that joining the corps will be a good way of seeing the world before we have to settle down. If there's going to be a war, and we believe there will be, we want to be in right from the start.'

Isabel glanced at the baron. So far he'd said little. If there was to be a war, and Andrew wasn't alone in thinking there would be, their German friend would be on the other side. She wondered what that would mean for the men's friendship. Had her brother even considered this?

'Have you spoken to George about your plans, Andrew?' her mother asked, with a frown.

Andrew's normally easy-going expression darkened. 'George may be head of the family, Mama, but I am my own man. I don't need him to tell me what I can and cannot do.'

'And what about you, Mr Maxwell? What does the earl say?'

'He thinks it will be good for me,' Simon answered. '"It'll make a man of you" were the words he used.'

'I wish I could see the world,' Isabel interjected. 'Men are so lucky.'

The baron turned his startling blue eyes on her. 'I would have thought you had an exciting enough life, breaking new ground. There are not many women doctors even in London, and none at all at Cambridge. I am impressed.'

203

The colour rose to her cheeks under his frank admiration. 'But you wouldn't necessarily approve if I were your sister, would you? Or you, Simon?'

Simon shrugged. 'I can't imagine my twin wanting to do anything except attend balls and luncheons. Dorothea will be content once she's married and her place in society confirmed. I see no similarity between you and her. I suspect a husband and children are not your priority.'

'And I suspect that many other women are more suited to being a wife and mother than I,' Isabel replied.

'But perhaps not as many suited to being a doctor,' the baron said, with a smile. 'All women can be wives and mothers but not all women can be doctors. If Dr MacKenzie has the gift for healing, as well as the intellect demanded by the rigours of the training, then she is following the correct path.'

'Every woman wants to be a wife and mother eventually,' Simon protested. 'Surely.'

Isabel took a sip of her wine. 'I don't intend ever to marry. My work is my life now. However, I can't see why a woman shouldn't work as a doctor, be married and have a family, if she wishes. Dr Elizabeth Garrett Anderson had a husband and three children while practising medicine perfectly well. We are living in modern times, after all.'

'Believe me, no criticism was intended,' Simon replied. 'I admire your ambition. I'm also envious that you can lead your life as you see fit. Not many can say that. When I'm finished with the army, there will be little for me to do. The truth is Richard doesn't need my help to run my father's estates. He's perfectly capable of doing that on his own.'

His words made Isabel pause. Simon, for all his wealth and position, was in some ways more tied to a life he hadn't chosen for himself than many women were.

'What are your plans, Baron Hoffman?' Isabel asked. 'Will you be in Edinburgh for a while?'

'My position is to last for twelve months at least.' He paused. 'Unless war is declared before then, in which case it's likely that I will be recalled to my hospital in Halle.'

'And if there is a war, will you join the fight?' Isabel asked.

There was an uneasy silence and the baron's eyes lost some of their sparkle. 'I sincerely hope there isn't one, Dr MacKenzie. Although I am proud to be German, I am a doctor first and foremost and our job is to treat the sick and injured, regardless of birth, nationality or wealth, as I'm sure you'd agree.'

'I intend one day to be a surgeon,' Isabel said, ignoring her mother's pursed lips and quick shake of the head, 'although at the moment that's almost impossible for a woman, unless she's fortunate enough to secure a position at the London School of Medicine. Perhaps, when we get the vote, we'll be able to make changes to the way women study medicine.'

'I see from the paper that the suffragettes are causing quite a stir again,' Andrew interjected. 'At least Isabel doesn't feel the need to join in their campaign.'

'Oh, I would, my dearest brother, if I thought it wouldn't affect my chances of getting on in medicine.' She evaded her mother's eyes. 'The suffragettes are fighting for the rights of all women. Do you know how difficult it is for us to be part of a man's world? Even if a man has half the brains of a woman, he finds it easier to do almost anything. As the baron pointed out, neither Cambridge nor Oxford will let women graduate. They can take classes and sit examinations but they are not granted degrees, even if their results are much better than those of the men they study alongside. How can that be right? At least now, thanks to my female predecessors, I can graduate with a degree and practise medicine – even if I cannot be a surgeon. We women have a long way to go before we have control over our lives and we can't have a say as long as only men make the laws of the land. We need the vote and we will get it one day.'

Her cheeks flamed as she realised she'd been on her soapbox for a good while and everybody was staring at her, her mother with disapproval and dismay, Andrew and Simon with amusement and the baron with frank admiration.

'Forgive me,' she apologised. 'I do tend to go on a bit when I feel strongly about something.'

The baron laughed and raised his glass to her. 'Well said, Dr MacKenzie. I sympathise entirely. Why doesn't Edinburgh let women train as surgeons? We have women surgeons in Germany and they are, in most cases, as competent as their male colleagues.'

'They won't even let women enter the theatres at the Royal Infirmary,' Isabel replied.

'In the meantime,' Andrew's grin was wide, 'they fight with one another for surgical experience at Bruntsfield Hospital. I understand, from what Isabel has told me, that the jostling to assist in theatre can become quite undignified at times.'

'If you wish to learn surgical techniques,' the baron smiled, 'I should be happy to teach you. I am to operate at Craigleith poorhouse tomorrow and I should be honoured to have you assist me.'

The chance to assist a surgeon of Dr Hoffman's standing didn't come along very often. Isabel would happily have given every piece of jewellery she possessed for the opportunity. 'Nothing would give me greater pleasure,' she replied, hiding her excitement. 'I understand that the resident there, one of my female colleagues, is often left to operate on her own. And, like me, she has little training in surgical technique. You may find, however, that the medical superintendent is opposed to having a woman assist with a major surgical procedure.'

'I will have whomever I wish to assist me,' the baron said, raising his eyebrows. Behind his easy charm, Isabel could detect steely resolve. This was a man who wasn't used to being told what he could and could not do. 'However, I leave the decision to you. I shall be there at eight, if you wish to join me.'

The servants cleared away Isabel's almost untouched plate and placed a bowl of blancmange and strawberry compote in front of her. She swirled her spoon in the blancmange until it was stained with red sauce, wondering how soon she could escape to her room without appearing rude.

'When were you last in Skye, Mrs MacKenzie?' Simon asked Isabel's mother politely.

'We haven't been back since my husband died. Too many sad memories, I'm afraid. Apparently the earl and countess no longer visit the island either,' she said to Isabel, then turned back to Simon. 'We were so sorry to hear about your brother.'

Simon dabbed his mouth with a napkin before placing it back on his plate. 'Like you, Mrs MacKenzie, Mama can't bear to return. Richard is the only member of the family to go to Skye now, although the renovations to our house in Glendale are complete and it's much more comfortable there than at the castle. With Charles still missing, the responsibility of the estate falls to Richard, and Father is glad to leave those matters in his hands.'

Startled, Isabel dropped her spoon in her bowl and a splash of strawberry compote landed on the tablecloth. Like blood, she thought distractedly, wishing she could get up and leave the room.

'Charles is missing?' she said, conscious her voice sounded strained.

'Yes. Had you not heard?'

'I'm sorry, my dear,' her mother put in. 'I'd quite forgotten you knew nothing of this. It happened around the time Papa died and you were confined to bed.' She turned to Simon. 'I would have called on Lady Glendale, but...' she bit her lip, '...with my dear William gone and Isabel so unwell...'

'Please, Mrs MacKenzie, think nothing of it.

You had your own troubles to deal with. I know Dr MacKenzie was greatly mourned by the islanders.'

'Thank you. We miss him dreadfully.' She touched the corner of her eye with her handkerchief.

'I believe you met my brother, Miss MacKenzie,' Simon continued.

It was as if someone had tipped cold water down the back of Isabel's neck. Was it possible Simon knew what had happened? Was he trying to tell her he knew more than he was saying?

'Yes. Your sister, too, at the coming-out ball your mother held for me. I didn't know him well.' Isabel was amazed that her voice sounded normal. She wished they would change the subject and talk about something else. Anything would do.

'Charles went riding one day and only his horse returned. We searched everywhere but never found him. It was thought at first that his mount might have unseated him,' Simon said, holding out his wineglass to be refilled, 'although I never saw a stream or a fence he couldn't take, even when he was in his cups ... and then there was the business of the crofter's son – MacCorquodale.'

For a moment Isabel thought she would stop breathing. 'What business?'

'The day Charles went missing MacCorquodale was seen fighting with him. When the police went to question him, he'd disappeared. Gone to Glasgow, according to his mother, though the police found no trace of him there.'

'Damned suspicious, if you ask me,' Andrew said.

'Archie MacCorquodale?' Isabel could barely force the words past her lips.

'Yes. That was his name.'

'No!'

Everyone looked at her in surprise.

'Archie MacCorquodale would never hurt anyone.' But she was remembering Charles's face. He had had a bruise under his eye and he'd said something about seeing Archie and her kiss. Could they have fought? If so, it must have been before Charles attacked her, and he had been very much alive then. Should she say something? But then she'd have to admit she had seen Charles that day.

'Isabel!' Mama's voice held a warning.

'Did you know this MacCorquodale fellow?' Andrew asked.

'We were friends – when we were children.'

Her heart was hammering so hard against her ribs that she could hear its dib-dab sound in her ears. Her temples ached and she raised a hand to her head. She glanced at the baron. When she caught his frown of concern, she dropped both hands to her lap and twisted them tightly together.

'If he had nothing to fear from the police, why did he run?' Simon said.

'He always talked of leaving Skye.' With an immense effort Isabel forced her expression into one of indifference. 'Perhaps Charles will yet turn up safe and well.'

Simon shook his head. 'I don't believe so. It has been almost five years.'

'Perhaps we should speak of other matters,'

210

Mama said quickly. 'This is too distressing for us all.'

Simon picked up his glass. 'Of course. Forgive me. I have been thoughtless. Happily I can see that you made a full recovery from your illness, Dr MacKenzie. I'm glad. I know your brother is very fond of you.'

'Isabel's as strong as a horse,' Andrew interjected. 'It would take more than a nasty case of scarlet fever to see her off. Our Papa might have survived, had he not been injured in the chest during the second Boer War.'

'Andrew! We agreed to speak of less painful subjects!' their mother reproved him.

'Sorry, Mama.' Andrew rose from his chair and went to kiss her cheek. 'I promise I won't say any more about it.'

Always ready to forgive her favourite son, Mama patted his hand and smiled.

Isabel's heart rate was slowly returning to normal. If Simon or his family had had the faintest inkling of Charles's attack on her, somebody would have said something long before now. And if Archie had left the island, it must have been because he'd always intended to.

Isabel's mother rose from the table. 'We should leave them to their port, Isabel. Gentlemen, perhaps you will join us in the drawing room when you are ready.'

'My parents are holding a small gathering tomorrow evening at their house in Charlotte Square and request the pleasure of your company,' Simon said, as the men got to their feet. 'Dorothea will be there, too, and I'm certain she would wish to renew your acquaintance, Miss MacKenzie. May I let them know that you will attend?'

'Please thank your parents, Simon, but I'm afraid I don't go out in the evenings,' Mama replied, 'but Andrew and Isabel will be delighted to accept. Isabel can put aside her tedious medical books for one evening.'

Isabel's pulse was racing again. It was bad enough meeting Simon but she simply couldn't come face to face with any more of Charles's family. She rose to her feet, clutching the back of the chair for support. 'I'm afraid I'm unable to be there. I have–' She raised her fingertips to her temple. She could barely think, her head was throbbling so painfully.

'Are you feeling quite well, Dr MacKenzie?' the baron asked quietly.

'A headache, that is all. Now, gentlemen, if you'll excuse me, I shall go to my room.'

Isabel stumbled upstairs and dismissed Ellie as soon as she'd helped her undress. She sat down at her dressing-table and brushed her hair with short, vicious strokes.

She shouldn't be glad that Charles might be dead but she was. That way he'd never be able to hurt another woman. It was the one thing she'd worried about whenever the memory of Charles's attack had pushed its way into her head.

And Archie was suspected to have played a part in Charles's disappearance. It was horrible.

The scene with Charles replayed in her mind. They'd been on the ground. She'd hit him with the rock and when he'd clutched his head, she'd scrambled from underneath him and ran. Unless she'd hit him harder than she thought ... No! He was most definitely alive when she'd left him. If something had happened to him it had to have been after he'd attacked her. He'd been drinking and in no state to be riding. His horse had likely thrown him into a bog or over the cliff.

Should she tell someone what had happened that day?

It would be different if they'd arrested Archie. Then she would have had to go to the police, although the thought of repeating what had happened nauseated her. If reporting Charles's attack would have brought shame on her and her family five years ago, to do so now, with Archie missing and foul play suspected, would destroy her, her family and her career. And for what?

There was a tap on the door and her mother came in. 'I came to see if you are all right,' she said.

'Just a headache, Mama. It will be gone by morning.'

Her mother came to stand behind her. 'Darling, you should not talk politics at the table. Men see you as a little ... odd as it is. One day you might wish to get married, and...' she lowered her voice, '...I'm afraid you will put off suitable young men.'

If only Mama knew that the very idea of a man holding her made her feel ill. With Papa gone, she should have been able to tell Mama what had happened to her. She was the woman who had given birth to her and who had been there all her life – or most of it. She longed to tell her, to put down her burden and say, 'Do you know what Charles did to me? Do you know that I feel

213

spoiled inside?' Then perhaps her mother would put her arms around her – no, not that, perhaps touch her cheek and say, 'It wasn't your fault. You're still the girl you always were.'

But she couldn't, of course not. Mama wouldn't know what to do, without Papa to tell her. She might even blame Isabel, say that she shouldn't have been walking on her own, that it was her fault for thinking she was different and that the rules of society, which existed to keep her safe, didn't apply to her.

No, the burden was hers and hers alone.

'I'll do my best, Mama,' she said.

Chapter 20

The next morning, Isabel ran into the hall at Craigleith Hospital and shook the rain from her umbrella. Several people were sitting on benches, some holding packages in their laps, others staring ahead as if they no longer had the energy to take in their surroundings.

A porter, with a long white beard that covered most of his face, slowly rose to his feet. 'What can I do for you, Miss?'

'I'm here to meet Dr Hoffman,' Isabel said. 'I'm Dr MacKenzie.' She loved saying that. Dr MacKenzie. She doubted she'd ever get tired of it.

The porter didn't so much as raise an eyebrow. Here, of all places, he had to be used to female doctors. The resident was always female. The

214

poorhouse was one of the few places a woman doctor could be certain to find a position.

'He's in the doctors' room, Doctor. First door on the right.'

She knocked, and a female voice bade her enter. Inside the room was a woman of around thirty or so in a suit, Dr Hoffman and a nursing sister.

'Dr MacKenzie,' Dr Hoffman said, with a little bow. 'I'm so glad you decided to join us.' He turned to the other two women. 'Miss MacKenzie is to assist me in theatre today.'

The woman in the suit, which was similar to Isabel's, held out her hand. 'How do you do? I'm Dr Howse and this is Sister Goody.'

'I hope I'm not putting you out,' Isabel said. She hadn't met Dr Howse before but could imagine her chagrin at finding that Isabel was to assist Dr Hoffman.

'Of course not,' Dr Howse replied. 'Although I did hope to assist myself. Perhaps you could act as anaesthetist while I help Dr Hoffman.'

Isabel hadn't come to act as anaesthetist, as Dr Howse would very well know. She glanced at Dr Hoffman, who was listening to the exchange with his arms folded and a slightly bemused smile.

'Normally I would be happy to act as anaesthetist,' Isabel replied firmly, 'but I feel that this time, as Dr Hoffman invited me personally to help, I should pass that honour to you.'

Dr Howse's eyes flashed, but Isabel returned her gaze calmly. 'I'm convinced,' she continued, 'that there will be other opportunities for you to act as Dr Hoffman's assistant. And, besides, judging from the number of patients waiting in the corridor to see you, you have a full day's work ahead.'

Now, unless Dr Howse was prepared to argue and risk losing face, she had no alternative but to back down. Isabel felt a pang of sympathy for her, but Dr Howse would have done exactly the same had she been in Isabel's shoes. Every woman had to fight for her career and Isabel would never realise her dream of becoming a surgeon unless she seized every opportunity to operate.

'This is all most irregular,' Sister Goody protested.

'Irregular or not,' Baron Hoffman responded, 'it is what I wish.'

'Very well,' Dr Howse replied. 'I shall, of course, be happy to act as anaesthetist. In the meantime, as Dr MacKenzie has pointed out, I have patients to attend to. I assume you wish to examine your patient first.' She looked at Dr Hoffman, who nodded. 'In that case, I shall meet you in theatre in an hour.'

As Dr Howse marched out of the room, followed closely by Sister Goody, Isabel caught the baron's eye.

'You were not joking when you said last night that women doctors fight over patients,' he observed.

'If I wish to be a surgeon,' Isabel replied, aware her cheeks were red, 'I must have operating experience. I may never have another opportunity to watch someone of your skill.'

'Somehow, Dr MacKenzie, I doubt you're trying to flatter me. Now, shall we go and see our patient?'

In the ward, around forty men were either playing cards at a table in the middle of the room or sitting on chairs while three women, in workhouse grey, fussed around them, trying to get them into bed. Isabel suppressed a smile. It didn't seem to matter which hospital or ward one was in, the sister always liked to have the patients in bed and ready for the doctor. Sister Goody swept towards them. No doubt this was why she'd been in a hurry to leave them. She might not have bothered for the women doctors but Dr Hoffman was clearly another matter.

Sister led them to the bed nearest the door. A man in his early sixties was lying on his side, clutching his stomach and groaning.

'Please sit up, Kennedy,' the nursing sister said sharply. 'The doctor is here to see you.'

Goody by name, but not by nature.

As the man struggled onto his elbows, the baron reached across and pressed him gently back. 'Lie there, Mr Kennedy. I'll do the work.' He looked over his shoulder. 'Are there screens, Sister?'

'I'm afraid not, but Kennedy won't mind.'

Dr Hoffman frowned. 'We spoke about screens before, Sister. I prefer my patients to have privacy while I'm examining them.'

'And, as I said, our little infirmary is short of funds. We do what we can with what we're given. Now, if you'll excuse me, I must get on.' The rebuke, mild though it was, had brought two spots of colour to her cheeks.

Isabel was relieved when she departed. She'd heard about poorhouse conditions: that there

217

were only two trained nurses to look after almost four hundred patients; that most of the nursing was carried out by untrained paupers; the only doctor was expected to see to all the patients, assess those needing admission to the workhouse as well as carry out operations. Undoubtedly an impossible task.

Dr Hoffman stood back from the bed. 'Would you like to examine our patient and tell me what you think?'

Isabel studied the man. Papa had always said it was important to do that before anything else. Mr Kennedy was gaunt and had a smear of encrusted blood at the corner of his mouth.

'You've been bringing up blood, Mr Kennedy?' Isabel asked, feeling for his pulse. Rapid and shallow. A possible sign of shock.

'Aye, Miss. This last month or so.'

'What colour is the blood?'

Mr Kennedy looked to Dr Hoffman, as if asking for his help. 'Red, Miss. What other colour of blood is there?'

'Bright red? Or dark, like coffee.'

'Come to think of it, it's a bit like coffee. Not that I've ever drunk much of the stuff. I prefer my ale.'

'And you have pain?' She dropped his wrist. 'Let me feel your stomach.'

'Feel away, lass. Anything to make the pain go away. It hurts something terrible.'

Isabel had been watching the way Kennedy moved and had noted the rigidity of his abdominal muscles even as he spoke. She palpated the lower right of his abdomen across then upwards, all the while watching his face. He winced as she pressed in the centre, just below the ribs. 'Is that where it hurts?'

'Aye, lass. Like buggery. Begging your pardon, Miss.'

'I think he has a perforated ulcer,' Isabel said to the baron.

Dr Hoffman nodded, looking pleased. 'And your treatment?'

'I'm assuming you're thinking of operating.'

'And you'd assume correctly.'

'I'm not having no operation!' Mr Kennedy protested, clearly terrified. 'You cut me open and the only way I'll be leaving here is in a box.'

'Mr Kennedy,' Dr Hoffman said calmly, 'as I explained yesterday, an operation is your best chance. If we don't remove the ulcer it will continue to bleed. And if it continues to bleed...' he glanced at Isabel, '...well, we don't want that.'

'I'll be fine without any operation,' Mr Kennedy protested again, his eyes wild and staring. 'Just give me summat for the pain. That's all I want. You doctors just want to practise on the likes o' me, and I'm telling you, you can't.'

'Mr Kennedy, if you don't let us stop the bleeding you will die,' Dr Hoffman said baldly.

Isabel took the man's hand. 'The treatment Dr Hoffman is suggesting is a new procedure but has been very successful in Germany. There are not many surgeons in this country with the skill and experience of Dr Hoffman, so you're very lucky to have him as your surgeon.'

Mr Kennedy looked up at Isabel. 'What would you say, lass, if I were your da? Would you let the

219

doctor operate?'

'If you were my father I would have no hesitation in recommending the operation. It's your only chance. You could live for many more years if you let us stop the bleeding. There's nothing else we can do, I promise you.'

Mr Kennedy stared into Isabel's eyes and she returned his gaze steadily. She couldn't promise him he'd survive the operation, but she did know he wouldn't last much longer without it.

Mr Kennedy sighed. He lifted his spittoon and spat a glob of bloody mucus. 'Very well, then, Doctor. Do what you think best.'

Dr Hoffman patted his shoulder. 'I'm going to check that the theatre is ready for us. I shall see you down there shortly.' He gestured to Sister Goody, who scurried over to them. 'I'd like this man to be taken to theatre as soon as possible, Sister.' He turned away and Isabel followed him out of the ward.

The theatre was small but adequately, if not lavishly, supplied.

Dr Howse was waiting for them, already wearing her long white theatre gown and hat. Isabel and Dr Hoffman scrubbed up and slipped into their white gowns and hats. After that they pulled on sterile rubber gloves.

A wary but resigned Mr Kennedy was brought into theatre by Sister Goody and settled on the operating table. He struggled a little when Dr Howse administered the chloroform but after a minute or two he was unconscious.

Dr Hoffman sliced into Kennedy's belly. It was

immediately obvious that there was a perforated ulcer, the stomach contents almost bursting out through the abdominal incision.

'Why don't you take over, Dr MacKenzie?'

Pleased to be invited, Isabel lifted a scalpel and, running through the anatomy of the upper abdomen in her head, cut away the perforation. When she had finished, Dr Hoffman sutured the cut ends of the stomach together. He turned to Isabel.

'Are you happy to close the abdomen, Doctor?'

She nodded, took the needle-holder and dissecting forceps from him and closed the wound. She was thrilled with her first attempt at surgery.

But if Dr Hoffman was impressed, he didn't show it. All she got was a brief 'Good', as she placed the final suture and applied the dressings. As Kennedy began to come around, Dr Howse left them to see to her other patients.

When the operation was over and a groggy Mr Kennedy had been returned to the ward, Dr Hoffman looked at his watch. 'I have to go back to the Royal. I could drop you at home on the way.'

'Yes, please,' Isabel said, eyeing the pouring rain through the small window. 'But first I must clean up here.'

'And I must leave instructions for Dr Howse regarding Mr Kennedy's care. I'll meet you at the front door. I shall be but a few minutes.'

Once they were in the carriage, Isabel studied Dr Hoffman from under her lashes. He was an excellent surgeon and teacher. 'Thank you for allowing me to assist you,' she said.

'The pleasure was mine. You have the delicate

touch of a surgeon.'

Isabel felt a pulse of delight at the compliment.

'If you wish to assist again, I shall be pleased,' Dr Hoffman continued.

'I should like that very much.'

Dr Hoffman leaned forward until his knees were almost touching Isabel's. 'Good. Now, am I to see you this evening? At the Glendales' party?'

'I know you'll think me dull, but I have a great deal of reading to catch up on.' Despite her mother's wishes, she couldn't bear to spend an evening with Simon and his family. What if they spoke to her of Charles? How could she possibly smile and not let her revulsion show on hearing his name?

A small smile played on Dr Hoffman's lips. 'My dear Dr MacKenzie, I doubt anyone could consider you dull.'

Chapter 21

The baron's courting was slow and gentle but unrelenting.

The spring weather was warm, and as summer approached, it became hot. Hotter than anyone could remember. With her studies behind her, Isabel was freer than she had been in years to attend tennis parties, lunches and dances. Until now she had avoided social occasions, pleading her studies or work, but with Maximilian her constant companion she found herself truly enjoying everything Edinburgh society had to offer. Occasionally she would go out walking with him, always accompanied by Ellie, who would discreetly lag behind, and on Sundays he would join Isabel and Mama for the morning service at St Giles Cathedral.

Most afternoons he called at the house in Heriot Row and took tea with them. Sometimes he stayed for dinner, and she found herself listening out for the doorbell. When it rang she would put aside her book and go into the drawing room, where she'd find him listening attentively to her mother.

Whenever she could she went with him to the poorhouse and assisted him with his scheduled surgeries. Increasingly she operated while he watched, guiding her hand with his own if ever she hesitated.

He had made it clear he wanted more than her company at the operating table, and in the beginning it had frightened her: she had sworn never to marry. But, as he made no mention of this, she could hardly raise the subject. She told herself that he would return to Germany one day, and in the meantime she was gaining valuable practice as a surgeon. She had made no promises to him, or shown him anything but polite friendship, so her behaviour could not be faulted – but that did nothing to dispel her unease that she was playing false with him in some way.

Christmas had come and gone, and because of the experience she'd gained from assisting Maximilian, she was increasingly allowed to do small operations on her own at the Bruntsfield Hospital. Whenever thoughts of Charles or Archie crept into her head she pushed them away. There was nothing, she'd decided, to be done.

True to their word, Andrew and Simon had joined the Royal Flying Corps and become pilots. The corps kept them too busy for more than the briefest visits to Edinburgh and, as Simon's family had returned to London, Isabel had avoided any further invitations to the Maxwells' house in Charlotte Square.

Maximilian was delighted when she practised her German on him, even if, at times, he couldn't altogether hide his amusement when she mispronounced a word or chose the wrong one. Although they were never alone his hand would often brush hers or their eyes would meet as they smiled over some little incident they had both thought amusing.

As summer wore on there was more talk of war, although they never spoke of it.

One day in July she returned home to find him in his habitual position in the drawing room. However, instead of his usual smile, he looked pensive, and she saw a sadness in his eyes that made her heart wobble.

'I wonder, Mrs MacKenzie, if I might have your permission to take your daughter for a walk tomorrow. I have never been up Arthur's Seat and I would like to before I leave Edinburgh.'

'Leave?' Isabel's breath caught in her throat. She had known, of course, that one day Maximilian would return to Germany for good. But not yet. Please, God, not yet.

He grimaced. 'My hospital is insisting that I return.'

'Why?'

He tossed his half-smoked cigar into the fire. 'They are recalling all doctors. It seems that the threat of war is increasing.'

Isabel sank down on a chair. 'You think it will come to that?'

'I hope not.' The shadows in his eyes told her everything she needed to know. He was certain there would be war. 'But what do you say?' he continued. 'Will you come with me tomorrow? It promises to be another fine day.'

'Isabel likes to walk,' her mother said, excited and delighted. 'As long as her maid goes too, of course.' She turned to Isabel. 'You must wrap up warmly, my dear. The wind can be cold on top of the hills.'

Isabel hid a smile. Her mother still didn't think she was old enough to make decisions for herself. In this warm weather it was unlikely she would require a coat. She was far more likely to feel over-heated in her layers.

'I should like very much to walk up Arthur's Seat with you,' Isabel said. If her time with Maximilian was running out, she wanted to be with him as much as she could.

'Now that that's settled,' her mother said, with a satisfied smile, 'won't you stay and have supper with us, Baron?'

The next morning was, as Maximilian had predicted, another perfect early-summer's day.

Isabel hadn't slept well. She'd been unable to stop thinking of the look in Maximilian's eyes when he had suggested the walk. Would he pro-

225

pose? If he did, what would she say? They had many interests in common, apart from medicine, and she found him easy company. She liked the way his eyes creased at the corners when he smiled, his ferocious intelligence, his manner towards his patients, the way he listened to Mama, as if he were fascinated by what she had to tell him, but most of all she liked how he made her feel as if she were the most captivating woman in the world. In so many ways he reminded her of her Papa.

But she'd sworn she wouldn't get married. The thought of the physical act that came with marriage terrified her. Could she respond to him as she was supposed to? She knew that the act of love with the right man was supposed to be gentle and satisfying, and she kept telling herself that Maximilian would never touch her as Charles had, but still her mind shied away from the thought of any man's hands on her naked skin.

But Maximilian cared for her, perhaps even loved her. He was a rare man, someone who valued women as equals, and who could make her happy.

Ellie came into the room to light the fire and help her dress. For once Isabel was undecided about what she should wear. But, as if she knew today was special, Ellie had brought in Isabel's new dress, a beautifully cut pastel blue silk. Even though she took little interest in the latest fashions, the beading on the bodice was exquisite and the touches of the finest Parisian lace on the sleeves and neck just right.

With expert hands, Ellie arranged her hair so

that it curled softly against her cheeks. The maid stood back and surveyed her handiwork. 'Oh, Miss, you look beautiful.'

Isabel smiled. 'Thank you, Ellie.' She did feel beautiful.

By the time she had finished breakfast, she knew what she would do. If Maximilian proposed marriage, she would say yes. She would love and cherish him and be the best wife possible. Her spirits rose as she thought of them working together as they cared for their patients. They would end their day by the fire talking of medicine and then... Her thoughts shied away again. She wouldn't think about that.

Nevertheless, she was glad that Ellie was to accompany them. She would never again make the mistake of being alone with a man before she was married. In becoming a doctor she was already bordering on the cusp of what respectable women could do, and she couldn't afford the merest whiff of scandal to be attached to her name. She had come close once to having her reputation ruined and her dream of becoming a doctor shattered, and she would never allow that to happen again.

Ellie jumped up beside the driver while Maximilian settled Isabel into the open carriage, tucking the skirt of her dress out of the way of the door. His hands brushed against her thighs, and even through her clothes, her skin tingled.

'How has your week been?' he asked, somewhat stiffly for him, as they set off towards Arthur's Seat.

Isabel was almost halfway through her residency at Leith Hospital. She had been lucky to get the position: there was so much competition among the women for decent jobs and Leith was currently the only hospital in Edinburgh apart from Bruntsfield that accepted female doctors. But Dr Inglis had been so impressed with her – not least because of her growing surgical skills – that she had recommended her for a position. Most of Isabel's fellow graduates had taken posts as missionary doctors or as residents in poorhouses and asylums. A lucky few, who had financial backing from their families, had set up in practice.

'I love it,' she said honestly. 'Do you know I performed a Caesarean section a few days ago. Mother and baby are doing so well that I may be able to discharge them in a few weeks.' She was glad they were talking about medicine. It eased the churning in her stomach.

But when Maximilian smiled down at her, her heart thudded against her ribs.

'So you've told me – several times, in fact.' He laughed when she opened her mouth to protest. 'But I don't mind hearing about it as often as you wish to tell me. I like the way it makes your eyes light up.'

He reached over and touched her cheek with his finger. 'I hope that light never leaves your eyes, *liebchen.*' Then he bent his head and murmured in her ear, 'There is something I must talk to you about. Perhaps we can shake off your maid for a little while when we get closer to the top.'

'Ellie will make herself invisible if I ask her to,' Isabel said, her heart beating like a trapped bird. 'I have no secrets from her.' That wasn't true. She did have a secret from her, the one she couldn't share with anyone. A cloud scudded across the sun and the daylight dimmed.

'What is it?' Maximilian asked, looking intently at her. 'You looked sad for a moment.'

Sometimes she had the impression he could see into her soul. She made herself smile. 'If I'm sad, it's because you'll be leaving soon.'

Perhaps she shouldn't be so forward, but she couldn't bring herself to dissemble. If Maximilian cared for her, she needed to let him know that she cared too. And if he didn't? It was better that she knew it.

'I like the way you always say what you think. I find it refreshing.'

'It's easier to speak one's mind. Oh, for a world in which men and women can cut to the heart of the matter,' Isabel said. 'Talking as if in code is too complicated.'

'That is another thing I admire about you. You're not worried about convention. I could never admire a woman who cared more for what society thought of her than for doing the right thing.'

If possible, her heart beat even faster. If Maximilian knew her secret, he wouldn't think so highly of her.

The carriage stopped at the foot of the hill, which was already crowded with vehicles of all shapes and sizes. Arthur's Seat was a popular place for the people of Edinburgh to walk.

Maximilian helped her down and, with Ellie following a discreet distance behind, they set off up the hill. The path was busy, and Isabel and Maximilian nodded to acquaintances as they passed. As they walked, they talked about the latest surgical procedures and how chloroform and X-rays were making surgery safer. Once more, Isabel felt herself relax.

As they climbed higher, the air became colder and most other walkers fell away, apparently feeling they'd gone far enough. Maximilian checked his stride so that Isabel could keep up with him, but she was a fast walker and determined that he would make few allowances for her.

'You're quiet. I suspect you're thinking about what I said, that our two countries might go to war.'

'I don't want to believe it! What possible gain is there for us in fighting each other over territory? Don't we each have enough? The talk in the papers is that Germany is looking for an excuse to take over the Hungarian empire. What does that have to do with us?'

They had come to the top of the hill and stopped to look out over Edinburgh. The castle was to their right, the old town with its tablecloth of smoke immediately below, and a little further on, the New Town where Isabel lived with her mother.

'I believe, my dear, that there is every chance we might find ourselves at war. I don't think they would be calling me back if it wasn't almost certain.'

'But do you have to go? You must be able to stay in Edinburgh. The hospital needs surgeons of your calibre. And, as you said, your mother is English.' Isabel had met Maximilian's mother once when she had come to visit her son in Edinburgh. She had stayed in the North British Hotel but had come to tea with Isabel and her mother at Heriot Row. Isabel had found her charming – if a little condescending. Mama had discovered that Maximilian's family was one of the richest in Germany; her delight and hope had been obvious.

Maximilian looked over his shoulder. 'Ask your maid to stay behind,' he said. 'Then come a little further with me.'

He touched her hand and she shivered.

Maximilian was immediately concerned. 'Are you cold?' Before she could reply he had taken off his jacket and laid it across her shoulders. The wind had gained in strength with every step they had taken, but she knew it wasn't the cold that was making her hands shake.

Ellie agreed readily to sit on a rock and wait for them, and Isabel let Maximilian lead her away from the track to a hollow where they would be hidden from anyone passing.

When he pulled her into his arms, she rested her head against his chest. Apart from her father and Andrew, it was the only time she'd been held in a man's arms. Without warning, an image of Archie flashed into her head. He'd held her, too, and kissed her. There had been nothing frightening about his kiss except the way it had made her feel. However, she didn't want to think of Archie.

Maximilian's hands were on the small of her back, pressing her close. A delicious warmth spread through her body. She was surprised by how safe she felt in his arms. Perhaps now she could put away the memory of Charles for ever.

'You must know I care deeply for you, Isabel,'

231

Maximilian whispered into her hair. 'I think I fell in love with you the moment I saw you, and as I have come to know you, I fall more in love every day.'

Isabel's heart sang. She cared for him too. Maximilian would never hurt her.

Tentatively she raised her face. He cupped it in both hands and pressed his lips to hers. Suddenly, sickeningly, the memory of Charles's mouth on hers flooded back. Before she could stop herself, she jerked away.

Maximilian looked at her with surprise. 'Please forgive me,' he said. 'I forget myself.'

'It's just...' What could she tell him?

He pressed a finger to her lips. 'You don't have to say anything. I let myself forget for a moment that you are a gentlewoman and not experienced in love-making. I should not have tried to kiss you until we are engaged to be married. Now, say that you will forgive me.'

He looked so remorseful and disappointed that her heart ached for him. Wasn't it time she drew on that courage her father had believed she had and told him why she had pulled away? But what had Maximilian said about becoming engaged? Had he proposed or not?

'I have to admit I'm a little confused,' Isabel admitted, with a shaky laugh. 'I'm not certain of whether we are to be married or even engaged. As you said, I have little experience in such situations.'

Instead of dropping down on one knee or even returning her smile, his expression darkened. 'My darling,' he said, 'we cannot be engaged. At least, not yet.'

Isabel's head was spinning. 'Why not? You said you loved me.' Then a thought occurred to her that made her heart sink. 'Is it because you are a baron and I am only a doctor's daughter?'

He laughed, but without humour. 'I wouldn't care if you were a servant. I will marry the woman I want, and I want you.' His eyes softened. 'But I cannot ask you at the moment. I cannot even ask you to promise yourself to me. At least, not until I'm convinced that there will be no war.'

Isabel stared up at him, dismayed.

'You must finish your clinical training and I must go back to Germany. Even if they allow you into Germany as my wife, what if I go to war and don't return? You would be alone in a strange country. I can't do that to the woman I love.' He tipped her chin so he could look into her eyes. 'I'm a selfish man. A better man would have gone without declaring himself, but I couldn't bear the thought that you might marry someone else before I could return to you. I will not ask you to wait for me, but I had to tell you that I loved you.'

'And I love you,' Isabel said softly. 'I will wait for you to come back, however long that takes.'

'We cannot even be engaged,' Maximilian said. 'I don't want you to promise me anything. I only want you to know that I love you and one day I'll come back for you. If you meet someone you can love before then...' he hesitated, '...although I hate the thought of you in another man's arms, I would understand.'

'Oh, Maximilian, do you think I'm so fickle? Of course I'll never love anyone else. I shall be here waiting for you when you return. As you say, with my work I have plenty to keep me occupied, although if you do go to war I shall worry about you. You must promise me that you will come back safely to me.'

She took his hand. 'We have left Ellie alone long enough. We must return to her, if we don't want people to gossip.'

As they turned to go, she tipped a smile at him. 'We could have a practice together in Germany when we're married. I'm certain there are as many there who need our help as here.'

Maximilian drew his brow together. 'What do you mean?'

'You know I've dreamed of starting my own practice. I didn't see how it was possible without funds, but you have money. I know it's not considered seemly for a woman to talk of such things but you already know that I am not seemly, so for us to set up a practice together should not be difficult.'

Maximilian's frown deepened. '*Liebchen*, that is not possible.'

Alarmed that she had taken too much for granted in speaking of their future when they were not officially engaged, Isabel stumbled over her next words. 'I know that you're a surgeon, a great surgeon, and naturally you will take up a prestigious appointment in Germany once you're able to, but I could send the rich patients to you and perhaps you could spend an afternoon or two consulting at our practice. Or perhaps I will join you in the operating theatre as a surgeon.' The vision filled her with joy and she forgot to be anxious. 'We'll be the Drs Hoffman!'

'But, my dear, as my wife, you will not be able to practise.'

'Fiddlesticks! How can they stop us? I know they don't like women doctors who work in hospitals to be married, but we can do as we wish. You told me that Germany has always been far ahead in its treatment of female doctors. You told me that the first woman graduated in Germany in the eighteenth century. Germany is clearly more modern in its thinking than we are in this country.'

Although Maximilian's frown had disappeared, he still looked puzzled. 'But, Isabel, it is I who do not wish you to practise. Naturally I wish you to finish your clinical training, but once we are married you will be the Baroness Hoffman and the chatelaine of my estates. You may, of course, do as much voluntary work as you wish, but to work as a doctor? I'm afraid that is out of the question. Besides,' he lifted her chin with one of his elegant fingers and smiled down at her, 'God willing, you will have our children to care for. So, you see, you will be far too busy to work.'

Isabel couldn't believe what she was hearing. 'But that is all I've ever dreamed of, Maximilian! I haven't spent five years learning everything I need to know about medicine not to use my skills. You said yourself that I'm a good doctor. I'm not the kind of woman who will be content to spend her days holding dinners and luncheons. You know that. When we have children we will employ a nanny to help, and naturally I shall be with them whenever I can.'

Her heart was hammering, but this time it was not a nice feeling. Could Maximilian not see that she would never abandon medicine?

'It is not for debate, my dear. When we marry, you will no longer practise medicine.' His tone left her in no doubt that he meant what he said.

'I thought you approved of women studying medicine,' she cried.

'I do. You know that. Only those women cannot be my wife. You must see that it is impossible. But, Isabel, you will not miss it. When we are married I will give you everything your heart desires.'

'Except the one thing I truly want, Maximilian.' Her throat was tight. 'You will deny me that?'

'And you would deny me my right as your husband to have you by my side, caring for our home and children?'

The hope and excitement she had allowed herself to feel were leaking away. She had dared to believe Maximilian was different from other men, but he was as bound by convention as everyone else. He wasn't the man she had thought he was.

'I'm sorry, Maximilian, but if you will not allow me to be a doctor, then I cannot be your wife.'

Maximilian returned to Germany a few days after his declaration – she couldn't even call it a proposal – and sometimes Isabel wondered if she'd done the right thing in refusing him. Was there something wrong with her, unnatural, even, that she was prepared to deny herself, and him, the chance of a home, children and love? Other women were satisfied with that so why couldn't she be? But she knew the answer. Medicine was in her blood and she couldn't be truly happy unless she was working as a doctor. She prayed that Maximilian would, in time, come to understand that. If he loved her – if he truly loved her – he would love everything about her. And that included her need to be a doctor.

He'd called once, just before he'd left for London on his way to Germany, and she'd allowed herself to hope that he'd changed his mind and had decided he couldn't live without her. But her hopes had come to nothing. He'd asked her once more if she would give up medicine when she became his wife and she'd told him no, sadly, but firmly.

She waited for a letter from him, to tell her that he'd made a mistake, that once the war was over, they'd meet again. But as the days passed without a word she began to feel angry. He'd led her to believe that he was different, that he shared her disdain for convention. She'd been wrong. Maximilian wasn't the man she had thought he was.

Chapter 22

Edinburgh, August 1914

Two weeks after Maximilian had left, the unthinkable happened: Britain declared war on Germany.

Andrew had been one of the first to be sent to Europe and Isabel was terrified for him. Her mother was proud to have her son fighting for his country, but Isabel knew she was frightened that he wouldn't come home. She prayed that Maximilian was safe in Germany. It was inconceivable that the two men she loved most might one day be forced to kill each other, and she tried not to think about it. Instead, she threw herself into her work with even greater vigour, finding some comfort there.

Her days as the resident house physician at Leith Hospital followed a similar routine. Every morning a probationer nurse knocked on her door to warn her that Mr Galbraith was about to pass through the gates of the hospital, and that morning was no different.

She tossed back the covers and leaped out of her narrow bed in the doctors' residence, before opening the curtains to let in the sun. As the medical resident, she was expected to live in the hospital. Her room, not much bigger than a cupboard and sparsely furnished, was in the attic above the women's medical ward.

After washing in the basin of warm water the ward maid had brought to her room, Isabel dressed hurriedly in her serviceable skirt and jacket. She arrived at the top of the stairs just in time to meet Mr Galbraith.

Side by side they entered the ward.

'Good morning, Doctors,' Sister said. 'Would you like some tea, Mr Galbraith, before you start?'

Isabel groaned inwardly. She hoped he would say no. The tea-taking process was such a waste of time and she still had specimens from last night to look at under the microscope.

'Not today, Sister,' Mr Galbraith said, to Isabel's relief. 'There's a meeting of the hospital governors this afternoon that I have to attend. Now that we're at war, we have to make plans.'

Most people expected the war to be over by Christmas, but Isabel wasn't so sure: the papers reported that the fighting was so fierce they had lost many more men than they'd expected. It was believed that others would soon be conscripted.

As soon as rounds were over and her duties on the ward concluded, Isabel made her way to the outpatient reception area. This was the part of the day she liked best. Here, without the specialists looking over her shoulder, she could talk to the patients and treat them as if they were people. Unfortunately the number waiting for her attention meant she couldn't spend as much time with them as she would have liked. She was pleased to see that the nurse working alongside her was Maud. Nurse Tully was quietly efficient, but always had a word for each patient. She also had a wicked sense of humour.

'Dr MacKenzie, I'm glad it's you. We have quite a crowd in.'

'In that case, Nurse Tully, shall we get started?'

The nurse grinned. 'With an extra pair of hands we might even get through this lot before we close the gates.' She had a snub nose and her mouth was probably too large for her to be considered beautiful but her irrepressible good nature, ever-ready smile and willingness to help had endeared her to Isabel.

'Does it ever end, Nurse Tully?' Isabel asked,

several hours later. 'We've been at it all morning and still they keep coming.'

'We could work night and day and still there would be more patients to see. Although,' she dropped her voice to a conspiratorial whisper, 'it's rather good fun, isn't it? If only Matron allowed us nurses more time off, life would be perfect.'

Isabel suspected most people would be outraged to hear someone refer to treating the sick as 'good fun', but not her. She agreed with Maud. Nothing in life was as interesting as fighting disease or so rewarding as saving lives.

The day passed with a relentless round of patients as Isabel and Maud worked side by side. There were the usual numbers with tuberculosis, a fair number with scarlet fever, who were admitted to the fever wards, as well as cuts, broken limbs and a million other ailments, serious and less so.

Her last patient was a little boy who had been brought in by his older sister. The child's swollen stomach immediately alerted Isabel. When his sister, who wasn't much better nourished, stripped the clothes off her brother, his ribs were clearly visible through his skin.

'Now, little man, what's your name?' Maud asked.

'Johnny,' the girl answered for him.

'And your name is…?'

'Patricia.'

'How old is Johnny, Patricia?'

'Not sure, Miss. Five, I think.'

Five! The child looked no more than three.

'Could you open your mouth, Johnny, so the

doctor can have a look inside?'

Johnny clamped his lips together and shook his head. It was the first deliberate movement he'd made since Isabel had entered and she was heartened. If he'd been completely unresponsive it would have indicated that they were probably too late.

But Isabel didn't need to look in his mouth to know that the child was suffering from starvation. The textbooks advised wholesome food and fresh vegetables, but how was this child to have them?

Isabel turned to the sister. 'Where are your mother and father?'

Patricia seemed frightened.

Isabel tried a smile. 'It's all right. I'm not going to hurt you. I need to admit your brother to hospital for a few days so we can make him strong. But, first, I need your father's permission.'

'I can look after Johnny, Miss. Just tell me what I need to do.'

Isabel straightened. 'You can't look after him. It seems to me that you can both do with some nourishing food. When did either of you last eat?'

'Don't know, Miss,' Patricia mumbled.

Isabel was at a loss.

Maud crouched in front of the girl. 'Are they gone, love?'

A tear ran down the girl's cheek and she nodded.

'When?' Maud persisted.

'A month ago. It was the typhus. Please, Miss, don't tell the parish. They'll make us go to the poorhouse. Then me and Johnny will be separated.'

'But if you can't get enough food, you can't stay

241

on your own,' Isabel said.

Maud took Patricia's hand. 'I know it's frightening, but it's the best place for you and Johnny. You'll get enough to eat and a bed to sleep in.'

'They'll take Johnny away from me, Miss, and give him to someone else. Please, Miss, he's all I got now.'

Maud and Isabel shared a look. The child was right. Even in his emaciated state, Johnny was an angelic-looking child. The workhouse routinely fostered out children under eight and there would be no shortage of people willing to take the boy. Isabel also knew that, once the novelty of having a sweet-faced child had worn off, the children were often unceremoniously returned to the poorhouse. It wasn't a good system, but it was the best they had.

'Let's not worry about that for the moment,' Maud said. 'Why don't we take you and your brother in here for a few days and get your strength up? Then we'll see what's to be done. In the meantime, I'm going to give Johnny some milk and ask one of the nurses to give you both a bath.'

The girl looked doubtful.

'Johnny needs to be looked after,' Isabel said firmly. 'You've done the best you can, but he needs more than you can give him. You see that, don't you?'

One of the nurses came to fetch Isabel and she had to leave the children in Maud's care. When she'd decided to be a doctor, she'd thought she would be curing people and sending them home. Of course, there had been many times when she had done just that, but more often she was fighting an enemy that wouldn't respond to her medical skill: poverty. The people she'd seen on Skye with her father had been poor, but they had always had enough to eat. And there was always an adult willing to look after a child, even if it meant stretching what little they had to the barest minimum. On days like today, she missed Skye terribly, although she knew she would never return. The island was spoiled for her.

She was kept occupied for the next few hours, setting bones, dressing wounds and ordering patients' treatments. Often she'd have to retire to the small room to do her tests or mix a bottle of medicine.

Eventually the patients had all been seen and the porter had closed the gates.

Maud came to find Isabel in the doctors' room where she was writing up her notes. 'Cup of tea?'

'I'd love one. How's Johnny?'

'In the children's ward with his sister. Don't know how long they'll stay, though. Someone from the workhouse is coming to see them tomorrow.'

Maud must be tired, Isabel thought. The nurse had started her day at five thirty that morning and now it was eight in the evening. She knew the nurses got very little time off, but she looked almost as fresh as when Isabel had first seen her this morning. 'How do you do it, Nurse Tully, seeing children like Johnny and his sister day after day and then that girl with the incomplete abortion? She'll die, you know, and there's nothing we can do to stop it.'

'We can't think like that,' Maud said cheerfully.

'We can only do our best. Patch them up and send them on their way. Anyway, I won't be doing it for much longer. I've joined the Scottish Women's Hospital. I'll be on my way soon enough to France or Serbia or wherever they decide to send me.'

Isabel had heard the rumours. When war had first broken out, Dr Elsie Inglis had approached the British Army and offered her services. Apparently she'd been turned away but, undaunted, had immediately sought out the French and Serbian governments and offered herself and her unit – to be staffed entirely by women. They had both, it was reported, accepted immediately. Now she was touring the country, recruiting.

'Do they still need doctors?' she asked.

'I'd say so. Look, Dr Inglis is speaking in Edinburgh tomorrow evening. Why don't you come with me and hear what she has to say?'

Isabel was intrigued. Going to war would give her so many opportunities to advance her surgical knowledge, opportunities that simply weren't available here. She'd be in Europe, helping the wounded soldiers, and in the same continent as Maximilian, doing the same as he was. And maybe she would see Andrew.

A thrill ran down her spine. She knew she had to go.

'Count me in,' she said. 'I only hope that they haven't filled all the positions already.'

Chapter 23

Isabel had to push her way through the throngs lining the Royal Mile. If she hadn't been expected at the hospital, she would have joined the crowd as they cheered the regiment, which, with pipers in front, was marching towards Waverley station. Even the drizzle and cold autumn wind didn't dampen their enthusiasm. Most of the women were laughing as they tossed flowers into the path of the soldiers. But some were running alongside, crying and reaching out for a last touch of a loved one's hand.

It was incredible how excited everyone was by this war. Didn't they know that many of the men marching down the road with embarrassed smiles on their faces would never return? Hadn't they read the papers? The fighting was worse than anyone had expected.

But the truth was, she was excited too. In a month she would be joining a unit of the Scottish Women's Hospital in Serbia. Dr Inglis had agreed to take her. There would be no pay for junior doctors and Isabel was expected to finance her own journey but, if she could fund herself, Dr Inglis had said she would be glad to have her.

The money wasn't a problem. It might have been if she'd had to rely on George, but Isabel still had some of what her father had left her. Would he be proud of her for going to war? Or would he be sorry that she was following in his footsteps? She remembered only too well how his face had darkened when he'd talked of his time in the Boer War.

An officer picked up a child in his arms and tossed it into the air. The crowd roared its approval. Another soldier wrapped his arm around the waist of a young woman, who giggled and looked at her friends in triumph.

The sound of boots on cobbles added their beat to the wail of the bagpipes. As the men disappeared down George IV Bridge, they were followed by the crowd. For a few minutes the street was quiet. Then the carriages and carts trickled back onto the road, and shopkeepers brought out their stalls. Business as usual. There might be a war but, as everyone kept saying, life had to go on.

Chapter 24

Jessie was roused by banging on her door. Although only half awake, she knew it would be someone looking for the howdie. Inevitably word had spread that she was a nurse with midwifery experience and, decent midwives being in short supply on this side of town, the women called her whenever they needed help. With Seamus gone, the work kept her from drowning in grief, although every time she held a newborn her heart would break all over again. At least every baby she saved made up, just a little, for losing Seamus.

Quickly, so that the banging wouldn't wake Tommy, Jessie jumped out of bed, shivering as her bare feet hit the cold floor. Her home suffered from chronic damp that no amount of heat from the stove could banish. Picking up her shawl and wrapping it around her shoulders, she opened the door to find a barefoot lad there, wearing a cap and breeches. He was hopping from foot to foot and blowing on fisted fingers in a futile attempt to keep warm. 'Are you the baby woman?' he asked.

'Yes. Is it your mam?'

The lad nodded. 'She says can you come. But you have to be quick.'

'What's her name?' Jessie asked, without much hope that she'd recognise it. She was always trying to get the women to tell her as soon as they knew they were pregnant, but for many reasons, mainly money, or lack of it, few did.

'Mrs Morrison.' The boy stopped hopping for a few minutes. 'We're on Water's Close. Number sixteen. The top flat. Could you hurry, Miss? Mam's making an awful noise.'

'I know where it is. You run back. Make sure there's a big pan of water on the stove. Tell her I'll be there as soon as I'm dressed. Off you go, now.' She gave him a gentle push and closed the door. Water's Close, on Water Street, was one of the poorest tenements in Leith and was often referred to with cynical humour as Rotten Row.

Jessie lit a candle and Tommy stirred in his sleep. Over the last months he'd become used to her being called out at all hours. At first he'd protested that he didn't want his wife to work,

247

but when she'd turned on him, telling him she had to do something to stop herself thinking about Seamus, he'd relented.

When she'd first started attending births, Tommy would wake up and watch her as she got dressed. Sometimes, wanting to make sure she was safe, he'd walk her to the house. But since Seamus's death something had changed between them. They had become awkward with one another, afraid to speak of Seamus, too careful not to talk about the things that mattered, and eventually he'd stopped coming with her. It was just as well. There was nothing he could do and he needed all the sleep he could get before his twelve-hour shift down at Leith docks.

He rolled over and she pulled the blanket over his lean, work-hardened body.

Once she had enjoyed making love to Tommy. She had never felt closer to him than when they were in their bed wrapped in each other's arms. On a Saturday night, when they were first wed, she would fill the tin bath with hot water from the stove. He would strip off his clothes, his white skin a startling contrast to the dirt on his arms and face, and she'd soap his back and neck. Although she liked the smell of grease on him, she always insisted that he bathed to be ready for church the next morning. Sometimes, when she was washing him, he would reach out for her and pull her on top of him. She would protest, but he would carry on removing her wet clothes, item by item, while kissing her and touching her body in the way he knew she liked most and found impossible to resist. When they were both naked he would take her to bed and afterwards they would lie together and talk for a while. Then he would get dressed again, in clean clothes although not his Sunday best, and go out to join the other men at the public house, leaving her to her cleaning and baking, or whatever else she had to do in preparation for the Sabbath.

Not that there had been much love-making since Seamus had died. She kept pushing him away, protesting that she was too tired, but the truth was she couldn't bear the thought of bringing another child into the world only for it to die. She couldn't rely on the methods her mother had told her stopped babies coming. If they were any use, women wouldn't keep having babies when there wasn't space or food for the ones they had. No, the only way to stop having babies was not to make love. But that was part of being married.

She still loved Tommy, of course she did, but the distance between them had only grown when, a week ago, he'd told her he'd volunteered for the army. How could he even think of leaving her when she was still grieving for their dead child?

It took her only a few minutes to pull on her heavy dress and stockings. She always kept her bag ready so there was no need to check it. She tucked her hair into a cap, shrugged into her coat and kissed Tommy's unshaven cheek. Then she let herself out of the room and stumbled downstairs.

Outside, the gas lamps gave off a ghostly light. The smoke from the coal fires of thousands of homes shrouded what little light the lamps gave off in a dense fog that rarely lifted on this side of Edinburgh. It made Jessie long for the blue mountains and clear, sharp air of Skye. Maybe if they'd lived there Seamus wouldn't have died. But there was no point in thinking like that. All the wishing in the world wouldn't bring her baby back. She pulled her coat tighter and peered into the smog. She knew these streets well, having attended dozens of births over the last few months.

As her heavy brogues beat a rhythm on the cobbles in the silent street, she wondered what would face her when she got to Water's Close. Mrs Morrison clearly had one child already, the lad who had come to rouse her, and he was at least seven, which meant there would likely be another three, possibly four children. That was good. First babies were the worst. You never knew with them. But if a woman had successfully delivered once, there was no reason to think she wouldn't do so again.

A lot depended on how the mother had looked after her health. The money she was given at the end of the week, after her man had been to the public house, was little enough and most used what was left to feed and clothe their children. A large number of the women had rickets from their own undernourished childhood. Rickets was bad. A twisted, malformed pelvis made it difficult – sometimes impossible – for them to give birth.

Mrs Morrison's son was waiting for her on the step of the close. He'd been joined by three other children. A girl, no more than five, held a baby in her arms, while a grizzling toddler huddled into the crook of the boy's arm.

'Have you not asked one of your neighbours to take you in?' Jessie asked. It was far too late for the children to be out on the street. One of the few advantages for families living squashed together in the tenements was the camaraderie that existed among the women.

'My da said not to,' the boy answered. 'He had to go to work, but he told us to wait here until you came.'

Jessie crouched by his side. 'What's your name?'

'Billy. And that's Annie holding Baby.' He nodded towards the little boy at his side. 'This one's called Charlie – you know, after the prince.'

'You can't stay out here, Billy,' Jessie said. 'It's not safe. Come on, let's go and knock up one of the neighbours.'

Billy looked frightened. 'I told you, Da said not to. He says they're nothing but a load of nosy bitches.'

Jessie knew what that meant. No doubt Da was used to giving his wife a few slaps to stop her asking for money. Mostly the other women kept their noses out of family squabbles but occasionally one or two would have a go at the husband. But Jessie wasn't going to let Da get in the way of making sure the children were looked after for the night. Depending on how the birth went, it could be hours before they were allowed back inside. However, with barely enough room in the one-roomed flats for a bed and a couple of chairs, it would be impossible for Jessie to work with four children under her feet. And it wasn't good for children as young as this to hear their mother scream with the pain of pushing a baby out.

Jessie knocked on the first door at the top of the steps leading into the close. After a few minutes it was answered by a large woman with a disgruntled expression. 'Whit is it?' she asked. 'Do ye not know it's the middle of the night?' She peered at Jessie, then gave a resigned sigh. 'You're the midwife? You've come for Agnes. Is it her time?' She glanced over Jessie's shoulder and noticed the children. 'Yous better come away in, then. It could be a while before your mammy can let you back.'

As the silent children trooped inside, Jessie picked up her bag again.

'Are you needing help?' the neighbour asked.

'I'll call down if I do,' Jessie said, with a smile. Behind the grumpiness, it seemed there was a soft heart. 'Thanks for taking the children.'

'Aye, well. She'd do the same for me. It's him I cannae stand.'

None of this reassured Jessie. With a bit of luck the baby would come long before Agnes's husband was back from work.

Jessie knocked on the door and let herself in. The room, lit by a single lamp, was in almost complete darkness. Only when she moved closer to the bed could she make out a woman with dark hair and resigned eyes. 'Thank Christ you're here,' Agnes Morrison said. 'I don't think it'll be long now, but it hurts like buggery.'

Judging by her red face and the drops of sweat on her top lip, the contractions had to be strong and she wasn't far from delivering.

As Jessie unpacked her bag she took in the surroundings. The room where Agnes lived with her husband and four children was no bigger than

Jessie's, and hers was cramped enough with only the two of them.

But Jessie knew that Agnes would cope as most women did, some with considerably more children – up to ten in some families. As many as five would share the only bed and the others would make do with pull-out beds in the space that served as sitting room and kitchen. In the morning, the beds would be put away and the children sent out to play while the women got on with the endless chores of washing, cooking and cleaning. It was likely that this newest baby would sleep in a drawer until it got too big. After that it would join the parents in the bed, while the older infant was allocated the floor, most often in an empty orange-crate. These women were used to making do. If only they didn't have so many children perhaps they'd have a chance at a better life, but the men would never stop demanding their rights, and as long as they did, the women would carry on get-ting pregnant.

'I'm Jessie,' she said, discarding her coat. 'I see you have a pan on the stove. Good. Now, why don't you lie down so I can have a look at you? I'll just put my instruments on to boil.'

Jessie dropped her scissors into the pan. That was as far as her instruments went, but it sounded more reassuring to pretend there were several. Then she took a clean apron out of her bag and put it on. She had also brought a freshly laundered towel and sheet, but from what she could see in the hazy light of the one gas lamp above the stove, the sheets on the bed were reasonably clean.

'I'll light this other lamp, if that's all right,' she said. 'I need to be able to see what I'm doing.' A second lamp would be an extravagance for Agnes, but it had to be done. 'Your children are with the neighbour downstairs.'

Agnes grunted as a contraction swept over her. 'My man will no' like that.'

'Seeing as he's not here, it can't matter. Anyway, I'll deal with him if he comes back.' Jessie wasn't scared. However badly some of the men treated their wives, they would never dare lay a hand on them when the howdie was around. Unfortunately she couldn't stop them once she had left. Sometimes she would stay a couple of days with the mother to help her cope with the new baby, but that wouldn't be possible in this already over-crowded room.

Jessie pulled up Agnes's nightdress and gently palpated her abdomen. Good. The baby was lying normally. 'The head is down,' she told Agnes. 'You were quite right. It won't be long now.'

Agnes grunted as another contraction hit her. With their first, mothers screamed with the pain and the shock, but Agnes had been through this several times before. And judging by her black eye, she was used to suppressing cries of pain.

Jessie would have liked to break a poker over the heads of men like Agnes's husband. Thank God her Tommy would never dream of laying a hand on her.

'Lift your knees,' Jessie instructed, after she had washed her hands in water as hot as she could bear, 'and let them fall apart. I'm going to have a wee feel to see how far along you are.'

Agnes did as she was asked, her face contorted with pain and concentration.

Jessie slipped her fingers into the birth canal and felt for the cervix. It was almost completely open. Her instincts had been right. Agnes's baby would arrive shortly. 'Only another little while and you can start pushing. But not until I tell you, all right?'

Agnes nodded.

Jessie spread out the clean towel on the kitchen table ready for the baby. The stove was burning well, heating the room. Often the babies were small and needed the heat from the fire. Jessie examined Agnes again. This time the cervix was fully dilated. 'You can put one of your feet on my shoulder if it helps,' she said. 'The next time you feel a contraction I want you to push, and when I say stop, stop.'

She had found that if she eased the baby's entry into the world slowly there was less chance of tearing. Tears down below could mean weeks of pain for the woman when she was expected to carry on looking after her family. Wounds might also become infected.

With the next contraction, Agnes pushed. From her position at the end of the bed, Jessie saw something dark appear at the opening of the birth canal. As the contraction eased, the baby disappeared again. This was the part she loved. In some ways she was like one of the conductors she'd seen in the Botanic Gardens, leading the brass band in the free open-air concerts.

'You can rest for a bit, Agnes, until the next contraction.'

She laid a hand across Agnes's taut abdomen. She would feel the uterus tightening almost as soon as Agnes did.

After another couple of contractions the baby's head popped out. To Jessie's dismay the cord was wrapped tightly around its neck. 'One more push, Agnes,' she said. She wished she had someone, preferably her mother, to help, but she was on her own and would have to do the best she could. When, with a final push from Agnes, the baby slipped out, Jessie unravelled the cord. The baby was a dusky shade of blue. Her heart hammering, she flicked her finger round the inside of the tiny mouth to check for any obstructions, then bent her head, placed her lips over the nose and mouth and blew gently.

'What is it?' Agnes pushed herself up on her elbows, straining to see what Jessie was doing. 'Why isn't it crying?'

Jessie couldn't stop what she was doing to answer. She blew a few more times, watching the miniature chest rise with every breath. Then the baby's chest squeezed in an attempt to draw in a breath. She raised her head. When the child gave a feeble cry, she felt dizzy with relief.

After rubbing the baby down, she wrapped it in the clean towel and passed her to the mother to feed. 'A wee girl, Agnes.'

Disappointment pulled at Agnes's mouth. 'He was hoping for another boy. He'll no' be very pleased with a girl.'

Stupid man. As if fathering boys were an indication of manhood! Jessie hoped that he wouldn't take out his disappointment on his wife.

'You get her feeding while I finish off down below. You're going to have to give me another push in a minute.'

When she had delivered the placenta, Jessie cut the cord. Then she wrapped the afterbirth in newspaper for Agnes to dispose of later. She washed her hands again and packed away the scissors. She would boil them when she got home.

'I want you to stay in bed as long as you can and get some rest,' she told Agnes.

'You've got to be kidding me, hen. He'll be expecting his breakfast on the table same as always when he comes in off the night shift.'

'I'll make you a cup of tea before I go, then. Perhaps your neighbour will keep the children for a few more hours so you can get some sleep. I'll ask her on the way out.'

From her bed, Agnes gestured towards a pile of coins on the table. 'It's all I've got, for now. I'll try to get some more for you when you come back.'

Jessie always returned to check up on mother and baby for a few days afterwards. She was paid for the delivery, and for each visit after, or that was the idea. In reality, the women could only pay her half of what they were supposed to. Sometimes they would offer her a few haddock or whatever they had instead of money, but Jessie usually refused. Now it seemed to be getting about that she was an easy touch, but she couldn't leave the women to give birth on their own when she could help; neither would she refuse to come back and check up on them. Still, it would be nice if she were paid properly every now and again. God knew she and Tommy needed the money, if they were ever going to get themselves out of their own small room.

'Don't worry. This will do fine.' If she refused to take anything, it would be almost as bad. Most of the women were fiercely proud, and anything that could be construed as charity was resented. At least she could add the few coins to the small pile she had already collected. Another ten years, she thought despairingly, and they might have enough to move into a bigger flat, in a better street. If Tommy hadn't joined up, he might have got the supervisor's job down at the docks, which would have meant a terraced house with a separate bedroom and more money. Maybe then she would have risked having another child.

Once she had finished making the tea and tidying up, she checked Agnes again. To her horror she saw a spreading red stain on the sheet. At this stage bleeding should have been minimal. If Jessie couldn't stop it, the mother might die. 'Agnes, I'll have to call for a doctor,' she said, keeping her voice calm and matter-of-fact. 'I'll have to leave you for a few moments to go for help.'

'Whit is it? 'Whit's wrong?'

'You're bleeding a little more than I'd like. You may need the doctor to give you something to stop it.'

Ignoring Agnes's frightened eyes, Jessie hurried downstairs and knocked on the neighbour's door.

'Send Billy or someone to the hospital for a doctor. Whoever you send has to tell them it's a post-partum haemorrhage and they must hurry.'

Billy appeared in the doorway. 'I'll go, Missus.'

'Run as fast as you can, Billy. There's no time to waste.'

Jessie hurried back upstairs. Not knowing if a doctor would come in time, or even if a doctor would come at all, it was up to her to control the bleeding. 'Do you have some clean pillow cases, Agnes?' she asked.

Agnes pointed to the sideboard. 'You'll find a couple in there.'

Working quickly, Jessie ripped them into strips. Then she rolled each strip into a wad and used them to pack the entrance of the birth canal as tightly as she could.

After she'd finished, she checked Agnes's pulse again. It was rapid and weak. If she continued to bleed there was no more Jessie could do for her, and those poor mites downstairs would be motherless.

Just as Jessie was giving up hope that a doctor would arrive, there was a brief knock on the door and a slender figure holding a leather medical bag stepped into the room. Although it had been years since she'd seen the doctor's daughter, Jessie recognised her straight away.

'Someone sent for a doctor?' Isabel said, wiping her feet on the mat. When she raised her eyes, her face paled in the half-light. 'Why, it's Jessie MacCorquodale! You're the midwife!'

For a moment, shock rendered Jessie speechless.

Isabel unwrapped her headscarf and started undoing the buttons of her fashionably cut coat. Her face was thinner than Jessie remembered, emphasising her high cheekbones and making her lips seem fuller. Despite the shadows under her eyes, she was more beautiful than ever. No wonder Archie had been besotted with her.

Jessie's heart thudded. At last she could ask Isabel what had happened that day on Galtrigill. But now was not the time, not while Agnes was bleeding to death.

Jessie found her voice as she took the coat from Isabel. 'It's Stuart now, Miss – I'm married.'

'Congratulations,' Isabel said, rolling up the sleeves of her pin-tucked blouse. 'And can you believe that I'm Dr MacKenzie now, Jessie? But we'll talk properly later. What's the problem?'

Jessie quickly explained what had happened and what she had done so far for Agnes.

Isabel nodded her approval while she felt Agnes's pulse. 'You've done everything right. She's fortunate to have you looking after her. Now, I have some ergot in my bag. It will help the uterus contract and should control the bleeding. If it doesn't, we'll have to take her to hospital.'

Isabel took a syringe from her bag, drew some fluid from a small bottle and injected it into Agnes's arm. 'We'll know in the next couple of minutes whether it's working.'

The women waited in silence, watching Agnes closely for signs of collapse. Then Isabel checked the wadding in Agnes's birth canal and nodded. 'The bleeding seems to have stopped,' she said. 'Well done, Jessie. If you hadn't acted so quickly, it might not have turned out so well.' She smiled again. 'You were always a natural at this. I remember my father had a great deal of confidence in you.'

Once, Isabel's praise would have meant everything to Jessie. Now, thinking of Archie and his admiration for this confident and privileged woman, her words only made Jessie feel patronised and resentful. Whatever had happened on Skye, it hadn't affected Isabel. She had gone on with her charmed life. Admittedly Jessie didn't know that Isabel had had anything to do with Archie's sudden departure, but she just had a deep, unwavering intuition that she had.

As soon as Agnes was sleeping peacefully, her baby wrapped snugly in her arms, Jessie offered Isabel a cup of tea.

Isabel tucked a lock of hair behind her ear. 'Thank you,' she said, after a brief hesitation. 'I'd like to stay here until I'm certain she won't start bleeding again.' She removed a pile of clothes from a rickety chair and sat down, with a sigh. 'What a day! It's good to be finally off my feet.'

Jessie set the kettle on the stove to boil. She had to ask Isabel about Archie, but she wasn't sure how. 'I still have the book you gave me the last time we saw each other,' she said, choosing her words with care.

'Oh, Lord, Jessie! I was meant to pass on the address of the people my father found for you but until now I'd quite forgotten. After he died, everything was so ... so confused.'

'It wouldn't have mattered if you had. In the end I couldn't leave Mam. She was sick and, with Archie gone, I had to stay. Did you know he's no longer on Skye?'

Isabel ran her tongue across her lips. 'Yes. Where did he go?'

261

'He's in America. At least, he was when I last heard from him.'

'America! He always talked of going there.'

Was she mistaken or did Isabel look relieved?

'Anyway, with Archie gone and Mam sick, I couldn't leave her on her own and I couldn't take her with me. She died a few years ago.' Jessie watched Isabel closely for her reaction, but apart from another little flicker in her eyes, there was nothing except sympathy in her expression.

'I'm sorry,' Isabel replied, 'Yet you found a way to become a nurse.'

Jessie poured water into the teapot and left it to brew. 'When Mam passed away, there was nothing to keep me on Skye so I came to Edinburgh. I tried to get a position at the Royal Infirmary, but they wouldn't take me because I didn't have enough schooling. Besides, they wanted me to pay them for my training and I didn't have the money. In the end I found a job as a nurse at Craigleith.'

'I didn't know you were at Craigleith! I used to go there on occasion to help in theatre.'

'I was there for three years. Although the Royal Infirmary wouldn't have me, the workhouse wasn't so particular about whom they took on.' But she didn't want Isabel to think she wasn't a real nurse. Despite everything, she still wanted her approval. 'I did a good job there. A new matron started just before me and she wasn't happy with the way things were run. Together we made the wards as good as anything you'd find in the Royal Infirmary. The matron had trained at the Glasgow Infirmary and she knew what she was about, so I had a decent training.'

She turned back to the stove and, using the cups and saucers she found above the mantel, poured the tea.

'Why did you leave?' Isabel asked, taking her cup from Jessie.

'I met my husband, Tommy. They don't like nurses to be married.'

'Do you miss it? Nursing in a hospital, I mean. Of course, you still have your deliveries, and I'm sure the women of Leith have cause to thank God that you're here to help.'

'I didn't miss it at first. I was too happy about getting married and having a baby...' She tailed off.

Agnes's baby stirred in her sleep and Jessie went over to the bed to check on her and her mother. The baby had already gone back to sleep, a little bubble of milk still on her lips.

'You have a child?' Isabel said, when Jessie returned to her chair.

'I had a son,' Jessie replied shortly.

'Had?' Isabel repeated. 'Oh, Jessie, what happened?'

Jessie took a sip of the scalding tea. 'He died. Diphtheria. I took him to the hospital. It was a woman doctor who saw him. She was useless. I kept telling her she needed to make a hole in his throat to help him breathe, but I reckon she thought the likes of me wouldn't know what they were talking about. But Seamus was my baby. If I'd had the stuff the doctor had, I would have saved him. I know I would.'

'I'm so very sorry,' Isabel said softly. 'What was the doctor's name? Do you remember?'

263

'I'll never forget it. Dr Harcourt.'

Isabel pursed her lips. 'I know her. She's left now. Set up a practice in the New Town, I understand.'

'I pity her patients.'

Isabel leaned across in her chair and touched Jessie's hand. Her fingers were frozen, despite the warmth in the room. 'We doctors are human, Jessie,' she said. 'We can't always save everyone, no matter how much we want to.'

'She could have saved Seamus, but she panicked. Not like you. You didn't panic when Agnes was bleeding. Dr Harcourt would have.'

'We can't know what she would have done,' Isabel said, rising to put her cup next to the sink.

'What kind of doctor are you?' Jessie changed the subject. What had happened had happened. It was no use harking after what couldn't be changed.

'I'm a resident at Leith at the moment. I finish there in December.'

'Will you stay on at the hospital?'

Isabel shook her head. 'It's difficult for a woman to get a permanent position in a hospital, unless it's children and mothers or one of the asylums. Besides, I've always wanted to be a surgeon. If there's one good thing about this war, it's that women can get experience they can't get anywhere else. There's a female unit going out to the front line and I've asked to go with them. That way I'm bound to get some practice as a surgeon.'

'Won't you be scared out there with all the fighting, Dr MacKenzie? Don't you have someone here who cares about you?'

'Oh, do call me Isabel, Jessie. We've known each other long enough. And, no,' a shadow crossed her face, 'there is no one, except my mother, whom I'll be leaving behind.'

A piece of wood in the fire hissed, and a laugh echoed in the street below.

'My Tommy's volunteered – the fool. I told him not to, but he wouldn't listen. He said it was his duty.' Jessie clicked her tongue. 'His duty? What has the government ever done for us?'

'I'm sorry you feel that way, Jessie. We all have to do our duty, especially now.'

Jessie had had enough. Who was Isabel to preach to her? The strain and grief of the last years and months gathered inside her like a storm. 'Duty? Please don't tell me about duty. I did my duty to my mam. I was the one who stayed behind when Archie went away. I was the one who put away my hopes and dreams to do my duty. You sit there, qualified, rich and happy, but you don't know the first thing about people like me or our lives. You were happy enough to look down on us when you were in Skye, going about with your dad as if you were Lady Muck. Did it make you feel good, knowing you could go home to your comforts any time you wished? You were happy enough to have Archie for your friend when it suited you. You didn't care that he loved you. Did you even notice?'

Isabel got to her feet, holding onto the back of the chair, as if for support. 'You're wrong, Jessie. I cared for Archie. He was my friend. And I never looked down on the islanders. If anything, I envied them and you. You may find it hard to believe but

I was lonely. Archie was the only person who made me feel I belonged.'

Jessie couldn't stop herself. She fought to keep her voice low. She didn't want to wake Agnes or her baby. 'You were there on Galtrigill the day Lord Maxwell went missing, weren't you? But did the police question you? Of course not. You were the doctor's daughter and above that sort of thing. But Archie was only a crofter's son. I don't know what happened that day, but if Archie had anything to do with it, I know it was because of you.'

Isabel's eyes had widened with shock. 'I can't think what you mean.' She crossed to the bed and bent over Agnes again, her back to Jessie.

'That day, when you went to say goodbye to Archie, did you see Lord Maxwell?' Jessie asked. She wouldn't let Isabel go without getting some answers.

Isabel's back stiffened. 'It was so long ago. What can it matter?'

But Jessie couldn't leave it. 'You were on Galtrigill. So were Archie and his lordship. Did you see Archie fight with him?'

'I saw Archie...We said our farewells. I was ill in the days before we left Skye. I didn't even know Lord Maxwell was missing until a couple of years ago.'

'Did Archie confess his love for you that day? Is that what happened?'

Isabel turned. Even in the half-light Jessie could see the dark red staining her cheeks. 'You have no right to question me!' she said, lifting her chin.

'I need to know what made Archie leave me

266

and Mam!' Jessie cried. 'Did Archie ask you to be with him and you turned him down?'

Isabel sighed. 'Yes. I did.'

So Jessie had been right about that.

'But you can't think that Archie had anything to do with Charles Maxwell's disappearance. You can't believe he would hurt anyone. You're his sister!' Isabel rushed on. 'You must know he always wanted to go to America. He was always talking of it. He wanted to make something of himself.'

'He was something already!'

'It wasn't enough for him.'

'And not enough for you either.'

Isabel shook her head sadly. 'No. I wish I could say different.'

Jessie frowned. Perhaps that *was* why he'd left? He'd been spurned by the woman he loved. It would have been enough to make him more determined to make something of himself. In that case, his leaving had had nothing to do with Lord Maxwell's disappearance and everything to do with his hopeless love for Isabel. Wasn't it what she'd always guessed? That her foolish brother was in love with a woman he could never have?

Isabel's hands were shaking as she picked up her coat. 'The bleeding's stopped completely. She'll be fine now. I must go back to the hospital. If you need me, send a message to me there.' She paused with her hand on the door handlle. 'If there is ever anything I can do for you, Jessie, I live at twenty-four Heriot Row.'

As the door closed gently behind her, Jessie realised that Isabel hadn't denied seeing Charles

Maxwell that day.

The driver was waiting outside to take Isabel back to the hospital. Although she would have preferred to walk, especially tonight when she needed to think about what Jessie had said, Leith wasn't safe for a woman alone at night. The ship-building continued through the night and prostitutes waited on street corners for when the workers stopped for a break. In addition, vagrants and paupers huddled in the streets, waiting for an opportunity to relieve the unsuspecting of their purses or wallets. Although it was an unwritten rule that they would never touch the nurses or female doctors, the nurses had their uniforms to identify them, while the doctors wore plain skirts and blouses.

It had been a shock seeing Jessie again. Especially when the constant talk of war had put all thoughts of Charles Maxwell and Archie out of her mind these last weeks. Who would have thought that her and Jessie's paths would cross again after so many years – and in Leith, of all places? It wasn't that odd when she thought about it. There were few places either of them could train and Edinburgh or Glasgow was the choice of most.

Isabel knew she was putting off thinking about the words Jessie had thrown at her. The Jessie she'd known on Skye would never have spoken to her like that. She remembered Jessie as a girl with an impish smile and mischievous eyes. She had grown into a competent nurse, but the light had left her along the way. Losing a child was bound to do that. If ever she thought her own life was exacting, she had only to look at the ordinary women of Edinburgh to see how difficult it could be.

But why had Jessie asked whether she'd seen Charles? Did she know Charles had attacked her? But how?

Archie *had* been nearby. She'd only been walking for about fifteen minutes when Charles had found her. What if Archie had heard her scream or seen Charles follow her? What if he'd come to her aid, only to find that she'd escaped, and had fought with Charles? Could Archie have killed him? Her heart banged painfully. It would explain why he had left suddenly for America and never been back. The Archie she knew would never have left Jessie alone to manage the croft and look after their sick mother. Not unless he feared for his liberty or his life. It was obviously what Jessie suspected.

Although the thought of her childhood friend witnessing her shame made her feel ill, the idea of him having had anything to do with Charles's disappearance was worse. If Archie were to blame, she should tell the police what had happened that day. But then, even though Charles had attacked *her*, her reputation, and probably that of her family, would be ruined. Certainly she would be disbarred from practising medicine again.

If Jessie believed Archie had harmed Charles because of her, no wonder she was so angry.

Tears pricked her eyes. Jessie's words had made very clear that she thought her selfish, patronising and indulged. And, to an extent, she was right.

She had intruded on the islanders' lives, not out of any real need to help but to ease her own loneliness and satisfy her curiosity in medicine. Her cheeks burned. Papa *had* indulged her, but she had helped many people with her skills since then and was about to have another chance to put the needs of others before her own. *But,* a little voice whispered, *isn't the true reason you're going to war because you want to further your knowledge of medicine?*

She sat up straight. Such thinking was pointless. It didn't matter why she was going to war. All that mattered was that when she got there she did everything in her power to save the lives of the men in her care.

As for the truth about Charles... Nausea clawed at her stomach. One way or another, although she didn't know how, she needed to find out.

She couldn't ask Jessie. What about Andrew?

But Andrew and Simon were in France, somewhere on the western front. They had gone out with the RFC almost as soon as war had been declared. Andrew wrote to their mother often and she had the address of his base in Marne. But this wasn't something she could ask in a letter. What if she were mistaken and Archie had had nothing to do with any of it? And how could she explain why she wanted to know more about Charles's disappearance without telling Andrew about his attack on her? And if she did, would that spoil the friendship between Andrew and Simon? The two men were close. Andrew's letters always mentioned Simon. He'd even gone so far as to say that he knew nothing could ever happen to him as long as he had Simon as his wingman.

Her head was throbbing and the jarring of the carriage over the cobbles made her headache worse. If only Papa were still alive she could ask him what to do. Or if Maximilian were here... But even if Maximilian hadn't left her, she could never tell him of Charles's attack. Charles's hands had soiled her in a way that would repel decent men.

No. If she wanted to discover the truth, it was up to her and no one else. And she had to know. If Charles was dead and she was responsible in any way, she would have to admit to what had happened. A shudder ran up her spine. Even if it meant she lost everything.

Jessie waited until Agnes was awake enough to feed her baby before she left. She stopped at the neighbour's to ask if she could keep the children until eight o'clock when Agnes's husband would be back from his night shift at the yard. Luckily the harassed-looking woman agreed.

Outside, it was getting light and the streets were filling. Jessie was still shaking, and whenever she thought of what she'd said to Isabel, she felt sick. She wanted to believe that Archie had left because he wanted to make a life for himself that might one day include Isabel, but she couldn't shake the feeling that that wasn't the whole truth. If it were, he would have written with his address or even sent for them. Unless ... unless it hadn't worked out for him in America and he was too proud to say so.

That was possible but, deep inside, she was still

convinced that Isabel knew something about Lord Maxwell's disappearance. Something that might help Archie. Although he was safely out of harm's way in America, if he ever tried to return to Scotland, she had no doubt that the police would arrest him even though six years had passed. But if Isabel knew something, she wasn't saying.

Traders were setting up their stalls at the side of the road from heavily laden carts. The men on night shift were returning home, their hats pulled low against the rain that was falling now in earnest. At this end of Edinburgh most of the men were employed, like her Tommy and Agnes's man, down at the shipyards. It was heavy work and not well paid, but it was work and most were glad to have it.

Thinking of Tommy, she increased her pace. If she was quick she'd be home before he left and there might be time for a cuddle. She'd never shared her fears about Archie with him and wasn't sure why not, only that some things were better not talked about. Even with the man she loved. And she did love him. She'd been daft to let things cool between them.

When she let herself in she was pleased to find him still at home. He was dressed, ready for work.

'Hello, love,' he greeted her warily. 'How did it go? Everything all right? Did she pay you?'

Jessie showed him the few coins in her hand and he frowned. 'That all? It's hardly worth it.'

'I'll add it to the rest. You'll see – one day it'll help us get something. It's better than nothing, Tommy.'

'I wish you didn't have to work,' he said. 'No

man likes to think that he can't provide for his wife.'

'We've talked about this before, Tommy. I like delivering babies. Besides, if you hadn't been so hard-headed about signing up with the army, you could have had the supervisor's job down at the yard. Then we'd have had money enough.'

He pulled her towards him and wrapped his strong arms around her waist. 'Don't go on about that, love. You know I had no choice. All the other boys were signing up and half of them are daft enough to get their heads blown off if I'm not there to look after them.'

And what if *he* didn't come back? Had he thought of that?

He nibbled her ear and whispered, 'Come back to bed, darling. I woke up thinking about you...' His fingers were at the ties of her dress, working away, loosening them. He would be going soon. Her Tommy, whom she loved with all her heart and soul. It had been a long time since she'd lain with him, felt his naked skin on hers, felt him inside her.

He had slipped her dress off her shoulders and was kissing the base of her throat, working his way down to her breast. As the liquid warmth between her legs increased, she pressed her body to his. He raised his head and gave her the wide smile that melted her heart. Then he picked her up and carried her towards their bed.

Chapter 25

Two weeks later, Jessie watched quietly as Tommy finished making the adjustments to his uniform. He was leaving for a training camp in England. From there he would go to France.

He looks fine, she thought.

He turned to her as he buttoned his jacket. 'Are you all right?' he asked.

'No,' she said quietly, hating herself for not being able to forgive him for leaving her.

He walked across to her and knelt in front of her, his kilt fanning around him. She felt the roughness of his calloused hands as he placed them on either side of her face. She pressed her cheek against his palm. 'I wish you weren't going, Tommy.'

'I know, my dear, but I have to. I can't stay here and let others do the fighting for me.' It was the conversation they'd had several times since Tommy had burst into their flat, his cheeks red with excitement, and told her he'd joined the Seaforth Highlanders.

'You could stay,' Jessie said, even though she knew he couldn't change his mind. 'You volunteered, Tommy. You could've waited until they called you up.'

'I couldn't, Jessie. It's not going to last long and I want to be there while I can.' He placed his head in her lap and she stroked his hair with trembling hands. How could she bear it if he didn't come back?

'If you'd waited until after they'd given you the supervisor's job we could have got one of the flats with a front room. We would have been able to rent it out, Tommy, and make some money.'

'I know. But it's not as if—'

'It's not as if we have Seamus to worry about any more. Is that what you were about to say? But one day there will, God willing, be other children. And when there are, I want them to have more than we did, Tommy. I want them to have an education, to have a chance to make something of themselves. I don't want them growing up not knowing if there'll be enough to eat. I don't want them growing up without a father.'

Guilt settled around her like a cloak. Her ambition had led to Seamus's death. If she hadn't wanted to put money aside for his education she would never have taken in washing and brought diphtheria into their home. Tommy had never said anything to make her think he blamed her, but she blamed herself. Oh, she blamed herself. Maybe Tommy going off to war was her punishment. Maybe she shouldn't want so much. Why couldn't she have been satisfied with what she had? Tommy and her baby. They had enough to eat, clothes on their backs, shoes on their feet, the odd penny to go out for the day on Sundays. Why did she always want more than God had seen fit to give her?

'I'll be back on leave. You'll see, Jessie. And you'll get my pay.'

'I don't want you to go!' Jessie pushed his head from her lap and jumped to her feet. 'I want you to stay with me, here, where you'll be safe.'

'Dear, you know I can't. I've signed up.' He clambered to his feet. 'I have to go now.'

Of course she knew it was too late. Once you'd signed up there was no getting out of it. She pulled off her apron, laid it across the chair and forced a smile. 'I know, darling. You mustn't mind me.' She looked around the little room. 'Have you got the pieces I made you?'

Tommy patted his knapsack. 'Aye. The bacon ones will go down a treat.'

They looked at each other. Jessie saw him as she had when she'd first met him at the poorhouse, standing there with the sweetie packet in his hand, a guilty smile on his face; she saw him again when he'd first kissed her, then when they'd stood in front of the minister, her in the dress she'd been secretly sewing for weeks, him in his only suit, his new shoes making him hop from foot to foot; on their wedding night, the way he'd taken her into his arms and, gently at first but then with a passion that had taken her breath, made love to her; the way his smile had almost reached from ear to ear when she'd told him she was pregnant; the look of wonder when he'd first held Seamus ... the look on his face when he'd realised Seamus was dead. So many memories.

The pain of him leaving ripped through her.

Then they were in each other's arms and her tears were soaking the front of his cambric shirt. She could feel its roughness, smell the particular scent that was all Tommy. Feel his wiry arms around her as he held her and told her he loved her, that he would be back before she knew it.

And then the door clicked shut and he was gone.

Tommy had been in France only a few weeks when the telegram arrived. Jessie's hands shook as she opened it. She didn't have to read it to know what it said. There was only one reason people like her got telegrams. Finally she opened the single sheet of paper.

WE REGRET TO INFORM YOU THAT CORPORAL TOMMY STUART OF THE SEAFORTH HIGHLANDERS IS MISSING IN ACTION AND PRESUMED DEAD. WE OFFER YOU OUR SINCERE CONDOLENCES.

Tommy was dead.

Her darling Tommy wasn't coming home. Not ever.

Was he frightened in those last moments? Was he in pain? Had he called out for her? She wrapped her arms around her body and hugged herself, trying to stop the shaking.

What would she do without him?

Agony pulled her soul apart. She was vaguely aware of a high-pitched sound until she realised it was her: she was keening. Deep, racking sobs robbed her of breath as she rocked back and forth until she had no more tears left.

She sat until night fell. Then she lit the oil lamp. Her eyes fell on the bed that she and Tommy had shared. How could she continue to live in this room, which had once held happiness but for evermore would be a reminder of everything she'd lost?

She read the telegram again. PRESUMED DEAD. Hope flared. They couldn't be sure. Hadn't Mrs McPherson's John been presumed dead and turned up safe and on the mend in a military hospital? Couldn't the same thing have happened to her Tommy? Maybe he'd banged his head and didn't know who he was. That could happen. Maybe they'd made a mistake. With all the confusion, it was bound to happen. Wouldn't she feel it if he were dead?

She rummaged in the drawer of the sideboard until she found what she was looking for. Then she went to the door and took her coat from the hook. She wasn't going to give up on her Tommy until she knew for sure that he wasn't coming back.

Chapter 26

Isabel was making a list of everything she would need for Serbia when there was a knock on her bedroom door and Ellie hurried in. 'Please, Miss, there's a woman in the kitchen who says she has to speak to you. Mrs Walker tried to send her away but she wouldn't go.'

'Is it someone needing my help?' Isabel asked. 'Doesn't Mrs Walker know by now not to send them away?'

'This woman isn't hurt, Miss. She just keeps saying she needs to speak to the doctor.'

'I'll come down straight away.'

Downstairs, she was alarmed to see Jessie slumped at the kitchen table, with red and swollen eyes, tear tracks visible on her cheeks, despair radiating from her in waves. Isabel was filled with a sense of foreboding. 'What's happened, Jessie? Is it one of your mothers?' She crouched at Jessie's side and took her hands. Despite the heat blasting from the kitchen range, they were frozen and Isabel tried to rub some heat back into them.

Jessie took a shuddering breath. 'No, it's not that.' She held out the piece of paper on which she had written Isabel's address. 'You said I should come to you if I needed anything.'

Puzzled, Isabel drew up a seat at the table and, ignoring the housekeeper's disapproval, sat down. 'And I meant it. Tell me how I can help. Take your time.'

Apart from the clashing and clanging of pots from Mrs Walker, the room was still.

'It's my Tommy,' Jessie said at last. 'He's missing. I got a telegram. It says they think he's dead.'

'I'm so sorry Jessie.'

Silent tears rolled down Jessie's cheeks. The rattling of the pots and pans stopped, and after a few moments, a cup of tea appeared on the table in front of her.

'Is there anything I can do?' Isabel asked, after Jessie had taken a sip or two.

Jessie looked at her. Despite the tear stains, her expression was resolute. 'Yes, there is. You said you were going to help in the war. Well, I want to go too.'

PART THREE

FRANCE AND SERBIA, 1914–19

Chapter 27

France, December 1914

Jessie was cold. So cold that her breath froze and she had to stamp her feet to keep her circulation moving. She huddled deeper into her greatcoat. She still felt hollow inside, as if someone had scooped out her innards with a big spoon, but neither her bruised heart nor her numb fingers and frozen toes could quite banish her rising excitement.

It was hard to believe that only a month ago she'd been in Edinburgh and now she was in France, part of the Scottish Women's Hospital. Two days earlier the unit had gathered at Victoria station in London, all of them identifiable by their grey skirts and jackets with tartan facings, their uniform. At first Jessie had thought that her ill-fitting, itchy grey suit was a hand-me-down, but when she saw the other women, equally dowdy and uncomfortable in theirs, she realised that someone must have paid a second-rate seamstress to make them. Despite their uniforms, though, there was no mistaking that most of the unit were ladies.

Jessie's cheeks burned. When she'd been introduced to Lady Arabella, she'd curtsied before she could stop herself. Lady Arabella had whispered something to her companion and they'd laughed.

It hadn't been long before her embarrassment had turned to irritation. The way the women had continually jumped off the smoke-belching train, as it waited to depart, with 'Hold the train, someone, I just have to get some sweets,' or 'Darling, tell the nice driver we can't possibly leave until I have some more tea,' would have tested anybody's patience. Every moment they were delayed made Jessie grit her teeth in an agony of frustration, although she knew it was soft-headed to believe that the sooner they got to France, the sooner she would find out what had really happened to Tommy.

Her heart ached. Was there any chance he was still alive? She wasn't ready to stop hoping. There was so much death: so many men had been blown up and their bodies never found. How could anyone know for certain who was dead and who wasn't?

At last, after more than a day and night of travelling, they were at Royaumont Abbey, not too many miles from Paris.

'So this is to be our hospital.' The refined tones came from the red-headed woman beside her. She'd caused quite a stir when she'd arrived at the station, dressed not in her uniform but in a beautifully tailored dark green suit and smart shoes. She'd also brought several trunks, despite the clear instruction that they were allowed only one. However, when she'd been told to change and send the extra trunks home with her driver, she had agreed without argument.

'It's an impressive building,' the red-haired woman continued.

In front of them, the cream stone of the abbey shimmered in the failing light. It was, Jessie thought, one of the most beautiful buildings she'd ever seen, with its arched lower windows of stained glass, separated at regular intervals by high columns in the same stone. A small wood shielded the abbey from the road, and in the middle of the circular driveway leading up to the entrance, there was a pond with swans and ducks.

'Right, everyone.' The medical officer, Dr Ludlow, a plump woman with short hair and bright blue eyes, clapped her hands for attention. 'As you no doubt have gathered, this is to be our hospital. Let us see what we have.' She strode into the entrance hall, followed by the group of excited women. The chatter stopped as they looked around in dismay.

There was little indication of the grandeur they had seen from outside. Every surface was festooned with cobwebs and dust, and piles of rubble lay on the dusty, straw-covered floor. Evidence of a hasty departure lay in discarded wine bottles, paper and cardboard and, curiously, a single hob-nailed boot.

'The German uhlans bivouacked here as recently as two weeks ago,' Dr Ludlow said. 'Needless to say, they didn't find it necessary to clean up after themselves.'

Some of the women peered into the gloom anxiously, as if expecting the enemy to come out of the shadows.

'There is no one here now, of course,' Dr Ludlow added sharply.

It was even colder inside the building than it

was outside and, to Dr Ludlow's evident frustration, there was no electricity. She paused to light some lanterns to pass around and, as the women held them high to see better, their faces grew longer and their excitement dissipated.

They followed Dr Ludlow up and down several staircases peering into each room with increasing doubt. The abbey was a mishmash of different-sized rooms; the high, vaulted ceilings meant it was freezing – the antiquated stove in the kitchen seemed unlikely to give out much heat; and the beautiful stained-glass windows would be impossible to black out.

'There is more to do than I'd thought,' Dr Ludlow said, when they'd finished exploring. 'I realise that most of you are here to look after the injured when they arrive, but first we're going to have to get this place shipshape. We have to be ready to receive patients by Christmas.'

Jessie shared a glance with another nurse. At that moment it was difficult to see how they could be ready for patients so soon. Christmas was less than three weeks away.

'I know that many of you have never had to do housework before, but everyone will have to help,' Dr Ludlow continued, when nobody spoke.

Of the other nine nurses, two had trained at the London, three at the Edinburgh Royal and one at the Western in Glasgow. The other three, as far as Jessie could gather, had worked in private homes and had had little formal training. Even so, she suspected that they thought themselves a step or two above her. When they'd asked her where she'd trained and she'd told them, they'd raised delicate eyebrows. Most hadn't even known that the workhouse had an infirmary.

Life would be tough, but training at a workhouse had its advantages: if anyone knew how to deal with difficult living and working conditions it was her.

The next couple of days were so busy that no one had time to do anything except work, eat and fall into bed. Jessie was sleeping in one of the cells that had once accommodated monks, sharing with three of the other nurses. If they hadn't been so physically exhausted, they wouldn't have been able to sleep for the cold. Most had given up trying to change into nighties and slept fully dressed. Those who had them used their fur coats as extra blankets. Those who didn't simply piled every spare item they owned on top of themselves.

The cook who, to Jessie's amazement, turned out to be the daughter of the Earl of Strathaven, provided meals for them with only three pans, no dishes and a single knife. It secretly amused Jessie to see the ladies tucking into their dinner with no more than a spoon, but they didn't complain and she was starting to feel a grudging respect for them.

In the mornings they had to crack the ice on their jugs of water before washing. Hot water was in short supply and had to be brought from the basement kitchen up several flights of stairs by which time it was cold.

But Jessie couldn't regret coming. The work left her little time to dwell on the past. Coming to the abbey and living within its walls was settling something inside her. For the first time since Seamus had died and Tommy had gone missing, she had come to believe that she could, one day, if not be happy, at least find a way to live. Perhaps here, where the monks had once worshipped, she would even find her way back to God.

This afternoon she was scrubbing stairs. The beautiful red-haired woman from the first day was kneeling next to her, her usually immaculate tresses falling in wisps around her face. With still only the promise of electricity, they had to work by candlelight.

'How many more, Sister?' Her companion groaned, as she sat back on her haunches.

'About fifteen, I think,' Jessie replied. It still felt awkward to work alongside women who were used to being pampered by servants and, judging by the way this one was dabbing at the steps, they'd be here for the rest of the morning.

Jessie dipped her cloth into the water and wrung it out. 'Tell you what, Maxwell,' she said, 'I'll do the first scrub, then you give it a final going-over.' It still felt strange to be addressing these aristocratic women by their surnames.

Her companion tucked her hair behind her ears and grinned. 'Are you suggesting, Sister, that I'm no good at this?'

Jessie smiled back. 'It would take less time if I was to do it on my own. No offence, Maxwell.'

'None taken. Nevertheless, I came here to help and help I shall.' She eyed her fingernails with dismay. 'If Lord Livingston could see me now, I doubt he'd still be so keen to marry me.' She dropped her cloth into the water, wrung it out and started again. Jessie had to admire her perseverance, even if she couldn't find a good word to say about her technique.

'Your voice reminds me of the way the servants spoke in our house on Skye,' Maxwell continued. 'Are you from there?'

The question took Jessie so much by surprise that she stopped mid-scrub. Maxwell. From Skye? Dear Lord, the only female Maxwell she knew who had a house on Skye was Lady Dorothea Maxwell, daughter of the earl and sister of the man whose disappearance they wanted to question Archie about. She had to prevent her making the connection.

'I – I was there when I was much younger,' Jessie said, 'but I've lived in Edinburgh these last years. That was where I trained as a nurse.'

Thankfully, Lady Dorothea seemed content with her answer and didn't pursue that line of questioning. Jessie was known only as Sister Stuart so there was no reason for anyone to link her to Archie MacCorquodale.

They worked in silence for a while, Jessie's heart still beating a tattoo against her ribs. Why, oh why did she have to be working with this woman of all people?

'Did you leave anyone special behind, Sister?' Lady Dorothea asked eventually.

Jessie sucked in a breath. 'No, my lady. My husband was with the Seaforth Highlanders and went missing in the battle at Mons.'

'Forget that "my lady" nonsense, Sister. Remember, you're supposed to call me Maxwell, at least while we're here, even if it does sound too ridiculous.' She glanced at Jessie. 'I'm sorry about your husband. So many men dead already.'

'I haven't given up hope he might still be alive. He's only presumed dead.'

Lady Dorothea's eyes were soft. 'You could be right, Sister. There's nothing wrong with hoping.'

'What about you, Maxwell? Do you have anyone in the war?'

A shadow crossed Lady Dorothea's face. 'My brothers. Richard and Simon. Simon's a pilot with the Royal Flying Corps and Richard is with the Scots Guards.'

'Are they all right?' Jessie bit her lip. 'I mean – have you heard from them recently?'

'They write. Mostly to Mama and Papa. They were both alive ten days ago.'

Jessie hauled the tin bucket up a few more steps. 'You must worry.'

'I do, but not as much as Mama and Papa. You see, they've already lost one child – my eldest brother Charles – and are frightened they'll lose another.'

Jessie was glad that Lady Dorothea was now behind her and couldn't see her face. She was sure it must be blood-red.

'I'm the only daughter,' she continued. She gathered her skirts and came to join Jessie on the next step. 'Sometimes I wish I were a man. I'd like to be flying planes too.'

Despite the nerves fluttering in her stomach, Jessie had to smile at the thought of this elegant woman, with her slim fingers, flying a plane.

'When do you think we'll get our first patients?' Lady Dorothea asked.

'Dr Ludlow said we have to be inspected by the French authorities first. Then they'll decide whether we're ready to take patients.'

Lady Dorothea wiped a hand across her brow. 'I wish they'd hurry up. I suspect I shall be better at looking after the wounded than I am at scrubbing. At least, I hope so.' She rubbed her shoulders and grimaced. 'My body already feels worse than it ever did after a day's hunting. Much worse.'

They had reached the top step. Although Jessie didn't feel tired, they'd been hard at work since seven this morning and she knew Lady Dorothea couldn't have done much physical work before now. And supper wasn't for another three hours. 'Why don't we stop for a cup of tea?' she suggested. It was pointless, and possibly dangerous, to work these well-bred women too hard – at least until they became used to it.

Lady Dorothea dropped her cloth and rose stiffly to her feet. 'What an excellent idea,' she said. 'A cup of tea is exactly what we need.'

Jessie wrung her cloth out and picked up the pail.

'I'll wait in the sitting room, shall I?' Lady Dorothea said, smoothing down her crumpled skirt.

Jessie paused. It was clear Lady Dorothea expected her to make the tea. But here Jessie was senior to her. As an orderly it was her job to make it, not Jessie's. She knew if she didn't stamp her authority now, she would never regain it. She looked Lady Dorothea in the eye, hoping her nervousness wasn't showing, and raised an eyebrow.

Lady Dorothea stared back, puzzled. Then, to

Jessie's relief, she laughed. 'Oh, forgive me, Sister. It's I who should make the tea! Of course. I wasn't thinking.' She took the pail from Jessie's hand. 'I'll refill this while I'm doing it, shall I?'

Jessie wondered if Lady Dorothea had ever made a cup of tea in her life. If not, it was time she found out how. But right now the woman was exhausted.

'Tell you what, Maxwell,' Jessie said, resisting Lady Dorothea's attempts to tug the pail from her. 'I'll get rid of this while you make the tea. Then I'll join you in the kitchen for a cup before we get started again.'

When she grinned at her, Jessie had the not entirely welcome notion that she was going to like Lady Dorothea Maxwell.

Chapter 28

France, January 1915

Despite their optimism, it was after Christmas before the abbey was finally passed fit to receive casualties. The women had worked tirelessly, stopping only for Christmas Day. Although everyone had done their best to make it festive, hanging garlands of holly over the stair banisters, and cook had surprised them with a full Christmas dinner, Jessie had tried to pretend it was just another day. She was glad she hadn't had to face it alone in Edinburgh: it would have been unbearable without Tommy and Seamus.

At last the abbey looked like a hospital. Electricity had been installed, the X-ray room equipped – albeit with an old soup kettle for developing the films, coal stoves found for every ward, and every bed perfectly made with grey blankets and scarlet coverlets. They had also created an operating theatre upstairs and a receiving room close to the front entrance. Every instrument, trolley and shower room gleamed so brightly it was almost possible to use the surfaces as mirrors – which was as well because mirrors were rare and highly sought after.

However, nothing could have prepared them for the state of the wounded soldiers. Covered with mud, it was difficult to distinguish individual features or even the colour of their uniform trousers. Blood had soaked through their makeshift dressings turning them brown until it was impossible to know what was a wound and what was mud.

Each patient was taken into the receiving room where his uniform was gently removed and placed in a bag to be fumigated. Their soaking puttees had contracted and had to be cut off, revealing blue and red marbled feet or, worse, they were black with gangrene. The men didn't complain. Not once. Not even when the removal of their frozen puttees must have been agony. When the rancid smell of faeces filled the room, Jessie knew instantly that frostbite and dysentery – not shrapnel – were going to be their first challenge.

The men, mostly not quite twenty, had to be blanket-bathed before their wounds could be cleaned and bandaged. Her first patient, a young

Frenchman, cried with shame when he realised he'd soiled himself.

'Hush,' Jessie whispered, as she washed him, exposing only a small area of his body at a time. 'Everything will be fine. You mustn't worry.' She knew he probably couldn't understand what she was saying, but she hoped her tone would soothe him. One of the orderlies popped her head around the screens and blushed when she saw that Jessie was washing the young soldier's private parts. Jessie hid a smile. They would have to get used to the sight of naked men.

While the nurses saw to the patients, the orderlies were kept busy bringing cups of tea, cigarettes and urine bottles. In a break Jessie looked up to see Lady Dorothea holding a bedpan at arm's length, looking aghast but resolute.

The hours flew by, and by evening all the men were bathed and their wounds dressed. Those who could were sitting up in bed drinking beef tea or smoking while others, too weakened by dysentery, were being given sips of water by the orderlies. Jessie looked around with satisfaction. Her fellow sisters were walking the ward, checking the patients and setting the orderlies scrubbing again.

It was a beginning. Of course, at the moment, there were almost too many nurses for the number of patients, but everyone had coped well. No one had fainted, no one had run away and, most importantly, no one had died. She only hoped the same could be said for the other wards.

From then on they received patients in increasing numbers. And as Dr Ludlow had decided that they should fetch the patients with their own ambulances, five of the orderlies, including Lady Dorothea, had been appointed chauffeurs – or shovers, as they called themselves. The remaining orderlies were shared out between the wards, and as most of them were put on night duty, Jessie and her fellow sisters were kept busy.

Soon the unit was taking patients directly from Creil station and had to deal with men who had stomach-churning wounds, the like of which none of the staff had ever seen before. The chauffeurs brought back indignant reports of the conditions at the station, where wounded men had to lie on straw in a draughty building for as long as twenty-four hours before they were allocated to a hospital.

The wards were kept spotless. When they weren't seeing to patients they were scrubbing, but thankfully the orderlies were in charge of fumigating the lice-infested uniforms.

The doctors had decided that the best way to deal with frostbite, caused by the men having to stand knee-deep in mud for days at a time, was to swathe the feet in cotton wool and flannel. But this seemed to make things worse: more often than not, the feet turned black after a few days and had to be amputated.

Jessie was frustrated: they were going about it all wrong. One winter when the snow had come, she and Mam had been in the MacKinnons' kitchen when the father and sons had come down from the hills. Their feet were red lumps of frozen meat, but when they had gone to warm them over the open fire, Mam had stopped them. Instead she had massaged their feet with a solution of alcohol and herbs and they had got better. Jessie had done the same in the poorhouse more than once and it had been effective there too. But when she'd suggested to the matron that they try this, she had looked at her as if she was soft in the head.

'I tried it in my last position, Matron, and it seemed to help. Let me try it on my ward. Half of the men can have the usual treatment, and half can have mine. That way you can see for yourself that it works.' Jessie held her breath. It wasn't usual for a nurse to question a matron and certainly never the doctors.

Matron looked thoughtful. 'It's worth a try. It can't make the men's feet any worse. I'll give you four days. If there's no improvement, you'll have to go back to the old method. Are we clear?'

'Yes, Matron.'

It would be more work in an already busy day, but Jessie set the orderly on her ward to the task immediately and, to her delight and satisfaction – she had had no doubt her treatment was the right one but had wondered if the men's frostbite was too advanced – it had worked. Around a third of her patients went on to need amputations, but the rest got better. Soon all the nurses were using Jessie's method. It hadn't hurt her reputation either: some of the nurses had looked down on her before, but now they often asked her advice.

She was learning all the time. She became adept at cleaning pus-filled injuries, and had learned to harden her heart when she, with the other women, had to hold down a patient to clean his wounds. But often in the night she would be sleepless, thinking about the frightened eyes of men who were no more than boys and cried out for their mothers, wives and sisters.

She prayed that if Tommy were still alive someone was caring for him, too.

Chapter 29

The Gare du Nord was chaotic.

Isabel stepped onto the platform and stretched to ease the stiffness from her body. More than a week had passed since she'd left Edinburgh and the journey had melted into a blur. The train to London, the long wait at Victoria station, surrounded by pale-faced women saying goodbye to their loved ones, the nightmarish voyage across the Channel, which had taken three times as long as it should have done as the captain had woven his way to avoid the German U-boats, had been exhausting.

Even before the ship had sailed into port, and despite the thick mist that shrouded the coast, the marquees of the British Army had appeared on the coastline, like a vast, haphazard city. As she'd stood on deck with the other passengers and surveyed the scene with dismay, the true enormity of what she was doing had sunk in. But at last she was here. Her tiredness and trepidation vanished. In a few days she'd be with the unit in Serbia, playing her part.

Seeing there was no chance of a porter, she

picked up her bag. In addition to French and British soldiers, the station was mobbed with refugees, and women in every type of uniform it was possible to imagine.

'Isabel! Over here!' a familiar voice shouted over the din. All she could see above the heads on the crowded platform was a hand, but when the crowd parted briefly, there was Andrew.

She dropped her bag and ran towards him. Her brother enveloped her in a hug so tight she couldn't breathe. When he released her, she stood back to study him. He was wearing the dress uniform of an officer of the Royal Flying Corps and it suited him. She doubted there were many women who wouldn't find Andrew handsome in his peaked cap and polished leather boots, although she cared less for the pencil-thin moustache he now sported.

She hugged him again. 'How long do you have?' she asked.

'Four hours. Then I have to report back to base.'

'Only four hours? I thought you'd have a couple of days at least.'

'I'm sorry, sis. I hoped we'd have more time too, but they need every pilot they can get their hands on at the moment.' He grinned. 'It's so cheering to see you. How's Mama?'

'Desperately worried about you. She sent you a new scarf and some tea, and Mrs Walker insisted I bring you some socks she knitted.'

Andrew picked up her bag. 'Simon's waiting in the motor-car. He used his charm to requisition one for the weekend. He managed to get himself some time off too.' He looked down at her, his brown eyes anxious. 'You don't mind, do you? He doesn't have anyone else to spend his leave with since Dorothea doesn't get much time off to see him. Did you know she's with the Scottish Women's Hospitals too? She's working as an orderly in an abbey barely twenty miles from here.'

'Of course I don't mind Simon joining us.' Isabel squeezed Andrew's arm. She'd expected that Simon would be with him but she was still disappointed. She'd hoped for some time on her own with Andrew.

But the news that Dorothea was in France with the Scottish Women's Hospital was worse. The abbey Andrew referred to had to be Royaumont and that was where Jessie had been sent.

The day after Jessie had turned up in her kitchen Isabel had taken her to the headquarters of the Scottish Women's Hospital and introduced her to the recruiting officer. They'd been delighted to secure a nurse with experience, especially one with Isabel's personal recommendation. She'd received a short note a few days later from Jessie to say she'd been taken on and was going out with the first unit to Royaumont Abbey near Paris. Dear Lord, Lady Dorothea and Jessie would be working and living together. Did either woman know who the other was?

It wasn't difficult to spot Simon. Even with his hat on, his red hair was like a beacon. He vaulted over the door of the car and came to greet her with a smile. 'Andrew's been like a cat on hot bricks waiting for you to arrive.' Taking her bag from Andrew, he threw it into the back seat. 'You climb in beside me, Isabel. Andrew will manage in the back.'

Within minutes they were winding their way through streets crowded with soldiers and nurses of every description. There were the FANYs in their beautifully tailored uniforms, finished off with brightly coloured silk scarves, and VADs in their blue dresses and white aprons. In fact, every possible nursing uniform was represented. Among them, the French soldiers, some in scarlet breeches, some in blue, strutted with a casual arrogance.

Andrew nodded in their direction. 'Someone should tell them that their red breeches make them into targets for the Germans. If we can spot them easily from our planes, the Huns must be able to see them from miles away too.'

Isabel had to hold onto her hat with one hand and the door with the other to stop herself being flung around like a sack of peat as Simon careered past the Arc de Triomphe.

'I tried to book you into the Hôtel Claridge,' Simon said, 'but it's being used as a hospital by the Women's Hospital Corps. All the rest of the hotels – even the Ritz, would you believe? – have been requisitioned for army use. Had to use my father's name to get you a room in a small hotel off the Champs-Élysées. Not quite the ticket, I know, but the best I could do in the circumstances.'

'Using his papa's influence *and* a pile of money,' Andrew corrected, with a smile. 'There's practically not a bed to be found anywhere in Paris, Is.'

'You must let me pay for my room,' Isabel protested. The thought of being beholden to the Maxwells horrified her.

Simon shook his head. 'Let a lady pay for herself? Not as long as I live and breathe.'

A liveried doorman came to take their bags as soon as they pulled up outside the hotel, and Simon tossed him the keys to the motor-car.

With Simon on one side and Andrew on the other, Isabel ran up the steps into the cool, calm interior of the hotel.

'What do you say to a spot of lunch, Is?' Andrew asked.

'I say yes, but I have to freshen up first. I'm covered with dust.'

'Go on, then, but don't be long. Simon and I will wait for you in the foyer.'

By the time she returned, they were holding drinks. She stood for a moment, watching them as they chinked together their gasses of brandy. They looked frozen in time, two confident young men who had the rest of their lives in front of them. Isabel swallowed the lump in her throat and pasted on a smile. She had only a few hours with Andrew and she was determined not to waste a precious moment in worrying about the future. She did, however, want to get him alone so she could talk to him about Charles – but how?

Time rushed past as they chatted over lunch, and for short periods Isabel was able to forget that Simon was Charles's brother and that there was a war on.

They were drinking coffee when Simon saw someone he recognised across the street and, with a quick 'Would you excuse me for a moment?' he left them alone.

'Are you truly all right?' Isabel asked Andrew.

He raised an eyebrow and smiled, but not before Isabel saw something in his eyes that made her shiver. 'Don't worry about me.' He looked off into the distance. 'We don't do much, really. Fly over the enemy lines and report back on their position, mainly. To be honest, the life of an airman is luxury compared to the PBI.'

'The PBI?'

'The Poor Bloody Infantry. At least when we tootle home at the end of a day's flying it's to a warm bed and decent food.' He leaned forward. 'It's rum up there in the clouds. One feels like the king of the castle – hardly aware that there's a war on unless some Hun takes a potshot at us.'

'They shoot at you? Oh, Andrew.'

'Don't worry, their aim is as bad as ours.' He frowned. 'This war isn't what any of us expected. But I doubt Papa, if he were still alive, would be happy to know you're here. I can't imagine what George was thinking about, letting you come.'

'George didn't *let* me come, Andrew. If he'd had his way, I'd be safe at home in Heriot Row doing embroidery or at most rolling bandages. Fortunately, I still had some money from what Papa left me. Not much, but enough to pay my way here. I couldn't not come. Don't you see? There'll never be another chance like this for women doctors.'

'You think you've seen it all, my dear sister, but...' Andrew paused. 'Look, never mind about that. As you say, you're here and I can tell you're determined to stay.' He took her hand. 'Just promise me you'll stay safe and away from the fighting.'

'Oh, Andrew, that's where we're going to be. As close to the front line as possible. It's where we're needed most.'

Andrew sighed and released her hand. 'Just be careful, Is.'

Isabel glanced to where Simon was talking animatedly to a woman in FANY uniform. She had to speak to Andrew about Charles now, before Simon returned.

'Andrew, do you remember the evening when you first brought Simon and the baron to dinner at Heriot Row?'

'Yes. What of it?' His beautiful face darkened. 'I wonder where Maximilian is. This damned war makes enemies of us all.'

Isabel started. 'Have you seen him?'

'No. And if I did, I'd probably have to blow his head off.'

'You wouldn't!'

'Most likely he'd blow mine off too, if he wasn't a doctor. Let's hope we don't meet again until this is over.' He raised his cup to his lips and sipped. 'Let's not talk of that. What were you saying about Maximilian and the night I introduced him? Did you come to care for him very much?'

Isabel was surprised. Andrew had never mentioned Maximilian's name in relation to hers before.

'I know Mama hoped you would marry,' Andrew continued. 'I suspect she thought that by marrying him you would restore the family's rank by becoming a baroness. But I'm glad it came to

303

naught. If you'd married him, you'd be the enemy.'

'There was no hope of us marrying,' Isabel said. 'Once, I might have thought...' she lowered her eyes, '...but in the end, he and I were not suited.'

'He didn't mislead you? Because if he did...'

'No, he only ever treated me with courtesy. Maximilian is an honourable man. You were not mistaken in your friendship with him.'

Andrew looked at her quizzically, but before he could probe further Isabel pressed on. 'Andrew, there's something...' She had to tell him what Charles had tried to do to her, even if he despised her for saying nothing before – but he was distracted, looking over her shoulder. She turned to see that Simon had finished talking to his companion and was walking back to them.

'What is it, Isabel?' But Andrew wasn't really listening. He stood up and thumped Simon on the back. 'Who was that beauty, my friend? Couldn't you have introduced us? Or did you want to keep her all to yourself?'

'That beauty happened to be Lady Millicent, one of Dorothea's friends,' Simon said, taking his seat. He leaned back and hooked his arms behind his head. 'They travelled over together, but went their separate ways after that.'

As Simon ordered more coffee, it seemed her opportunity to tell him about Charles had gone. Perhaps it was for the best. Why worry Andrew when soon he'd be going back into battle? It wouldn't be fair.

All too soon it was time for the men to return to their base. Her heart ached. This might be the last time she saw her brother.

When they were outside the hotel, Andrew ran into a fellow officer, leaving her alone with Simon.

'Look after him, won't you?' she whispered.

Simon held her gaze. 'I'd trade my life if it meant saving his.' He glanced at Andrew, who was giving the doorman some money, and the adoration in his eyes made her reel.

So that was how it was. She'd heard about men like him. People whispered about them in drawing rooms, but no one ever acknowledged it aloud.

'Does he know how you feel?' she asked, trying to keep the shock from her face.

'No. And he must never find out.' Simon gripped her wrist so tightly she almost cried out. 'Promise me, Isabel, that you'll never breathe a word. If he guesses and the rest of the squadron comes to suspect... For God's sake, promise me you won't tell.' He looked at her with desperate eyes. Andrew was walking back to them. 'I shouldn't have said anything. Maybe it was the brandy – or because you're his sister and love him too. Perhaps it's because I don't know how long I'll survive this bloody awful war–'

He stopped as Andrew joined them. There was only time for Isabel to give Simon a slight nod. Of course she wouldn't betray his secret: she was too used to keeping one of her own.

A flurry of kisses and hugs, a final toot of the horn, and they were gone.

Chapter 30

The following day, after Isabel had breakfasted on pastries and French coffee, she decided to explore Paris. She hadn't been to the French capital before and was eager to see a little of it before she had to leave. Her train to Rimini wasn't until six that evening. From there she would take a boat to Salonika and another train north to Kragujevatz where she was to join the unit.

She strolled along the Champs Élysées towards the Arc de Triomphe. The wide boulevards, trimmed with elegant apartment buildings, were swarming with carriages and street vendors hawking their wares. People ambled down the busy streets, stopping to admire the shop displays as if they didn't have a care in the world. From a glance in the café windows, many still found time to enjoy coffee or lunch. Apart from the sandbags protecting homes and businesses, it was hard to imagine that, only weeks earlier, the German Army had been on the city's doorstep, causing the French government to decamp south.

The bustling atmosphere did nothing to shake the darkness that had descended on her. She wished she was working. Then there would be no time to think, no time to worry about whether she would ever see her brother again, whether Maximilian still thought of her – or if he was even still alive.

As for Simon, how perverse life was. That her brother's best friend, who clearly loved him more than a friend should, was the brother of the man who had attacked her.

She paused as a motor ambulance turned in front of her. Wasn't the rue François where the Hôtel Claridge was? If so, that was where the Women's Hospital Corps – a unit also staffed wholly by women – was setting up a hospital.

After a moment's hesitation, she decided to go and see for herself. It was possible she would know one of the doctors there, and it would be interesting to find out how they were coping. When she saw two ambulances and men in civilian clothes taking stretchers into a building, she knew she had found the right place.

As she drew closer, a man appeared outside the front door and pulled a silver case from his jacket. He propped a leg against the wall, tapped a cigarette on his hand and bent his head to light it.

There was something disturbingly familiar about the curly dark hair. When he lifted his head to blow smoke into the freezing air, she knew she hadn't been mistaken. It was Archie. Here? In Paris?

Her heart lurched. She wasn't ready to see him – at the very least she needed a few moments to collect herself – but before she could move his gaze fastened on her.

'Isabel?' His wide mouth stretched in a smile. 'Isabel MacKenzie?' He threw his half-smoked cigarette on the ground and strode towards her. 'So it *is* you! I thought for a moment that I was dreaming.'

He was different in a way she couldn't put her finger on. Perhaps it was the stubble that darkened his cheeks or the lines on his face that hadn't been there before, but he seemed older than his years. He was broader too, his body more muscular than she remembered, and the leather jacket with the red-on-white insignia of the Red Cross seemed almost too tight for his shoulders.

He was looking at her as if he still couldn't believe it was her. 'You've cut your hair,' he said finally. 'It suits you.'

Despite her agitation, his words made her smile. After all this time, that was the best he could do. 'Thank you. I find it easier to manage when I'm working.'

'Working?'

'I'm Dr MacKenzie now.' She couldn't keep the pride from her voice.

'Dr MacKenzie, eh?' He raised an eyebrow and studied her with those intense, blue eyes. 'I knew you'd do it. You were always determined to get what you wanted.'

She flushed as the memory of the last time they'd met spooled before her mind's eye, like a reel of a moving picture. Their kiss, the argument – then, sickeningly, the incident with Charles.

'But, Archie, what are you doing here?'

He frowned as if her words hadn't been what he'd expected – or hoped for.

'I mean...' she tried to compose herself, '...in Paris! Of all places!'

'I'm a driver for the American Hospital in Neuilly. We've been transferring patients from our hospital to here. What about you?'

They were talking as if they were strangers.

'I came to meet my brother, Andrew. He's with the Royal Flying Corps. I had lunch with him yesterday. I hoped to spend today with him, too, but he was called back to his squadron.'

God – Simon! Did Archie know he was here? Did he even know that the Glendales and the police were looking for him?

'You came to Paris to see your brother?' Archie asked, looking puzzled.

'I'm on my way to Serbia. I'm to join a field hospital there.' A thought struck her. Did Jessie know her brother was here? She'd be thrilled to find him again. 'Archie, I saw Jessie recently in Edinburgh. She's here in France too.'

'You saw Jessie?' Archie's face lit up. 'She's in France? Is she well?'

Isabel laughed. 'One question at a time. She's a nurse. She's working with the Scottish Women's Hospital, too, in a unit about twenty miles north from here.'

'So she became a nurse, after all! Good for her – look, let's find somewhere to sit. I'd suggest a café but I'm on duty.' When she hesitated, he added, 'Please? I want to know about Jessie. I want to know everything.'

Isabel followed him into a high-ceilinged marble hall brightly lit by crystal chandeliers. She stepped aside to allow two stretcher-bearers carrying a wounded soldier to pass. Despite the heavy bandages on both of his arms the injured man was smoking a cigarette and grinned cheekily at Isabel, calling something in French that she didn't catch but that made the men carrying him laugh. As

Archie led her to a couple of ornately carved chairs out of the way of the scurrying nurses, she thought frantically about what she would say to him.

'How did you come to be working with an American unit?' she asked, when they were seated.

'I was in Paris on business when war was declared. I'm American now, so when I heard they had set up a unit in Neuilly and were looking for ambulance drivers, I volunteered. But never mind all that just now. Tell me about Jessie.'

'You haven't heard from her?'

He closed his eyes briefly. 'Not for years.'

Isabel bit her lip. 'She's not had it easy, Archie. She married and had a little boy – Seamus – but he died. And that's not all. Her husband was one of the first to join up. He's missing in action, presumed dead. I am so sorry to have to tell you this.'

He smacked a fist into his hand making her jump. '*A Thighearna!* I should have been there to look out for her!'

Isabel stretched out a hand towards him, her fingers not quite reaching his. 'Why *did* you leave? Did it have anything to do with Charles Maxwell?'

She held her breath as he studied her with guarded eyes. 'Why do you ask me that?'

'Because I heard that the police wanted to question you. He disappeared and Father thinks you had something to do with it.' When he stayed silent she continued. 'That day, the day we parted, did you see him?' If he denied it, she would know she couldn't trust anything he said.

'I did. He saw us kissing. He said... Never mind

310

what he said. I pulled him from his horse and punched him.' So it had been Archie who had given Charles the bruise. 'The man was a coward. He wouldn't fight with me so I let him go.'

Her breath came out as a long sigh. So Archie had fought with Charles, but she believed him when he said he'd let him go. However, his explanation didn't altogether make sense. Why would Archie leave just because someone had seen him fight with Charles?

'You could have told the truth. You were only defending yourself.'

He laughed harshly. 'Justice in your world is not the same as it is in mine. The word of a crofter doesn't mean much against the word of an earl's son. If Lord Maxwell had told the policemen I'd hit him, they would have arrested me and I wasn't about to let that happen.' He shrugged. 'I always wanted to go to America. I just went a little sooner than I'd planned.'

She studied him intently. She had the feeling he was keeping something back. 'Is that truly the only reason you went? Did you know that Charles hasn't been seen since that day?'

'No.'

'They think ... they think he must be dead and that you had something to do with it.'

His eyes never wavered from hers. 'What do you think?'

Should she tell him about Charles's attack? Every fibre of her being rebelled against it, but she'd sworn to get to the truth.

'The day we met...' her face burned as she thought of their parting, '...after I left you,

311

Charles, he...' She swallowed. 'It was horrible.'

'Go on,' Archie prompted.

'He followed me. He tried to...'

Archie reached for her hands and she welcomed the warmth of his fingers. 'Did he hurt you?'

'I managed to get away from him before he could. I think he meant to...' She hurried on before she lost her courage. 'It was as well he was drunk – otherwise...' She pulled her hands from Archie's grasp and twisted her fingers together to stop them trembling. 'I didn't know he went missing that day until years later, and that was when I discovered they were looking for you ... and that you had left Skye. Then I met Jessie. She asked me if I'd seen you fighting with Charles.' She sucked in a steadying breath. 'I thought about it later. When I saw Charles he had been fighting, that much was clear, so then I wondered...' Archie's eyes hadn't left her face. She swallowed and she forced herself to continue, '...if you'd seen him attack me and if...' She tailed off.

'What did you wonder?' His voice was soft but there was a thread of steel in his tone. Then she saw realisation dawn in his blue eyes. 'You think *I* might have killed him?' He laughed harshly. 'My God, Isabel. You of all people...'

She could tell by the incredulity in his face that he was telling the truth and felt lighter than she had for months. Whatever had happened to Charles, Archie had had nothing to do with it and therefore neither had she. Now she was with Archie again, her fears that he'd harmed Charles because of her seemed absurd and she was mortified.

'Of course not,' she lied. 'He was drunk. He was probably thrown from his horse. Perhaps he fell into the sea. Maybe he ran away. Perhaps he was ashamed – or frightened I would tell someone.'

'In one respect you're right,' Archie said. 'If I had come across him when he had his hands on you, I probably would have killed him. Men like him don't deserve to live.'

Nevertheless, the police and the earl were still looking for Archie. He wouldn't find them so easy to convince. 'But don't you care that, if they find you, they'll question you?'

'They won't find me.' He reached across and touched her hand. 'Forget about his lordship, Isabel. Leave the past where it belongs. Isn't there more to worry about now, with this damned war?'

He was right. It was time to put the past behind her.

'Now I've answered your questions, I want to know more about Jessie.'

Isabel was instantly ashamed. She'd been so obsessed with her need to know about Charles that she hadn't stopped to think about Archie's need to hear about his sister.

At that moment, an older man came strolling towards them. He tipped his hat to Isabel. 'Excuse me, ma'am.' His voice sounded strange, as if each syllable was being drawn out. 'Scotty, you're needed to go up the line.'

Reluctantly Archie got to his feet. 'I have to go. Can we meet tomorrow? There's so much I want to ask you.'

Isabel shook her head. 'My train leaves at six this evening.'

'Dammit.' He hesitated. 'Why don't you come with me now? You can help with the wounded I bring back. God knows they could do with someone to look after them. And you can tell me about Jessie on the way.'

What he was suggesting was crazy. She had no experience of dealing with casualties. She didn't have her medical bag. Her heart banged against her ribs. But to treat wounded men was why she'd come and Archie deserved to hear everything she knew about Jessie.

He leaned his head to the side and grinned. 'Unless you're frightened?'

Immediately she was transported back to the day on Skye when she'd first met him and he'd dared her to follow him over the cliff. The same heady excitement surged through her and she smiled back. 'What are we waiting for?'

As they bumped their way up the road the explosions grew closer and Archie turned to her. 'Don't worry, we won't get too near the fighting, only as far as the casualty clearing station. But stay close to me.'

To her surprise, she felt calm and ready for anything.

Archie had to pull over every now and then to let a convoy of vehicles with red crosses emblazoned on the side stream past.

'We pick up the stretchers they have for us. I can take four. Most will have temporary dressings – some will have had emergency operations. My job is to get them to the American Hospital as quickly as possible.' He had to raise his voice to be heard

314

above the noise of cannon. 'That's our side fighting back.'

It was hard to believe that Paris was only a short distance away.

'What happened to Jessie's baby?' Archie asked.

'Diphtheria.'

'Poor lass. If I get time off I'm going to see her.'

'She'd like that.'

Archie was concentrating on steering the ungainly vehicle over the icy road. Isabel studied him. In the years since she'd seen him, he'd changed. He'd always been self-assured but now there was an ease about him that hadn't been there before.

'Tell me about America,' she said.

'It's a great country. A man can make of himself what he will. I started with nothing, but now I own land and am planning to grow grapes.' She heard the pride in his voice. 'That's what I was enquiring about in Paris. But when the war broke out I knew nothing was more important. I've a good partner. He'll keep things ticking over until I get back.'

Isabel grabbed the edge of her seat as they hit a pothole and the lorry bounced.

Archie slid a look at her. 'And you, Isabel? Are you glad to be a doctor?'

'You knew I could never do anything else.'

'So you kept insisting,' he said drily.

A short while later they came to a field dotted with canvas tents. Men, with armbands bearing a red cross, scurried around carrying stretchers, laying them on the ground, then hurrying away. A doctor, identifiable by the white coat he wore

315

over his officer's uniform, bent to examine each patient and would either call someone over to take the casualty inside or make a note on a piece of cardboard before tying it to the injured soldier's lapel. Occasionally he would look at a man and shake his head. Then someone would lift the body from the stretcher and add it to a row of sheet-covered corpses.

Archie yanked on the handbrake and leaped out. 'Wait in the back, Isabel. I'll fetch whoever they have for me. Try to keep them alive until we get them to hospital.'

He ran to a canvas tent and spoke to a doctor. Isabel's heart was thumping so hard she felt nauseous. She told herself that the adrenalin flowing through her veins would sharpen her senses. Haemorrhages. That was what she would be dealing with. As Archie had said, the casualty clearing stations patched the men up as best they could for transfer to hospital. She would have to keep an eye on the wounds. Watch for sudden bleeding. Apply pressure if needed.

Already her first patient, a lad of no more than eighteen with a bandaged right thigh, was being loaded into the back. Isabel felt his pulse. It was a bit quick but otherwise steady. The dressing was still almost white, so the bleeding was under control for now.

The next injured man had a bandage covering the whole of his face apart from a small gap around his nose and mouth to let him breathe. More bandages shrouded his torso and upper arms. He was badly burned and, her heart sinking, Isabel knew his chances were almost non-existent.

She bent over him. 'I'm a doctor,' she said. 'Hold on until we get you to hospital. You'll be fine then.' She repeated her words in French. She had no idea whether he could hear her, but if Andrew was badly wounded, she'd want someone to offer him reassurance – even an empty promise.

The third casualty made her stomach clench. His right leg was missing below the knee. The stump had been bandaged but bright red blood had soaked through and his pulse was rapid and weak. He needed a solution of saline, even though it was unlikely to make much difference.

Her last patient climbed into the back of the truck unaided. He smiled tiredly through his mud-spattered face. 'Are you the nurse?' he asked in French. Isabel didn't bother to correct him. As he was relatively uninjured she needed his help.

'Can you watch this soldier here for me?' she replied, also in French, pointing to the soldier with the thigh wound. 'If blood starts soaking his bandage, let me know.'

Archie came around to the back. 'Are you going to be all right?'

'I'll be fine. Just get us to the hospital as fast as you can. Try not to bounce too much.'

Archie closed the tailgate, and a few moments later the lorry lurched away.

On the way back, Isabel kept a close eye on her patients, although in the rear of the lorry, with no equipment to speak of, there was little she could do. The boy with the burns moaned softly and she whispered words of encouragement.

Finally, the nightmare journey was over and hands were reaching out to unload the casualties.

A soldier lifted Isabel down and she hurried along beside the stretcher of the boy with the missing leg.

As they got to the theatre, she was stopped by a male orderly. 'I'm sorry, Miss, but you can't go in there.'

'She's a doctor,' Archie protested.

The man raised his eyebrows. 'No women, sir, except our nurses.'

Isabel suppressed a scream of frustration. She wanted to see her patient through his treatment, but as the stretcher was wheeled away and the doors closed behind him, she knew arguing would only waste precious time in getting the boy to the operating table.

She was about to turn away when a young surgeon in a white gown and hat opened the door. 'You may watch if you wish, Doctor,' he said. 'Just keep out of the way.'

Inside, Isabel took a gown from the outstretched hands of an American Red Cross nurse and slipped it on.

'My sister's a doctor,' the surgeon said. 'She'd kill me if I tried to keep you out.'

Another nurse was hanging a bottle on a stand next to the patient. It looked like blood.

'You're giving him blood?' Isabel asked, surprised. As far as she knew, early attempts to replace lost blood with some from a donor had almost invariably ended in death when the donor's blood had coagulated in the patient's veins, causing a large clot or thrombosis.

'It's his only chance. One of our doctors here has established a technique with which we can

318

prevent the blood from clotting by mixing the donor's blood with a solution of sodium citrate. We've started to use it on moribund patients in casualty clearing stations. It doesn't always work, but this fellow has lost too much blood to survive without it so I'm going to take the chance.'

Isabel was intrigued. If he was right, the methods they were using could have far-reaching consequences. The *Lancet* had reported that most wounded soldiers died from blood loss.

'We'll give him one transfusion now and another after the operation,' the surgeon continued, as another stretcher was brought in with a man who was conscious. 'This man has the same blood group and has agreed to be our donor.'

Fascinated, Isabel watched as the doctor instructed the donor to grasp a rolled-up bandage and keep pumping his fist. Then he made an incision in the vein, inserted a cannula and the patient's blood flowed into a flask. Powder had been added to the flask, which was then shaken, and the blood was given to the injured patient in the same way saline was normally provided.

The surgeon watched for a few moments as it trickled into his patient. When he was satisfied, he indicated to the anaesthetist to put the patient under and began to operate.

After the patient's amputated stump had been cleaned, the dead tissue excised and re-bandaged, he was given more blood.

'Now it's in the hands of the gods,' the surgeon said, pulling off his gloves. 'We wait and see. But at least he has a chance.' He handed her a bottle. 'Take some citrate solution – you never know when you might need it.'

Now the excitement was over, Isabel wanted nothing more than to lie down and sleep, even on one of the hard benches. But she had to get back to the hotel. Her dress was stained with the blood of the wounded soldiers and her hair was full of dust. She desperately needed a bath, and she'd have to hurry if she wasn't going to miss her train, which was due to leave in a couple of hours.

As she stepped out into the dark winter evening she met Archie, who was bringing another stretcher. His face was dark with fatigue but, when he saw her, his expression brightened.

He passed his end of the stretcher to an orderly who was waiting by the door. 'When will I see you again?' he asked. He stepped aside to allow more stretcher-bearers to pass.

'I don't know... I can't see how it would be possible.'

They looked at each other for a long moment.

'Will you write to me?' He reached into his pocket for a piece of paper and a pencil. He scribbled something and handed it to her. 'If ever you need me, you know where to find me.' His eyes roamed her face as if he were trying to memorise every inch.

'I'll try.' She swallowed hard. For some reason she wanted to cry. 'What about Jessie? Will you see her?'

'I have twenty-four hours off next week. I'll go then.'

'Archie, remember Lady Dorothea Maxwell is there. Perhaps I could write to Jessie with your address and she could come to you?'

'I won't let anything stop me seeing my sister.'

They stood in silence for a few moments.

'Look after yourself, old friend,' Isabel said, then stepped out into the frosty night.

Chapter 31

As the reputation of the hospital at the abbey grew, the number and severity of the casualties increased. Jessie was learning how to keep an eye on several men at once, even though most were seriously ill following operations to remove mangled and frostbitten limbs that were past saving.

The nurses were too busy to do anything except fly from patient to patient, and they came more and more to rely on the orderlies, who handled the horribly injured men with the same equanimity they must once have shown when dealing with awkward social occasions. When the orderlies weren't helping bathe the patients, they gave the men bottles to urinate in, helped them eat and drink, and write letters home to their loved ones.

But mostly the *poilus*, the common French soldiers, turned to Jessie. Even though she could speak barely a word of French, it was as if they recognised that she understood them and their lives in a way the aristocratic nurses and orderlies never could. Recently British soldiers had been arriving too and Jessie searched every mud-encrusted face for Tommy. Once the soldiers had been treated, she would ask if they'd come across the Seaforth Highlanders. So far, the answer had always been 'No.'

Sometimes, after she'd finished for the day, she would go into the cloisters and sit for a while. When she looked up at the clear night sky sprinkled with stars, with the fountain burbling in front of her, she could almost believe she was back on Skye.

Tonight the silence was broken by a loud sniff and a strangled sob coming from one of the stone benches in the shadows. Jessie moved quietly to see who was crying.

It was Evans. The only friendly conversation Jessie had had on the journey to the abbey had been with this orderly – a long-limbed woman, who was as tall as a man and had what Mam would have described as an unfortunate face. She had sat down next to Jessie, brought out her Bible and asked if Jessie would pray with her. Afterwards Elizabeth Evans had confided that she was engaged and had been planning to go out to Africa to work as a missionary with her future husband when war had been declared. Their plans would now have to wait until it was all over.

Now Evans was holding her Bible and whispering to herself, as tears ran down her cheeks. Thinking she was praying, and therefore entitled to her privacy, Jessie was about to creep away when Evans gave another gulping sob.

She couldn't leave her. Perhaps she had had bad news from home.

Jessie moved to the bench and sat down beside the gangly orderly. She waited for her to stop crying before she spoke. 'What is it, Elizabeth? Is there anything I can do?'

Evans dabbed her eyes with a handkerchief and sniffed loudly. 'Oh, don't mind me, Sister. I'm just being silly. I'll be fine in a minute.'

Jessie was unsure of what to do. She still didn't want to leave her, not without finding out more.

'News from home? Your fiancé?'

Evans shook her head. 'Everyone is well.'

'It's been a difficult few weeks for us all,' Jessie said, 'getting used to being here.' The truth was she hadn't found it hard, but Evans had come from a safe, warm, privileged home.

'It's not that. I can put up with anything as long as I'm doing the Lord's work, but does Sister Lafferty have to make it so hard? She's always telling me to do this and do that, and before I'm even halfway through the first task, she's given me another. Then she complains that I haven't finished anything she's asked of me. I'm useless. Maybe the unit would be better off without me. I'm slow. I know it.'

Jessie hid a sigh. Sister Lafferty was from the London Hospital and fancied herself above all the other nurses, but Jessie had seen her work and suspected her arrogance concealed a fear that she didn't know quite as much as she liked the others to think she did.

'You're bound to be slow at first. Goodness knows, all you orderlies are doing a grand job.'

The orderly sniffed again. 'Do you really think so?'

'I'm sure of it. You all work hard without a word of complaint.' Well, not too much complaining: some were more willing than others.

Evans smiled shakily. 'I wish I was on your ward. Your orderlies say that you're the best out of all the sisters to work with. You never lose your temper and you're always willing to show them what to do instead of barking at them.'

Jessie was delighted. She had tried hard to remember that the orderlies were mostly new to the job. Some had had experience as VADs before the war, but none had dealt with injured men. Even when she wanted to scream with impatience, she bit her tongue and instead showed them how she wanted things to be done. It had paid off. Soon her orderlies were adept at changing dressings and some were even able to clean wounds under supervision.

'I admire you all,' she said honestly. 'I was brought up to do physically hard work so it's nothing to me. When I worked in the infirmary at the workhouse I started under a sister who always found fault with whatever I did. It used to make me so nervous that I'm sure I made mistakes I wouldn't have done if she'd left me alone. I swore then that when I became a sister I would treat my staff well. Although,' she warned, 'I've never been able to tolerate slackers. But you're not a slacker, are you, Evans?'

'I don't think so. I work as hard as I can. I'm so tired all the time. That's why I keep falling asleep.'

'Dry your eyes now,' Jessie said, 'and go to bed. You'll see. It'll look better in the morning.'

They had been accepting patients for a month, and Jessie was just finishing a dressing on a young soldier with shrapnel wounds to his face when

Dorothea Maxwell appeared at her elbow.

Jessie had seen little of her over the last weeks. The chauffeurs were all housed in rooms above the stables, and as their hours were different from others', they tended to keep themselves to themselves, sharing a small dining room and eating at different times.

'There's someone outside who wants to see you. He wouldn't say who he was.'

Jessie's heart raced. Could it be Tommy? Had she been right all along and he was still alive? Had he come to find her?

But it seemed that Maxwell knew what she was thinking. She squeezed Jessie's shoulder. 'He's not a soldier, Sister. I'm sorry.'

The disappointment made Jessie's throat tighten.

'All he would say was that he was with the American Hospital near Neuilly,' Lady Dorothea continued, 'and that he needed to see you.'

An American unit? Could this man have news of Archie? Next to finding out that Tommy wasn't dead, it was what she longed for most.

'Will you cover for me?' she whispered. 'I'm not supposed to be off duty for another hour.'

'Just go. If Matron comes looking for you, I'll tell her you're counting linen or something.'

Jessie quickly finished what she was doing and tucked her patient in. Then she wrapped her cloak around her. Over the last few weeks the snow had thawed but it was still bitterly cold outside.

She ran down the stairs and into the courtyard where visitors were asked to wait. A tall figure was pacing up and down the cloisters with his back to her. At first she wasn't sure but when he turned her heart stopped.

'Archie?' she whispered. Then, as a glow like a burst of sunshine spread through her, she launched herself towards him. 'Archie! Is it really you?'

He opened his arms and she went into them. 'Hello, Jessie.' His voice was different, with a slight, unfamiliar drawl.

When he let her go, she led him to one of the stone benches and they sat down. 'What are you doing here?' He wasn't in uniform so he couldn't be with the army.

'I was in Paris on business when the war broke out. I decided to stay and do my bit by driving ambulances for the American Hospital.'

Paris on business? There was so much she wanted to know that she couldn't think where to begin. 'How did you find me? I didn't have an address for you so I couldn't tell you where I was going. How is America? Are you all right? Tell me everything!'

He laughed. 'Whoa. Slow down. I'll tell you everything. I just want to look at you for a moment.' He held her at arm's length and studied her. 'My little sister. All grown-up.' He grinned again. 'Look at us! Who would ever have thought we'd both be looking after the injured – not,' he added quickly, 'that I do much except patch them up and drive them to the nearest doctor.'

'But how did you know I was here?'

'I met Isabel in Paris and she told me.'

Jessie tried to ignore a stab of envy. Had he

been in touch with Isabel all these years and not her? His own sister?

Now that the first flush of pleasure of seeing him alive and well was over, the anger that had been burning inside since he'd left flared again. 'Why didn't you write to me when you got to America? I couldn't write to you. Not even when...' She bit her lip. Although she was furious with him, he didn't deserve to be told about Mam's death before she could prepare him. 'Archie, Mam got sick and I couldn't even let you know.'

Dread flickered in his eyes. 'If I'd known she was ill, I would have tried to come back to see her. How is she?'

'Oh, Archie. She's gone. She died five years ago.'

He sucked in a breath. 'Mam dead? Oh, no, Jessie.'

Jessie laid her hand on his and squeezed. 'She'd been ill for a long time. She knew months before you left but wouldn't let me tell you. She didn't want anything to stop you going.'

'I wish I'd known.'

'Would it have made a difference?'

'Did you get the money I sent you?' Archie asked after a pause.

'Oh, aye, I did.' Her anger rose again. He hadn't answered her question. 'But you never put a return address. Did you forget about us so easily or...' She hesitated. They couldn't talk here. Not where they could be overheard. Although they were talking in Gaelic, it was possible someone would understand what they were saying. She stood up. 'Let's walk. We can talk more freely in the gardens.'

As soon as they were out of earshot, she turned

to him. 'I have to ask. Did your leaving have any-thing to do with Lord Maxwell's disappearance?'

Archie shook his head. 'What is it with you women? When I saw Isabel she asked me the same thing. God, Jessie, I'm your brother. How can you ask me that?'

Isabel? Why would she be asking? Because Jessie had asked *her*. That must mean she knew as little as Jessie did about what happened that day. Jessie shook her head in frustration. Had she doubted her brother all these years for nothing? 'I ask because he went missing the day you left. His horse returned home without him. At first everyone thought he'd fallen and the earl had everyone out looking for him, but they couldn't find his body – or any trace of him.'

'Isabel told me. But why do you ask if I had anything to do with it?'

'Because a policeman came looking for you a day or two after you'd left, Archie. It seems Lachie McPhee told some garbled story about seeing you pull him off his horse. It turned out he was only repeating what Flora had told him, and apparently she denied ever saying such a thing.'

'There you are, then.'

'But the policeman didn't like it when Mam told him you'd gone away. She didn't tell him you'd gone to America, Archie. She made up some story about an argument and you going off to Glasgow in a temper. She lied, and Mam would never lie for no reason. She was too scared of going to Hell.'

The dark look on Archie's face deepened. 'Mam lied for me?'

'She wouldn't tell me why. The night you left,

328

your knuckles were bleeding and you had a mark on your face, so I knew you must have fought with his lordship, whatever Flora did or didn't say. Then you never sent an address. Is it any wonder I worried you'd had something to do with his disappearance?'

Archie shoved his hands into his pockets. 'I did hit him. He said something...' He shook his head. 'Never mind that. I would have thrashed him, but he got back on his horse and rode off.'

Jessie wanted to believe him, but there was something in the way he was avoiding her eyes that made her uneasy.

'The night I left, Flora McPhee came to the house,' Archie went on. 'She'd been on Galtrigill and had seen me pulling the man from his horse. She was glad someone had stood up to him. She hated him for refusing to acknowledge the baby she'd had by him, but she came to tell me she'd told her father she'd seen us fighting. As soon as Lachie heard that Maxwell's horse had returned without him, he said he was going to tell the earl what she'd told me. Flora knew the police would take a dim view of my fight with Lord Maxwell even if he turned up safe and sound. And if they discovered his body – even if his horse had thrown him – she guessed I'd get the blame of it. So she came to warn me.'

That made sense. Flora had always had a soft spot for Archie, while Lachie McPhee hated him and Dad.

'I used the ticket of John McPherson's brother who died, and kept his name,' Archie continued. 'His first name was the same as Dad's. I'm

Calum McPherson now, although the men in the unit call me Scotty.'

'And why didn't you write?'

'I never trusted Effie in the post office not to read my letters – everyone knows she can't let one be delivered without having a look first. That's why I never put a return address.'

Although what he was saying made sense, intuition told her that he wasn't telling her the whole truth. If he had had nothing to do with Lord Maxwell's disappearance, there was still something he wasn't telling her.

'I wondered if you might have left because of Isabel,' she said.

'Why would you think that?' he asked sharply.

'Because she told me you'd confessed your love to her and she'd refused you.'

Archie frowned. 'It seems to me that you and Isabel have too much to say to one another.'

Jessie blushed. She hoped Archie would never find out exactly what she had said to the doctor. She was now ashamed of her outburst.

'But, Jessie, let's not talk about them any more. Let's talk about you.' Archie eyed her with admiration. 'My little sister a nurse!'

'And once a wife and mother. Oh, Archie, I lost them both.'

'I know, Isabel told me that too. I'm sorry, Jessie.' He placed his hands on her shoulders. 'I wish I'd been there to help you. And not even to be at Mam's funeral...' His eyes were anguished. 'Leaving you both is the thing I regret most about going to America. I wish I could have met Tommy and your wee boy.'

'You'd have loved them, Archie, and they would have loved you.'

'You could come with me to America when this is over. There's nothing to stop you now. I've made money, Jess. I have a motor-car, my own house with two bedrooms and an inside bathroom, and some land. You should see America. You can be whoever you want to be.'

Jessie smiled. 'Perhaps one day, but I'm not ready to give up looking for Tommy. You must have heard stories of people who thought their husband or son or brother was dead, but he turned up eventually.'

'Oh, Jess,' the sympathy in his eyes made her blood freeze, 'I'm not saying don't give up hope but don't count on finding him alive. So many men have been killed and they can't even find...' He looked at his feet. 'Forget I said that.'

'You were going to say that they don't always find the bodies, weren't you? You were going to say that sometimes there isn't a body left to be found. I know that, Archie. I didn't before I came here, but I do now. Until the war is over, though, and all the men have returned home, I'm going to believe he's in a prisoner-of-war camp or doesn't know who he is. They say many men have lost their memories and Tommy may be one of them. His captain wrote to me and told me that no one saw what happened to him. That's what I'm holding on to.'

She looked at her fob watch. She'd been away for some time, but Matron could go hang. There were enough staff on the ward to look after the patients and Jessie could be spared for a little longer.

Then another thought struck her. 'Lady Dorothea's here, Archie, Lord Maxwell's sister. She's working as an ambulance driver, same as you. What if she finds out who you really are and tells someone? They can still arrest you – even if there's a war on. You need to leave.'

His mouth settled into the stubborn line she knew so well. 'I'm not going anywhere, Jessie. Not until the war's over.'

'Oh, Archie, don't you see you have to? Not just from here but from France. It's too dangerous. Go back to America where you'll be safe.'

Archie placed his finger under her chin and tipped it so that she was looking into his eyes. 'I'm not leaving,' he repeated. 'I've only just found you again and I'm needed here.'

'But–'

'No buts. I'm staying and that's all there is to it, but I won't come back to the abbey, if that will make you feel better.' He pulled a notebook from his pocket, ripped out a page and wrote on it. 'That's my address. Ask anyone where to find Scotty and they'll tell you.' He folded her hand over the scrap of paper. 'For God's sake, Jess, look after yourself.'

Chapter 32

Serbia, January 1915

Isabel held up her dress as she stepped over the mud. After almost three days of being on a train, boat and another train she was finally at Kragujevatz and so close to the front line that every now and then a flash lit up the rain-filled sky.

The town, with its light stone buildings built around narrow muddy streets, was not the most attractive Isabel had ever seen but its location, surrounded by high mountains, was breathtaking.

'It reminds me a bit of Skye,' Isabel said to her companion. She had met Dr Alice Sinclair in Salonika and the two women had travelled together, the rest of the unit having arrived the week before. Dr Sinclair was older than her and had been qualified for several years. That much she had found out when they'd shared supper on the train before going to sleep. She prayed that she wouldn't let herself down in front of these more experienced women.

'Is that where you're from?' Alice asked.

'Not exactly. My father had a practice there before he died.'

They picked their way through the cobbled streets until they came to a small building. Alice glanced at the address on a letter she took from her pocket and frowned. 'This is it,' she said. 'Home for the next few months.'

They stepped into the hall to find a woman wearing the uniform of the Scottish Women's Hospital walking towards them. She was younger than Dr Sinclair, perhaps in her mid-thirties, and had a long face that some might have found un-attractive and overly severe, if it hadn't been for the mischievous light in her dark green eyes.

She held out her hand. 'Good. Two new recruits. I'm so sorry, I meant to send someone to meet you, but it's been dreadfully busy here.' She peered behind them hopefully. 'Do tell me you've brought some nurses with you?'

'Sorry. It's just us,' Isabel replied.

'I'm to tell you that HQ is working on getting more staff to you,' Alice said. 'In the meantime, we've to do the best we can.'

The woman frowned, then smiled. 'Forgive me, I'm forgetting my manners. Cecilia Bradshaw, chief medical officer for my sins. Now, first things first. I'll show you to your room. I imagine you'll be wanting a bath.'

They followed Dr Bradshaw along a corridor. 'We've been given this place as our billet,' she said. 'It's basic, but clean.' She opened a door onto a large room. 'This used to be one of the wards. We're using it as a staff dormitory. The kitchen is outside. Find a bed and make yourselves at home. We use the hall downstairs as a sort of living room for when we have time off – not that there's much of that. Everything is still in a bit of a muddle here, I'm afraid. We've taken over a school as our sur-gical hospital and have agreed to take responsibility for another two hospitals as soon as we can. That will bring our bed numbers up to more than two hundred. The Serbian nurses, bless them, are untrained so pretty much useless. Happily we do have Austrian prisoners whom we're using as orderlies, so we're just about managing.' Dr Bradshaw was looking at her watch. 'The other hospitals the Serbians run are in a bit of a state so as soon as we can we're going to have to sort them out too.'

Isabel's head was reeling with the effort of taking it all in. She didn't know what she'd expected – injured men, of course, but organised hospitals, not this ... disarray. She and Alice exchanged a look.

If Dr Bradshaw noticed their dismay, she gave no indication of it. 'Now, what surgical experience do you have?'

Alice looked at her feet. 'None, Doctor.'

'I have a little,' Isabel said, 'mainly gynaecological but some abdominal procedures too.' Thanks to Maximilian. To her surprise, thinking of him no longer pained her.

Dr Bradshaw seemed pleased. 'Then you have more surgical experience than most. Have you ever amputated?'

'No, Doctor, but I've read as much as I could about anatomy and surgery.'

A brief smile crossed Dr Bradshaw's face. 'You'll find you become adept at operating while consulting a medical textbook. I'll start you, Dr MacKenzie, in dressings until I see what you're made of. Dr Sinclair, I could use you in the fever hospital.'

Isabel tried not to show her disappointment. She would have preferred to be allocated to theatre immediately, although dressings would be better than medical. Alice still looked stunned and disbelieving.

Dr Bradshaw glanced at her watch again. 'Forgive me, Doctors, but I'm due in theatre. Do have the rest of the day off. Unpack, have a bath, explore the town.'

Isabel was about to protest that she'd rather start work, but the doctor held up a hand. 'Take the time off. It may be the last chance you get for a while, and I prefer my staff rested with their wits about them when they come on duty. Supper's at eight. The kitchen isn't ready yet so we take our meals at the hotel across the road.' Then, with a final piercing look from her green eyes, she turned on her heel and swept out of the room.

'Goodness,' Alice said. 'She reminds me of a whirlwind.'

Isabel found what appeared to be an empty bed and sat down. The springs groaned and the straw from the mattress stuck into her legs even through the protective cover of the mattress. She took off her hat and laid it beside her.

There were six beds, four of which, judging by the female paraphernalia, were already occupied.

Alice was setting her belongings on the small table next to the remaining vacant bed.

'More than two hundred beds,' she muttered. 'And they said there'd be a hundred.' She picked up her toilet bag. 'I'm going to find the bathroom and then I'm going to sleep.' She paused in the doorway. 'Can you remind me where it is? I have no sense of direction, I'm afraid.'

'In the courtyard, I believe,' Isabel replied.

After Alice left, Isabel replaced her hat. She would wait until later to have her bath. Now she wanted to explore the place where she'd be living for the next few months.

She stepped back onto the crowded street, negotiating the uneven cobbles as best she could while trying to keep the hem of her skirt out of the mud. The high-pitched cry of a pig rang through the air as a soldier in Serbian uniform walked past, carrying the poor animal by its hind legs. He smiled cheerfully and touched his cap in a brief salute.

She passed a hotel with several Serbian officers standing outside drinking and was halfway up the road when she heard a familiar voice.

'No. A turkey,' the woman said, in a Scottish accent. 'Not one of those scrawny chickens. I simply must have a turkey.'

Delighted, Isabel hurried over to the woman and tapped her on the shoulder. 'Maud?'

The woman whirled around. 'Dr MacKenzie! Well, I'll be blowed.' She ignored Isabel's outstretched fingers and hugged her instead.

'I knew you'd been sent to join one of the units,' Isabel said, 'but I never dreamed it would be here.' Maud hugged her again and Isabel's throat tightened. Until now she hadn't realised how much she had wanted to meet someone she knew, and that it was Maud Tully made it all the more pleasurable. 'I was given permission to come via Paris so I could spend a few hours with my brother. Otherwise I would have been here last week. Have

I missed much?'

Maud tucked Isabel's arm through hers. 'Lots! Let's find a cup of tea – not that it tastes remotely like it – and I'll tell you everything.' Maud led her back towards the hotel, threading her way through the Serbian officers at the door, then ushered her into a small sitting room. 'They keep this little nook for us,' she said. 'The Serb officers are lovely, but they do tend to become rather over-zealous when they see us. They know that Dr Bradshaw would have their guts for garters if they followed us in here. She's perfectly sweet, but rather strict about us not mixing with the men.'

The women exchanged small-talk about Edinburgh and people they knew until their tea arrived.

'What's it really like here?' Isabel asked.

'It's ghastly, yet sort of thrilling at the same time. We work so hard we can hardly stand by the end of our shift. Mostly we just fall into bed – sometimes without even undressing.'

'Do you get many wounded?'

'More than we can cope with. Are you quite sure you want to hear all of this when you've only just arrived? It might make you take the next train home.' Maud cocked her head to the side and grinned.

'Go home? Not a chance,' Isabel replied. 'I can't wait to get started. Tell me everything.'

A shadow crossed Maud's face. 'We arrived a week ago, expecting to be working in hospitals that were neat and clean. The reality couldn't have been more different. It was grim.'

Isabel leaned forward, intent on not missing a word.

'We couldn't understand at first why stretchers with patients were lying in the streets in the freezing cold,' Maud continued, 'but we simply couldn't walk past them, even though we'd been travelling all night and still hadn't reached our accommodation. Dr Bradshaw marched straight into the Serbian hospital, for that was what it was, and demanded an explanation while the rest of us went among the stretchers, giving hot drinks and checking on the wounded.' She shuddered. 'Some of the men were dead, others were near enough dead and those who weren't looked as if they might die at any moment. When Dr Bradshaw came out of the hospital, her face was white. Apparently this was the way things had been for the last few months. The Serbian doctors just couldn't keep up with the demand for beds. I'll admit it was an eye-opener for us. We'd all been so excited to be here and what we found was a shock.'

Maud looked into the distance. 'Dr Bradshaw was as grim as I'd seen her. She gathered us up and marched us to our billet. She told us to unpack and rest, then said she was going to the hospital that was to be ours and would report back when we met for supper. But we couldn't rest. Not after we'd seen what we had. To a woman, we insisted that we'd go with her. We made her wait until we'd changed into our uniforms and then we marched out of our accommodation, like so many ducklings following their mother.' Maud paused again, smiled wanly and took a sip of tea.

'The surgical hospital was crowded. It was supposed to be for a hundred but there must have been nearly twice that number crammed in. The men were filthy, lying two to a bed. The nurses hadn't the vaguest idea how to look after them and didn't seem to have heard of fresh air. The stench was so awful we had to cover our faces with our handkerchiefs. We took off our cloaks, rolled up our sleeves and got stuck in. The first thing we did was break the windows that were jammed fast with paint and age to get fresh air in – you should have heard the grumbling. But the Serbian doctor was pleased to see us. The poor man had been working almost single-handed on the wards while two others tried to keep up with the operations.

'We worked until we were fit to drop, but the ward was so filthy and the patients so neglected it was difficult to see how we could get everything into shape. We left that night a much more subdued bunch than when we'd arrived. At supper we made a plan. We would move the patients into one half of the hospital while we organised the other. We knew it would be a squash but it was the only way. We would use the Serbian nurses to clean and the orderlies to bathe the men. Although they're Austrians they're so sweet. Some were only captured because they refused to fight the Serbs, you know, so they aren't any trouble. They don't try to escape or anything.

'Anyway, for a week we scrubbed and cleaned until we thought our backs would break. But you should see the hospital now. It's really quite respectable.'

'I can't wait.'

'It's not just the wounded that are the problem

here. There's typhoid, typhus and cholera. Did you see that building opposite our lodgings?'

When Isabel nodded, she continued, 'It's a hospital for recurring fever, although most of the patients also have wounds. It's run by a Serbian doctor – except he's not even a doctor, just a fifth-year medical student.' Maud smiled wistfully. 'He's really rather lovely. He comes to have tea with us sometimes so you'll meet him.'

'Why don't we help?'

'I believe that's Dr Bradshaw's plan, now that we have the surgical hospital in order. If you like, I'll show you the Serbian fever hospital when you've finished your tea.' Maud frowned. 'Unless you'd like to rest first. You must be exhausted.'

'I'm far too excited to sleep.' Isabel set her cup on its saucer and stood up. 'Let's go at once.'

The first thing that struck Isabel as they stepped inside the fever hospital was the stench: a cloying mixture of carbolic, unwashed bodies and decaying flesh. It was far worse than anything she'd experienced in the worst slum tenements in Edinburgh.

She followed Maud into the first ward on the right. The smell there was even worse. There were no beds, only straw mattresses jammed too tightly together to walk between them. Some patients were sitting up, smoking and chatting, while others lay quietly except for the occasional moan.

'There are four wards like this,' Maud whispered, 'and the doctor sees to them all. Look, there he is.' She pointed to the far end of the room where a man with a shock of dark hair was leaning over a patient and listening to his chest. He said something Isabel couldn't hear and the patient laughed. When another patient called, the doctor turned. Catching sight of Maud, he smiled widely. He stepped over the mattresses, taking care to avoid standing on anyone, and came towards them.

'It is Sister Tully,' he said.

'Dr Popović, may I introduce Dr MacKenzie?'

'Please excuse... I would shake your hand but first I need to wash them.'

'Dr Popović does almost everything,' Maud said, who was clearly taken with him. 'He attends to all the men, gives them medicine, works the X-ray machine, dresses their wounds – he even sees outpatients. Don't you think he's clever?'

Isabel was appalled. Only one doctor to do it all! And as for the conditions... The ward needed a good scrub, the men needed baths and the windows should have been opened. 'What is wrong with these men?' she asked.

'Typhoid, mainly, but also cholera and dysentery.'

'And the treatment?'

Dr Popović shrugged. 'Not so much. Mostly the patient runs a temperature for a week. If he has no wounds or other conditions, he usually survives that. Then there is a week of normal temperature, followed by a second week of fever. Sometimes there is a third. I have orderlies to help me. They feed the patients, sometimes even wash them, but they are not trained to do anything.' He smiled apologetically. 'Forgive, but you ladies must excuse me, I have more patients to attend to.'

'Will you come to tea with us tomorrow?' Maud asked.

He dipped his head. 'If I am able. Yes, I will be pleased to come.'

'You have to take time off, Doctor,' Maud said firmly. 'We shall expect you. At two? I am off between two and four.'

She took Isabel's arm again. 'Let's leave Dr Popović to his patients. We'll see you tomorrow, Doctor.'

Outside, Isabel took deep lungfuls of air. 'It's appalling. How can he hope to treat patients in those conditions?'

'You think that's bad?' Maud said. 'It's a lot worse in some of the other hospitals. Now, let me show you ours. I think you'll be impressed.'

After what she'd seen, the surgical hospital where Isabel would be working was a relief. It was a two-building block with several wards of around thirty patients in each. They were set out in the Nightingale style Isabel was used to, with plenty of space between each bed. The patients were tucked in, the crimson covers stretched so tightly it was impossible to see how anyone could move so much as a toe. The wards were spotlessly clean, with not even a dirty cup to mar them. Cold, fresh air drifted through the open windows. It was difficult to imagine that only a week ago conditions had been similar to those in the fever hospital they'd just left.

'The men say they're more likely to die from pneumonia in our wards than anything else.'

Maud grinned. 'They're naughty. Whenever we turn our backs they close the windows. They are simply not used to fresh air. There are more beds in sheds in the courtyard – mainly officers and re-cuperating patients. The theatre is in the back block. The doctors operate two at a time, but there's a lull at the moment. There hasn't been much fighting over the last week, although there's a rumour that it won't stay quiet for long.'

Maud placed her hands on the small of her back and stretched. 'I'm due on the evening shift. I should get some rest.'

'I'm sorry. I shouldn't have kept you so long.' Isabel was instantly contrite.

'I'm just pleased that you're here,' Maud replied, with a smile. 'But you should rest too. You'll not get much from now on.'

Chapter 33

The next day, although Isabel was awake at six, it appeared she was the last to rise. The other beds were made and Alice was nowhere to be seen.

When her bare feet touched the floor it was as if she were stepping on ice. A plump woman wearing a greatcoat was jabbing furiously at the basin of water with a spoon. She glanced behind her when she heard Isabel's bed creak. 'Oh, hello. You must be one of the new doctors. I'm Dr Sylvia Lightfoot. Not so much light of foot as heavy of body, as you might be able to tell.

Trained at the London Hospital.'

Isabel smiled. 'Dr Isabel MacKenzie, trained at the Edinburgh Royal Infirmary.'

Dr Lightfoot raised an eyebrow. 'One of the pioneers? Good for you.'

'What are you doing?' Isabel asked, throwing her coat around her shoulders.

'The water's frozen again and there's no hot to melt it. Mrs Cavendish says she needs it all for breakfast and if I want some I'll have to wait. She says she's tired of us all pinching her hot water, and the next time a kettle goes missing, she'll lock the kitchen door.' She gave the frozen water another vicious jab. 'I don't mind the mud. I don't mind the hard work. I don't even mind the straw mattresses with the straw that pokes into one, jabbing and pricking and stopping one from getting to sleep, but I do mind not being able to wash.' Dr Lightfoot turned to Isabel. 'Sorry,' she said. 'I'm not at my best in the morning.' She held out her hand. 'How do you do? I'm delighted you're here.'

Isabel smiled, despite chattering teeth. It was so cold in the room that ice had formed on the inside of the windows.

'Most of us don't bother undressing at night any more,' Dr Lightfoot said. 'It's too damn – excuse my French – cold. If you brought a fur, use it as an extra blanket.'

'How long have you been here?' Isabel asked, dressing as hurriedly as she could, adding several layers until she knew she resembled a pudding more than a doctor. Perhaps Dr Lightfoot wasn't as corpulent as she appeared.

'The same as everyone else – a week.'

'How do you find it?'

'I love it. Apart from there not being enough water to bathe.' Dr Lightfoot flung the spoon onto her bed. 'I give up. Unless...' she slid a glance at Isabel, '...unless you fancy taking your chances with Mrs Cavendish and fetching us some water. Oh, do say you will. If she catches you, you can tell her you're new. She can't blame you.'

'Show me the way!'

Isabel managed to sneak a kettle of boiling water and once she and Dr Lightfoot had washed, each taking their turn behind a curtain at one end of the room and exposing themselves to the cloth a small area at a time, they made their way to the dining room. As far as Isabel could work out, the nurses were accommodated in their own quarters.

'This used to be the hall when it was a hospital. We use it as the dining room. We run a strict regime here. Breakfast is at seven for those on day shift and seven thirty for those coming off night shift. It's usually not much more than porridge, bread and tea, but it's enough to keep us going until lunch.'

Isabel took a seat beside Dr Lightfoot while an older man in the grey-blue uniform of an Austrian soldier served tea and porridge.

'Johannes looks after us here,' Dr Lightfoot said. 'He doesn't speak much English but we understand one another well enough. We're blessed to have some good men to help us.'

Johannes grinned and nodded vigorously.

There were several nurses at one end of the table, orderlies in the middle and the doctors, including Isabel, at the other end, all keeping up a stream of easy chat as Johannes served them. Dr Lightfoot made introductions but the only name Isabel could remember was that of Margaret Guthrie. She was a sister in her mid-forties, whom Isabel had met when she was working at the Royal Infirmary. Sister Guthrie had been capable if demanding, with a dry sense of humour, and Isabel was pleased to know she would be working alongside her.

Excited and nervous in equal measure, Isabel tried to ignore the fluttering in her stomach and force herself to eat. Everyone had finished when Maud dashed into the room. Buttoning her cuffs she took the empty chair next to Isabel. 'I had to wait ages to get some water,' she hissed. 'Not that Matron believes that's any excuse! Now I shall have to do without breakfast.' She reached over and took a slice of thick dark bread from the centre of the table that no one had touched. When she bit into it, she grimaced. 'Ugh. But needs must.'

At seven twenty exactly there was a rapping of a spoon on a plate and the dining room fell silent.

'Matron,' Dr Lightfoot whispered to Isabel. 'She allocates the nurses to the wards and then our MO briefs us as to where she thinks we're needed.'

The process took less than five minutes. As Dr Bradshaw had promised, Isabel was allocated to dressings and Alice Sinclair to the medical ward. The women all rose and there was a clatter of spoons and cups as they cleared away their breakfast dishes.

Maud smiled at Isabel. 'Catch up later?' With a

347

rustle of her grey uniform, she hurried away.

'Come with me,' Dr Lightfoot said. 'You should start in General Surgical. Then I suggest you go to Heads followed by Abdominals. After that you may have to come back to General to do those who are being dressed twice a day.' She grimaced. 'I keep hoping they'll put me on the convalescent wards for a day or two, but no luck so far. They tend to keep Dr Murdoch there as she's a bit of a menace if she gets too close to actual wounds – she came straight to us from a resident's post at one of the asylums, poor thing, but it does mean she's very good with the men suffering from neurasthenia.'

Isabel had heard rumours about this new and baffling condition that affected men on the front. They couldn't sleep, couldn't speak and often had to be fed as if they were children. Some appeared not to be able to move their arms or legs, although their limbs were uninjured. Recently people had started referring to the condition as shell-shock.

Isabel was allocated a nurse and a decent-sized room off the general surgical ward, with a couch, a dressing-table stocked with bottles and bandages, and a trolley with syringes. The nurse, who introduced herself as Elliot, was a slim, cheerful woman from Australia. 'We don't have enough morphine or chloroform to go around at the moment,' she said. 'We used it all in the first week just to get the bandages off the men. You should have seen them. Stuck to the wounds like cement, they were. All the anaesthetic we have left is being saved for the worst cases and for theatre. We start with the ambulatory patients to give the sisters on the ward time to get the patients washed, then do the dressings there.'

Elliot pointed to a man who was mopping the floor. 'This is Kurt, one of the Austrians. Doesn't have a word of English, I'm afraid.'

'*Sprechen Sie Deutsch?*' Isabel asked.

Kurt broke into a wide smile and replied in the same language. 'Yes, of course. My home is only a small distance from here.'

'Crikey, you speak German,' Elliot said. 'Wait until the others hear. Most of us haven't a clue.'

'One of the few benefits of a finishing school in Switzerland,' Isabel replied drily.

They rolled up their sleeves and were soon immersed in a steady stream of dressings. Although none of the soldiers spoke English, Kurt was able to translate Isabel's German well enough to make the Serbians grin with delight.

'They keep trying to talk to us in Serbian,' Nurse Elliot said, her quick, gentle hands never pausing as she rebandaged wounds that Isabel had cleaned, 'even though they know we can't understand. But don't you agree that they're rather handsome?'

Isabel suspected a reply wasn't required.

When they'd cleaned, disinfected and redressed the wounds of all the walking patients they went into the ward, accompanied by Kurt.

Their first patient was lying in bed, his sheets tented over his right leg. His heavily bandaged left arm was missing below the elbow but when he opened his eyes and saw Isabel he launched into a stream of Serbian that had Kurt grinning widely.

'What's he saying?' Nurse Elliot asked, as she undid the dressing on his arm.

'He says that the doctor is the most beautiful woman he has ever seen and he has decided to marry her,' said Kurt.

Isabel's cheeks burned. 'Something about wanting to marry me.' Deciding it was better to ignore the comment, she bent her head over the wound on her patient's arm.

But Elliot had no such qualms. 'And you tell him from us that if we have any more of his nonsense he'll be out of here in two shakes of a monkey's tail.'

Kurt looked baffled and Isabel hid a smile. She didn't think she was going to translate. Her patient continued to smile and chat in Serbian through what must have been a painful few minutes while Isabel cleaned his arm. When she unwrapped his leg, it took all her training to prevent her showing how shocked she was. The stump was hot and swollen, the suppurating flesh turning black at the edges.

She exchanged a glance with Nurse Elliot, whose cheerful smile had disappeared. Within seconds it was back. 'No point in letting him know how bad it is, Doctor,' she murmured. 'I'll put his name down on the list for theatre, shall I?'

Isabel nodded. For a moment she couldn't speak. One of her first patients and it didn't look good. She cleared her throat. 'Could you tell this soldier, Kurt, that we're going to have to take him back to theatre to try to remove the black bit on his leg? It will probably mean it has to come off above the knee, I'm afraid.'

As she rewound the bandage, Kurt translated. Her patient looked grim for a moment, then spoke to Kurt. 'Alexandrovitch says,' Kurt said, with a glint in his blue eyes, 'that he will go to the operating room but only if you are with him. He says that if he is going to die, it should be with a beautiful woman looking into his eyes.'

Isabel managed a smile in return. 'Tell him I'll be there. First I have other patients to see.' She peeled off her gloves. 'Oh, and tell him I have no intention of letting him die.'

When Isabel returned to Alexandrovitch, Dr Lightfoot was taking his temperature. There was a look on the doctor's face that chilled her. 'This patient is going to theatre, Doctor,' Isabel said, with a smile at Alexandrovitch.

'I haven't quite decided.'

'But—' Isabel started to protest but Dr Lightfoot took her by the arm and led her out of earshot.

'He's too ill to survive the operation,' Dr Lightfoot said quietly. 'He's already showing signs of sepsis and there are too many who need operations who will survive. I'm going to leave him until the end of my list and then decide. We have barely any anaesthetic as it is.'

'But you must operate! If you leave him he'll almost certainly die. The gangrene will spread through his body if we don't stop it.'

Dr Lightfoot looked regretful. 'I can't spare the anaesthesia. And if we go ahead and operate without it, I don't think he'll survive the shock in his weakened condition.'

351

'We could try to give him blood. I watched the American doctors do it in Paris and it worked.'

'It's been tried before and it's killed more patients than it's saved. We can't risk it.'

Isabel wasn't prepared to give up. She'd promised Alexandrovitch he would get better.

'I'd take the chance of operating if it might save him.'

Dr Lightfoot shook her head. 'You young doctors are so brave – so willing to try new things.' She held up her hand when Isabel started to protest again. 'If the shock doesn't kill him, the sepsis will. Nevertheless if you wish to operate and he agrees to have the procedure carried out without anaesthesia, you're welcome to try.'

The thought of amputating her first limb was bad enough, but to do it with the patient awake made Isabel's stomach churn. However, Alexandrovitch wouldn't live if she didn't take off his leg and it was up to her to make the right decision for her patient. She had no choice. There was no other way to save his life.

She returned to his bedside and, with Kurt translating, explained what she planned to do.

'He asks what will happen if you don't take his leg,' Kurt said.

Alexandrovitch hadn't even flinched when he'd been told he'd be fully awake and able to feel every cut of the knife.

'The infection will spread to the rest of his body, and he'll become increasingly septicaemic and die.'

'This operation – it could kill him anyway?'

Isabel nodded, and waited until Kurt translated

once more.

'He wishes to know if he might still survive without it?'

'It's possible,' Isabel admitted, 'but unlikely.'

'If he were your brother, what would you advise him to do?'

'To have the operation.'

Alexandrovitch looked thoughtful. He reached under his pillow and brought out a small statue of a blue-robed Madonna. He pressed his lips to the small figurine and mumbled something in rapid Serbian under his breath.

Kurt looked at Isabel, his dark eyes troubled. 'He says that the Scottish doctors have served them well. He will take his chances. He prays that Mother Mary will watch over you both.'

Isabel's hands were shaking as Sister Elliot helped her put on her rubber gloves.

Alexandrovitch was lying on the table staring up at her with a half-smile. Dr Lightfoot was carrying out another operation on the other side of the room so at least she wouldn't be alone for this, her first major unassisted operation.

Elliot passed Alexandrovitch a piece of sterilised cloth to hold between his teeth and had arranged for four of the Austrian orderlies to be there to hold him down when the pain became too bad.

Signalling to Elliot that she was ready, Isabel lifted the special amputating knife and prepared to make her first incision. She would have to make it without hesitation and cut deeply. Any other way would hurt Alexandrovitch more. Taking a deep breath, she nodded to the orderlies who had positioned themselves at each corner of the table.

'Hold him tight,' Isabel said, relieved to hear that her voice wasn't shaking. 'Don't let him move – not even a fraction.' She lifted the scalpel and sliced through Alexandrovitch's flesh.

The operation went better than she could have hoped. Dr Lightfoot left one of the other doctors operating on her patient and came to help. As Isabel cut, Dr Lightfoot used the battery-operated galvaniser to seal off the blood vessels. To everyone's relief, Alexandrovitch passed out when Isabel started sawing through the bone.

'Well done,' Dr Lightfoot murmured, when they'd finished. 'Neat work. Have you done much operating before?'

'A little. No amputations, though. Except the tip of a finger.'

'I'm surprised. You have the hands and cool nerve required of a surgeon.'

Now that the operation was over Isabel felt sick, but she was thrilled by the praise from the more experienced doctor. 'It's what I always wanted to do.'

Dr Lightfoot smiled. 'I'll speak to Dr Bradshaw and see to it that you spend more time in theatre, then. God knows, you'll get all the experience you need here to turn you into a first-class surgeon.'

Chapter 34

France, February 1915

Jessie crept back to her ward after dinner. She was so exhausted she could hardly stand, but earlier that day, a young soldier from Skye had been brought in with both legs missing and most of his face bandaged. There had been nothing the doctors could do for him, except clean his wounds and make him comfortable. The soldier wasn't expected to survive and had been sent to Jessie's ward to die.

She'd never met him before, as he came from Sleat in the south of the island and she was from the north, but when he'd heard her speak, he'd clutched her hand. 'Stay with me, Sister. Please.' He was terrified and Jessie couldn't blame him.

Although the ward was busy, and comforting the soldiers was a task normally left to the orderlies, Jessie pulled up a chair next to his bed.

'Donald, isn't it?' she asked softly, in Gaelic. The ward was lit only by paraffin lamps as, in an effort to save power, they kept the electric lighting off when they weren't expecting casualties. Although the flickering light made it difficult to see what they were doing, at this time of night Jessie preferred it. It was more soothing for those who were awake and in pain.

'Yes, Sister. Donald Stuart.'

'You have the same surname as me,' Jessie replied, with a smile.

'I'm not going to make it, Sister, am I?'

'Now, where did you get that idea?' Jessie chided, as her heart constricted. 'Don't you know that we have no intention of letting our soldiers die?'

Donald's grip tightened. The strength of his fingers almost made Jessie cry out. 'Whatever you say, Sister.' He sighed.

It was clear to Jessie that he knew she had lied. 'Tell me about yourself,' she said. 'Have you a girl back home?'

'Aye, I do. Mairi's her name. We're to be wed on my next leave.'

'Mairi's a pretty name.' Jessie's throat felt as if there were pebbles in it.

'Will you tell her, Sister – I mean, write to her? Tell her that it wasn't too bad in the end and that I didn't suffer.' His hand squeezed hers again. 'At least she won't have to decide whether she could marry a man without legs and missing an eye.'

'If she loves you, she'll just be glad to have you home.'

'But she won't be having me home, will she?'

No, Jessie thought wearily, she won't. This damned war. 'Why don't I write a letter for you?' she suggested.

'What can I say?'

Jessie thought for a moment. What would she have liked Tommy to say?

'Tell her you love her, that you miss her and are looking forward to seeing her again.'

'Even if I do leave here alive, there's no chance

356

I'm keeping her to her promise to marry me.' At least he was calmer now and seemed to have some hope that he would survive. Hope was all Jessie had to give him.

'I don't think you should worry about that right now. Let's just write her a letter and wait and see.'

Jessie stood up. Her stomach growled. It had been a long time since she'd eaten but she couldn't leave Donald. At least, not yet. 'I'll fetch a paper and pen, shall I? I won't be a moment.'

By the time she returned a few minutes later, Donald was sleeping. She felt for his pulse. It was weak and thready. It wouldn't be long now. She settled herself into her chair to wait.

An hour later, Donald stopped breathing. Jessie called one of the doctors to make out the death certificate. As she set about preparing Donald's body, she became aware of someone standing behind her.

'I've brought you some tea.' It was Evans. After their chat, Jessie had gone straight to Matron and asked for the orderly to be transferred to her ward. Expecting an argument, she'd been relieved when she had acquiesced with a smile. 'But,' she'd warned, 'don't ask me again. We can't have all the orderlies working on your ward, Sister Stuart.' It was as near to a compliment as she'd had from the matron but it was enough. Evans had been thrilled to find herself with Jessie and, with her unfailing smile and willingness to turn her hand to anything Jessie asked of her, was a pleasure to work with.

'Poor devil,' Evans said softly. 'Perhaps it's better

this way. At least he'll be with God.'

Jessie swung around. The night had taken its toll on her. 'Better for whom?' she said bitterly. 'Better for the fiancée who won't have to marry a man who could never work again? Better for the mother who waits for a letter, praying to God that her son is still alive? Better for his sisters?' She gripped her hands together to stop them shaking. 'This damned war. It takes our loved ones and keeps on taking them. Day after relentless day we nurse the poor things, only to see them die regardless of what we do. We don't even have enough morphine to help those who are dying meet their Lord free of pain and with dignity. Oh, I can see it's better for us. Every time one dies we have a bed to put another poor soul into. Every hopeless case means we have more morphine to spare for those who, one day, after we fix them up, might be returned to war. A war that shows no sign of ending.' Her voice caught on a sob. She was so tired of seeing men die and she'd only been there for two months.

When Evans's face blanched, Jessie tried hard to regain her composure. The orderly didn't need to see her anguish. Evans set the cup and saucer down on the bedside table and squeezed her shoulder. 'Steady on, old girl. If we weren't here, many more would die. That's what we have to remember. Look, you must be exhausted. How long have you been on duty? Fifteen hours? Sixteen? No one can keep going like that. Why don't you go to bed and I'll see to Corporal Stuart here?'

Jessie shook her head, annoyed and embarrassed that she had lost control. All of them were

358

in the same position. Most of the staff had at least one family member fighting and every death hit them all hard. But she was going to carry out her last duty to Corporal Stuart. She might be weak with hunger and fatigue but she was going to prepare his body. Apart from the letter to his fiancée, it was the last thing she could do for the young soldier. 'Thank you, but no. I will see to him.'

'Then I shall help you,' Evans said firmly.

Together they washed Donald Stuart's body gently, as if he were still alive and too much pressure could still hurt him. When they'd finished, they wrapped him in a shroud and, with the help of the night nurse, got him onto a stretcher. Jessie wrote his name and regiment on a card and attached it to the shroud with a piece of string. In his locker she found a letter from his fiancée with a return address and slipped it into the pocket of her uniform. Donald's commanding officer would write to his mother, but she would write to Donald's Mairi, keeping her promise to tell her that he had died bravely and without pain.

The mortuary was a fair distance from the ward, and Donald's stiffening corpse was heavy, but somehow between them they managed to carry the stretcher through the moon-lit cloisters and down the stone steps where they laid his body next to those of the other men who had died during the night.

The two women stood looking down at the neat line of the recently dead and bowed their heads as Jessie said a brief prayer. As she did so, a cool hand slipped into hers and squeezed. The unexpected gesture almost made her cry again.

'Come on, Sister, time for bed,' Evans whispered. 'You're on duty in a few hours' time.'

Jessie managed a small smile. 'As are you.'

Just then the sound of a horn blast tore through the room. More injured were on the way and sleep would have to wait.

Chapter 35

'You simply must come!' Dorothea Maxwell insisted, stretching out her hands to the fire. It was mid-afternoon and they were in the sitting room with nurses and orderlies, seeking the miserly warmth from the log fire. As each took her turn to stand in front of it, Jessie was reminded of how her mother used to have a couple of irons in the embers. When one had cooled she had exchanged it for a hot one.

Tomorrow would be her first day off. Some had already had a day free, venturing into Paris to have dinner at an Italian restaurant before the opera, while others had taken the opportunity to explore the trenches.

'I'm tired,' Jessie protested, hiding a yawn behind her hand. 'I have my uniform to wash and a hundred other chores to catch up with.' Anyway, she wanted to save her days off to see Archie. She'd had one letter from him since they'd met, asking her to come and see him last week, but as she'd been on duty she'd been unable to go.

'You've been wretched since that soldier died, Sister. A good luncheon will buck you up,' Evans interjected.

If only her life could be made better by a good meal, Jessie thought. And why Donald's death had shaken her more than all the others she didn't know. Perhaps it was the Skye connection. Or because, in him, more than in any of the other injured soldiers, she'd seen what it might have been like for Tommy. Sometimes the only way to keep going was to try to forget that the wounded men were someone's brother, husband or son.

Lady Dorothea smiled beguilingly. 'You can do your chores at some other time. We have only one day off a month so we should make the most of it. A whole day and an evening out in Paris – who could resist? Surely not even you, Sister Stuart. Besides, I told the Americans I'd bring as many of us as I could.'

Jessie's heart jolted. When Lady Dorothea had suggested a trip into Paris to spend time with a group of officers she'd met, she'd assumed she was talking about British men. 'Americans?'

'Yes, the doctors from the American Hospital and the Harvard Unit. We keep bumping into them when we fetch the patients from the station. They're such darlings.'

Had Lady Dorothea met Archie, then? But, of course, even if she had, she would know him as Calum McPherson – or Scotty.

'If it makes you feel better, think of it as your duty,' she continued. 'They need as much cheering up as anyone else. 'And...' she dropped her voice, '...they're so handsome and so much fun.

Much less stuffy than our own officers, I have to say.'

Dear God, Jessie thought wearily. Did Archie truly understand the risk he was running by staying close to Paris? The nurses and doctors from all of the units often bumped into one another. If he insisted on staying, there was a good chance that he and Lady Dorothea would meet. Now she had no choice. She would have to go with them. She had to warn him. His new name wouldn't hold up for ever.

'Very well. Count me in,' Jessie said, as Evans vacated her spot at the fireplace for Jessie to take her turn. 'What time are we leaving?'

'Jolly good. I think we should plan to set out around nine o'clock to get there in time for luncheon. The roads are pretty crowded and we might get stuck behind army trucks.' Lady Dorothea tapped her lip with her finger. 'Now, what on earth are we going to wear?'

'Our uniforms, surely,' Evans said. Although they had dispensation to wear their own clothes when they were off duty, most chose not to. Uniform brought too many advantages, such as free train travel.

'Not this time.' Lady Dorothea looked horrified. 'I've had enough of this dreadful grey. We should dress up for once.'

Jessie thought of the only good dress she'd brought, the one she kept for church, although it was showing signs of wear. She would look like Lady Dorothea's maid if she wore it, and although she shouldn't have minded, she found she did. Here at Royaumont, with everyone doing the same job and wearing the same uniform, it wasn't always easy to tell who was a lady and who wasn't. 'I like my uniform. The MO prefers that we wear it when we're out.'

'Poppycock!' Lady Dorothea said. 'Our esteemed MO can say what she likes when we're on duty but I simply refuse to go into town looking like a partridge. And,' she leaned forward, a sparkle in her blue eyes, 'come to think of it, I have just the thing for you. You're a little shorter than I, but it should fit. It's a russet skirt with the sweetest little jacket that would go with your colouring perfectly. I don't know why I even brought it. It clashes dreadfully with my red hair.'

Jessie didn't want to wear one of her cast-offs, no matter how kindly meant the offer was. 'Thank you, but I'd still rather stick with my uniform.' Reluctantly, she left her position near the fire. 'If I'm to come with you, I should go and find some water to do my laundry.'

The next day, Jessie found herself squashed into the front of the truck between Lady Dorothea, who was driving, and Evans. She was anxious. Although it was unlikely that Archie would be one of the party they were meeting for lunch, it was possible that the American doctors would know him. Last night she'd decided to make her excuses as soon as they arrived in Paris and find Archie before there was a chance of them meeting unexpectedly. She had to try to persuade him to leave France.

'I hope you won't mind if I don't join you for lunch,' she said, grabbing the front of the truck as it gave a particularly sickening lurch to the left, 'but I need to do some shopping.'

Lady Dorothea waited until the vehicle was straight once more. 'Shopping? What a wonderful idea. If the boys haven't arrived I'll come with you, although I don't think Evans will be up for it.'

The last thing Jessie wanted was to go shopping and particularly not with Lady Dorothea. 'Evans sleeps like the dead,' she said. 'I've never seen anything like it.'

The orderly was slumped against the passenger door and not even the erratic progress of their journey had made her do more than protest mildly in her sleep. It was hardly surprising that she was dead to the world: they'd all been dragged out of bed at four in the morning to help with a new influx of injured. Lady Dorothea and Jessie had been summoned too but, unlike Evans, they seemed to manage better without sleep.

'Poor darling,' Lady Dorothea said. 'She's such a trouper.'

They shared a smile that turned into a shriek as they headed into a pothole that threw them up in the air.

'I think it's better if I go shopping alone. You won't want to miss your friends.'

Lady Dorothea looked at her curiously. 'My darling girl, if it weren't for the fact that it's you, I'd swear you're trying to shake me.'

For all her apparent flightiness, she was sharp. How could Jessie get rid of her without making her more suspicious? 'Where are you meeting everyone?' she asked.

'At Pierre's Café. It's really the only place left to

get something decent to eat.'

'Is that close to the American Hospital?' Jessie asked.

'About half a mile, I think. Why do you ask?'

'I just wondered,' Jessie said. She could walk that distance easily.

'Ah, I know why you're trying to shake me. It's the man who came to see you at the abbey. He was wearing the insignia of the American unit. I remember now! You never did tell me who he was. A bit of a dish, I thought. So, do tell, where did you meet him?'

Jessie thought quickly. 'At the Gare du Nord the day we arrived. When all of you went for a walk, I stayed with the luggage. I – er – I went over on my ankle and he stopped to help. When he came to the abbey to see me, he didn't know I was married. I told him not to come again.'

How many more lies would she have to tell?

'But, Jessie...' Whatever Lady Dorothea saw in her face seemed to change her mind. 'Perhaps he'll be at luncheon.'

'I doubt it. He's an ambulance driver. Didn't you say it was the doctors we were meeting?'

'Not just them. Didn't I tell you?' Lady Dorothea looked at her – Jessie would have preferred her to keep her eyes on the road. 'My brother Simon's stationed at Marne and he's been given forty-eight hours' leave to spend in Paris, so he'll be there too with his friend.'

Her words did nothing to dampen Jessie's anxiety.

Lady Dorothea pouted. 'I did ask the MO if I could have a couple of days' leave but the battle-

365

axe refused point-blank.'

Jessie knew she didn't mean it. Everyone adored Dr Ludlow. She was a tough disciplinarian, but worked as hard, if not harder, than anyone else.

'You must be looking forward to seeing your brother,' Jessie said casually.

'Why don't you join us when you've finished your shopping?' She stopped talking as she man-oeuvred the truck past a line of refugees trudging along the road. 'Poor things,' she said. 'Rotten Huns forcing people out of their homes.'

'We'll see.' Jessie's heart was racing. She hated deceiving Lady Dorothea by not admitting who she really was. 'But won't you want some time alone with your brother?'

'Oh, don't be silly. His friend will be there, so it isn't as if we were going to have lunch on our own in the first place.' She smiled. 'I'm not sure Simon would know what to say to me after the first ten minutes anyway. Except to tick me off for coming to France. I have no doubt Mama and Papa will have asked him to persuade me to go home. They think I'm mad not to have stayed in London and married Lord Livingston.'

'What's he like, your Lord Livingston?' Jessie asked, seizing on the chance to change the subject.

Lady Dorothea shuddered. 'He's not too bad, if you can ignore his squint and the moustache that curls at the ends in the most peculiar fashion. But I dare say I could have got around those if he wasn't so utterly boring.'

Jessie laughed. She liked Lady Dorothea. She said exactly what was on her mind and, unlike some of the others, had no airs and graces. 'They can't make you marry him, surely,' she said.

Dorothea turned to stare at her, her eyes off the road for so long Jessie feared that this time they would certainly end up in a ditch.

'My dear Sister Stuart, don't you see? I have to marry someone.'

It was almost eleven when they pulled up outside a grand-looking hotel.

'I can't imagine the doorman is going to be best pleased to have our truck parked here,' Jessie said.

'I don't care a fig what he thinks,' Lady Dorothea replied, with a lift of her chin. It was at times like this that Jessie was most reminded of the aristocrat she was.

She shook Evans awake while Lady Dorothea pinned on her hat, an elaborate concoction with an ostrich feather, then the three of them clambered out. Lady Dorothea tossed the doorman a smile. 'Keep an eye on our motor vehicle, please. Don't let anyone go near it. There's many a unit who would steal it if they had half a chance.'

If the doorman was surprised to see a woman in an afternoon dress of deep green silk and an elaborate hat emerge from the dusty truck he gave no sign of it.

'I'll leave you here,' Jessie said, glad that she'd worn her uniform, as had Evans. If she hadn't, she would have felt like a pigeon next to Dorothea's peacock.

'Do come and meet Simon and his friend first.' Before Jessie could protest, Lady Dorothea had linked arms with her and Evans and steered them up the grand staircase. Although the last person Jessie wanted to meet was another member of the Maxwell family, it appeared she had no choice.

Inside, the grand salon was crowded with Allied soldiers and women either in uniform or dressed, like Lady Dorothea, in sweeping skirts and tight-fitting jackets. Laughter and the sound of tinkling glass filled the smoky room. Lady Dorothea stopped behind a tall man with red hair, who was surrounded by glamorous women, some of whom were holding long cigarette holders, and tapped him on the shoulder.

'Simon!'

The officer spun around. 'Dorothea! Darling sis, how well you look!' He kissed her cheek. 'Andrew's here too. Somewhere.' He looked around but, whoever Andrew was, he had been swallowed by the mass of bodies.

'Sister Stuart, Evans, may I introduce my brother, the Honourable Simon Maxwell.' She gave him a teasing smile. 'Although I don't know how honourable he's managing to be around all these charming French women. I hear they love a pilot.'

'How do you do, Sister Stuart, Miss Evans?' Simon replied. 'Please ignore my sister. She tends to talk a load of tosh.'

'You're a pilot?' Evans asked, looking more alert than Jessie had previously seen her. 'Is it terrifying? Or thrilling?'

'A bit of both,' Simon said easily. He smiled at Jessie. 'It's you nurses who deserve the most thanks. We're all so grateful that you're here.'

Jessie blushed, feeling awkward. She didn't

know how to take part in the conversation without showing herself up. Worse, she felt such a fraud.

Lady Dorothea stood on tiptoe and waved. 'There they are. Our American boys.'

Thankfully, Archie wasn't among the group and Jessie was able to slip away, promising she'd return well before it was time to go back to the abbey. She left Evans in conversation with Simon, who had been joined by a dark-haired man also in the uniform of the Royal Flying Corps.

She found the American Hospital after getting lost several times. When she asked for Scotty she was shown into a small room and instructed to wait. It wasn't long before she heard footsteps and her brother flung open the door with a wide grin.

'Jessie! I was beginning to think I'd have to go back to the abbey if I wanted to see you.'

She held up her face for his kiss. 'You must promise me you'll never go there again, Archie. Lady Dorothea and her brother are having lunch only a short walk away. Good grief, she even knows some of the American doctors. You must leave France. She could come across you at any time.'

'If she does, she will know me only as Calum McPherson, or Scotty. You worry too much.'

'And you worry too little,' she retorted. 'If they discover who you are, they could still arrest you and put you on trial.'

His expression darkened. 'Then I shall make it my business that they don't. I've no intention of being taken back to Scotland like a beast in chains. But, Jessie, let's not quarrel. As luck would have it, I have a few hours free before I'm on duty again. Why don't I show you Paris?'

Jessie knew the determined look on Archie's face well enough to know that it didn't matter what she said. Her brother would stay in France and nothing she could say would have the slightest effect. She sighed and took his hand. 'Come on, then. I want to see everything.'

Jessie loved it all: the Champs-Élysées, with its frighteningly expensive shops, the river with the boats and finally the Eiffel Tower. They walked until her feet ached before taking tea at one of the little cafés. Archie told her more about his life in America.

'If a man's prepared to work, there's nothing to stop him making a decent living or buying land, as long as he can raise the money to pay for it. Can you believe I own land, Jessie? Land that no man can take from me.'

'How did you afford it? Is land that cheap in America?'

'Not especially. I have a business partner and he puts up the funds. He's rich and I know how to work hard. We will grow grapes or oranges. We might even build houses on it. One way or another, in a few years' time I expect to be rich.'

'Rich enough to take a wife?'

He shook his head. 'There has only ever been, and will only ever be, one woman for me.'

Jessie clicked her tongue in exasperation. 'Isabel MacKenzie! I thought after all this time you'd have forgotten her. Why won't you accept she's not for you?'

Archie toyed with his knife. 'One day, as I always promised, I'll be her equal.'

'What then? Even if she comes to think of you the way you want her to, she'll never leave Scotland for America – not for a man suspected of murder.'

She was exasperated. Couldn't Archie get it into his head that hankering after Isabel MacKenzie was like hankering after the moon?

It seemed not. He looked her in the eye and grinned. 'I'm a MacCorquodale, Jessie. And the MacCorquodales have always had a weakness for a lost cause.'

Chapter 36

As time passed, the abbey received increasing numbers of casualties and the women were rarely given sufficient time off to make the trip to Paris. Tempers were fraying and there had been the odd spat between doctor and nurse, nurse and orderly and even some tension between the MO and her doctors. Jessie didn't let it worry her. With so many women living in close quarters with one another, it would have been a miracle had there been no fallings-out. She was making her way to her room when the cry 'Post!' rang through the abbey. The delivery of mail never failed to cause excitement. Unless it brought bad news it raised everyone's spirits.

371

Jessie hesitated with her hand on the banister before turning to join the crowd of chattering women surrounding the postman. Perhaps this time there would be a letter with news of Tommy.

She hung back, unwilling to join the scrum. As the names were called out, the women fell upon their letters and retreated either to their rooms or to the courtyard to read them in solitude. There was nothing for her. Disappointed, she turned away. Lady Dorothea, she noticed, had been one of the lucky ones and had taken a seat next to the fountain. Jessie smiled at the look of happy anticipation on her face. Then, to her dismay, the woman's hands fell to her lap and sadness replaced delight.

Quickly Jessie crossed to her and crouched by her side. 'What is it, Maxwell?'

She shook her head. The hand holding the letter was trembling and her eyes were wet with unshed tears.

Her alarm growing, Jessie asked again. 'What is it? Is it bad news?'

Over the last two months, three of the women in the unit had received the letters everyone dreaded, informing them that loved ones had been killed.

'It's a letter from my papa,' Lady Dorothea said quietly. 'He writes to tell me that the body of my eldest brother Charles has been found.'

Shock jolted down Jessie's spine.

'Charles went missing years ago, and although we suspected he must be dead, I confess I hadn't given up hope that he was alive.'

'I'm sorry.' She gripped her hands together lest

Lady Dorothea noticed they were shaking.

'It's even worse than we expected. It seems that Papa was right all along and that he was murdered.'

'What makes you think that?' Jessie's voice sounded odd even to her own ears but it seemed Lady Dorothea was too distraught to notice.

'Poor Charles had been buried. There was a storm on Skye last week. A wild one. It blew part of a cliff away near Galtrigill and one of the crofters discovered what remained of Charles. He must have been buried there all this time. I can hardly bear to think of it. Poor Mama.' Apart from the tremor in her voice she appeared calm, almost unnaturally so. 'Papa won't rest until he has brought my brother's murderer to justice.'

Dear God. 'I'm so very sorry,' Jessie whispered. She took one of Lady Dorothea's cold hands in hers. 'Come, let me take you to your room. You should lie down.' She looked into Dorothea's blue eyes and sucked in a breath at the emptiness she saw there.

'I can't rest. I'm due to go on duty.'

'Don't be a goose,' Jessie said. 'No one will expect you to work today. Not after such news.'

Lady Dorothea rose to her feet. 'What use would it be for me to lie in my room? I'll only have too much time to brood. Besides, there are only three of us who can drive the ambulances, and if I don't help, what of the men on the battlefield who are waiting for someone to bring them here? I can't help Charles, but I can help save others.' She smoothed the folds of her grey dress and smiled wanly. 'I ask you to say nothing of this to anyone. At least, not until I come back off duty.'

'But–'

'Please, don't argue with me, Sister.' She raised her chin, and, once again, Jessie was reminded that behind the easy-going manner was a woman who was used to having her way. And even more used to doing her duty.

Jessie squeezed her hand. 'You know where to find me if you need a friend,' she said simply.

Lady Dorothea nodded and, head held high, walked away.

Jessie waited until she was out of sight before she buried her head in her hands. Lord Maxwell had been killed and his body buried on Galtrigill. If Archie hadn't killed him, who had? Now the Glendales had evidence that their son had been murdered, they would never rest until they found Archie and brought him back for questioning.

She had to warn him. Surely now he would see that he had to return to America.

Chapter 37

Serbia, February 1915

Isabel and Maud, for once off duty at the same time, met to go for a walk. The day was fine and mild, the weak sunlight doing its best to dry the slush that still lay on the street.

They stepped over a muddy stream, then followed the road upwards, lifting their skirts, which, to keep the hems free of the incessant mud, they had shortened daringly above their ankles. After days spent in sour-smelling, stuffy wards the fresh air was balm for Isabel's soul. At the top of the hill they paused to look down. Close to the town, the hills were brown and barren but as they rose higher they turned a lush blue.

It might have been Skye, Isabel thought, realising that, for the first time since Charles's attack, she could remember the island with longing rather than distaste.

From where they were standing they could see the red roof of Kragujevatz beneath them and, almost hidden in the hollows of the valleys, other smaller towns and villages.

Maud stopped to pick some primroses. 'I might give some to Milan,' she said slowly. 'I doubt he finds much opportunity to go walking.'

'How is your Dr Popović?' Isabel asked.

Maud blushed. 'He's not my Dr Popović.'

But Isabel guessed that Maud cared more for the young man than she liked to admit. It wasn't difficult to see why. Milan was tall and powerfully built, with expressive, dark eyes and a beautiful smile. He'd come for tea twice since she'd been there and had spent the whole time sneaking glances at Maud with his soft brown eyes.

'Would it be so bad if he were?' Isabel asked.

Maud turned away to look over the valley. 'I know it's an awful cheek to ask, but have you ever been in love?'

Isabel hesitated. 'No. At least, I don't think so.'

'Then you couldn't have been.'

375

Perhaps Maud was right. If she had truly cared for Maximilian, she would have given up everything to be with him. To her surprise she realised that she had hardly thought of him over the last few weeks.

'I think I might love Milan,' Maud continued. 'Whenever I see him, I feel light inside, as if someone has lit a candle in my heart.'

Isabel smiled.

'Have you ever kissed someone?' Maud continued.

'My mama and my brother,' Isabel replied wryly. At that moment the memory of Archie's lips on hers came back so sharply she could almost feel the imprint, almost taste his mouth, almost smell the sea in his hair. 'There was someone once...'

Maud spun around. 'Who? A lover? Oh, my goodness, where? When? What was it like?'

Isabel laughed, wishing now that she'd lied. Somehow, out here, among all the death and suffering, things that once seemed so important appeared less so. 'It was a very quick kiss, but I have to admit I liked it. Of course, I shouldn't have been kissing anyone, but I can't regret it.'

The clatter of oxen hoofs on cobbles in the town below filtered up to them on the cold winter air. Maud came to stand beside Isabel and wound her arm around her waist. 'Do you think it will be different when we go home? Now we've been out here on our own, they can't expect us to go back and be the way we were. Perhaps Mama and Papa might come to accept a Serbian son-in-law.'

'So you're serious about him.'

'Yes,' Maud dropped her arm and faced Isabel, 'I rather think I am. But please,' her grey eyes were anxious, 'don't tell anyone. They would send me straight home.'

One girl had already been sent packing for becoming engaged to a Serbian officer, and Dr Bradshaw had warned them all that the same fate awaited anyone who was even seen out alone with a man.

'Don't worry,' Isabel squeezed her shoulder. 'You can trust me to keep a secret.' If only Maud knew.

'There's never an opportunity for us to meet privately – unless,' she glanced at Isabel from under her lashes, 'you'd agree to chaperone us.'

'I'd be happy to, if you could arrange it for when I'm free.'

Maud's smile lit her face. 'I'm thinking of writing to Mama about him.'

'Perhaps that would be wise.'

They lingered for a few more minutes, but it was cold without the shelter of the hills so they took a different route down to the village. They stopped at a cake shop for some pastries and walked through the market, Maud carrying her flowers and Isabel their purchases. They had to step out of the way as bearded Serbs, wearing brown sheepskin hats shaped like beehives, drove bullock carts down the street.

'When we first arrived, there were so many of those carts,' Maud said softly, 'all carrying dead soldiers. We called them the death-carts.'

'They're still dying,' Isabel replied, 'but not nearly so many.' Her thoughts turned to Alexandrovitch, who had recovered from his operation and showed no sign of septicaemia. Since she'd amputated his leg, she had spent most of her working day in theatre.

Maud smiled sadly. 'We're helping to make a difference, even if it feels like too little.' They stopped outside the entrance to the Serbian Military Hospital. 'Have you met Dr Ross?'

'She came to tea once,' Isabel said. 'She's a remarkable woman.' Dr Ross had left her private practice to come to Serbia. Everyone had heard her tales of daring adventures, once being captured by brigands. Now she was working in the Serbian hospital with a number of Greek doctors. There were more than a thousand patients and often three men with different infectious diseases had to share a bed. The death toll was enormous.

'Shall we go in? Take her some cake?' Maud asked. 'It must be horrible for her to be on her own so much.'

They stepped into the hall, gagging as the smell of unwashed bodies and disease flooded their nostrils. An Austrian orderly went to let Dr Ross know they were there.

Isabel was shocked when she appeared. Since she'd last seen her, she had lost more weight from her already too-thin frame and there were dark shadows under her eyes. Isabel could have sworn her hair had turned grey in the last two weeks.

'Dr MacKenzie, Sister Tully, how lovely to see you. Unfortunately I don't have time to entertain you.'

'You must stop for a few minutes and have tea and cake, Dr Ross,' Maud said. Isabel could tell that her friend was as taken aback as she herself had been at Dr Ross's altered appearance.

'You shouldn't be here,' Dr Ross replied. 'I'd blame myself if either of you came down with an infection.'

'It's a risk we run even in our hospital,' Isabel protested.

'No, it is not. Your hospital is clean and you have proper sanitary arrangements. None of that exists here.'

'Come back with us, then,' Maud pleaded. 'Dr Bradshaw would be happy to have you in the unit.'

Dr Ross drew a hand across her face. 'Would you leave your patients to die?'

'Of course not,' Isabel replied. It was unthinkable.

'Then, my dears, you will understand. Neither can I.'

It was only a week after their visit to Dr Ross that news came that typhus was rampaging through Serbia again, wiping out whole villages and large tranches of the Serbian Army.

And not just the Serbs. Two doctors and three nurses from their own unit had been placed in isolation. The atmosphere in the unit was grim, and became grimmer still when they heard that Dr Ross had died from the disease. It was even worse among the Serbian medical staff. News trickled in that the Serbian doctors, working in overcrowded hospitals and with no way to isolate infected patients, were dying almost as rapidly as their patients. Milan was sent to help at the military hospital in Belgrade, and Maud admitted that, although she hated to be parted from him, she was relieved to see him moved away from the typhus raging in and around Kragujevatz.

Dr Bradshaw called the staff together. Her face was drawn and she had deep shadows under her eyes. 'We need help,' she said. 'You will be aware that we're in the throes of a typhus epidemic. I understand that there are around five thousand cases in Serbia alone – not just among the soldiers but the civilian population too. People are dying at a rate of almost two hundred a day. Dear Dr Ross isn't the only doctor who has died. In the last three weeks the Serbians have lost twenty-one doctors in Valjevo alone. I've written to Dr Inglis asking for more nurses and doctors but, as we have to deal with the epidemic now, I'm going to establish a new typhus hospital in one of the old barracks. I need an experienced nurse to take charge of it.'

The women looked at one another. They all knew what running a hospital of typhus patients could mean.

Dr Bradshaw's eyes came to rest on Sister Guthrie. 'Sister Guthrie has volunteered to take charge. I'm sure you will all join me in wishing her the best of luck.'

The women filed out in hushed silence. Isabel went up to Sister Guthrie and took her chilled hands in hers. 'Are you sure about this, Margaret?'

The older woman shivered. 'No, but what else can I do? None of us can turn our backs now.'

Chapter 38

France, March 1915

Jessie knew she had to return to Paris to warn Archie that Lord Maxwell's body had been found, but her request for a day off was denied. There was great excitement at the abbey: Dr Inglis, the founder and chief medical officer of the Scottish Women's Hospital, was expected and everyone was needed to get the unit looking its best for her.

In addition, they were kept busy day and night with the unremitting flow of casualties from the front, and when patients weren't taking up their time, the nurses and orderlies scrubbed, then scrubbed again.

Apart from her anxiety about Archie, Jessie was worried about Lady Dorothea. She had taken a week's leave to attend her brother's funeral, but since she'd come back she'd been weak and listless. Jessie was worried that she had returned to duty too soon. She was keeping an eye on her, but it was difficult when there was so much to do.

To her relief, Dr Ludlow needed someone to collect supplies from Paris and agreed that Jessie, who had had only one day off since she'd been there, could go too. She sent a message to Archie, asking him to meet her in the Tuileries gardens.

He grinned broadly when he spotted her sitting on a bench near the fountain. He wouldn't be so happy when he heard what she had to say.

'Where to today, Jess?'

'I'm content to stay here and admire the Louvre,' she replied, reluctant to spoil his mood. 'It's hard to imagine how big it must be inside. They could fit the whole of Skye into just one wing. And did you see the Gare du Nord? It's even grander than Edinburgh Castle and it's only a railway station.'

'One day I shall build houses that are even more elegant than these fancy Parisian apartments. After the war, I shall send for you and we shall stay in the grandest hotel in Paris. Would you like that?'

'I'd love it.'

He picked her up by the waist and swung her around. 'And you shall have any dress you wish and your own motor-car. Servants, too, of course. They'll curtsy to you and you'll say, "A cup of tea, please," in that fancy accent you have now from spending time with aristocrats.'

'I don't speak like them!' Jessie protested.

'Yes, you do. A little. But to me, sister, you were always a gentlewoman.'

'Thank you, kind sir.' Jessie bobbed him a curtsy.

Despite everything that had happened, it seemed that Archie, at least, was happy. But she could no longer put off what she had to tell him. 'I have news for you, Archie. It concerns Lady Dorothea and her family.'

His eyes grew watchful. 'You've come to care about her, haven't you?' he said.

'Yes,' Jessie said. 'She's a good woman, an honourable one.' She shuddered. 'It makes it so much worse that I'm keeping secrets from her. I doubt she'll ever forgive me, should she find out.'

'There's no need for her to know, is there?'

'That's what I have to tell you. Lord Charles has been found – at least his remains have – in a shallow grave.'

She glanced at him. He was motionless, his face carved in stone.

'How was he found?'

Jessie's skin prickled. He didn't seem surprised to hear Charles had been killed.

'Does it matter? What is important is that he must have been murdered and now the Earl of Glendale will pursue his death with new vigour.'

Archie's eyes darkened. 'Maxwell deserved to die.'

It was as if someone had poured freezing water down her neck. 'What do you mean?'

He placed his hands on her shoulders. 'Remember what Dad always said? A man without honour is not a man at all. Do you believe I am a man of honour?'

She nodded.

'Then all you need to know is that I did only what a man of honour would have done.'

Dear God in Heaven. 'You know what happened to him, don't you? Please tell me you had nothing to do with it.'

'I can't.'

'Can't or won't? Lord, Archie, you know I would never betray you.'

His mouth twisted. 'Even if you think your brother a murderer?'

'But you do know something, don't you? I'm

tired of these evasions and half-truths, Archie. Tell me the truth.'

He gripped her arm. 'I can't tell you what truly happened, Jessie. You must trust me.'

'Must?' She shook her head. 'Why can't *you* trust *me* enough to tell me the truth?' She tugged herself free of his grip. 'I won't see you again. Not until you're prepared to tell me what really happened. All of it. Every last thing. Until you can see that you owe me that...' She blinked away angry tears. 'You must make your choice Archie. Your honour or your sister.'

When he didn't reply, she knew she had her answer. 'I won't come and see you again,' she said softly. 'It wasn't safe before and it is even less so now.' She took his hand in hers. 'I ask you one more time to tell me that you are innocent of that man's death.'

When he remained silent, she touched his beloved face with a fingertip. 'Then it is goodbye, Archie. I pray to God to keep you safe.'

She left him in the gardens. When he didn't call after her or try to change her mind, she thought her heart would shatter into a thousand pieces.

Why wouldn't he tell her what had happened? He hadn't denied killing Charles but she couldn't believe he was a murderer. He had to be protecting someone. And there was only one person he'd risk his life and liberty for: Isabel MacKenzie.

As she walked along the Seine, her head was spinning with unanswered questions. Unless Archie told her the truth, she was powerless to help him.

Dr Inglis was a great deal smaller than Jessie had imagined, but such vitality and energy flowed from her, it made her appear ten feet tall. Once she had inspected the abbey and declared herself happy, she called a meeting of all the staff who weren't on duty. The dining hall was buzzing as everyone took their seats. Some had already met the famous doctor but those who hadn't were looking forward to meeting the leader of the Scottish Women's Hospitals.

Dr Ludlow waited until supper – a simple meal of bread and cheese but with roast pork in Dr Inglis's honour – was over, before rapping on her cup with a spoon.

'Ladies,' she said, as a hush fell over the room. Jessie smiled: in the time she'd been there she'd never heard all the women quiet at once. 'May I introduce Dr Inglis to those who haven't had the privilege of meeting her? I know you are aware of what she has achieved in a very short time, but there is more to be done.' She glanced down at the woman on her right. I shall let Dr Inglis tell you more.'

There was thunderous applause as Dr Inglis rose to her feet. She waited, a smile on her austere face, for the clapping and cheers to die away.

'Good evening. I thank you all from the bottom of my heart and on behalf of the government of France for joining us. To date, the Scottish Women's Hospital has three units and all are leaders in their field. We have the lowest incidence of infection and amputation.' She waited as the listening women applauded again. 'That is, as you will know, no small feat given the conditions we are working in. But our work is far from over. The war shows no sign of ending and we have many volunteers back in the United Kingdom eagerly awaiting the opportunity to join us. However,' she looked around the room, seeming to pause and hold each woman's eye, 'we have lost staff too. Our unit in Serbia has been particularly badly hit. Two doctors and three nurses have died from typhus.'

Jessie's heart thudded against her ribs. Might Isabel have been one of the doctors who had died? Even if she had something to do with Lord Maxwell's death, she hoped not.

'Therefore,' Dr Inglis continued, 'I am here to ask for volunteers to go there to make up the numbers. The abbey is so well run that it would be better for new recruits to start here and some of our more experienced staff to go to Serbia. I will not make any of you go. I simply ask, at this moment, for volunteers. I do not pretend that whoever goes will find life there easy, or without its dangers. If you choose to volunteer, I prefer that you do so in the full knowledge of the risk you will be taking. I don't wish you to make up your mind immediately. I would prefer you to sleep on it, or come and speak to me about it, if you prefer, but I should tell you that I plan to spend time at the unit myself once I have finished here.'

Dr Inglis had barely drawn breath before Lady Dorothea was on her feet. 'I'll go, if you'll have me.'

Dr Inglis consulted with Dr Ludlow before she replied. 'There's little need for shovers in Serbia at the moment. I've asked for funds to buy motor ambulances, and when we have them I shall need you to drive them. In the meantime, we require you here.'

Lady Dorothea sighed, but she knew, as did they all, that Dr Inglis, their leader, had the final say.

Jessie raised her hand. 'I'll go.' She couldn't bear to stay in France, not if she had to see Lady Dorothea every day, knowing she was deceiving her, and not if she couldn't see Archie.

As soon as the words were out of her mouth, Evans sprang to her feet. 'I should like to go too,' she said quietly.

A slow smile crossed Dr Inglis's face erasing the fatigue etched on her face. 'In that case,' she said, 'it's settled. Pack your belongings and be ready to leave in a day or two.'

Later, Jessie wrote to Archie telling him of her new address. Although she was still angry and hurt that he wouldn't confide in her, she couldn't bring herself to leave without letting him know where she was. She hesitated over whether or not to tell him that a couple of doctors had died, although she had been able to establish that Isabel hadn't been one of them. In the end she decided against it. If he knew staff were dying in Serbia, she wouldn't put it past him to come to the abbey to try to stop her going.

They had to pack while still working the twelve-hour shifts, but as Jessie had little with her, apart from her uniform and the small woollen blanket that had belonged to Seamus, it didn't take her long to gather her belongings together. She was glad that Evans was going too. A woman with little imagination but relentless good humour, she was easy and pleasant company. In addition, despite her remarkable aptitude for falling asleep whenever and wherever she got the opportunity, she was a hard and willing worker. Since she'd come to Jessie's ward, she had never once complained. The injured men adored her. Although she was plain, and prone to reading aloud to them from her Bible, most seemed to find something of those they had left behind in her kind and gentle manner.

But most of all, Jessie admitted, she liked having her as a friend.

Chapter 39

Serbia, March 1915

The journey took days rather than the hours it should have done. The smell of decay mingling with disinfectant permeated the stuffy train and Jessie was grateful when at last they arrived in Kragujevatz. They were met at the station by a woman who introduced herself as Sister Maud Tully.

'Are we glad to see you!' she said, with a wide smile. 'Although I wish there were ten of you.'

'Is it very bad?' Jessie asked.

'Quite, quite horrible, but we're coping, which is more than can be said for the Serbian hospitals.'

A bullock cart with a white cross painted on one side and a large wooden cross at the front trundled past.

'That's a death-cart,' Maud said, her blue eyes troubled. 'You'll get used to seeing them day and night, unfortunately.'

Evans brought her ever-present Bible out of her pocket, kissed it and bent her head in prayer.

'If she's going to do that every time we pass a corpse,' Maud whispered, with a mischievous smile, 'we're never going to get to our hospital.' Nevertheless, she waited until Evans was ready to move on.

'Dr Bradshaw has put you both on night duty on the relapsing fever ward – it's also where the hopeless cases are sent. I'm afraid we're so short-staffed that you'll have to start tonight. I do day shifts there, so I shall be giving you the report. I'll let you poor things get settled first, though.'

At seven thirty, after a supper of vegetable stew and beef tea, Jessie and Evans presented themselves for duty.

Maud looked up from her desk, her bright eyes shadowed with fatigue. 'Good. Did you manage to sleep?'

Although Jessie had managed only an hour or two, she was certain that Evans would have had more.

'Most of the men are doing well. There's just two I'm worried about – they have injuries as well as fever. Dr MacKenzie will be joining us for a ward round as soon as she's finished in theatre. Evans, would you be a darling and see to the men's Oxo?'

Jessie started at Isabel's name. Although she'd

389

known she would come across her, she hadn't expected to see her so soon. She waited until Evans had hurried away.

'Dr Isabel MacKenzie?' she asked.

'Yes. Do you know her? She's one of the surgical stars and a dear friend.'

'It was Dr MacKenzie who helped me join the unit,' Jessie said.

'Then she'll be delighted to make your reacquaintance.' Maud glanced over Jessie's shoulder. 'In fact, here she is.'

Jessie turned. It had been months since she'd last seen Isabel and she was shocked at how much weight she had lost. But they were all much thinner than they had been when they'd arrived on the continent.

'Dr MacKenzie, I believe you know Sister Stuart,' Maud said, with a tip of her head. 'She and Elizabeth Evans, an orderly, have come from the unit at Royaumont to help, brave souls.'

'Why, Jessie,' Isabel held out her hand, 'it's so nice to see you again.'

'And you, Doctor.'

'We'll catch up later,' Isabel said, 'once we've seen the patients. I'm sure Sister Tully's looking forward to her supper and bed.'

'Sister Tully can think of nothing she'd like more,' Maud replied, with a smile. 'Shall we make a start with the two boys I'm most concerned about?'

They stopped at the bed of a young man whose head was covered with a bandage with only a slit for his mouth. He was lying listlessly, his fingers fiddling with the edge of the sheet.

'This is Andreas,' Maud said. 'He's an Austrian soldier who was shot in the head. He also has relapsing fever.'

Isabel said something to him that Jessie guessed was in German. The young soldier smiled a little at the sound of her voice.

'How long has he been in hospital?' Jessie asked.

'I can't remember,' Andreas replied, in English. 'Many months, I think. Only a few days here.'

His hand snaked out from under the covers and Isabel took it. For a moment Jessie had a vision of the young man pointing a gun at Tommy and pulling the trigger, but she pushed the image away. This boy was someone's brother, someone's son, perhaps someone's husband. 'You're far from home,' Jessie said gently.

His mouth trembled and she suspected he was trying not to cry 'Please, Doctor, would you do something for me?'

'I'll try,' Isabel soothed.

'Could you write to my fiancée? She hasn't heard from me since I was captured. I can't see to write myself and the sisters don't know German. No one else will do it for me.'

'The Serbian orderlies tolerate the Serbian-speaking Austrians – many of them were neighbours before the war – but they loathe the true Austrians or the "Schwaba", as they call them,' Maud whispered to Jessie.

'Of course I will, Andreas,' Isabel replied, 'but I'd like to look at your wound. When I've finished with my other patients I'll return and write your letter for you.'

He squeezed her hand. 'Thank you.'

When Maud unwrapped Andreas's bandages, Jessie had to bite her lip to stop herself crying out. The soldier's face was partly missing – his nose was gone and part of his cheekbone was exposed. He stared up at, the roof with unseeing eyes as Isabel inspected the wound. She shook her head and Maud wrapped a clean bandage around his injuries.

After Isabel had spoken to him in German, they stepped away from the bed.

'There's nothing more to be done for him except to make him as comfortable as possible,' Isabel said. 'That letter to his fiancée needs to be written quickly.'

The next patient, two beds down from Andreas, was a Serbian soldier who, according to Maud, had been transferred earlier that day. He, too, had been in the Serbian military hospital for several weeks.

'This is Milo,' Maud said, drawing the screens around him. 'I need you to look at his back, Dr MacKenzie.'

Milo, who was on his side, looked at them with wide, frightened eyes.

'We'll be as gentle as we can,' Maud said softly. The boy just blinked. He probably had no idea what Maud was saying but must have heard the pity in her voice.

When she lifted his pyjama top, Jessie bit her lip again. She was used to seeing the most awful wounds, but this was so much worse than anything she'd seen. Milo had a bedsore that must have been there for months. Almost a third of the skin on his back had fallen away, exposing the vertebrae of his lower spine.

'What do you think?' Maud whispered to Isabel. 'Is there anything we can do for him?'

'I'll consult with the other doctors, but, no, I'm sorry, Sister Tully. I think it's too late. With some of the others we can excise the infected flesh if there's enough tissue left to heal, but there is nothing left here to cut away.'

Maud's eyes filled. 'He's only a baby. He doesn't even cry – he just lies there looking at me with his sad eyes. I can't bear it.'

Isabel took her arm. 'You must bear it, for his sake. I'll ask Dr Lightfoot to have a look but I'm certain she'll say the same as I. We can't save everyone, Maud, no matter how much we wish to.'

'I wanted to save this one. He reminds me of my brother. They're of a similar age. Milo's only sixteen. This beastly, senseless, stupid war.'

'I hate it too,' Isabel said. 'But we have to do our best for those we can help.' She walked to the other side of the bed, and crouched by Milo's side. 'I'll be back,' she said. 'It is going to be all right. *Dobra* – you understand?'

Jessie found her voice. 'We can't just let him die!'

Maud looked at her sympathetically. 'None of us wants any of our boys to die. If only we had got to him sooner he might have had a chance, but if Dr MacKenzie says nothing can be done, it usually means nothing can be done. She's developed quite a reputation here for saving hopeless cases.'

'I'm sorry, Sister Stuart. All we can do is try to

393

make his last few hours as painless as possible. I'll prescribe the morphia for him. Give him as much as you think he needs.'

A little later, they finished walking the ward. After Maud had gone off duty, Evans passed round hot drinks and urine bottles, then dimmed the lights. She asked if they would like a cup of tea and Isabel accepted with a smile, and said, 'Join me, Sister Stuart. Then I shall write Andreas's letter for him before I go off to bed.'

They took seats at the table at the end of the ward. Isabel closed her eyes briefly, but when she opened them again, the energy and vitality Jessie had always known were back. 'How are you?' Jessie asked.

'I'm well. And you?'

'The same.'

Isabel picked up a pen and started to write her medical notes. 'Did you see Archie when you were in France?'

'He came to the abbey, and I saw him twice in Paris.'

Isabel put her pen down and leaned forward. 'How is he?'

'He's well too.'

Isabel sighed. 'I suggested he stay away from the abbey. I heard that Charles Maxwell's sister, Dorothea, was there.'

'He came anyway.'

Isabel smiled. 'Archie has always done as he wishes. I doubt he'll ever change. He wanted to see you so much I suspected that nothing would stop him.'

'You could have knocked me over with a feather

394

when I realised Lady Dorothea was one of the orderlies. At least, she was then. She's a shover now.'

'Didn't she recognise you?'

'No. Why should she? She'd never met me or Archie before. And I'm Sister Stuart. She has no reason to connect me with Archie MacCorquodale.' Jessie hesitated. 'Did you know they found Lord Maxwell's body?' She watched Isabel closely.

'His body?' Isabel gave a sigh that seemed to come from the depths of her soul. 'So he is dead. Where did they find him?'

'Buried in a shallow grave on Galtrigill.' Jessie deliberately didn't soften the words. 'Now they know for certain Lord Maxwell was murdered, they'll search for Archie harder than ever.'

'Charles was buried?' Isabel paled. 'That means someone did kill him,' she said, almost to herself. 'I can't say I cared for him but I wouldn't wish him a violent death.'

Jessie knew that she wasn't lying. If Archie had killed Charles Maxwell, she genuinely didn't know. 'I can't help but wonder what really happened,' Jessie said, before she could stop herself. 'Whether Archie had anything to do with it.'

Isabel's head snapped up. 'No, Jessie! He told me he had nothing to do with whatever happened to Charles and I believe him. Surely you do too?'

Jessie kept her face expressionless. She couldn't possibly share her fear with anyone, particularly not with Isabel. Yet every instinct in her body was screaming that there was something Isabel was keeping from her. But what?

'All I know is that neither Lady Dorothea nor

her brother must ever find out who Archie is,' Jessie managed.

'His secret is safe with me,' Isabel said. 'I would never put harm his way. Now, here is Evans with our tea. Let's talk about something else.'

Chapter 40

Serbia, May 1915

Isabel peeled off her gloves and wiped a hand across her forehead. The small operating theatre was heating up in the midday sun. Her armpits were damp and a trickle of sweat ran down between her breasts. One more poor soldier would have to find a way of living without a leg. Sometimes she wondered if they were doing these young men a favour. What kind of work would this man, once a farm worker, find, now that he was so cruelly disabled?

But it was futile to worry about what would happen to them once the war was over. Her job was to save as many lives as possible. She was busier than ever, particularly since typhus was still killing thousands.

The nurse untied Isabel's gown and tossed it into the laundry bin behind them. Then, with the help of two orderlies, they lifted their patient onto a stretcher so he could be taken to the ward. Isabel would look in on him that afternoon. But for now, with no more patients waiting to be operated on, she had time to herself. Not far away there was a lake. She'd find Maud and see if her friend would accompany her for a swim. Water to wash with was in short supply, and she longed to immerse herself. If there was one thing the women all looked forward to when this hellish war was over, it was a decent bath.

She stepped out into the bright sunshine, screwing up her eyes against the glare. In the distance the ever-present thud of shells continued, making the ground shudder beneath her feet. She hardly noticed it any more. Even at night, when it was at its worst, she slept deeply. It was hardly surprising after she'd spent hours on her feet.

She walked down the narrow street, pausing to enjoy the sun on her face. As usual, at this time of day, the street was crowded with off-duty staff and soldiers. At the hospital, the nurses had brought outside any patient who was fit enough to be moved, sometimes still in their beds. It made an incongruous sight, but they took every opportunity to shower the men with fresh air. Sometimes Isabel wondered if they thought it could cure any ailment.

A truck drew up in front of the army barracks and two men jumped out. They turned and Isabel's breath caught in her throat. She stopped.

Unbelievably, it was Andrew and Simon. She had written to Andrew many times but had received only one reply. She'd tried to tell herself that no news was good news, but now, seeing him alive and well, she knew she had been terrified for him.

She hurried over to them and threw herself into

her brother's arms.

'We thought you'd be surprised.' Andrew grinned when she let him go. There were new lines around his eyes and mouth, but he was still her dear beautiful brother.

Simon was standing a step or two behind, keeping a polite distance until brother and sister had greeted each other.

'Lieutenant Maxwell, it's good to see you again.' She was surprised to find that she meant it.

'You too, Isabel.'

Isabel tucked her arm into Andrew's. 'Now, tell me, what are you doing here?'

'We're here to help the Serbian Air Force. We had a few days' leave and we thought we'd spend it with you. We left our kites at headquarters in Nish and begged the use of a motor for a few days and room in a tent with the American Red Cross in Mladanovatz.'

'You have a few days?'

'Seventy-two hours. Not enough time to go home, but enough to come and see you. I always knew that being a pilot would come in useful one day.'

Dr Bradshaw released Isabel from her duties while Andrew and Simon were there. When Isabel had tried to argue that she needed only a few hours, Dr Bradshaw had been adamant. 'I need my doctors refreshed,' she said. 'You haven't had any leave yet and you're exhausted.'

'We're all exhausted,' Isabel had protested. 'And there's so much to do with this latest typhus epidemic.'

Dr Bradshaw smiled tiredly. 'I know. This unit has been through a great deal and I wish I could send you all home for a couple of weeks' rest. Sadly, that's not possible.'

'I could work in the mornings and take the afternoons off.'

'You'll do no such thing. You have seventy-two hours, Dr MacKenzie, and if I catch even a glimpse of you on the wards, I shall put you on report.'

The two women shared a smile, knowing that Dr Bradshaw would do no such thing. She might try to run her unit along military lines, as Dr Inglis wanted it, but she had enough knowledge of her staff to realise that the best way to keep them happy was to allow them their independence – with the exception of becoming attached to one of the soldiers.

And Isabel did want to spend every moment she could with Andrew.

As the sun was shining, she coaxed a picnic from the cook. Andrew and Simon had brought cheese and cold meat from Paris, so they were well served.

After they had picnicked, Andrew stripped down to his long-johns and jumped into the lake. Simon shook his head when his friend tried to persuade him to come in.

'How is he?' Isabel asked. Although there were glimpses of the carefree young man Andrew had been, they seemed few and far between. Often when she glanced at him he was staring into the distance as if he were somewhere no one else could go.

Simon gazed longingly at him and Isabel prayed, for his sake, that only she could see the naked love in his eyes.

'He doesn't sleep. Come to think of it, neither do any of us.' Simon's hands trembled as he shook out a French cigarette. 'The Huns like to have a go at us when we fly over their trenches, and now that their engineers have found a way of mounting machine-guns on the front of their kites that can fire through the propellers, their damn pilots are having a go at us too.'

'Is it very bad?' Isabel whispered.

'It's not good. One poor chap was shot down yesterday.'

'Oh, no!'

'Forgive me,' Simon said quickly. 'I didn't mean to alarm you. You mustn't think the same thing will happen to us. He'd only had eight hours' flying time. Andrew and I have much more experience. Your brother flies as if he were born to it. No one can catch him.'

A shiver ran down Isabel's spine. She couldn't bear to think of anything happening to Andrew. 'Have you seen Dorothea recently? Is she well?' she asked.

'We see her whenever we have time. Sometimes in Paris, sometimes at the abbey.' Simon's eyes were bleak. 'Of course, I saw her at Charles's funeral. Mama and Papa didn't want her to leave again. They worry about us.'

Isabel's mouth went dry. 'Are you any closer to discovering what happened to your brother?'

'We found his remains buried on Skye.'

Isabel swallowed the nausea that had risen to

her throat. 'I'd heard,' she said. 'One of the nurses in the unit was with Dorothea when she received the news.'

'Until we can find the MacCorquodale fellow and are able to question him, then, no, we don't know for certain what happened. But Papa is convinced MacCorquodale killed Charles. He spends much of his time trying to get Scotland Yard to hunt for him, but with the war on, there's not much appetite for conducting a search. Papa has a private detective on it and I doubt he'll give up until he has MacCorquodale in his hands.'

Apart from Andrew's splashing and the call of the birds, there was silence. All of the joy went out of the day. Would Charles haunt her for the rest of her life?

'Come on, Simon,' Andrew called from the water. 'Don't be a sissy.'

Simon gave Isabel a smile of apology. He removed his jacket and boots, then jumped into the lake.

The remainder of Andrew's leave rushed by. Isabel found that the more time she spent with Simon, the more she appreciated his dry sense of humour, and his love for Andrew comforted her. Thankfully, Charles wasn't mentioned again and neither was the war. Instead the three of them, occasionally joined by Maud, Evans or some of others, talked only of happier times. However, as Isabel watched Simon and Andrew playing cricket with the nurses, she kept having to push away the foreboding sense of doom that clung to her like a shroud.

When, finally, it was time for them to leave, she thought her heart would break. 'Come back soon, Andrew,' she said, as he flung an arm around her.

'As often as I can. Chin up, old girl. I don't intend to let the Huns get me.'

But as he leaped into the lorry alongside Simon, she wondered if she would ever see either of them again.

Chapter 41

The weeks passed quickly and Jessie found the work no harder in Serbia than it had been at Royaumont, although the patients they were dealing with were different. Andreas had come through his latest bout of fever and, although he still said little, he was heartbreakingly appreciative to Jessie and the other nurses for any small task they did for him. Milo, to everyone's relief, had died a few days after Jessie arrived. At least with the morphia his passing had been peaceful.

She saw little of Isabel, who roomed with the other doctors, and for that she was grateful. She was pleased to find she had been billeted alongside Maud, who ran a tight ward and was always cheerful and ready for a chat when they found themselves off duty at the same time.

As the days grew warmer, the flood of patients with typhus eased. Soon there was less to do on the wards and more time for relaxing. They filled the days with games and dances, the recuperating patients joining in while those who were too sick to leave their beds were wheeled out to watch from the shade. The women adored the Serbs and one in particular sought out Jessie whenever he could. Although she did her best to discourage him, telling him she was married, he smiled, pretending not to understand.

She hadn't given up hope of coming across someone who could tell her what had happened to Tommy. Every week she wrote to Captain Steel, his commanding officer, asking if there was any news of her husband, and every week she received a letter back telling her that he was sorry but there was still no information. She wrote to Archie, too, telling him as much as she could about Serbia while staying on the right side of the censors. She hadn't heard from him recently and fretted.

She dabbed at her throat. All day she had been feeling seedy. She'd tried to ignore it, but it was getting worse.

Evans, who had been darting concerned looks her way, came to ask her to look at a dressing. Although Jessie longed to go to her room to rest, there were still two hours left of her shift. If only she could make it to the end, a good night's sleep would sort her out.

But as she fumbled with the dressing, she was finding it increasingly difficult to concentrate.

'Are you perfectly well, Sister?' Evans asked. 'You look a little flushed.'

'I have felt better,' Jessie admitted. 'Perhaps I should sit down for a moment.' The floor seemed to be shifting under her feet and she was grateful for the discreet support of Evans's arm.

'I'll fetch a doctor,' Evans said.

'No! They have enough to do. I'm just a little tired. That's all. A glass of water will keep me going.'

As Evans hurried away, Jessie lowered her lids. A few minutes' rest and she'd be able to carry on.

When she opened her eyes, she was in bed on the staff sick bay, with Isabel bending over her, looking concerned. Evans was hovering behind, peering over the doctor's shoulder.

Jessie tried to toss aside the blankets but she was too weak. The room was far too hot.

'Lie still, Jessie,' Isabel said softly. 'You're ill. You need to rest.' A cold cloth was placed on her forehead. 'Stay with her, Evans. I'll look in again as soon as I can, but in the meantime keep her as cool as possible.'

It was ridiculous her lying in bed when there were patients who needed looking after. Jessie attempted to push away Isabel's hand but found she could barely lift her arm. She closed her eyes. A little sleep, and then she would get up.

When she came to, Archie was in a chair by the bed. She must be dreaming. It was impossible that he could be here. Hadn't he gone to America?

'Archie? Is it really you?'

Archie's eyes were red, as if he'd been bending over a sooty fire. Didn't he know better? 'Hush, Jess. You have to rest.'

'Rest? Don't be silly. Not when there's baking to do and Daisy to milk.'

'Jessie, you're not at home in Skye. You're in

404

Serbia. But I'm really here and I'm not going to leave you until you're better.'

A figure bent over her, blocking him from her view. Cool hands felt for her pulse and laid a cold wet towel across her head. It felt so good, but she wanted to see Archie. She needed to know she hadn't dreamed him.

Thankfully, the figure moved away. It looked awfully like the doctor's daughter. What was she doing here? But her head was pounding and thinking was too much effort.

'I'll go and get Evans, Archie.' It was definitely the doctor's daughter's voice. 'I expect her fever to break soon.'

'And if it doesn't?' Archie's voice was ragged. He reached out and grabbed Isabel's wrist. 'For God's sake, Isabel, don't let her die.'

Die? Who was going to die? Jessie struggled to open her eyes. If someone was dying, she needed to help them. There was a click as the door closed. Even though she summoned all her strength, she couldn't move. But somebody was dead. 'Ah, Lord Maxwell is dead,' she said. There was something about those words that troubled her. 'Somebody killed him.'

Archie, if indeed it was him and not an apparition, spoke softly in Gaelic: 'You have to fight this, Jessie. I need you. You're all I have left.' His voice caught on the last word and he cleared his throat. 'Please, Jessie, you have to live. I can't let you die thinking your brother might be guilty of murder.'

Jessie couldn't think who or what he was talking about. Of course she didn't think Archie was a

405

murderer. Archie was her brother, the son of a Martyr of Glendale, and if he'd killed anyone, he would have had good reason. There was a war on, after all. She remembered that now. She was trying to stay conscious so that she could make sense of what he was saying, but she was so tired. It was as if she were being pulled into a dark hole as deep as Dunvegan Loch and she was powerless to resist.

'You see, Jessie, I didn't kill Lord Maxwell. He was already dead when I found him.'

When she next woke, Isabel was there and Archie was in the chair with his elbows propped on his knees. He looked almost happy.

'How are you feeling, Jessie?' Isabel asked.

Jessie tried to speak but her tongue was dry and her throat raw.

Archie came behind her and lifted her into a sitting position while Isabel held a cup of water to her lips. Never had anything tasted so good.

When she'd had enough she lay back, exhausted. 'What's wrong with me?'

'You've had typhus,' Isabel said, 'but you're better now.' Fragments were coming back to her. Evans sitting next to her holding her hand, Isabel bending over her looking worried, Archie talking to her in Gaelic, his voice low and reassuring, making her think once or twice that he was Dad.

What had he said? Something about finding Charles dead. Or had she dreamed it?

'You've been ill for two weeks and you'll be off your feet for a while longer, I'm afraid,' Isabel said. She looked exhausted, almost as if she, too, were ill. 'Now, if you'll excuse me, I'll leave you two alone.'

When Isabel had left, Jessie turned to Archie. He was grey with fatigue. 'How is it that you're here?' she asked.

'Isabel sent for me.'

'You came all this way just to see me?'

'I'd walk across the Atlantic, Jess, if I had to.'

'Have I really been ill for two weeks?'

'You have. You were very sick.'

'And you've been with me all that time?'

'It took me three days to get here after Isabel telegraphed me, but I've been here for ten days now.'

'What about your work in Paris?'

'Do you think I could stay away? Anyway, they need ambulance drivers here as much as they do in Paris, if not more. The American Hospital is so swamped with volunteers they've set up a rotation system. Three months' duty at a time.' He half smiled. 'So I'm going to stay here for the next six months. The Serbs need people to retrieve their wounded from the battlefield and, understandably, they don't want to use women.'

If Jessie had had more energy she would have argued with him. So far, the women had done as well – if not better – as any male unit. But she had something else on her mind. Something that couldn't wait.

'Archie, when I was ill I thought you said something strange.' She licked her dry lips. 'You said when you found Lord Maxwell he was dead. What did you mean?'

Archie leaned back in his chair and pulled a

hand through his thick hair. 'I thought you were going to die, Jessie. Forget what I said.'

'I can't, Archie. I don't want to forget. You have to tell me the truth this time. Please.'

Archie stood up and started pacing the small room. There wasn't far for him to move as there was barely enough room for Jessie's bed and the bedside table, but that didn't stop him doing a passable impression of a bear in a cage she had once seen in the Grassmarket.

'You should know that I couldn't let you leave this world thinking your brother a murderer. You should also know that Isabel saved your life. She's spent every hour she could tending you. If I'm to tell you what happened, you must promise me on the souls of those you've loved that you'll never repeat what I tell you.'

Jessie nodded, too weak to respond.

'I did fight with Maxwell – that much is true. He was out riding. I suspect now that he was on the look-out for Isabel. He saw us kiss.' He closed his eyes, as if thinking back. 'It was a quick kiss, two friends saying goodbye for the last time.'

Jessie doubted that but held her tongue.

'When Isabel and I parted, he rode towards me and said something about her that no man should say of a woman. I pulled him from his horse and punched him. He didn't put up much of a fight. As Dad used to say, cowards and bullies back down easily when challenged. But he'd been drinking and there was a wildness in his eyes. When I saw him ride off in Isabel's direction, I followed.

'He was mounted and I was on foot, so even though I ran, I was well behind him. Then I heard

408

a scream. A few moments later, Isabel appeared from one of the copses – the one near the cliff. She was running as if the devil himself was behind her. I had to get to Maxwell to stop him following her.' He took a deep, shuddering breath.

'And you found him.'

'Yes. He was lying on the ground. At first I thought he'd passed out, but when I got closer his eyes were open and staring. There was a bloodied rock next to his head and a piece of white petticoat still in his hand. That was when I knew that Charles had attacked Isabel and she had killed him.'

Bile rushed to her throat. Whatever she had thought, in all her imaginings she had never suspected this. '*Isabel?* All this time it was *her?* How could she lie about it, knowing you were suspected?'

'Because she doesn't know she killed him – and she must never find out. When I saw her, she was running as if she expected him to appear at any moment. She did admit that Charles attacked her when I saw her in Paris. I'd stake my life she had no idea and still doesn't.'

'What did you do?'

'I stayed by the body, thinking. I knew it was possible that Isabel would report the attack – if not to the police then to her father. They would look for Charles, and when they found him, she would be accused of his murder.'

'But if she had killed him, it had to be in self-defence. Could they blame her?'

'I couldn't take the risk. At the very least there would have been a trial. Even if she wasn't found guilty, she would have been ruined.

'I waited until dark and then I buried him. I buried the rock and the piece of petticoat separately. His horse was still tied to a tree so I let it loose and sent it on its way. I hoped people would believe that it had thrown him over the cliff. Then I went home.'

'Why didn't you throw his body into the sea? No one would've suspected her then.'

'I couldn't. If I carried his body from the copse anyone might have seen. It was still light.'

He was right. Out of the shelter of the trees, a person could be seen for miles.

'Later that night Flora McPhee came to the door. She told me and Mam that she'd seen me fight with Maxwell and that she'd told her dad. When they'd heard that his lordship was missing, Lachie said he'd go to the earl and tell him what Flora had said. He'd had no love for our family since Dad had threatened him with the police if he didn't stop hitting his wife. He was too drunk to go that night, but Flora knew he would as soon as he was sober.'

'But you ran away. The police would have had only Lachie McPhee's word that you'd been there. Everyone knew he was a drunk and, besides, if anyone had a grudge against Charles Maxwell it was him. It was his daughter his lordship had disgraced.'

'Don't you see, Jessie? I couldn't let him take the blame either. If I'd done that, I'd have no self-respect or honour.' He shook his head. 'No, the only way I could defend myself was to tell the police that he'd attacked Isabel. And in burying the body

410

I'd made it worse for her. Now they'd never believe that his death was an accident. Don't you see? At best they'd think I'd killed him because of her, and at worst they'd decide she'd helped me hide the body. Either way, her life would be over. I couldn't allow that to happen. Not for a man like him. The only thing I could do was leave.'

It explained everything – Archie's evasiveness, the feeling she'd had about Isabel too.

'Did Mam know?'

'She was there when Flora came to the house. She agreed it was best for me to go.'

Jessie's head was aching. Isabel had killed Lord Maxwell and her idiot brother had diverted any suspicion that might fall on her to himself. If the police found him and he was brought to trial, he would certainly hang.

'You must have loved her very much,' she said.

'Yes – and, God help me, I love her even more now.'

For the next few days, Jessie drifted in and out of sleep. Sometimes her dreams were filled with men's corpses, looking up at her with pleading, empty eyes, and she would start awake, her heart thudding until soothing hands shushed her back to sleep. At others her dreams were of Seamus and Tommy, the three of them at their home in Leith. Seamus would be playing on the floor while she sat on Tommy's lap, happy and content. Waking from that dream was worse than the others.

The periods she spent awake grew longer: she saw less of Isabel and Archie, and more of Evans who attended to her every need. When she was alone, she thought of what Archie had told her.

Isabel had killed Charles Maxwell. The woman her brother loved would, if her secret was ever revealed, be tried with him for murder. What would she have done had she been in Isabel's position? It was an easy question to answer. She would have fought. She would have done whatever was necessary to save herself. How could she blame Isabel?

But it was Archie whose life was in danger. If he were ever arrested, would Isabel come forward and speak for him? And if she did, what then? Even if the court believed Archie's story, Isabel might be arrested and face death. Even if she were found innocent, her reputation and that of her family would be destroyed. But what of the reputation of Jessie's family? Did that not count? She was the daughter of a Martyr of Glendale, and Archie was his son. At one time they had been as highly regarded in their community as Isabel and her family were in theirs. Now people would turn away from them, and her parents' memory would be stained.

Her thoughts whirled, giving her no peace, always coming back to one immutable fact: she had promised Archie on the soul of her dead son. To break that promise was unthinkable. Archie was safe, as long as no one found out who he truly was. He had made a new life for himself in America – a good life, by all accounts. There was nothing to be gained from telling anyone what she knew, so Isabel would continue to lead her charmed life, unhindered by the knowledge that she had killed someone and left another to take the blame.

Would Archie have behaved honourably if he had exposed Isabel to save his own skin? No. Their father had believed a man's honour was the most important thing he had. It was the only thing that no one could take from him. He, too, would have risked his life to save the woman he loved.

How, then, could she blame Archie? She wished only that he had never set eyes on the doctor's daughter.

Chapter 42

Isabel was in the hall drinking tea when Archie walked in.

When Jessie had first fallen ill, she had wondered if she'd pull through. She'd written to Archie immediately and hadn't been surprised when he'd turned up a few days later. To her dismay, as soon as she'd seen him, still crumpled from his travels and frantic about his sister, her heart had done something complicated inside her chest.

He, on the other hand, had barely looked at her.

Seeing him every day had been strange ... and disturbing. Now she knew what Maud had meant about feeling as if someone had lit a candle in her heart. This beastly war. It made everything so much more intense. She couldn't fall in love with

Archie. Whatever Maud had said about the war changing everything, a marriage between them was still impossible, and not just because of the difference in their stations. When the war was over, she'd return to her life and he to America.

'How did you find Jessie today?' she asked.

'I suspect she'll be back on the wards before long.'

'She's strong and determined,' Isabel agreed.

'Will you walk with me?' Archie's voice appeared to be coming from a long way off. 'I've a few minutes to spare before I have to get back to the field hospital.'

Isabel was so tired she didn't know if she could speak, let alone walk, but she couldn't say no. She wanted to be with him for as much time as they had left. 'Of course,' she said, rising to her feet.

They walked through the town in silence, following the road as it rose towards the hills.

'Thank you,' Archie said.

She looked at him in surprise. 'For what?'

'Caring for Jessie. Letting me know she was ill.'

'It's what I do, Archie.'

'You didn't have to nurse her yourself.'

'I wanted to.'

He placed a hand under her elbow as she stumbled on a loose rock. His touch made her tremble.

'When will you go?' she asked. She didn't want him to.

'As I told Jessie, I'm not leaving. I can work for the American Red Cross in Belgrade as easily as I can in France. Besides,' he smiled grimly, 'the

414

Serbs need help more than anyone and I've always had a weakness for a hopeless cause.'

When he sent her a sideways look she knew he was referring to the day he'd asked to court her. Her heart thumped hard against her ribs. Did he still care for her?

'I want to be near Jessie,' he continued. 'I lost her once and came close to losing her again. I'm all she has now.'

And me? Isabel wanted to ask. Do you want to be near me? The sun was high in the sky turning the hills blue. 'Do you ever think of Skye?' she asked.

'Often.'

'Do you regret that you'll never return?'

Archie stopped and looked down the valley. 'No,' he said finally. 'Scotland wasn't kind to me. America is my home now.'

'What about Jessie? The war won't last for ever.'

'I hope she'll come to America when the war's over. She can be a nurse there.' He turned to her. 'You must be tired. Shall we sit for a while?'

When she nodded, he shrugged out of his jacket and placed it on a rock with a flat top. They sat side by side, Isabel unbearably conscious of his leg against hers. Although she knew she should move away, she stayed where she was. Perhaps it was because of the heat, perhaps it was because she was tired, but all of a sudden she felt like crying.

'What will you do after the war is over?' Archie asked.

'I'll continue as a doctor. I might even find a position as a surgeon in a hospital. It's what I've always wanted.'

He gave her a searching look. 'You've changed.'

'Have I?'

'You're softer. Less sure of yourself. More like the woman I hoped you'd be.'

'In what way?' At one time his words would have offended her, but now she was curious to know what he meant.

'Do you remember that day we met on the moors?' he asked.

'As if it were yesterday.' Although she barely remembered the girl she'd once been. The girl who had thought life was hers for the taking.

'I'd never met anyone like you,' he said. 'You looked at me as if I were some sort of strange animal you hadn't seen before.' He touched the tip of her nose. 'I don't know how you managed to look up at me, yet down at the same time.'

She burned with shame. She had thought him forward when he'd fallen into step beside her, because she was the doctor's daughter and he a crofter's son, yet it hadn't been long before she'd found herself seeking him out. She remembered the easy way he had held himself, despite his bare feet and darned clothes. 'I thought you were won-derful,' she admitted, 'so real, so much part of the world in a way I wanted to be.'

'You thought me wonderful, but not fit to court you.' His voice was flat. 'I hoped that the Isabel I thought I knew would have the courage not to care what society thought.'

'It was when I ignored the rules that I found myself in trouble,' she reminded him quietly.

The memory of Charles's hands on her flesh rushed back and she shuddered. There was little

416

to be gained in remembering that day and even less by longing for what could never be.

She rose to her feet. 'We should go. I'm due back on the wards soon.'

Archie stood too and gripped her shoulders. 'You can trust me never to hurt you, Isabel. Do you not know that? There's nothing you could do or say that will change how I feel about you.'

His words should have surprised her, but they didn't. She could see his love for her in his eyes. She wished she was stronger, that she could let herself love him back.

'Don't, Archie,' she said softly. 'Don't love me. I can bring you only pain.'

Chapter 43

As soon as she was back on her feet, Jessie returned to work. She had kept her promise to say nothing of what Archie had told her to anyone but, certain that Isabel would see the knowledge of what she'd learned in her eyes, she tried to keep away from her as much as was possible in this strange life where they were all thrown together.

The summer days continued to pass with little activity on the front line.

Every day one of the staff would make a trip into town and come back loaded with pastries, and almost every night, before going to bed, they would gather in the sitting room for tea and cake.

The women would chat about the lives they'd left behind and Jessie would listen, fascinated. How could anyone fill their days with nothing but balls and dances, dinners, museums and helping with the village fête?

If they weren't busy, neither was Archie. Twice a week he would collect her and as many others of the staff who were off duty in one of the vehicles at his disposal and take them out into the countryside for a picnic. Sometimes he would come alone, at others with another ambulance driver or one of the young doctors from the Red Cross unit. Often he'd bring a letter for Maud from her Serbian. Maud had confided that when the war was over they intended to marry.

Jessie noticed that Isabel would never join the others in their plea to be taken to the lake or to the nearest town. Instead she would hang back, with a wistful expression on her face. Maud and Evans often formed part of the group and they would try to coax her to come with them, but she would say she had letters to write or laundry to do. Jessie suspected she was avoiding Archie, and she was glad. But if Archie noticed, he seemed not to care. Perhaps, at last, he'd stopped thinking about her. There were, after all, plenty of others in Kragujevatz who were happy to spend time in his company.

As summer turned to autumn, when everyone was restless because they hadn't enough to do, the fighting became fiercer and news filtered through that the Germans were expected to take back Belgrade. Dr Inglis had returned and, once more, the women were called together.

'We've been invited to set up a field hospital in Mladanovatz,' she said. 'It's closer to the front line than we are here but the renewed fighting means our services are needed there more than ever. As before, I ask for volunteers.'

Isabel's hand was the first to go up and Dr Bradshaw smiled at her. 'Dr MacKenzie, I was hoping you would volunteer. We need a surgeon.'

Dr Lightfoot raised her hand too, but this time the MO shook her head. 'I'm sorry, Doctor, but work nearer the front is more suited to the young.'

'Nothing wrong with my legs or my ability to operate,' Dr Lightfoot grumbled. 'Can't see why I shouldn't go too.'

'We need you here,' the MO said. 'Now, I require some nurses and orderlies. We're expecting more to arrive any day but I'd rather keep the new recruits here to begin with.'

Maud raised her hand. 'I might get a chance to see Milan,' she whispered to Jessie. 'And if Dr MacKenzie's volunteering, how can I say no?' She jabbed her in the ribs with her elbow. 'Come too, Jessie. We're in this together.'

Jessie smiled and raised her hand. Although it would mean working more closely with Isabel, how could she resist the chance to be closer to the fighting soldiers and the possibility of hearing a sliver of news about Tommy?

'If you're going, Sister, I'm blowed if I'm going to stay behind,' Evans said. 'You're my talisman.'

Several more volunteered, until they numbered twenty.

'Dr MacKenzie will be acting as chief medical

officer,' Dr Bradshaw said, 'although one of the more senior doctors will visit you as often as she can. I'd like you to be ready to go tomorrow. It will all be under canvas, I'm afraid, but you'll have everything you need exactly as it is here.'

They filed out and Maud tucked her arm into Isabel's. 'CMO! My dear, you're going up in the world.'

Isabel paused. 'I'm so glad you're all coming with me. Now I don't feel nearly as nervous.'

Jessie doubted that Isabel had ever felt nervous. Everyone spoke of the doctor's coolness in the operating theatre. Sometimes she wondered if Isabel had a heart.

As she was about to return to her ward, a nurse came towards them with a pile of mail. 'There's one for you, Sister Stuart.' When she held out a handwritten letter, Jessie recognised the writing: it was from Captain Steel, Tommy's commanding officer.

She took the letter and went to sit under an olive tree. She had come to dread opening Steel's missives. They never said anything different.

When she had finished reading she buried her face in her hands and sobbed. Just when she thought she had no tears left, she felt a shadow fall over her and looked up to find Isabel, Maud and Evans standing there, their faces tight with concern.

Isabel dropped to her knees beside her. 'Bad news, Jessie?'

'No. The best. My Tommy's alive.' She held out the letter. 'Read it, please, so I know it's real.'

Isabel took it, and when a smile crossed her face

Jessie knew she wasn't dreaming. There was no mistake. Tommy wasn't dead. He had been in hospital in Germany for some time, although the captain didn't know what his injuries were, before being transferred to a prisoner-of-war camp. The Red Cross had written to her in Edinburgh as well as to him.

She had always known that Tommy couldn't be dead, and now she had proof. Her beloved Tommy was alive and one day, when this wretched war was over, he'd be coming back to her.

Chapter 44

Serbia, early October 1915

The camp in Mladanovatz was indeed under canvas, and as the women struggled to pitch their tents, the wind whipped their skirts over their heads and blew into their hair. Jessie was glad that she had decided to cut hers.

The sound of cannon was louder there. Every few minutes an explosion would rock the ground beneath their feet, and when the wind dropped, the rat-a-tat of bullets could be heard distinctly. Soldiers filed past on their way to the fighting, and there was talk that the Allies would be coming to join the Serbian Army. Everyone prayed that this would be so. And not before time. The Serbians had put up such a valiant defence of their small country that it was inconceivable it should fall now.

Immediately they had set up the field hospital, they were inundated with patients. The men came in a continuous stream, most on bullock carts, wrapped in blankets, some carried on their comrades' backs or crawling on hands and knees. The injuries were heartbreaking: men with their torsos ripped open, their insides lying beside them in the mud, missing arms and legs, sometimes several limbs; men with faces half blown away and missing eyes. As soon as an injured soldier had been attended to, he was placed on a stretcher and sent to another hospital by train. Jessie tried not to think about the dying and the maimed as she held hands and dressed wounds, but for all of them, it was becoming increasingly difficult. At least she had the knowledge that Tommy was alive to sustain her. She wished he would write to her but knew it was possible that she would have to wait until the war ended before she heard from him.

It wasn't long before the carefree days of the summer were nothing but a distant memory. There were no more picnics or concerts as the staff worked tirelessly to keep ahead of the relentless flow of casualties. Shocking news of Edith Cavell's arrest on suspicion of spying had reached them and every Sunday there were prayers for her safe release. The mood was sombre in the camp and, as more and more news of atrocities reached them, hatred of the enemy solidified.

Jessie and Maud shared a tent, and although Maud longed to go to Belgrade to see her Serbian doctor, she had been forbidden to go by Dr Inglis, who had come to Mladanovatz to help.

The doctors, Isabel included, were operating constantly, often returning to the theatre after supper. Sometimes they had to work through the night, even though they'd been on their feet all day. The worst time to be on duty was dawn: in the dim light the staff would have to step over patients lying on mattresses on the ground and sometimes, on their way outside to incinerate bloodied bandages and blood-soaked pillows, they would trip over a basin or bag. Most patients died in the small hours of the morning, and there were always bodies to be buried before the others awoke.

There was too much to do to pay attention to the fighting, but Jessie worried about Archie. The worst of the fighting was taking place close to Belgrade only a few miles away and he was bringing the wounded back from the first-aid dressing station on the front line. He continued to visit when he could, but even he had lost some of his swagger.

Sometimes Jessie caught a glimpse of his dark head as he delivered another patient to their hospital but no sooner had he placed the stretcher on the ground than he was off again. Occasionally he would come into the mess and have tea with them.

'Your brother and Dr MacKenzie appear to be spending time together,' Maud said, one day, as they changed the dressings of a soldier who had shrapnel wounds to his abdomen, legs and torso. Isabel had been the operating surgeon and, as always, her stitching was neat.

Jessie looked up. 'I can't see when they would find the time.'

Maud's head was bent over their patient as she swabbed the wounds with carbolic acid. 'One can find time if one really wants to. I say good luck to them. We all need something to take our minds off this.'

'I don't think...' Jessie paused. She liked Maud, and hoped they would remain friends after the war, but gossip linking Isabel's name with Archie's could hurt them both.

They finished the dressings and left one of the orderlies to give the soldier a cigarette and a cup of tea. They moved to the sisters' table to write up what they had done.

'Things won't be the same after this, Jessie. We can't go back to how things were. It makes no sense. Our mamas and papas will have to understand that we're different women from the ones they knew.'

An explosion, so near it sounded almost right outside, deafened them.

'More wounded coming in!' Evans popped her head through the tent flap. 'No supper for us for a while.'

They worked on through the evening until all the wounded had been operated on and settled for the night.

They were heading for the mess tent, the whizzes and bangs of exploding shells lighting the sky, when Jessie saw Archie. Unshaven and splattered with mud and blood, he was walking alongside one of the British commanding officers. Instead of stopping to talk to her, he followed the officer into Dr Inglis's tent. Their leader had come a few days ago for one of her visits.

'You go on without me,' Jessie said to Maud. 'I want to find out what's going on.'

She loitered outside the tent and waited for Archie to reappear. When both men did, the major's mouth was set in a grim line. Paying no attention to Jessie, he turned to Archie. 'You know these women, McPherson, don't you?' he barked.

'I do,' Archie replied.

'Well, use your influence, man, and make them see sense. If they insist on staying, we can't protect them.' He stalked off without waiting for a reply. Jessie smiled. She could just imagine the scene between the major and Dr Inglis and had no difficulty in guessing who had come off worse.

Archie pulled his hand through his hair in the gesture Jessie knew so well. His usual ready grin was missing. 'He's right, Jessie. You have to go. The Austrians have retaken Belgrade. You've done a grand job but it's over for the Serbian Army. They've started retreating. The unit I'm with will follow soon.'

The tent flap opened and Dr Inglis swept past. 'Sister Stuart, please let the others know that I wish to speak to them in the mess. Eight thirty sharp. Only those who have to stay on the ward to care for the patients are exempt.' With a rustle of her skirts, she was gone.

'*A Thighearna*, is she always like that?' Archie asked, bemused. 'She gave the major a right earful just now. Said that no army could tell her what to do.'

Jessie grinned back. 'Dr Inglis is a tough bird, but we love her. No one works harder than she does. If she asks us to stay, we'll stay.'

425

The smile left Archie's face and he glowered at her. 'Jessie, listen. There's no telling what the Germans will do if they capture you. Hasn't the execution of Nurse Cavell taught you that? And the doctors here aren't even in uniform.' Two days ago they'd heard that the brave nurse had been executed by firing squad and that even at the last she'd refused to condemn the enemy.

'Yes, they are,' Jessie protested, determined to lighten his mood. 'They would never wear those horrible grey skirts and jackets unless they had to. You have to hear them complaining to know that it's a uniform.'

'It may be a uniform to them, but I doubt it will appear so to the Germans. You can't take the chance that they won't shoot the lot of you. Jessie, please, listen to me. This is no joking matter. You have to leave.'

Jessie studied Archie's face. He meant every word. But how could they leave when so many men still depended on them?

'We'll be all right, Archie. We'll go when Dr Inglis tells us it's time to and not a moment sooner.'

As Jessie had suspected, Dr Inglis wanted to discuss the major's visit with them. As soon as Jessie had left Archie, she went from tent to tent rousing women. Happily, most of the day shift were still awake, either chatting as they toasted bread in front of a stove or writing letters home. Once she had passed on Dr Inglis's message, she went to the wards to find the night sister. She appeared irritated to be robbed of her staff – even for an hour – but nodded briefly and told Jessie to leave it to her. No one would dream of going against Dr Inglis's orders, not even the night sister.

The women gathered in the dining room. Isabel was there, looking curious but unalarmed. Maud and Evans arrived together, the latter seeming more alert than usual. Some of the women clustered around Jessie, asking if she knew what the meeting was about.

'You'll have to wait for Dr Inglis,' she said, ignoring their pleas for 'just the tiniest snippet of what it's all about'. Whatever Archie said, Jessie wasn't going to be the one to influence anyone one way or another.

She looked around the chattering women. She would miss them when this was over. Despite the niggles that were an inevitable consequence of living together, they were a fine bunch, brave and uncomplaining, and Jessie was proud to be among them.

Everyone hushed as Dr Inglis strode in, followed by Dr Bradshaw.

'Good evening, ladies.' The habitual twinkle behind her usually severe expression was absent. 'Thank you for coming.'

Her audience waited patiently. Only the sound of the wind and the distant boom of cannon disturbed the silence.

'I've brought you here to update you as to the present situation and to ask you to make a decision.'

The tent filled with a low murmuring, and Dr Inglis waited until everyone had settled down again before continuing. 'The British consul came to see me this evening, to let me know that he thinks we should leave. The Serbian Army is in retreat and our safety can no longer be guaranteed.' She flashed one of her rare smiles. 'If I could have sixpence for the amount of times I've heard that I'd be a rich woman.'

Some of the women clapped, and others called, 'Hear, Hear!' Jessie glanced to where Isabel was sitting, her hands folded on her lap and her head cocked to one side as she listened. On Isabel's right, Maud smiled and raised a fist. Evans's eyes were closed as her lips moved in silent prayer.

'But this time he may be correct. If the army pulls out we will be unprotected, and there is a chance that, as the enemy draws closer, we'll find ourselves behind enemy lines. Despite what the major says, I don't believe that the German Army will treat us with anything but respect. But I cannot guarantee it. Especially now that we know what was done to our colleague, Matron Cavell.'

The room hushed once more.

'For this reason, you must all think carefully about whether you wish to stay. I will hold no one back who feels she must leave. That must be a private and individual decision.' She smiled again. 'I'm proud of each and every one of you. The units of the Scottish Women's Hospital have shown themselves to be unshakeable and, in many cases, the shining lights of the war. This is down to you and the high standard of care. One might say we have done enough, and for some of you, this will be the case. To you, I say, thank you and God bless you. But I intend to stay in Serbia. I cannot find it in my heart to leave when I'm still needed. I do not intend you to vote or even make a decision to-night. I wish you to think on it and let me know in the morning.' As she gathered up her papers, Jessie stood.

'I don't need to sleep or to think further. I'll stay,' she said.

'I shall also,' a familiar voice rang out. Isabel was on her feet. Instantly, Evans and Maud were standing. 'Me too.' Then, one by one, every woman in the room got to her feet.

'I will stay.'

'And I.'

'I'm not running. Don't they know they can't scare us away?'

Jessie's throat tightened and, for a moment, she thought she saw Dr Inglis brush a tear from her eye. But immediately the small, beloved figure smiled. 'I expected nothing else from you all. I will be in my office tomorrow morning, if anyone decides that they should leave.' With a final smile, Dr Inglis left the room.

There was one departure the next morning – an orderly from Royaumont whom everyone had worried about since her arrival in Serbia four weeks earlier. Lady Arabella Jones had been un-able to deal with the blood and pain she'd witnes-sed and had been transferred to kitchen duties, but even then she had gone about with a fearful, haunted expression. No one blamed her for leaving, especially as Lady Arabella was clearly so distraught about her inability to cope.

Dr Bradshaw and Dr Inglis were leaving too. Dr Bradshaw to Kruševatc and Dr Inglis to visit the high commissioner in Nish. In her absence, Isabel was to carry on as CMO in charge of the unit. The women had to be ready to pack up camp and retreat with the Serbian Army as soon as the word was given.

In the meantime, they would carry on as usual.

Chapter 45

A few days after Dr Inglis's departure, Isabel was repairing a tear to her skirt before retiring for the night when Maud walked in. The pity in her eyes sent a jolt down Isabel's spine. Her sewing forgotten, she jumped to her feet. 'What is it?' she asked.

'You must be brave.'

'Just tell me.'

'One of the soldiers has brought news from Belgrade. He says the Germans are firing on the stretcher parties. He says that two Americans – a doctor and one of the bearers – have been killed.'

'Archie?' It was all Isabel could force from her numbing lips.

'He doesn't know who. Just that the dead men are American.'

Dear God. Please let it not be Archie.

'Does Jessie know?'

'I told her. She refuses to believe it's him. She's insisting that God wouldn't do this to her – not when she's just got her husband back. She's gone to the chapel to pray.'

'I must go to her.'

'I don't think you should.' Maud reached out and touched Isabel on the arm. 'I don't know what the trouble is between you two, but I suspect she has seen how you look at her brother and doesn't like it.'

Isabel started. Had her feelings been so obvious?

'I have to go back to the ward,' Maud continued. 'Will you be all right?'

Isabel didn't try to pretend that she didn't know what Maud was saying to her. She nodded. After Maud was gone she very carefully folded the skirt she'd been sewing and placed it in her needlework basket. Then she put on her coat over her nightdress and replaced her shoes with wellington boots. It was all done very deliberately, each action steadying her a little, as if by doing each thing she had done for weeks she could keep this day exactly as the others.

She left her tent and headed away from the camp.

It was the same as every other evening – the mass of soldiers tramping past, although no longer singing. In their faces she read defeat. Staring straight ahead, lest anyone call out to her, she followed the little track that led down to the lake. The sun was setting so it was unlikely that anyone would be lingering there, but if she saw someone she would skirt the lake and make for the nearby copse. Over the weeks and months she'd tolerated never being on her own, but now she needed solitude.

As she'd hoped, the lake was deserted. She found a rock to lean against and spread her coat on the ground. What if Archie were dead and she

431

had missed her chance to tell him, just once, that she loved him? That she didn't know if she could be with him but she loved him.

And she did. She knew that now. When it might be too late.

What did her mother's disapproval – all of it – matter if she couldn't be with Archie? She could go to America, be a doctor there, and they could be happy.

Or could have been. If she hadn't let her stupid pride and her place in society stop her. How had she ever thought she would be embarrassed to call Archie her husband? She should be proud.

She sat there shivering until long after the sun had gone down, unable to bring herself to return to camp. She was still thinking of Archie when she heard branches snapping under feet. She sighed but didn't turn. She should have known that someone would come looking for her.

'Isabel?'

She whirled around. Archie, a bandage on one of his hands, was looking down at her. 'You're alive,' she whispered, hardly able to believe it was him. She scrambled to her feet and threw herself against him. 'Thank God.'

His arms tightened around her and she breathed in the smell of him. The sweat, the blood, the smoke. She didn't want to think of death, or of rotting wounds and discarded limbs, or the knowledge that life could be snuffed out like a candle at any time. But if it were to be, she wanted to know what it was like to be loved and to love in return. She wanted to imprint every bit of him on her memory.

She placed her hands on either side of his head and pulled his face towards her.

And then he was kissing her and she was pressing herself into him, needing to feel all of him against her. He was moaning into her neck, saying words in Gaelic that she didn't understand but knew were of love. He lifted her nightdress and when he touched the bare skin of her thighs, she stopped thinking. All she knew for sure was that she wanted him to touch her for ever.

Later, as they lay together in the grass, Isabel knew that she was fundamentally changed. How, she couldn't quite say, only that she couldn't – wouldn't – go back to the life she'd once treasured. She had never been more at peace than she was now, in Archie's arms. She blushed, glad of the darkness. She hadn't been passive when they'd made love – she'd been demanding. He'd been excited by her need and the words of encouragement she'd whispered to him when at first he'd tried to draw away from her. She had no shame with him, no anxiety that he would despise her for what they'd done, or for her wildness.

With the end of the war, a new world would come and she'd be part of it. All that she'd previously cared about, all that she'd thought mattered, had gone, as if blown away by the breeze. What mattered was the here and now, his hand in her hair, the warmth of his body, the sharing of air as they breathed in rhythm. She was no longer passive, a hollowed-out branch tossed on a sea, to be pushed wherever the wind sent her. With him beside her, she could be mistress of her own destiny.

'Perhaps I should have let you believe I was dead before now,' he said, with laughter in his voice.

She turned on her side and rose on her elbow to look at him. 'Perhaps you should,' she agreed. 'Does Jessie know you're safe?'

'She said she never doubted it.'

'How did you find me?'

'Maud told me you'd heard about the deaths and thought it might be me. She said I'd find you here if I wanted to.'

'Do you still love me?' She needed to know.

He traced her lips with the fingers of his un-injured hand. 'You need to ask me that?'

'No.' She caught his other arm in hers and pressed her lips to the skin above the bandage. 'What happened?'

'It's nothing. Just a graze. I was lucky. The man carrying the other side wasn't.' He kissed her lips. 'I wish you would go from here. It's not safe. They don't care who they fire on. It's all so desperate now.'

She smiled up at him, revelling in the desire and love in his eyes. She stretched like a cat knowing she was teasing him. 'You know we can't go,' she said, 'not while they're still bringing us their injured. In the meantime, why don't you make love to me again?'

Chapter 46

Jessie wondered if she was using up all her favours with God. He'd returned Tommy to her, then Archie. Not that she'd really believed Archie was one of the Americans who'd been killed two weeks earlier. Just as she would have known in her heart that Tommy was dead, she would have felt it if Archie had been killed. Still, she made sure to thank God in her prayers every night.

She was on her way to the mess tent when a motor ambulance pulled up. At last, one of the trucks they had been promised for weeks had arrived. A little late but welcome.

Isabel was waiting to greet the chauffeur. Jessie hadn't seen much of her over the last few days – or Archie, for that matter. She frowned. Come to think of it, recently, when she heard Archie was in the camp and went to seek him out, it was to find he wasn't there. And neither was Isabel. It was possible, of course, that they weren't together, but... A hollow feeling gathered in her stomach. She'd seen enough of Isabel over the last two weeks to become aware of a change in her. Despite the doctor's obvious exhaustion, her face was permanently aglow as if she were hugging a secret to herself. How could she have been so blind? It was all making sense now.

Even after everything that had happened, Archie still couldn't let Isabel go. And for what? When the war was over, she would return to her life in Edinburgh and Archie to his in America. Out here it was easy to forget how different their lives were. Her brother was mistaken if he thought it could be different.

When the chauffeur jumped down from the motor ambulance, Jessie's heart banged against her ribs. There was no mistaking the red hair. Of all the chauffeurs to bring the vehicle, it had to be Lady Dorothea. God help them all – Isabel had no idea that the woman she was about to greet was the sister of the man she had killed, albeit unknowingly. And everyone here knew that Archie was Jessie's brother. Could this mess get any worse?

Their voices drifted on the still air. 'Dr MacKenzie, if I remember!' She stepped towards Isabel and held out a slim hand. 'Imagine us meeting here, after all this time.'

'Dorothea!' Isabel sounded taken aback. 'So you're the shover we've been expecting. Welcome. You've no idea how pleased we are to see you and your ambulance.'

Jessie felt paralysed. She had to get a message to Archie, to warn him to stay away. But how?

A group of Serbian soldiers hurried over to Isabel and started gesturing animatedly.

Isabel shook her head, but each time she did so, the soldiers raised their voices and pointed in the direction of the fighting.

Maud came to stand next to Jessie. 'I wonder what's going on? Let's find out.' Before Jessie could protest, Maud had taken her by the arm and was puffing her along.

436

'Let me take one of the ambulances,' Lady Dorothea was saying. 'It's not far. I could be there and back in a jiffy.'

'It's too dangerous,' Isabel replied.

'We can't just leave them there to die!' she protested. 'The soldiers won't fire if we go.'

'Go where?' Maud interrupted.

'Sister Stuart! How lovely to see you again.' Her pleasure at seeing Jessie again was unmistakable.

'Maxwell! Nice to see you too.' It wasn't. It was awful. The soldiers were still talking to Isabel, their voices rising. 'What's going on?'

'Apparently there's been a terrible battle about three miles from the nearest casualty clearing station. They're trying to evacuate it while seeing to the wounded at the same time, but there are injured soldiers still out there with no one to help them.'

'We could go,' Maud said. 'Somebody has to do something! We're set up to be a field hospital, after all.'

Isabel chewed on her lip. 'We're quiet here. If anyone's going, it should be me.'

The fighting further north was so intense that the wounded were being taken by train to a field hospital further south. The only patients they were treating now were those with minor injuries.

'I'll go too,' Jessie said quietly. Her heart was hammering against her chest. 'Between us, we'll manage.'

'Very well,' Isabel said. Then she hesitated. 'But...'

'But?' Lady Dorothea repeated.

'As far as the clearing station, but absolutely no

437

further. I won't risk the lives of the women under my command. We'll wait there for the army to retrieve the injured, then bring them back here. If we can't, or if there's evidence that the fighting is moving closer, we will return at once. Is that clear?'

Maud grinned. 'Of course, Dr MacKenzie. Immediately.'

'Sister Stuart?'

'I'm ready.'

'Dorothea?'

'Count me in. But shouldn't we get a move on?'

It took them a little while to transfer their mobile equipment to the ambulance and for Isabel to let the other doctors know where they were going.

When they were ready they squashed into the front of the truck and within minutes they were on their way. The engine protested loudly as they bounced along the rutted track up the hill. Dorothea gripped the steering-wheel tightly as she concentrated on keeping the vehicle on its four wheels. 'Are you scared?' she shouted above the noise.

'Terrified. Of your driving, that is.' Isabel laughed. 'Keep your eyes on the road, for Heaven's sake.'

It seemed that, like her, Isabel was more excited than terrified. Jessie didn't believe that they were in any more danger than they had been these last few weeks. Three days ago they'd heard that a German plane had dropped a bomb just outside the hospital building in Kragujevatz, killing seven civilians, but mercifully leaving the hospital intact.

After twenty minutes of bone-shaking road, they drew up outside the casualty clearing station. Several trucks were parked haphazardly as men carried the wounded into the tents or placed them in the back of ambulances to be taken to the railway station.

Leaving Dorothea at the wheel, they jumped down and went to find the commanding officer.

'We've come to help,' Isabel said. 'I'm Dr MacKenzie, this is Sister Tully and Sister Stuart. We can take casualties back to our hospital.'

The CO was relieved to see them. 'We're retreating and need to get this place cleared. Go and find the medical officer and take as many as he thinks are fit to travel with you. Then return, please.' He grimaced. 'I need every ambulance I can get my hands on right now.'

A row of tarpaulin-covered stretchers lay on the ground and Jessie averted her eyes. Everywhere she looked there were injured men, some lying quietly, others crying out for help. A short distance away others sat smoking, looking about with blank and unseeing eyes.

Archie was kneeling next to a soldier, the barrel of a syringe between his teeth as he used his hands to tie a tourniquet around the bloody stump of the man's arm. Isabel and Maud hurried past into a tent and Jessie dropped to her knees beside her brother, taking the syringe from his mouth.

'What the hell are you doing here?' Archie had to shout to make himself heard over the cannon.

Calmly Jessie filled the syringe with morphine and injected the dose into the white-faced soldier.

439

'We're here to take the injured to our hospital,' she said, as she checked for a pulse. It was weak but regular. 'Archie, I have to warn you, the ambulance driver waiting for us is Lady Dorothea.'

Archie frowned. 'I can't worry about that now.' He turned back to the man on the stretcher. 'Just lie quietly, chum. I'll be back in a minute.'

He got to his feet and Jessie followed his gaze to another stretcher a few feet away. This time the soldier was unconscious, the spreading stain of blood on his bandaged abdomen a sure sign that he was still bleeding. But, to her shock, Archie stepped over him and knelt beside another, less severely injured man. 'What about this one?' she called after him. 'He needs medical attention urgently.'

Archie shook his head. 'We have limited supplies left. We have to help those who can be saved.'

Furious, she stepped over the stretchers until she was at the unconscious man's side. Crouching next to him she felt for his pulse. It was barely discernible. Then she looked at his wound. The bright red was rapidly turning brown in the heat of the sun. 'Don't worry, soldier,' she said, hoping he would know he wasn't alone and abandoned.

From all around, the sounds of men in pain, whimpers and loud curses, filled the air. Archie moved from soldier to soldier, stopping once in a while to summon a stretcher-bearer. Although the sun was still high in the sky, the air was thick with smoke and the smell of cordite.

Jessie looked down at her patient again. His eyes were open, his pupils fixed and dilated. Very gently she closed his eyelids and got to her feet.

When she returned to the ambulance Lady Dorothea was already cranking the engine. The back was filled with stretchers, three rows deep and two levels high, and Isabel was giving orders to Maud who was in the back.

'Are you ready to leave?' Lady Dorothea asked.

'I'm going to stay,' Isabel said. 'They could do with another doctor here.'

'And a nurse. I'm staying too,' Jessie added.

'It sounds as if the fighting's getting closer.' Lady Dorothea's hair had come loose from its pins and was swirling around her face. 'Perhaps it would be wise for us all to leave.'

Isabel shook her head. 'You're going to have to return for more. We'll come back with you then. Now, you and Maud go! Quickly!'

They didn't wait to see them leave as another two lorries pulled up with more wounded. As soon as they were unloaded Isabel made a quick assessment of each injury. She instructed Jessie to tie tourniquets or apply pressure to wounds, while Isabel directed the more seriously injured to the operating tent.

'They're not operating on hopeless cases,' Jessie said. 'They say they don't have enough supplies.'

'I will not leave men whose chances seem lost,' Isabel muttered. 'If the doctors here decide to leave them, I can't do anything about it, but I will not, cannot, make a medical decision based on anything other than the nature of the injury.'

Jessie wanted to hug her. Right now, working together, she couldn't care less what Isabel had done in the past. She was a great doctor.

Jessie was aware of Archie close by, his large hands deft as he bandaged wounds or injected morphine, until at last the tide of the injured began to slow and the line of waiting soldiers dropped to three or four.

While they worked, she was conscious of Lady Dorothea and Maud returning and leaving again, but she knew neither she nor Isabel would leave until all of the men had been taken from the casualty clearing station.

As soon as the immediate needs of the injured had been met, she sat back on her haunches and wiped the perspiration from her face. Although the noise of gunfire and cannon was more sporadic, it sounded closer.

Jessie glanced up to see Archie, his face grim, talking to a wildly gesticulating soldier. He patted the man on the back before approaching one of the captains standing near Isabel.

'There are wounded men not far from here, sir,' Archie said. 'Requesting permission to take a truck and see if we can rescue them.'

'It's too dangerous,' the captain replied. 'I need every man to help here. Permission refused.'

Archie's face was like thunder. 'Then I should remind you that I'm not under your command, sir. I'm going to go, but I need a doctor. I understand the medical officer in the first-aid station is in a bad way. There is no one else to help them.'

'It's impossible, man. The surgeons are all operating. I can't spare a single man. Neither can I stop you going on your own, but I advise against it.'

Jessie and Isabel looked at each other and

stepped forward. 'We'll come with you.'

Archie shook his head. 'It's too dangerous for women.'

Jessie looked at the face she knew almost as well as she did her own. 'I'm not scared.'

'Do you remember that day we met on the cliffs back on Skye?' Isabel said softly. 'You told me that climbing down was too dangerous, but it didn't stop me then. And you're not going to stop me now.' She touched his arm and looked him directly in the eye. 'Please, Archie, I need to do this.'

'I must insist that you return immediately to your hospital,' the captain said. 'I will not have the death of women on my hands.'

Isabel's face flushed with anger. 'But if we don't go, you'll have more deaths on your hands.'

'It's out of the question, and that's the last I'll say on the matter.'

'One of the good things about being a doctor with the Scottish Women's Hospital, is that we are not under your command either, Captain. If I wish to go, there is nothing you can do to stop me.'

The captain looked indecisive. Then he shook his head. 'As you say, I can't stop you. But I wash my hands of the whole business.' He placed his baton under his arm and stalked away.

'We'll collect who we can and then get out. Agreed?' Archie said.

Isabel frowned. Lady Dorothea and Maud had returned and were waiting for instructions. 'We'll need our motor ambulance as it has all the equipment and medical supplies – at least enough to keep the men alive until we can transport them back to Mladanovatz. They can go by hospital train from there.'

When Isabel explained what they were planning to do, Maud and Lady Dorothea insisted on coming too. Once more Archie tried to protest and once more he was thwarted. As the truck lurched forward, Jessie tried to ignore the hammering of her heart by thinking about what she might have to do in the next few hours.

'The first-aid station is around three miles from here,' Archie said. Instinctively they ducked as a shell whizzed over their heads and exploded next to the truck. Archie swore in Gaelic.

Lady Dorothea held onto the steering-wheel and, without taking her foot off the accelerator, kept the truck going forward.

It was the longest twenty minutes of Jessie's life. When she made out the Red Cross flag over the first-aid post she almost wept with relief.

'We don't have long,' Archie said grimly. 'We do what we can, then go.'

They jumped out of the truck, keeping their heads down, and hurried over to the station, dropping quickly into the trench. Several wounded men were lying in rain-soaked mud and Isabel, Maud and Jessie set about deciding who to treat first while Archie, and Lady Dorothea, went in search of the injured doctor.

Of the four men lying in the trench, one was dead from a bullet to the head, two had minor leg injuries and one had a severe abdominal wound that required surgery.

'Please get the two walking wounded into the back of the truck, then set up the operating tent.

When you've done that, come back for this man. I'll try to stop the bleeding as best I can while I'm waiting,' Isabel instructed.

Maud and Jessie nodded, their hands flying as they bandaged the two other men. Isabel placed a wad of swabs over her patient's abdominal wound. Jessie knew they would have to get it cleaned and the bleeding stopped but they could only do that in theatre.

Archie and Lady Dorothea returned from the doctor's dug-out and Archie shook his head. 'He died while we were with him. Nothing anyone could do, I'm afraid.'

Lady Dorothea's face had lost its colour. Whatever injuries the doctor had sustained must have been horrific to shake her.

'Can we get this man out of here?' Isabel asked. 'He needs surgery.'

'I'll fetch one of the stretchers.' Lady Dorothea turned to Archie. 'Forgive me, we haven't been introduced. I'm Maxwell.' Despite her pallor she held out a dusty hand.

'Scotty, ma'am. Pleased to meet you.'

There was no sign from Dorothea that she recognised him from the abbey. Jessie wondered if Archie truly appreciated the risk he was taking but there was little either of them could do except hope that she would never discover she'd just met the man sought in connection with her brother's death.

Ignoring the sounds of battle, they managed to get the injured man onto the stretcher and out of the filth of the trench. In the meantime, Lady Dorothea and Maud had pitched the tent and set up the mobile operating table with a large basin underneath to catch the blood. Sterilised instruments were set out on another table, with morphine and chloroform.

'I'll act as your anaesthetist,' Jessie said to Isabel. 'Like the day we helped your dad with Flora McPhee.' How long ago that seemed.

Isabel smiled. 'There's no one I'd rather have by my side. We made a good team that day.'

An explosion rocked the ground, sending an instrument spinning from the table.

'We should get out of here,' Archie said. 'Those guns can't be more than three thousand yards away.'

'We can't move him,' Isabel replied. 'He'll die for certain if we do.'

'Then Jessie, Maud and Maxwell must go. I'll stay to help.'

'I'm going nowhere,' Jessie said tersely, cutting away the wounded soldier's uniform.

'You can't help Isabel, Scotty,' Maud added. 'Sorry old chap. She needs us. Why don't you go with Maxwell and take the two men in the truck to Mladanovatz?'

'If you think I'm leaving any of you women alone here, forget it.' Archie motioned with his hand. 'Jessie, I insist you leave.'

Jessie's head snapped up. 'Archie MacCorquodale! I'm not your baby sister any more! I'm not leaving this patient and that's that!'

'Archie MacCorquodale?' Jessie hadn't heard Lady Dorothea come in. She was standing looking at them, frowning.

Jessie was horrified. Amid the fear, exhaustion

446

and frustration at the death and destruction around them, she'd forgotten herself.

'And you're his sister? But you told me you met him at the station in Paris.'

'We can talk about it later,' Isabel said. 'Right now, I need to operate on this man.'

Jessie's heart was racing as she placed the mask over their patient's face. What would Lady Dorothea do when she realised, which she was bound to at any moment, that Archie was the man they were looking for?

Lady Dorothea paled. 'Oh, my Lord,' she murmured, and stumbled out of the tent. Jessie knew she had worked out the truth. However, nothing could be done about that now. The injured man had to come first.

They fell silent as they concentrated on the operation. As soon as they'd finished, Jessie left Isabel and Maud to see to the patient and went in search of Lady Dorothea.

She found her sitting on an upturned crate with her eyes closed.

'Maxwell,' Jessie whispered, 'I can explain.'

'What was your name before you married?'

'MacCorquodale.' There was no point in lying any more.

'I can't believe you've been deceiving me all this time. Good Lord, Jessie, your brother's Archie MacCorquodale – the man my papa believes killed my brother. Did you think I wouldn't find out?'

'I hoped you wouldn't. Please, Maxwell, you have to believe me. Archie didn't kill your brother.'

Lady Dorothea smiled sadly. 'I might have if you'd told me this at the beginning. How can I believe anything you tell me now?'

'What will you do?' Jessie whispered. 'At least give him time to get away.'

'If he's innocent, he has nothing to fear.' She shook away Jessie's arm and began to walk towards the truck. 'I'll wait for you in the ambulance.'

Just then there was an explosion and Jessie was thrown into the air. She landed on her stomach with a thump that tore the breath from her body. Time seemed to stand still as dirt and rocks showered around her. She covered her head with her hands. Eventually she became aware that someone was shouting her name.

'Jessie! Jess, are you all right?' Archie's voice was muffled. 'Thank God,' he said, when she raised her head to let him know she was unhurt.

'The others?' Her voice was no more than a whisper. She scrambled to her feet. There was too much smoke to see clearly.

'The shell missed the tent. But we have to get out of here. We might not be so lucky next time.'

'Where's Lady Dorothea?' She looked towards where she had last seen her but there was only a hollow where the shell had struck.

'Stay here,' Archie ordered. 'I'll look for her.'

Jessie watched him with increasing despair as he ran in a half-crouching position towards the shell hole. There was no chance Lady Dorothea could have survived the blast. A droning noise filled the air and Jessie looked up. Two Serbian aircraft were flying overhead. One dropped in height and began raking the ground with gunfire. It wouldn't stop the advancing army but it might buy them a little time.

Archie had paused in front of what looked like a crumpled heap of rags. A few seconds later he raised his head and shouted, 'Jessie! Help me!' He swept the bundle into his arms and ran back towards the tent. When Jessie caught up with him, she saw he was carrying Lady Dorothea and that she was in a bad way.

In the tent, Isabel and Maud were shocked but unhurt. When Isabel saw Archie her face lit up, and in that instant Jessie knew that the doctor's daughter loved her brother as much as he loved her.

But when Isabel saw the unconscious Dorothea in Archie's arms, her face blanched. 'Quick, Jessie, let's set up another table so I can examine her. Maud, you stay with our patient. Shout if you need me.'

Archie laid his burden down and Jessie cut the lower half of Dorothea's dress before snipping away the elastic of her drawers and parting the material. Thick red blood pooled in the injured woman's groin.

'Hold the lamp over her,' Isabel said, before bending her head to examine the wound. 'Shrapnel's causing the bleeding. I need to remove it.' When Isabel lifted her head, Jessie saw the anguish in her eyes. 'And when I do she'll bleed even more. We have some saline left but I don't think that will be enough to save her.'

'Remember that transfusion you saw, Isabel?' Archie said. 'We could try it.'

Isabel's expression was bleak. 'I don't have any-thing. No blood. Nothing.' She glanced around, and as her eyes fell on her medical bag, she frowned. 'No, wait... The doctor at the American Hospital gave me some citrate solution. If we had blood I could risk trying to transfuse her.'

'But we do. You can use mine,' Archie said. 'The doctors have used it before. My blood seems to work.'

'I don't know,' Isabel said. 'We might kill her.'

'If we don't give her blood, will she survive?' Archie demanded.

Isabel shook her head. 'No.'

'Then it seems to me that we have no choice.' Archie gripped her shoulder. 'You can do this, Isabel. At least you have to try.'

Isabel smiled uncertainly, then seemed to give herself a shake. 'We need tubing and a bottle. A sterilised bottle. Do we have one?'

They didn't. Then Jessie had an idea. 'There's an empty antiseptic bottle – why don't we use that?'

While Archie rolled up his sleeve, Isabel rinsed the bottle with boiled water.

'Jessie, could you keep pressure on Dorothea's wound?' Isabel asked, smiling briefly when she saw that Jessie was already one step ahead of her. She swabbed Archie's arm and applied a tourniquet. Working quickly, she attached a length of tubing to a large-bore needle. She poured a little citrate solution into the bottle, put the other end of the tubing into it and placed it on the floor. Archie didn't even wince as she inserted the needle into his vein, checking it was in before she loosened the tourniquet.

'You'll be fine, Maxwell,' Jessie whispered. 'Hold

on.' Oh, God, this couldn't be happening. Lady Dorothea had found out who Archie really was, but Jessie didn't want her to die. She deserved better than this.

As soon as Archie's blood was running into the bottle, Isabel swabbed a large vein in the other side of Dorothea's groin and inserted a cannula into it.

'Now, Jessie, you'll have to let go so you can assist me,' Isabel said, her voice steady. 'Archie, hold the lamp over my surgical area. I know it won't be easy with the tube in your other arm, but I need both Jessie's hands free.'

Jessie concentrated on keeping the surgical field free of blood while Isabel explored the wound with forceps. She gave a triumphant smile as she removed a piece of metal. 'That's one. Let me check for any more.'

They held their breath as they waited. Every now and again the dull thud of an explosion came from outside but, to Jessie's relief, it seemed that the shells were falling less often. The drone of the aeroplanes was still audible too, although they appeared to be moving further away.

'Catgut, Jessie,' Isabel said, and Jessie used sterile forceps to pass her the suturing material. When she'd done that she placed her fingers on Lady Dorothea's carotid artery. The pulse was so weak she could hardly feel it, but it was there.

A few moments later, Isabel straightened. 'Jessie, if you dress the wound, I'll complete the transfusion.'

This, Jessie guessed, was the most dangerous part.

'When will we know?'

'Almost as soon as I start feeding Archie's blood into her. If anyone feels like sending up a prayer, please do so.'

Jessie closed her eyes and silently begged God to grant her one more favour. He'd taken Mam, Dad and Seamus, and although He'd returned Tommy and Archie to her, she asked Him for one more life. They waited – it was all they could do – but when Dorothea's pulse began to beat harder under her fingers she knew her prayers had been answered.

The shelling started again, closer now.

'We have to go,' Maud said anxiously.

Isabel pulled off her rubber gloves and dropped them on the floor. 'Let's get our patients into the truck.'

As soon as they'd transferred them to the ambulance, Archie cranked the engine until it spluttered into life. He heaved himself up on the step of the driver's door, but then he turned away and stared across the field, listening.

'What is it, Archie?' Isabel asked. 'We must hurry. There's no time.'

'There's a man out there. I can hear his calls for help. I have to go to him.'

'No, Archie. They'll shoot you.' Jessie was almost sobbing with terror. 'You're not in uniform. Let me go. They'll not harm a nurse.'

He gripped her arm. 'Please, Jessie. Listen to me. I have to do this. Call it restitution, if you like, but you must all leave now.' He turned to Isabel. 'Can you drive?'

She nodded.

He pulled off his Red Cross armband and put it on Isabel. When she tried to pull it off, he held her arm firmly. 'You must wear it. If the Germans catch you they may not believe you're a doctor. Now for God's sake, get out of here.' It was only then that Jessie saw Isabel wasn't wearing hers. She must have forgotten to put it on in the rush.

Isabel looked at Archie, and for a moment they held each other's eyes. She smiled slightly. 'Oh, Archie,' was all she said.

Before Jessie could speak, Archie passed her a revolver. 'Take this.' He leaned forward and hugged her. 'Be careful, *a gràidgh*, and take good care of Isabel.' He smiled again, but Jessie could see the torment in his eyes. 'I'll come back, you'll see.' Then he jumped down and started to run.

When Jessie made to follow him, Isabel grabbed her arm and pulled her none too gently towards the truck. 'We have to get Dorothea and the others to the hospital. They'll die if we don't.'

Jessie looked into the darkness. She could still go after him.

'Maud needs your help in the back, Jessie,' Isabel said quietly, 'and if anyone can survive, it will be Archie.'

All Jessie could do was nod.

'Now, Sister Stuart,' Isabel said, helping Jessie into the back, 'let's make sure our patients stay alive until we can get them to the hospital.'

Chapter 47

The camp in Mladanovatz was in chaos when they
finally rolled in. Women hurried between the tents,
heaping belongings and supplies onto wagons.
Men sat in the backs of trucks, their bandages
reflecting a ghostly light.

Before Isabel had brought the truck to a stand-
still, Jessie had jumped from the back. 'We need
some help over here. Now!'

Orderlies unloaded the two patients and stretchered them away to the wards. Jessie made to
follow, but Maud held her back. 'I'll stay with her
and make sure she gets onto the hospital train.
You're in no state to do any more.'

Maud was right. Jessie looked wearily at Isabel
as she joined them. Even in the dim light and
under the coat of dust and mud, her face was
white. 'I need to go back,' she said.

Jessie sighed, almost too tired to argue. 'You
can't.'

'I must.'

Jessie's heart felt as if it were encased in ice. 'If
I thought there was the slightest chance of
rescuing Archie, I would go. But there isn't. He's
behind enemy lines, and if he's alive he'll have
been captured by now. As it is, the enemy are
only just behind us and we have patients who
need us.'

Evans ran to them. 'We've been given orders to

evacuate to Kruševatc. Only those who can't be moved are to stay. Four nurses will remain with them. The rest of us are to leave with the patients.'

Isabel didn't appear to be listening. She started to walk away. 'They won't shoot me. I'm a doctor.'

Jessie yanked on Isabel's arm until she was facing her. 'The sun's going down. You'll be a figure in the dark to them.' She had to shout to make herself heard above the noise of cannon fire and exploding bombs. 'Even if they don't shoot you, remember what happened to Matron Cavell.'

Isabel's eyes were frantic and Jessie doubted she was hearing a word she was saying. 'For God's sake, Isabel. If you go after him, I'll have to go too. He'll never forgive me if I let something happen to you.'

Isabel slumped to her knees, her face awash with tears. It was the first time Jessie had seen her lose her composure. 'Then I'll stay here. I can't leave him.'

There wasn't time to argue. Some of the wagons, loaded with the wounded, were already leaving. Jessie crouched beside Isabel. 'Can't you see that if I thought there was a chance of saving him I'd go? He's my brother.' Her voice caught and she took a deep breath to steady it. 'Archie is a strong and determined man, Isabel. If anyone can survive, it will be him. If he can find a way back to us, he will.'

'I love him, Jessie.'

'I know. And for that reason you have to live. So he can find you when this war is over.'

When she raised her face, Isabel's expression was resolute. Although she was still pale, all other signs of her earlier distress had vanished. Jessie held out her hands and they got to their feet.

Evans was waiting impatiently. 'We're about to leave. I've fetched your bundles for you.'

'What about Kragujevatz?' Jessie asked. 'Can't we go there?'

'Apparently not. The Germans are expected to take it at any moment – if they aren't there already. Some of the staff have already left and our orders are to take as many wounded as we can and retreat to Kruševatc. The others will meet us there.'

Jessie frowned. 'Where's Maud?'

'She'll stay with Maxwell to make sure she gets on the hospital train. She's to be one of the nurses who will stay. I imagine she wants to be close to Milan.'

Jessie looked around the place she'd called home these last weeks. So much had happened, was still happening. When would this nightmare end? She turned on her heel and clambered into the back of the truck alongside Isabel and two nurses. There were four trucks carrying as many of the wounded as they could cram in and an equal number of ox-wagons piled high with supplies. The women who were staying behind with the patients who couldn't be moved saw them off with cries of, 'See you soon. Take care now, and God bless.' To hear them, anyone would have thought they were waving guests off after a party instead of facing the possibility of capture – or worse.

As the truck rolled out, Jessie watched the diminishing figures fade into the darkness. Archie was out there too. Perhaps dead. Perhaps wounded and calling for help. Evans's fingers twined around hers. 'Let us pray,' the orderly said quietly. 'They're in God's hands now.'

Jessie closed her eyes, hoping that God would hear her prayers just once more.

Dawn was breaking when the truck slowed to a crawl. Evans peered out of the back.

'Good grief,' she said. 'I've never seen anything like it.'

They all clambered over to have a look. As far as the eye could see there were old men, women and children on foot or riding in every kind of conveyance imaginable. There were wagons heaped high with beds, blankets, chairs, kettles and even live geese. A few lucky refugees had carts, but most carried their belongings or their children – sometimes both – on their backs as they trudged along. A boy led two calves, which were pulling a tiny cart with a baby strapped into it.

Interspersed between them were the ragged remains of the Serbian Army in their mud- and blood-encrusted uniforms and filthy boots, their eyes downcast. This was a defeated army and a defeated nation, and Jessie's heart filled with pity for them. But there was little they could do for anyone. What supplies they had, they needed for the injured men in their care.

With increasing horror she saw bodies by the sides of the road, their white faces and empty eyes staring upwards.

The road was abominable, churned to a river of mud and potholes. As the trucks crawled along throughout that relentless day, they took turns to jump down and offer what help they could to the sick and dying. But there were simply too many of them. One by one, men and women fell to their knees with exhaustion and hunger.

It was dark when the trucks stopped.

Jessie and Isabel got out to see what the problem was. The lights of the vehicles shone on the broken remains of a wooden bridge. They stared at it with dismay.

Behind them some soldiers appeared and went to investigate. When they returned it was clear from their agitated voices that there was a serious problem. One of the doctors, who understood a little Serbian, translated. 'There are planks missing halfway across. One of the gun wagons ahead must have damaged them. I don't see how we're going to get across.'

'We can't stay here,' Isabel said.

The doctor shrugged. 'They suggest we take the wagons across. Their wheels are narrower than those of the trucks so they should make it. In the meantime they're going to chop down some branches and try to repair the bridge.'

Jessie looked behind her. Several trucks and wagons belonging to the army had yet to cross. The Austrians couldn't be far away and every passing minute was bringing them closer.

'We must unload our supplies, put the injured into the wagons and get them across without delay,' Isabel said. 'At least then they'll be on the right side of the bridge. Jessie, you and the nurses will have to look after them. We can't leave our trucks. They could be our only shelter and I'm not leaving our equipment behind. I'll stay this side with the shovers until we get the trucks across.'

'I'll take the ox-wagons,' Jessie said. She managed a smile. 'I doubt anyone has more experience than I of making beasts do as they're told.'

By this time the others had gathered around, shivering in the freezing night air. Quickly, and without further discussion, they unloaded the supplies from the wagons, making space for the stretchered patients and heaping every available blanket on top of them. The men who were able to walk gingerly negotiated the creaking bridge to the other side. Evans and three nurses went with them.

Jessie leaped onto the front of the first wagon and lifted the reins. As the oxen lumbered forward, she tried not to think what would happen if the bridge gave way. There wasn't a chance that any of the injured men would survive a fall into the icy water below. To her relief, the cart made it across the bridge.

She was pleased to see that the soldiers, with the help of some of the refugees, had managed to cut a good amount of wood and had replaced the broken planks.

On the other side of the bridge, the engines were being started. Would the hasty repairs hold their weight? They held their breath as the first truck shot over the bridge. The chauffeur jumped out, looking relieved. 'Thought I should go as fast as I could,' she said. 'Same way I set a horse to jump a fence.'

She was followed by the remaining trucks. Then each patient was lifted as gently as the women could manage back into the trucks, and they were on their way again.

The hours ticked agonisingly by until the convoy came to a halt at a ruined village. Over every spare bit of ground, women sat huddled with their children. Their silence was almost worse than anything.

A nurse wearing the uniform of the Serbian Relief Fund hurried over. 'We used this place as a dispensary until a month ago. There may be some supplies left, but if there aren't at least you can shelter overnight in the houses.'

Many of the refugees had stopped too and were looking to them for guidance, the children's faces pinched with hunger, their lips blue with cold.

'I think the children should sleep in the houses,' Evans said. 'They need shelter more than we do. We can make do with the verandas, don't you think?'

From the rumble of guns, the enemy was only a few miles behind them and advancing quicker than expected. But they had to rest.

They settled as many of the children as they could gather in the houses. The parents would have to do as best they could. At least there was wood to make fires, which would give them some warmth. The women shared what food they had with the children, and once they were tucked in, they unrolled their mattresses on the veranda, huddling close to one another for warmth. There was no chatter, each woman either too wrapped up in her own thoughts or too exhausted to talk. Jessie closed her eyes as a wave of grief washed over her. In the gaps between distant explosions she heard women sobbing and wondered how many would be dead by morning. But they couldn't do more to help than they were doing already. She closed her eyes and let sleep claim her.

The next morning they were up before dawn. In the dark, they packed their belongings and set off again. The day followed a similar pattern to the one before. Every so often they had to jump out of the truck and help push wagons and vehicles out of the mud. The sound of guns and cannons was now a constant roar.

By the time they reached Kruševatc, they had spent forty hours on a journey that should have lasted four or five. The staff from other retreating units rushed out to take their patients from them. At least the men wouldn't have to spend another night out in the cold. For them the journey was over. They would be placed on trains to safety. And they would travel to hospital in relative comfort.

Dr Bradshaw, her eyes ringed with fatigue, hurried over to them.

'Thank goodness you made it. But you'll have to leave again tomorrow.'

'Can't we stay and help?' Jessie asked.

Dr Bradshaw shook her head. 'We expect the Germans to take the town at any moment and the retreating soldiers and refugees will need medical care along the way. My orders are to send as many as I can to Scutari. I'm keeping the smallest number of staff here to look after the men who can't be moved. We'll evacuate when we can.'

Jessie and Isabel looked at each other. Jessie

knew Isabel didn't want to leave either. Every step would take them further away from Archie.

'You must go. That's an order,' Dr Bradshaw finished, seeing their hesitation. They couldn't disobey a direct command. If Dr Bradshaw said they were needed to look after the sick and injured as they retreated, that's what they would do.

They managed to snatch a few hours' rest before they were ordered to move on.

The other women gathered around them, those staying pressing hastily written letters into their hands. Fourteen were coming with Jessie and Isabel: Evans, ten of the nurses and three orderlies. All young and fit. The five women Dr Bradshaw had chosen to stay were older.

What would happen to them? Would the enemy treat them with the respect they were due, or would they be shot as spies? There was no way of knowing.

After another gruelling day they reached a village and pitched camp in a field, trying to ignore the shells whizzing overhead. As more wounded arrived, they attended to them as best they could with their dwindling supplies.

That night, they sat around the campfire, feasting on roasted turkeys a grateful villager had given them.

'I can't remember when I ever tasted something so good,' Evans said.

But Jessie noticed that Isabel was only picking at her food. When there was work to be done, she appeared strong, but as soon as it was finished, the fight seemed to go from her.

Jessie added more kindling to the fire and lifted the blackened teapot. 'Tea, anyone?'

Evans, clutching her ever-present Bible, squinted in the dim, flickering light from the fire and held out her tin mug.

And so it continued, day after miserable day. Every morning they packed up and moved on, and every night they pitched their tents and treated the injured. The wounds were less severe than they had been a few days earlier, and the Serbian officers explained that the worst casualties had been left on the battlefield as the ambulance parties were being fired on. Jessie and Isabel exchanged a glance. They didn't need to be told.

Sometimes an influx of patients kept them busy through the night and they treated the men by the light of storm lamps. When they could, they saw to civilians too. But what the refugees needed more than anything was shelter and food, and although they couldn't provide shelter they shared the little food they had.

Often, just as they were ready to move on, more wounded poured in and they would have to unpack their tents and start work again.

At least it kept them from dwelling on their own misery.

The enemy was still hard on their heels. They heard that two hours after they had left one of the villages, the Germans had marched through. Then came the news they'd been dreading. Kragujevatz had fallen to the enemy and all the women still there had been captured and they worried that the same fate would await those left behind in

Kruševatc. It was their lowest point. Their only hope now was to continue over the Montenegrin mountains towards Scutari.

Hour after hour, day after day, week after week the horror continued. Thousands upon thousands of Serbian soldiers marched wearily beside the women's ox-wagons or rode on the horses pulling their gun-carriages. Always in silence. There was no laughter, no singing, no talking. Impeding the army's progress were thousands of women, children and old men, and amongst them hundreds of Austrian prisoners without guards.

Every day it became more difficult to buy anything to supplement the rations they had left. What they had, they shared with the children, but there was none to spare for the prisoners.

Throughout night and day, cars and trucks had to be pushed through the mud. Many died where they lay and news came that a thousand men had been left dead or wounded on the fields near Bargan.

As they trekked on, the rain and sleet turned to snow. A blockage at the front would stop the whole line. Frightened people, hearing the thunder of guns, would try to squeeze through the gap, making matters worse. Horses fell to their knees, exhausted and starved, throwing riders to the ground. Wagons stuck in deep mud and, to lighten the load, people threw down their possessions. Barrels of precious benzene, chairs, tables, even packing cases with food were flung aside. If a wheel came off, a wagon was abandoned in the middle of the road, slowing progress further.

As the convoy neared the mountains, the road

became impassable and they had to abandon the trucks – their only source of shelter from the driving rain and cold. Now the women had only the wagons and would have to sleep in the open.

Eventually they reached a gorge. On one side was a river, on the other a steep path up almost perpendicular mountains, too narrow to take their wagons. The night was black with neither moon nor stars to help them see their way. But they had no choice. With the Germans closing in behind them, and in danger of being cut off by the Bulgars attacking from the east, the only way was forward. They cut the carts in half and made them into two-wheelers, gathered the few horses they had left and set out again.

With only a little food remaining, no shelter and the freezing cold, Jessie wondered how much longer they could go on.

Chapter 48

They had been walking for twenty days when Isabel knew for certain that she was pregnant. She'd vomited her breakfast, just as she had the last few mornings. At first she had managed to convince herself that bad food and poor hygiene were making her sick, but now her breasts were tender and, despite the weight she'd lost, fuller.

She was horrified. She and Archie had made love only twice, yet she was pregnant with his child. She was unmarried and carrying a baby, with little or no prospect of marrying its father. She wrapped her arms around herself as a fierce glow spread through her. Despite everything, she could not regret this child. It was a part of Archie she would never lose. Leaning against a tree, she wiped her mouth as best she could. They were still miles from safety and were still climbing. It was possible they would all die on the frozen plains. Perhaps it would be for the best. No one would know her shame. To be an unmarried mother was unthinkable.

But as soon as the thought entered her head, she pushed it away. She had no intention of dying, and the baby inside her needed her so that he or she could live.

If it could survive this. The snow-covered mountain was littered with dead bodies, arms and legs sticking up, as if in some sort of macabre dance. Near the road, she could see the corpse of a child, still wrapped in a shawl, the little face blue. She wouldn't let her baby die.

She pulled her greatcoat tighter around herself. She wouldn't tell the other women unless she had to. They had enough to worry about, without having to help her. She thought of Archie and her father. Papa had said she was the strongest woman he knew. She could almost see their faces, urging her on. She smiled to herself, drawing strength from their images.

Whatever it took, she had to make it to safety.

Chapter 49

They continued into Montenegro – the Land of the Black Mountains – walking through the night until exhaustion forced them to stop. So many had died or given up along the way that they were now a skeleton column.

The track became increasingly treacherous and slippery. Wherever they looked, horses, oxen and people stumbled and fell, only to lie in the snow and freeze to death. To stop and help anyone now would mean death for those who still had hope that they would reach Scutari alive.

They trudged on, leading their one remaining horse and cart when the track became too narrow to be safe. The sound of cannon behind them told them that the enemy couldn't be more than a day behind. They could no longer afford the time to stop and rest during the day. They continued ever upwards in the snow, always on the look-out for bread from the few Serbian military stations along the way, but there was never any to be had as it was rationed for the remaining soldiers at the front. In the end they were forced to eat the meat of dead oxen and horses.

They scrambled across jagged rocks through mud and snow, over passes and between mountains thousands of feet high, through rivers with no bridges, until finally it became impossible to travel at night.

'We have to make camp soon,' Isabel said finally. 'We can't risk taking the paths in darkness.'

Jessie knew she was right. The tracks along the mountain were barely wide enough to take even their half-wagons. One slip would send them hurtling into the valley with no chance of climbing out again.

'But where?' Evans looked around at the endless expanse of knee-deep snow in dismay.

'See those trees a little up the side of the hill?' Jessie said. 'They'll give us some shelter. If we scrape away the snow we can make a fire.'

'We can't sleep there, surely,' Evans objected. 'There's nothing to stop us spilling down the hill.'

'If we place logs behind us they'll act as a wedge and stop us rolling,' Jessie replied.

Although they were exhausted, they set about scraping away the snow and foraging for dry twigs and branches for the fire. Then they fed a few leaves to the painfully thin horses. For themselves, they made tea with melted snow, and nibbled small chunks of stale bread and maize meal. At least they had something to fill their stomachs, unlike the refugees.

In weary silence, they unrolled their mattresses and started their preparations for the night, setting their frozen boots by the fire to thaw. Jessie thought longingly back to her first days in Royaumont – if she'd thought it cold there, it had been nothing compared to this.

Despite her exhaustion, sleep was difficult. She woke several times, lying shivering until she finally fell asleep again. Once, she woke and, needing to relieve herself, reluctantly slid out from under her covers. To her surprise, Isabel was silhouetted against the dark sky. Jessie stumbled over to her. They hadn't spoken much since they'd set out on their trek.

'You should be in bed,' Jessie said, teeth chattering in the freezing air.

'I can't sleep,' Isabel replied. 'Isn't it lovely? It's hard to believe that so much horror can exist alongside such magnificence.'

The mountains loomed up on either side, a haunting beauty in their jagged ridges.

'Come to bed,' Jessie coaxed. 'We have another long day in front of us tomorrow.'

'I'm going to have a child,' Isabel said suddenly.

Dear God! They were barely surviving as it was. 'Are you sure?' Jessie asked. 'I mean, we're all hungry. It wouldn't be surprising if your monthlies were disrupted.'

'I'm quite sure,' Isabel said.

The silence stretched between them.

'Is it... I mean, of course it's Archie's?'

Isabel smiled tightly. 'Yes, it is. Do you think badly of me?'

Jessie almost smiled. Compared to killing a man, a child out of wedlock was a relatively small sin. Warmth flooded through her: Archie would live on in his child.

'I'll lose everything,' Isabel whispered, 'my reputation, my career, but I can't bring myself to care. I have his child growing inside me and I cannot regret it.'

If ever Jessie had wondered if she would confront Isabel with the truth about Charles Maxwell, she knew now she never could. If the truth came out Isabel, the mother of her brother's child, might hang. She owed it to Archie to see that that never happened.

'You must sleep. And you must take more of the rations. I'll tell the others and they'll be glad to give up their share.'

'No,' Isabel said, her voice ringing out in the cold night air. 'You must say nothing. There is a chance I'll lose this child and, if I do, my reputation will have been ruined for nothing.' She lowered her voice. 'I don't know if a child can survive what we're going through, Jessie. I'm so weak, so tired, that sometimes I wonder if I can go on.'

'You must! If not for your sake, for that of the child you're carrying. For Archie's sake. Besides, I've nursed women who've had less nourishment and they've still managed to bring healthy babies into the world. One thing I do know about babies is that they're greedy devils. They take all they need from the mother, even if it saps her dry. I won't tell the others, if you promise you'll take food when you can. I'm stronger than you – no...' She held up her hand as Isabel made to protest, '...you know it's true. I'm used to having less food than I need and to being out of doors. Although,' she grimaced, 'I'm not used to this. No one could be used to this. You must take half of my rations. I'll manage.'

Isabel returned her smile. 'Did I ever tell you how much I admire you, Jessie? You're the woman most of us want to be, but can't.'

Jessie was moved. Isabel's words meant a great deal. 'Poppycock,' she replied, using one of Lady

Dorothea's favourite words, 'but thank you. I'll respect your wishes and not tell the others. However,' she held up an admonishing finger, 'if you don't eat properly, I'll be forced to tell them. Are we in agreement?'

Isabel raised an eyebrow. 'It seems I have no choice. Now, let's get some rest. We are going to need all our strength if we're to make it.'

Chapter 50

The first inkling Jessie had of the disaster was when Isabel screamed.

'Jump, Evans! Oh, God, jump!'

Jessie's head snapped up and she watched in horror as the wagon Evans had been steering slid backwards, its wheels slipping over the edge of the narrow track. The horse reared, its shrill, panicked cry rending the air as it fought against the weight pulling it downwards.

Evans made no effort to jump free. Instead she, the wagon and the horse disappeared from sight. Isabel looked at Jessie in horror. They rushed as quickly as the slippery snow and boulders would allow and looked over the edge.

Halfway down the mountain, the horse was kicking feebly in its death throes. Their belongings were scattered everywhere, some still rolling down towards the river. Worst of all, Evans lay motionless in the snow, her cloak spread around her like a grey tablecloth.

Jessie lifted her skirts. Beside her Isabel was doing the same.

'I'll go to her,' Jessie said. 'You can't take the risk.'

Isabel brushed her arm away. 'If she's alive she'll need my help.' Jessie didn't say anything. Supposing Evans had survived the fall it would be an almost impossible task, even with the soldiers' help, to get her back up the mountain. But they couldn't just leave her. And she could see from the set of Isabel's lips she had made up her mind.

Carefully the two women slid down the slope, the snow seeping into their coats. It seemed to take for ever to get to Evans, but it couldn't have been much more than ten minutes when they finally scrambled to a stop beside their friend.

She was badly injured – Jessie saw that at once. Her leg was twisted at an unnatural angle and her head was bleeding profusely. Quickly Isabel examined her as the ghastly cries of the dying horse rang in their ears. Unable to bear its suffering any longer, Jessie took out the gun Archie had given her, slipped out of her coat, folded it several times and placed it on the horse's head. Eyes tightly shut, she pulled the trigger. There was a soft thud and the horse jerked, then lay still.

She glanced back to where Isabel was bending over Evans. Isabel shook her head slightly. Jessie stumbled towards them, sinking up to her knees in the snow with every step she took.

Evans was barely conscious. 'That's torn it,' she whispered.

Isabel lifted her dress and, using her teeth, tore

off a piece of petticoat to wrap around Evans's head.

'We're going to get you out of here,' Jessie told her firmly.

Evans reached out and grasped her wrist. The fall had ripped the gloves from her hands and her fingers were icicles on Jessie's skin.

'Don't pretend,' Evans said.

'Nonsense,' Jessie replied, although her throat was aching so badly with the need to cry that she could hardly speak. 'I'll get some of the soldiers to help us. We'll have you up in a jiffy.'

'Then what?' Evans murmured. 'I'm going to die so I might as well die here. But stay and pray with me.' She coughed, her eyes tight with pain.

Jessie felt for a pulse. It was fast and weak. Evans was slipping away. She looked at Isabel, who shook her head again and, out of sight of their injured friend, pointed to the broken leg. Jessie knew what she was saying. Supposing they could get her back up the slope, the pain would be excruciating. They had no morphine, nothing to ease her agony. She was going to die, they both knew that. What was the point in her last moments being filled with pain?

'I'm not frightened,' Evans said. 'I'm going to meet my Maker.'

Jessie laid her coat over Evans. No, not Evans. Elizabeth.

Isabel removed her gloves and pulled them over Elizabeth's frozen hands.

'My Bible. It's in my pocket. Put it in my hands,' Elizabeth said. Every word was clearly an effort.

Jessie found it and opened it at Psalm Twenty-

473

three. Although she knew the words by heart, she bent her head over the book and began to read. As she did so, Elizabeth closed her eyes.

'Is she?' Jessie asked Isabel, when she'd finished.

Isabel placed her fingers on Elizabeth's carotid pulse. 'Not yet.'

Together they sat beside their friend until finally her breathing stopped. They looked at one another in despair. *How many more, Lord?* Jessie cried inside. *How many more do you need before you're satisfied?*

Slowly Isabel picked up Jessie's coat and placed it around her shoulders. Then she removed her gloves from Elizabeth's hands and slipped them back on. 'We can't leave her here,' she said. 'Maybe the soldiers will help us carry her body back up so that we can bury her.'

'Once they've finished stripping the horse of its meat, you mean,' Jessie replied, jerking her thumb behind her.

Isabel sighed. 'We've all become less human in this war, Jessie.'

'At least we can gather what remains of the cart to make a stretcher for her.' Carefully, as if Elizabeth could still feel pain, they lifted her body onto the planks tied together with their scarves. The refugees fell upon the rest of the cart and started scrambling up the slope with the precious wood tucked under their arms.

Without being asked, several soldiers trudged through the snow towards them. Wordlessly, they began to haul Elizabeth on her makeshift stretcher up the hill, leaving the two women to clamber after them. For a time, Jessie wondered if they would make it. Her feet were so cold she could no longer feel them. Perhaps it was easier to give in. She almost fell, but Isabel grasped her hand and pulled her on. Then Isabel stumbled and it was Jessie's turn to help her and so it went on, each of them falling only to be lifted by the hands of the other.

Finally, they were at the top. The path was still clogged with refugees and retreating soldiers. Someone had removed Elizabeth's boots and her bare feet were almost the final straw for Jessie. But those boots might mean the difference between life and death for a child and Elizabeth would have been the first to give them away.

With the help of the soldiers, they buried her in a makeshift shallow grave at the side of the road and said another prayer. Realising there was nothing they could do, the rest of their convoy had gone before them.

Now they were without horse, tents and even dry socks. They had a little food in the knapsack Jessie carried on her back, but that was all. If their journey had appeared doomed before, it would take a miracle to get them to Scutari alive now. And God, Jessie thought bitterly, didn't seem to be handing out miracles.

'We need to go on,' Isabel said finally. 'The longer we wait, the greater the chance that the Germans will be upon us. We have to make the most of the daylight.'

They turned away from Elizabeth's grave, and as the snow started to fall thickly, they huddled into their coats and started to walk.

For seven more days they continued their route,

along narrow valleys that ran between steep mountains of grey rock and jagged peaks, through thunder, lightning and hail. In one place they had to tramp over the bodies of three horses, one not quite dead. Although they were soaked to the skin and couldn't light fires in the rain, and Jessie worried about Isabel. They camped every night in the open and rose to find each morning identical. They spoke sometimes, not about their lives before the war, or the people they had lost, but about their time with the Scottish Women's Hospitals, reminding each other of the good times they'd had. If one stumbled, the other would slip her arm through her elbow until she, too, stumbled. What little food they had they shared. Jessie hardly felt hungry now.

Just when she wondered if they could survive more than another night or two, the path veered sharply to the left and all at once a brilliantly green stream stretched before them. 'We must be close to Lake Scutari,' she said. Her lips were cracked and sore, as were Isabel's.

Isabel attempted a smile. 'Thank God.'

They hobbled on for the rest of the day. The sleet had turned to rain and even that was easing when suddenly the mountains fell away. Open country stretched before them and below, at the bottom of the decline, glinting in the sunshine was the lake. After almost six weeks of more pain, hunger and heartache than Jessie had thought it possible to endure, they were safe.

At the bottom they found a boat to take them across Lake Scutari to the military headquarters and the port.

When they saw the lights of the town they were too exhausted to do more than raise a feeble cheer. They had survived the journey, but at what cost? Jessie would never be able to get the terrible images of the dead bodies out of her head, especially those of the children. And Archie, was he alive? Or was he dead and buried too?

As for Isabel, she had lost more weight. Instead of the bloom of pregnancy she was gaunt and paler than a Christmas rose. What would happen to her when she returned to Scotland, as she must? Would her family disown her or would they open their arms to her, simply glad that she had returned to them? Certainly she'd be struck off the medical register. Of that there was little doubt. But whatever happened with her family, Jessie would never abandon her. Isabel was carrying Archie's baby and she would do everything in her gift to care for them both.

When they arrived at the hotel, they were delighted to be greeted by a number of their unit who had made it before them. Old friends and companions fell upon them with cries of disbelief and joy. The hotel, although busy, found rooms for them, and that night would be the first in four months that Jessie and Isabel would be able to bathe. Although they had often discussed food on the long journey, they had talked more of how they were looking forward to a bath and clean clothes.

'Shall we meet for dinner?' Jessie asked Isabel, when they were alone again.

Isabel smiled faintly. 'I'm going to have a bath

and then I'm going to sleep. Don't be surprised if you don't see me for a couple of days.'

'You need to eat,' Jessie said firmly, 'and I intend to see that you do.' She lowered her voice to a whisper, lest she was overheard by anyone in the crowded lobby. Isabel's pregnancy couldn't be concealed for ever but there was no need for anyone to find out now. 'That baby is going to be born healthy if it kills me.'

'I have no doubt that it will be.' Isabel dropped her hand to her still flat stomach. 'Poor little thing. It hasn't had the best start.'

'As soon as I've cleaned myself up,' Jessie said, 'I'm going to see if I can find you a passage home. It might have to be on one of the hospital ships, but the sooner we get you there the better.'

'What about you?'

'I'll come with you, and as soon as I've seen you back safely, I'll return to wherever I'm needed.'

Isabel looked as if she were about to protest, but instead she touched Jessie's shoulder. 'I'll miss you.'

'And I you.'

Chapter 51

The next morning, clean, fed and rested, Jessie and Isabel walked down to the harbour.

'Another week at the most and we'll be home,' Jessie said.

'Can you bear to come back here?'

Even after everything, Jessie had no doubt that that was what she had to do. 'There's still nothing in Edinburgh for me until the war's over and Tommy's released. Besides, they're going to need experienced nurses more than ever.'

'I envy you,' Isabel said. A shadow crossed her face. 'I don't know what I'll do if I can't practise medicine again.'

It was on the tip of Jessie's tongue to tell Isabel that that was the least of her worries, but she bit back the words. If Archie was dead, and she feared he was, she was glad that he had known some happiness with the woman he loved. At least with the baby a part of him would live on.

'When the war is over, I'll come and help you with the wee one. And every leave I get I'll come and see you both.'

'I don't even know where I'll be living. Mama is unlikely to wish me to stay with her. Not when I'm expecting and unmarried.'

'Your mam will never put you out of the house,' Jessie said, shocked. 'No mother would do that to her daughter. Especially when she's carrying a child.'

'I don't suppose she will, although I can't see my brother George having anything to do with me.' Isabel smiled weakly. 'I have to admit, though, that that doesn't seem much of a loss.'

'You could always tell them that you married and he died. I'm certain you won't be the first to use that story.'

'No.' Isabel shook her head. 'It wouldn't be long before someone found out the truth. The women we travelled with know I'm not married.'

'You could say you married Archie secretly. People might believe that.'

'No, Jessie. I must simply face whatever I have to.' Her stoicism faltered. 'If only I could carry on working as a doctor, I'd have something. But don't worry about me. I've brought enough trouble into your life. I'll think of something.'

'You have the baby,' Jessie said. 'You'll see. It'll make up for a lot.' She reached across and pressed Isabel's cold hand. 'Archie's child. We're bound together now. Your troubles will always be mine.'

'You're a good woman, Jessie. You know that, don't you?'

Aye, well, perhaps she wasn't and perhaps she was. 'Family stick together and you're family now, so don't go all soft on me.'

The hospital ship was packed to the rafters with the injured and with soldiers returning home on leave. Jessie hadn't been able to secure them berths so they would have to manage as best they could on deck, but when some British officers realised that the two women were without a cabin, they offered their first-class one. A young captain took the lead. 'You ladies have done a wonderful job taking care of us, eh? My sister's a nurse and she'd never forgive me or Williams here if we let you sleep on deck.'

Jessie took up the offer without having to think twice. After what they'd been through, a deck-chair would have seemed the height of luxury but Isabel needed a proper bed.

Their borrowed cabin was cramped but comfortable. They laid out their few possessions, then decided to go on deck for some air.

On the dock, the ambulance trains were still unloading patients. Nurses, veils blowing in the wind, attended to them with quiet efficiency.

Suddenly Jessie heard Isabel gasp. 'Down there, do you see? The man sitting against the wall – the one with red hair?'

Jessie followed Isabel's pointing finger. It was easy to see whom she was talking about: only one man had red hair. Isabel whirled around and ran towards the gangway.

'Wait!' Jessie called. Either Isabel didn't hear or she was too intent on getting to the wounded soldier, but she didn't even turn.

By the time Jessie had pushed her way through the crowds, Isabel was kneeling by the man. He was wearing the uniform of the Royal Flying Corps.

'Simon, my God! Simon – don't you know me? It's Isabel – Andrew's sister.'

So this was Simon, Lady Dorothea's other brother. He didn't look well. His left arm had been amputated at the elbow and was heavily bandaged. When he saw Isabel, his face lit up. Then an expression of such grief crossed it that Jessie shivered.

Isabel must have seen it too. If possible, she paled even further. 'No, Simon. Please no! Not Andrew too!'

From the expression on Simon's face, it was clear that Isabel had guessed right.

'I'm so sorry, Isabel. Didn't you know? It happened two weeks ago. I wrote to your mama.'

But Isabel wasn't listening. Her arms were

wrapped around her body and she was rocking back and forth. Jessie stepped forward and held her. 'Come, Isabel. Come with me. Hush now. It will be all right. Hush now.'

Later, when she was in control of her emotions again, Isabel walked down to the ship's hospital intent on finding Simon. She had cried for the last couple of hours until it seemed there were no tears left in her. Now she needed to know exactly what had happened to Andrew. While she had been in her cabin, the last of the injured had been loaded and the ship had set sail. It swayed from side to side and she had to clutch the railings to stay on her feet.

From the hospital she was directed to a small lounge that had been set aside for the wounded officers. Simon was sitting at a table playing cards with his one hand. When he saw her he stood up and smiled wanly. 'My dear girl, how are you?' he asked.

'I've been better. I want to ask about Andrew. I need to know what happened to him.' She still couldn't quite believe that her beautiful, kind, clever brother was dead.

'Let's go on deck,' Simon said. 'We can talk more freely there.'

Isabel waited until they had found a quiet spot near the stern. The wind had risen once more, and all those left to find what shelter they could outside huddled under blankets.

'Tell me everything,' she said, 'if you can bear to.' The ship's motion was making her queasy but she tried to ignore it.

Simon stared out to sea. 'When we first joined the RFC we were mainly flying reconnaissance sorties, finding out where the enemy was and reporting back, that sort of thing. Remember when we last met, I told you they'd put forward-facing guns on their planes?' Isabel nodded. 'It turned into a scourge. But over the last six months they put better guns on our kites and we started getting into dogfights with the Hun. We knew it was only a matter of time before we bought it.'

She thought of Andrew's eyes the last time she'd seen him. Even then he'd known.

'Was Andrew ... was he scared?'

'We all were, but we didn't show it. And Andrew loved flying. He was good at it too. Better than I was, much better.'

'Go on,' Isabel encouraged him, although her chest was tight with the effort of keeping back the tears.

'We were up there, covering the Serbs' retreat. Trying to make it as difficult for the Hun as possible. All we wanted to do was to keep them off for as long as possible. But there were too many German planes. I went after one and got him, but when I looked back, there was another on my tail. Andrew must have spotted him because he came out of the clouds and shot him down. Then he waved at me. I saw his face, Isabel – he was that close. He was grinning from ear to ear. But we weren't paying attention. Another plane came from behind him. Andrew was still smiling when the other pilot shot him.' Simon's breath hitched. 'If he hadn't been looking out for me, he wouldn't have died. It's my fault he's gone.'

Isabel covered his hand with hers. 'You mustn't blame yourself. Andrew wouldn't want you to. You were his friend. Remember that day near the beginning of the war when we met in Paris?' Simon nodded. 'He told me flying was as close to God as it got. He would have been glad he died when he was flying and glad that he'd saved you. He loved you like a brother.'

'And I loved him. He was my world. My life. I don't know what I'll do without him.' Then Simon started sobbing. Deep, racking sobs that tore through his body. She put her arms around him and held him, letting her tears mingle with his.

In time, Simon's sobs eased and he released her with an embarrassed laugh. 'If my fellow officers could see me now, or learn how I truly felt about Andrew, they'd drum me out of the RFC.'

'Your secret is safe with me. God knows I have enough of my own. Did Andrew ever discover that you loved him – er – in that way?'

'No! He would have been horrified. He might even have pitied me and I couldn't have borne that. If I could, I would have died in his place – and gladly. I would still die if it meant I could be with him.'

'I think enough people have died, don't you, Simon? And it wasn't your fault. Andrew did what he believed he had to do.'

They stood in silence for a while, watching the white curves of the waves.

'What did you mean just now,' Simon asked, 'when you said that we all have secrets? I can't imagine you having any. You're far too sensible.'

'I wish I was.' Isabel hesitated. Why not share

her troubles with Andrew's friend? 'Promise you won't be shocked.'

Simon laughed harshly. 'I doubt there's anything about you that's more shocking than what you know about me.'

'I'm going to have a baby.'

Simon whistled between his teeth. 'Good God, that is a surprise. May I assume there's no husband?' He held up his hands when Isabel raised an eyebrow. 'I didn't say I disapproved.'

'*I* disapprove. And, more importantly, society will disapprove too.' She shuddered. 'I can't say I'm looking forward to facing everyone, but I could live with that if it wasn't for what it will do to Mama. She's lost her darling son and now she'll lose her place in society. She'll have nothing.'

'Any chance of marrying the father?'

Isabel shook her head. 'I suspect he's dead.' She closed her eyes as Archie's image swam in front of her. To have found love with him only to lose him. If it weren't for her baby, she didn't know how she could bear it.

Simon was quiet for a while. 'How will you manage?'

'I don't know. I have no money and no way to make any – they'll strike me off the medical register as soon as I tell them I'm to have a baby unmarried.' She laughed shakily. 'I'm afraid I shall be quite ruined.'

'And, by association, Andrew's memory will be tarnished too,' Simon said. 'I can't allow it.'

'I don't see how it can be prevented.'

Simon looked thoughtful. 'There is a way,' he said at last. 'We could marry.'

485

Isabel was so surprised that she laughed. 'What? Us?'

'Don't you see? It makes sense. My brother Richard died at the battle of Loos and with both my brothers dead, I shall inherit the title. If I survive the war, that is. But given that it's unlikely they'll send me back to the front without an arm, especially as I can no longer fly, there's every chance I'll make it. Mama and Papa will expect me to marry. No doubt they already have a selection of debutantes lined up for me. It wouldn't be fair for me to take a wife, not with me being the way I am, but I could marry you. I don't even wish to know the name of the man whose child you're carrying.'

'But I don't love you and you don't love me.' The very idea was out of the question.

'Which makes it the perfect solution. You know what I am and you wouldn't expect me in your bed. I see Andrew in your face, your mannerisms, in the way you smile. In you and your child, I'll have a little bit of him always with me.'

Isabel studied him. It was an absurd idea and yet... If they did marry she wouldn't be shamed, she wouldn't be struck off and her child wouldn't be born illegitimate and despised.

'You don't have to give me your answer now,' Simon continued, 'but promise you'll think about it. I'd be happy for you to carry on working as a doctor, as long as you were prepared to carry out the duties of Lady Maxwell when I needed you to. I'd acknowledge the child you're carrying as mine, my heir if it's a boy.' He looked at her, his blue eyes alight. 'At least think about it. We could ask the

486

captain to marry us – I hear it's been done before. Mama won't be pleased,' he shrugged, 'but we could tell her we married in Paris, on the spur of the moment, before I went on one of my sorties. It would take her time to forgive me, but she would in the end.'

It was madness. She'd be acting a part for the rest of her life ... and if Archie were still alive...?

Marrying Simon would put Archie out of her life for ever. Her heart shattered at the thought. If he were alive and came looking for her, would he understand why she'd done as she had? But what other choice did she have?

There was one other person who knew she was carrying Archie's baby and that her marriage would be a sham – Jessie. Until she'd spoken to her, she couldn't give Simon an answer.

'I'll think about it,' she said. 'You'll have my answer as soon as I have one to give.'

'Don't think about it for too long. The ship docks tomorrow afternoon. If we're to marry it has to be before then.'

Jessie was dressing for dinner, shaking the dust out of her worn and tattered uniform, when Isabel came back to the cabin. For the first time in weeks, her cheeks had a healthy glow.

'Is it breezy out there?' Jessie asked. 'We've been asked to join Captain Swift and his friend for dinner. As we separated them from their cabin, I didn't feel I could say no.'

'Jessie, there's something I need to discuss with you.'

She was instantly alarmed. 'Are you feeling all

right? Is it the baby?' She ushered Isabel to the only chair in the cabin and sat her down.

'Please don't fuss. I'm fine. A little nauseous, perhaps, but, yes, it is about the baby.'

There was something about the steely look in Isabel's eyes that frightened Jessie. She had the certain feeling that whatever Isabel wanted to tell her she didn't want to hear it. Nevertheless, she sat on the bunk, folded her hands in her lap and waited for her to continue.

'I've had a proposal of marriage.'

Whatever she'd expected to hear it wasn't that. 'Who from?'

'Remember the wounded pilot? The one on the quayside? Simon Maxwell?'

Something squeezed in Jessie's chest. 'You mean Lady Dorothea and Charles Maxwell's brother. The brother of the man who...' She bit her lip. 'You can't possibly be thinking of accepting him. Have you lost your mind?'

Isabel leaned towards Jessie, her brown eyes glowing with a fervour Jessie hadn't seen in a very long time. 'Don't you see? It's the answer to everything.'

'How can it be? How can you even think of marrying a man you don't love? What about Archie? I thought you loved him.'

'Archie may never return to us, Jessie. We have to accept that.'

'No, we don't. If Archie's alive, he'll find his way back to us. To you. To his child.'

'But is he alive? I know Tommy managed to come back to you, but two miracles don't happen in one lifetime. And even if, God willing, he's a prisoner, it will be the end of the war before he's released. I can't wait that long.'

Jessie pushed Isabel's hands away and jumped to her feet. 'Does Simon know you're carrying the child of the man they believe murdered his brother?'

'No, and he's made it clear he doesn't want to know who the father is. I told him he was dead.'

'You'll live the rest of your life as a lie. How can you even think of doing such a thing?'

'I'll do it because it's the *only* thing to do. Simon knows I don't love him.'

'Then why does he wish to marry you? Isabel, think about this.'

'I have no choice, Jessie. I can't have a child out of wedlock and still practise as a doctor. My family's reputation will be ruined, not just mine. It would kill my mother to be rejected by society. I'll do everything I can to make Simon happy. I'll be a faithful and loving wife to him. It's all he asks.'

Jessie couldn't believe that Isabel meant what she was saying. 'What if you're wrong?' she said quietly. 'What if Archie's alive and comes looking for you, only to find that you're the wife of another man? Can you do that to him? Can you hurt him in that way?'

'I can and I will, Jessie, because I must.'

In the end, Jessie couldn't dissuade Isabel from her course. But neither could she be a witness to a marriage she knew to be wrong. There was a coolness between them that Jessie knew would never leave. Isabel, as always, would have her way.

She wanted to shout at her, to tell her the truth, that she had killed the brother of the man she was marrying, but her promise to Archie was unbreakable. And if Isabel was right, and Archie was dead, she knew he would have wanted Isabel to protect herself and their child in any way she could. Her brother had always been a fool for this woman and there was no reason to believe he would ever be anything else.

By the time they landed at Dover, Isabel was Lady Maxwell and there was no going back.

Isabel was waiting for her husband at the top of the gangway when Jessie saw her. She moved towards Jessie and held out her hand. 'Please, Jessie, stay my friend. Try to understand why I've taken the course I have. I'll bring my child to see you whenever I can, and perhaps you'll visit us when we're in Edinburgh.'

Jessie wanted to turn her back on the woman she had come to think of as a friend but had caused so much trouble in her and Archie's lives, but she knew she couldn't. 'Let me know when the child is born. Promise.'

'I promise,' Isabel replied, and then, as Simon Maxwell appeared at her side, she turned and went with him down the gangway.

Chapter 52

Edinburgh, 1919

Jessie paused for a moment outside Craigleith poorhouse, or what was now the military hospital, and tucked a lock of her hair under her hat.

The last years of the war had passed quickly. Isabel had written to say she had been safely delivered of a baby boy, and Jessie had been glad. It had helped her bear her sorrow when, finally, she'd heard from Archie.

She fingered the letter in her pocket. He had asked that she forward it to Isabel, but the news it contained wasn't the kind to be conveyed in writing.

She had another letter with her, from Tommy. He didn't want to see her. He told her to forget him, to forget they were ever married.

Fear lay under the singing joy she felt that soon she would see her darling husband again. It had been almost five years since they'd last met, and if she'd changed so must he too. Could she convince him that they still belonged together?

She pushed open the heavy oak doors. It was at once familiar and different. Nurses hurried everywhere, their starched skirts rustling, their immaculate collars and cuffs a glaring white that was impossible for the nurses working at the front to achieve.

One stopped. 'Can I help you?'

She had that look, Jessie thought, the haughtiness, the certainty that she had seen in all the nurses when they had first gone to the front, a look that soon disappeared. She smiled. 'I've come to see my husband, Corporal Tommy Stuart,' she said mildly.

'Visiting hours aren't until four. I suggest you come back then.'

Jessie's smile widened. If this nurse, who couldn't be more than eighteen, thought she was going to wait until then, she was very much mistaken. 'I would like to see my husband immediately, Nurse.'

Perhaps it was the tone of her voice, perhaps the nurse recognised authority, but the girl's expression changed. Astonishment and awe crossed her face. 'You're one of the nurses who were out with the Scottish Women's Hospitals.'

Jessie cocked her head to one side. 'Yes, I was. How do you know?'

'From your medal.'

In her excitement Jessie had forgotten she'd pinned it to the front of her jacket.

'Gosh, wait until I tell the others! What was it like?'

What was it like? How could she possibly explain, and even if she tried, how could this young woman even begin to understand? 'It was thrilling,' Jessie replied, 'but, if you don't mind, I'd like to see my husband now.'

The nurse bobbed a curtsy. 'Of course. Right away. I'll just let Sister know.'

Before Jessie could protest that she wasn't interested in whether Sister wanted her on the ward or not, the nurse was gone. As she pushed open the internal doors, she stood back to let two doctors past. Jessie's breath stopped in her throat.

'Let me have your diagnosis and your suggestions for treatment, Dr Roberts, as soon as you've seen the patient. You will find me on the abdominal ward.'

Isabel scribbled something on a piece of paper, then looked up. Their gaze locked for what seemed an age but could only have been a moment. 'My dear Jessie.' She stepped forward. 'How good to see you again. Are you here to visit Corporal Stuart? Forgive me – of course you are.' She paused, her brown eyes anxious. Then she seemed to gather herself. 'As I wrote to you, be prepared to find him changed. I told him you were coming so he's expecting you. I'll take you to him, shall I?'

Jessie's mouth had gone dry and she found she couldn't speak. She nodded.

'When you've seen him, we shall talk more. One of the nurses will bring you to my consulting room.'

Yes, they would have to talk, although it wasn't a conversation Jessie was looking forward to.

She followed Isabel up a flight of stairs, past the fever ward where she had once worked. 'Your husband has made a complete recovery. At least physically.' Isabel paused with her hand on the banister. 'He didn't want us to tell you he was here, but of course we had to. He's fit enough to go home. He's on the convalescent ward for the time being.'

Jessie still couldn't speak.

493

Isabel pushed open the door to the ward and Jessie accompanied her inside. The room was bathed with sunshine and the balcony doors were wide open to let the fresh air flood in. Jessie remembered the arguments she'd had with Sister about that in the past. The beds were arranged down the side, but they were empty. The patients, many with limbs missing, sat at tables playing cards or smoking, some with cumbersome false hands and legs. They looked up with mild interest as Jessie and Isabel passed.

And then she saw him. He was in a chair on the balcony, slightly apart from the others, a blanket covering his missing legs. His eyes were closed as if he were sleeping.

'I'll leave you alone now,' Isabel said softly, then withdrew.

Jessie drank in the sight of him. His hair was longer than she remembered, a lock falling across his brow. His beloved face was still the same, and although there were lines around his eyes and mouth that hadn't been there before, he was still her handsome Tommy. She moved towards his chair and touched him gently on the shoulder. 'Tommy dear, it's me, Jessie.'

He opened his eyes briefly and closed them again. 'Go away. I told you and them I didn't want to see you.'

Jessie recalled the boy in France saying the same thing. Couldn't these men believe that women who truly loved did so regardless? 'Tommy, look at me,' she said. When he shook his head, she repeated her words more firmly. He opened his eyes and she saw fear and shame. 'I'm not going anywhere, husband, so you can put that notion out of your head.'

'How can you say that?' he asked bitterly. 'I'm no use to anyone. Not now. I'll never be able to work, never be able to look after a wife. If you stay with me, Jessie, you'll be a pauper alongside me.'

'I need you, Tommy. I can work. There'll be enough money for us to live on.'

'They won't let you work if you're married. You must divorce me. It's the only way.'

'I'm not going to divorce you, Tommy. The very idea is ridiculous.' She knelt beside him, her hands covering his. 'I love you. I prayed every day these last years that you'd come back to me, and God heard me. Do you think I'm going to let you go now?'

Something shifted in Tommy's eyes. He gripped her hands so tightly she almost cried out. 'You'll never leave me? Because if I come home to you, I'll never let you go. You have to believe I mean what I say. I'm not the man you married. I'm not much of a man any more. The only thing that kept me alive in the camp was that you were waiting for me. I wish I'd been killed instead of having my legs blown off, but maybe you're right. Maybe God did have something in mind when He kept me alive.'

Jessie was crying now and she didn't care who saw. Tommy reached out and pulled her against his chest. He was still Tommy. The feel of him – although he was thinner than he used to be – the smell of him, the warmth of him.

When she stopped crying, she looked up to find

his eyes damp. 'I'm not going to cry, Jessie. I'm already only half a man.' But this time there was a smile. It was tentative, as if he'd forgotten how to do it, but it was there. She snuggled against him. 'Funny how it was here we met and here that we should come together again.'

'Only this time, when I leave, I'm never coming back.'

She smiled up at the only man she'd ever loved and would ever love. 'Let's start thinking about getting you home then, shall we?'

After she had left Tommy, with a promise to return every day until he was ready to be discharged, a nurse took her to see Isabel, who was waiting in the doctors' room. Despite the bright sunshine outside, the room was chilly.

'How did you find him?' Isabel asked.

'He'll come home as soon as he can,' Jessie replied.

Isabel nodded. 'I knew if anyone could persuade him he still has a life, it would be you.'

'It won't be easy,' Jessie said. 'Our flat is on the second floor and I have no idea how I'm going to get him up and down the stairs. Then I'll have to find work. I'll see the matron here before I leave and ask if she'll take me on. Perhaps she'll find it in her to overlook the fact that I'm married.'

'When the war is over I plan to open a small practice,' Isabel said. 'I'd be honoured if you'd be my nurse.'

'Aye, well, perhaps. If I can't find anything else.' She smiled to take the sting from her words. 'How's the baby?'

'Richard Calum Andrew Maxwell is well.'

Isabel paused as a shadow crossed her face. 'He looks like his father – Archie, I mean. Lady Glendale keeps remarking that she's surprised he doesn't have Simon's red hair.'

'You called him Calum?' It was her father's name and the name Archie had gone by in France and Serbia.

'I wanted him to have something that belonged to Archie.' Isabel ran her tongue over her lips. 'I … I don't suppose you've heard anything?'

Jessie swallowed. 'You must prepare yourself.'

Isabel's face lost its colour. 'Tell me,' she whispered.

'His letter only found me recently. He sent one to you, too, and asked me to let you have it.' She brought the letter out of her pocket and laid it on the desk. Isabel made no move to pick it up.

'As we suspected, he was captured by the Germans. He wasn't wearing his armband.'

'He gave it to me,' Isabel said quietly.

'He was to be tried as a spy.' Jessie leaned across the table and took Isabel's hands in hers. 'I'm afraid, my dear, they planned to execute him.'

Isabel closed her eyes. There was a long silence. Outside, Jessie heard the sound of the tea trolley. Isabel pushed herself away from the desk, stood up and walked to the window, where she remained with her back to Jessie.

'If he hadn't given me his armband…'

Aye, well. Archie had done so much for this woman. He must have loved her greatly. 'He did what he had to. He always wanted to protect you. My brother was a man of honour. He couldn't have acted differently.'

'Can you be certain he was executed?'

'My dear, it's more than four months since the war ended. Do you not think if Archie was alive he would have found his way back to you? And to me?'

'Yes,' Isabel whispered.

When she turned again, her face was composed although her lips were white. She picked up the letter and held it to her breast before placing it in her pocket. 'If you don't mind, I'd prefer to be alone when I read it.'

'I understand.'

Isabel sat down. 'Tell me what happened after we parted.'

'I was sent back to the abbey. You heard that Dr Inglis and everyone was captured by the Austrians after we left them in Serbia?'

Isabel nodded.

'After three months the news came that they had been released unharmed. It turned out they hadn't been treated too badly. They had the same horrible journey as we did, but they all survived – you'll know that much.' She raised her eyebrows. 'What news of Lady Dorothea?'

'She recovered well, although she limps when she's fatigued. She intends to train as a lawyer when the war is over.' Isabel smiled faintly. 'She has done with Lord Livingston and claims she'll marry whomever she pleases. If she pleases.'

'What did she have to say about your marrying her brother?'

Isabel fiddled with the cuffs of her dress before answering. 'She was surprised, of course, but I don't think she minded.'

'Did she suspect it wasn't her brother's baby you were carrying?'

'If she did, she never said. Too well bred. She adores her nephew.'

'And did she ever tell anyone about Archie?'

Isabel shook her head. 'She remembers nothing of that day.'

Jessie hadn't been aware she'd been holding her breath until it came out in a long sigh. At least Archie's memory would not be tarnished further.

'Forgive me,' Isabel said, after another long silence. 'Would you like some tea?'

'No, thank you. I can't stay long. I have a lot to do before I can take Tommy home.'

Isabel reached out a hand. 'Please don't go just yet. Tell me more of what happened after we parted.'

Jessie blinked. She hadn't planned to leave without making some arrangement to see Archie's son.

'After I returned to Royaumont we had a pretty hard time of it. There were a few familiar faces. Maud was there. She's going to marry her Serbian doctor, by the way.'

'I'm glad.'

'Later, near the end, we were at Villers-Cotterêts, another hospital close to the front. We were there when the Germans advanced again, but we stayed until the last moment. They're calling it the Scottish Women's Hospitals' finest hour. That's where I got this.' Jessie fingered the medal.

'Your father would have been proud to know his daughter followed in his footsteps.'

'You know about him and the other Martyrs?'

'Archie told me. He would have been proud of you too.'

Jessie kept quiet. Her father would spin in his grave if he knew his only son had been thought a murderer. But, then, if he was with God and Mam in Heaven, he would know the truth.

Jessie leaned towards Isabel. 'Did you make the right choice, Isabel? Are you happy?'

'Happy? I suppose so. As happy as I have the right to be. Happier even. I have my son – a part of Archie no one can take from me – my work, and a husband who is loving and generous.' She stood too. 'Would you like to see the baby?'

'There's nothing I would like more, but won't your husband wonder? The war has changed us all, but for Lady Maxwell to invite a crofter's daughter to her home?'

Isabel lifted her chin in the way Jessie had come to know. 'You're not just a crofter's daughter, Jessie. You're the finest woman I know and the bravest. If I can never be your sister, I'd be honoured if you would consider me your friend.'

Her friend? The years rolled past as she remembered the first time she had seen Isabel, at school, then the day they had toiled together over Flora McPhee's baby, the patients they had battled to save, the long trek on which they had kept each other alive, Archie telling her he was carrying the blame for a killing Isabel had committed, the night Isabel told her she was pregnant with Archie's child and then that she was marrying Simon Maxwell. She was bound to this woman in so many ways, but could they ever be friends?

She doubted it. The shadow of Archie and Charles Maxwell would always lie between them. She could never look at this woman without remembering how Archie had suffered for her. That he had chosen to do so, willingly and clear-sightedly, did not make it easier.

But she could not turn away from Archie's son. She longed to see him, wanted to protect and watch over him, as Archie would have done, had he lived.

'Although, of course, you can never be acknowledged as my son's aunt,' Isabel continued. 'You do see that?'

Even now her last link to Archie was to be denied. As always, Isabel was to be protected.

'Please,' Isabel implored. 'I want Richard to know you.'

The choice was simple. If Jessie wished to see Richard it would be as a friend of his mother's, not as his aunt.

She stood and held out her hand. 'It's been interesting knowing you, and I wish you well. I would very much like to meet my nephew. Perhaps in the park one day.'

Isabel smiled sadly, understanding what Jessie was saying. 'I should like that very much.'

As the door closed behind Jessie, she turned her mind back to Tommy. *A Thighearna*, she had a lot to do. She realised she was smiling. The years ahead would be hard, very hard, but she had her Tommy and her work. It was enough.

Isabel sat in her garden at Charlotte Square in the dying light of the afternoon. Richard was examining some bushes with the same fierce intensity his father had had.

The letter Jessie had given her lay on her lap, her name written on the envelope in a bold, confident hand. Odd to think she had never seen his writing before. Summoning her courage, she opened it.

My darling,
I write to tell you that I have been captured and will be tried as a spy. If I am found guilty, I will be shot. But I'm not afraid. My only regret is that I will never see you again – never see you smile, never see the stubborn lift of your chin when you're cross but, most of all, never again will I hold you in my arms.

But at least I knew your love. Many men will die never knowing what it is to be loved the way I know you love me, and it gives me the strength I need to face my death with honour.

Be brave, my Isabel. Live your life the way only you can. Be the finest doctor you can be.

Despite what I have written I have not given up hope. My darling, whatever happens, I know one day we will meet again. Remember the words in the Song of Solomon? 'When the dawn breaks and the shadows flee.'
Until then, my love,
I love you.
Archie

While she'd been reading, Richard had come over to her. He tugged as her skirt. 'Mama, why are you crying?'

His face was so like Archie's, his eyes the same

502

shade of cobalt blue, his too-long hair, which she hadn't the heart to cut, like his father's, dark and wild.

'I'm crying because I'm sad.' She held out her arms and lifted her child onto her lap, holding him close to her. If only Archie could have known he had a child. If only…

But there could be no more thinking about the if-onlys.

Richard pulled away from her and took her face between his two small hands. 'I don't like it when you're sad. Papa says it's better to be brave.'

His papa. Simon. The only father he'd ever known or would know. If only she could tell him about his real father: 'Your papa was a brave man, a fine and honourable man.'

She wanted to do something to honour him. He had urged her to be the best doctor she could be. It had been her plan when the remaining soldiers were finally discharged from Craigleith to set up in private practice. But another idea was forming in her mind.

A shadow fell over her and she looked up to see Simon standing beside her. He was a good husband, kind and loving, but he wasn't Archie.

'My dear? Whatever is the matter?'

'It's nothing,' she said. 'You know that sometimes I get a little sad.'

'Is there anything I can do?'

'I should like to visit our house on Skye for a while.' If she couldn't tell her son about Archie, she could show him the place his father had loved.

'Of course,' Simon said. 'It's always kept ready.'

'I have another favour to ask. How would you feel about your wife starting her own small hospital for the poor? Here in Edinburgh. It would take money. A substantial sum.'

Simon smiled. 'Then it's fortunate that I'm a very rich man.' He lifted Richard from her lap and held out his hand to her. 'It's getting cold. Shall we go in?'

The sun was setting, casting long shadows across the garden. 'You go. I'll be along in a moment.' She smiled back at him.

Left alone again, she sat, remembering Archie. She reached into her pocket for her handkerchief and removed the petals of a wild rose from between its folds. She brought them to her lips before placing them in the envelope containing Archie's letter. Suddenly a cloud cleared from the setting sun and the rays shone directly on her, bathing her in light.

She closed her eyes. Yes, my darling love. *Until the dawn breaks and the shadows flee.* In the meantime I'll do my best to make you and your son proud.

She stood up and smoothed her dress.

There was work to do and a life yet to live.

Author's Note

Quite early on I knew I wanted to write about a Scottish woman doctor in the early twentieth century but when I started to research medical training at this time, I stumbled on the story of Dr Elsie Inglis and the Scottish Women's Hospitals (SWH).

As an ex-nurse, the name Elsie Inglis was familiar to me. I trained in Edinburgh and at that time the Elsie Inglis Memorial Hospital was still taking patients.

What I didn't know, however, was that at the outbreak of the First World War, Dr Elsie Inglis had gone to the British Army to offer her services abroad. She was promptly told 'to go home and sit still.' This however, wasn't in the Scotswoman's nature. Undeterred, she immediately approached the French and Serbian governments who accepted her offer with alacrity.

Within weeks she had recruited doctors, nurses, orderlies, cooks and chauffeurs for her women-only unit and by December the SWH units were in France and setting up a hospital at Royaumont Abbey. This was followed by units in Serbia until, at the end of the war, the Scottish Women's Hospital had fourteen units in total. They weren't the only all-women units, nor were they staffed only by Scotswomen. The SWH units included women from across the Commonwealth and even working guests from the USA.

Although many know the story of the women's units in France, less is known about their work in Serbia. Following the assassination of Archduke Ferdinand, the Austrians declared war on Serbia and by early December had occupied Belgrade. Two weeks later, the Serbian capital had been regained by the Serbian army and forty thousand Austrian soldiers captured. Many Austrian prisoners-of-war, particularly those who spoke Serbian, had no heart for the conflict and were content to live out the war as orderlies in Serbian hospitals. At that time, Serbian hospitals were over-crowded, badly run and had few, if any, trained nurses and welcomed the Scottish Women's Hospitals and other female units with open arms.

By October 1915, the Austrian and German armies had invaded Serbia and two weeks later, Bulgaria attacked from the east. The women, along with those from the Serbian Relief Fund, were forced to retreat across the Montenegrin mountains, along with thousands of refugees and soldiers, many of whom died along the way. Miraculously only one of the nurses died when her cart slipped down the mountainside.

The women who remained behind in Serbia, Dr Inglis included, were captured by the Germans and when they were eventually released they were forced to retreat too. (In fact Dr Inglis was captured a second time during the war, this time in Russia.)

No feat I describe in my book does justice to the resilience and courage of these women. There are however other facts I have changed slightly to fit with my story. In Part One, I describe the village of Galtrigill on Skye as being a cleared village. In fact it was Borreraig, the village next to it, that was cleared. Evidence of the clearances can still be seen all over the Highlands and Islands of Scotland.

Dunvegan Castle (Sir Walter Scott was really a guest) is still the home of the MacLeods. However, it was empty for a time. The 25th Chief, having given away a substantial part of his wealth to provide work and food for his people, was forced to take a job as a clerk in London and no chief resided at the castle again until 1929. The Maxwells are of course fictitious although there were many landowners just like them in Skye at that time. The story of the Glendale Martyrs is true.

The Americans were doing blood transfusions during the First World War – but it was still experimental and risky and therefore not widely used until much later. Antibiotics did not exist at this time. Infection killed more soldiers than bullets, bombs or shrapnel.

The Edinburgh Royal Infirmary was considered the leading hospital in Europe, even the world, at the beginning of the twentieth century. Women were not permitted to take lectures alongside men until 1916, four years after the date I use in the book. The attitudes to women medical students from their male counterparts and the professors was every bit as antagonistic –

if not more – as I describe.

Finally, I use the spellings of the towns as the women used them in their diaries, for example Nish and Kragujevatz.

If you are interested in finding out more about any of the topics I cover in my story, I include a list for further reading.

Selected Further Reading

Adie, Kate, *From Corsets to Camouflage* (London: Hodder & Stoughton, 2004)

Bell, E. Moberly, *Storming the Citadel: The rise of the woman doctor* (London: Hyperion Press, 1981)

Corbett, Elsie, *Red Cross in Serbia 1915–1919: a personal diary of experiences* (Banbury; 1964)

Crofton, Eileen, *The women of Royaumont: A Scottish Women's hospital on the Western Front* (Edinburgh: Tuckwell Press, 1997)

Culter, Elliot Carr, *A journal of the Harvard Medical School Unit to the American Ambulance Hospital in Paris, spring of 1915*

Eastwood, M. A & Jenkinson, Anne, *A History of the Western General Hospital: Craigleith Poorhouse, military hospital, modern teaching hospital* (Edinburgh: John Donald, 1995)

Krippner, Monica, *The quality of mercy: women at war, Serbia* (Newton Abbot: David and Charles, 1980)

Lawrence, Margot, *Shadow of Swords: a biography of Elsie Inglis* (London: Joseph, 1971)

Leneman, Leah, *In the Service of Life: The story of Elsie Inglis and the Scottish Women's Hospitals* (Edinburgh: The Mercat Press, 1994)

MacDonald, Lyn, *The Roses of No Man's Land*

(London: Penguin, 1993)

Marlow, Joyce (editor), *The Virago Book of Women and the Great War* (London: Little, Brown, 2009)

McLaren, Eva Shaw (editor), *A History of the Scottish Women's Hospitals* (London: Hodder & Stoughton, 1919)

Powell, Anne, *Women in the War Zone: hospital service in the First World War* (Gloucestershire: History Press, 2009)

Stevenson, David, *1914-1918, The History of the First World War* (London: Penguin, 2005)

Storey, Neil R. & Housego, Molly, *Women in the First World War* (Oxford: Shire Publications, 2011)

Whitehead, Ian R., *Doctors in the Great War* (London: Leo Cooper, 1999)

Other sources

The National Library of Scotland, Edinburgh

The Royal College of Surgeons, Edinburgh

The Mitchell Library special collections, Glasgow

Imperial War Museum, London

Musée de la Grande Guerre du Pays de Meaux, Paris

The *British Medical Journal*

The publishers hope that this book has given you enjoyable reading. Large Print Books are especially designed to be as easy to see and hold as possible. If you wish a complete list of our books please ask at your local library or write directly to:

Magna Large Print Books
Magna House, Long Preston,
Skipton, North Yorkshire.
BD23 4ND

This Large Print Book for the partially sighted, who cannot read normal print, is published under the auspices of

THE ULVERSCROFT FOUNDATION

THE ULVERSCROFT FOUNDATION

... we hope that you have enjoyed this Large Print Book. Please think for a moment about those people who have worse eyesight problems than you ... and are unable to even read or enjoy Large Print, without great difficulty.

You can help them by sending a donation, large or small to:

**The Ulverscroft Foundation,
1, The Green, Bradgate Road,
Anstey, Leicestershire, LE7 7FU,
England.**
or request a copy of our brochure for more details.

The Foundation will use all your help to assist those people who are handicapped by various sight problems and need special attention.

Thank you very much for your help.